Joy Dettman was born in country Victoria and spent her early years in towns on either side of the Murray River. She is an award-winning writer of short stories, the complete collection of which, *Diamonds in the Mud*, was published in 2007, as well as the highly acclaimed novels *Mallawindy*, *Jacaranda Blue*, *Goose Girl*, *Yesterday's Dust*, *The Seventh Day*, *Henry's Daughter*, *One Sunday*, *Pearl in a Cage*, *Thorn on the Rose*, *Moth to the Flame*, *Wind in the Wires* and *Ripples on a Pond*. *The Tying of Threads* is the sixth and final novel in Joy's Woody Creek series.

Also by Joy Dettman

*Mallawindy*
*Jacaranda Blue*
*Goose Girl*
*Yesterday's Dust*
*The Seventh Day*
*Henry's Daughter*
*One Sunday*
*Diamonds in the Mud*

Woody Creek series
*Pearl in a Cage*
*Thorn on the Rose*
*Moth to the Flame*
*Wind in the Wires*
*Ripples on a Pond*

# Joy Dettman

# THE TYING OF THREADS

First published 2014 in Macmillan by Pan Macmillan Australia Pty Limited
This Pan edition published 2015 by Pan Macmillan Australia Pty Limited
1 Market Street, Sydney, New South Wales, Australia, 2000.



Cataloguing-in-Publication entry is available
from the National Library of Australia
http://catalogue.nla.gov.au



Typeset in 12.5/16 pt Adobe Garamond by Midland Typesetters, Australia
Printed by IVE

*For Joan, sister poet of that dark old bedroom*

*and*

*for Lois, sister dependable, who pleaded with us to shut up and get to sleep*

# Woody Creek Characters, Past And Present

Jenny, born of a brief relationship between Archie Foote, the philandering husband of Gertrude, and Juliana Conti, a foreign woman who died in childbirth, was raised as the daughter of mad Amber and pompous Norman Morrison. Her early life was chaotic.

Margot, first born of Jenny's three daughters, dies in a house fire in 1977, and if not for fate and a fallen fence, Georgie, Jenny's second born daughter, would have burnt with her. Georgie escaped with her life and little else, and has since escaped Woody Creek.

Cara, Jenny's third daugthter, given at birth to Myrtle and Robert Norris, was drawn back to that town on the night of the fire. She has since disappeared with her two children.

Jimmy, only son of Jenny and Jim Hooper, claimed as a six year old by his grandfather, Vern, and later adopted by Margaret Grenville-Langdon (*née* Hooper), took his adopted English father's name and is now known as Morrison (Morrie) Grenville-Langdon.

# Woody Creek Characters Past and Present

[illegible]

# Family Tree

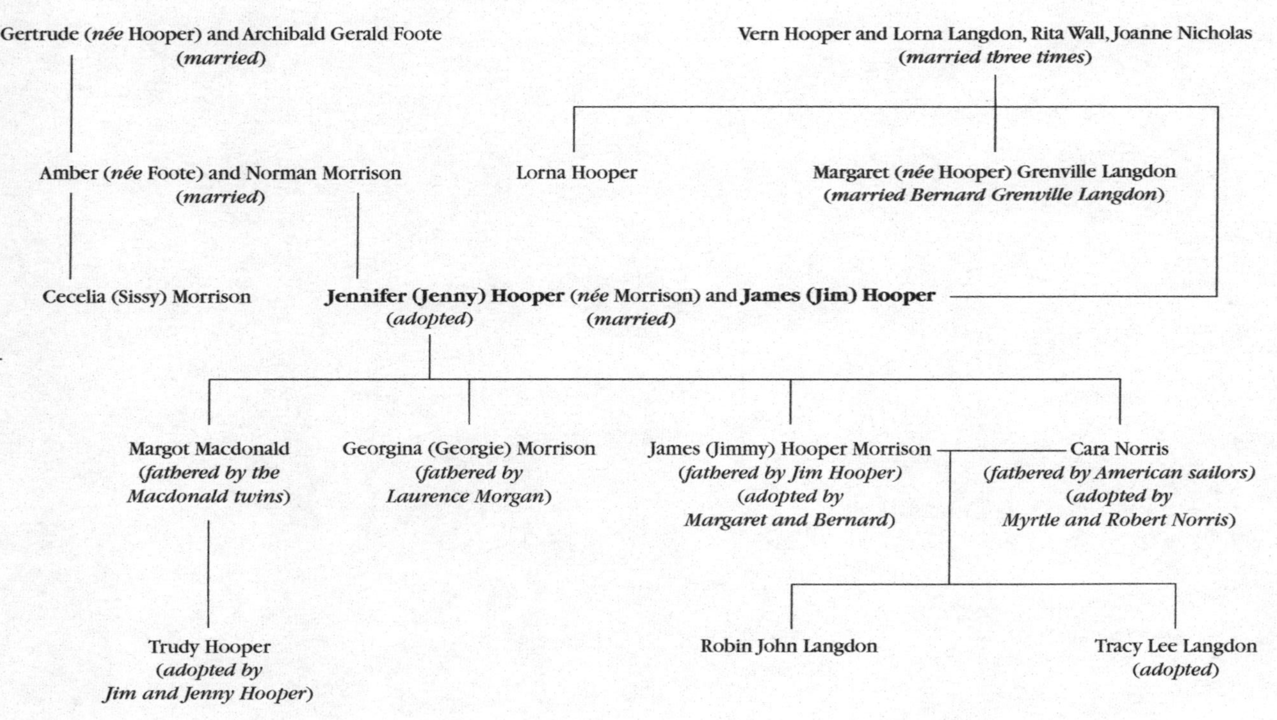

Gertrude (*née* Hooper) and Archibald Gerald Foote
(*married*)
Vern Hooper and Lorna Langdon, Rita Wall, Joanne Nicholas
(*married three times*)
Amber (*née* Foote) and Norman Morrison
(*married*)
Lorna Hooper
Margaret (*née* Hooper) Grenville Langdon
(*married Bernard Grenville Langdon*)
Cecelia (Sissy) Morrison
**Jennifer (Jenny) Hooper** (*née* Morrison) and **James (Jim) Hooper**
(*adopted*)
(*married*)
Margot Macdonald
(*fathered by the Macdonald twins*)
Georgina (Georgie) Morrison
(*fathered by Laurence Morgan*)
James (Jimmy) Hooper Morrison
(*fathered by Jim Hooper*)
(*adopted by Margaret and Bernard*)
Cara Norris
(*fathered by American sailors*)
(*adopted by Myrtle and Robert Norris*)
Trudy Hooper
(*adopted by Jim and Jenny Hooper*)
Robin John Langdon
Tracy Lee Langdon
(*adopted*)

# Part One

# THE STORM

The good seasons and the bad came in cycles to Woody Creek, the rich years when the rains came as required, when the crops grew tall, the sheep grew fat and the cows gave cream-rich milk. Then there were those other years when too much rain fell and the creek escaped its banks to spread for miles across low-lying land. A cow would swim, sheep drowned and crops turned to slime beneath mud-brown lakes.

The red gum forests surrounding Woody Creek celebrated the flood years, their roots drinking deep enough to sustain them through the droughts when passing clouds refused to give up their rain, and the crops wilted, and the cows grew gaunt and sheep lay down to die in dustbowl paddocks.

The bad heat had always come in cycles, that baking, blast furnace forty-degree heat that sucked the sweat and breath from Woody Creek, those days when children followed the shade and old men who had no more sweat to shed eyed the cemetery as friend not foe.

The town fathers had chosen land too close to town when they'd planted their first crop of the dead. Woody Creek had grown around it – and for reasons known only to those who lived there, was still growing.

A mill town, Woody Creek. Thirty years ago there'd been five sawmills in town and the bush mill; no man capable of labour was out of a job. By '78 only two mills were still cutting, Macdonald's and Davies', and unemployment figures were high.

Land was cheap there, and so it ought to be. Woody Creek had no rolling hills, no nearby ocean, no lake. It had a corner pub, a scattering of shops, acres of red gum forest – and the creek. It had Willama too, a large inland city a half-hour drive to the north-east, where a small building block two miles from the Willama post office might set you back four times what you'd pay for a good-sized block behind Woody Creek's cemetery, or down near the old slaughteryards where a bowling club was currently under construction. Its lawns would no doubt appreciate the blood and bone of generations of cow, pig and sheep.

By '78, the local butcher no longer slaughtered local cattle on local land. By '78, much of the meat eaten in Woody Creek arrived in town pleasantly presented on supermarket trays.

The council had built a swimming pool on the corner of Cemetery Road and Slaughter Yard Lane. Kids who used to cool off in the creek behind Dobson's and McPherson's land now congregated at the pool where their massed screams competed with Macdonald's screaming mill saws.

Back after the first war, old George Macdonald had built that mill on the outskirts of Woody Creek but, like the cemetery, the town had surrounded it. Its saws were silent during the week between Christmas and New Year and the silence was deafening, though not this year. Fire truck sirens had bellowed through the town that week.

Forest fires travelled hand in hand with those red north winds of drought years and there was not a lot a man could do to fight them. For a time it had looked as if Woody Creek might go up in smoke, but the wind had turned and sent that fire back on itself.

'God's hand was in it,' the old folk said.

'Why did he start it in the first place then?' the kids asked. Their generation wouldn't waste their Sundays in church. They'd marry there. They'd attend burial services there.

There were two funerals at the Anglican church today, old Pop Dobson's and Margot Morrison's.

'It's such a bad day for it,' Maisy Macdonald said. 'It reminds me of when we buried old Cecelia Morrison. The temperature peaked at a hundred and fifteen that day.'

'You would have all been dead, Nan,' her twelve year old grandson said. 'You would have been sizzling like bacon if it ever got that hot.'

Kids today knew so much more than their grandparents would ever know – and they knew so much less. They'd never heard of Fahrenheit, but knew that the forty-four degrees Celsius promised by the television weather man last night made it too hot to go outside.

Jenny had parked the car in the shed, for its shade, not the car's protection. It was a write-off, the insurance company said. Jim had ordered a new car, and been waiting for days for a call to pick it up.

She backed it out to Hooper Street, named for Jim's family; they'd built on that corner before the street had a name. Once again she looked for Georgie's red ute. She'd been looking for it all morning – listening for it for days.

She expected to see the ute parked out front of the church. No red ute. Only four cars there – and the undertaker's car and the hearse – and Margot's funeral was due to start at one thirty and Jenny needed Georgie at her side today.

Five days since she'd had her stitches removed – and Jenny had to phone the hospital to find out that much. Not one word from Georgie.

'She's not coming,' she said.

'She's an adult, Jen, and we need to get in there,' Jim said.

An old red-brick building, the church stood on the corner of South and Church streets, and today, surrounded by dead lawn, it looked abandoned. Little Jenny Morrison had sat at Norman's side on its hard pews each Sunday of her childhood. These days she entered that door only for funerals.

They were close to its shade when another fire truck bellowed through town.

'Something's burning again,' she said.

'It's the day for it,' Jim said, stilling his feet to listen. By the sound of it, it was heading towards the bridge, to the west of town. There wasn't a lot left to burn out that way.

An atrocious day for a funeral. It would have been worse had the church been crowded. No crowd there to say goodbye to Margot Macdonald Morrison. Few had known her, fewer had sighted her these past ten years.

Elsie and Harry Hall were there with their sons. Teddy and Lenny Hall would carry the coffin. Maisy Macdonald was there with four of her eight daughters and two adult grandsons, also pallbearers. John and Amy McPherson, Robert Fulton, his elderly mother and Miss Blunt. Jenny nodded to them as she walked by to the front-row pew.

The minister, sweating in his vestments, didn't waste time.

For two days Jenny had attempted to write something meaningful for him to say about Margot. All she'd come up with was how she'd loved to win when they'd played cards and how two little girls had slept side by side as babies and how they'd lived together in Granny's house.

She'd made no mention of Trudy. In life, Margot had denied giving birth to her and few in this town knew she had. Elsie and Harry and their kids knew, and Georgie – and where was she?

Again Jenny glanced over her shoulder, half-expecting to see Georgie standing in the doorway. Only the undertaker, sweating in his dark suit.

Georgie had lost everything that night. She'd damn near lost her life. If Harry and Elsie hadn't known which room she'd slept in and if Raelene hadn't knocked down the chicken wire fence, the police couldn't have got near that window to break it and drag Georgie out.

There was nothing left of Granny's house. Not a stick of a wall. Not the shape of a door. The chimneys and the kitchen stove, accustomed to heat, had survived the inferno and that was all.

Jenny forced her mind back to the coffin. She'd chosen a white coffin. As a twelve or thirteen year old, Margot had developed a germ fetish and become obsessed by white. She'd only wear white underwear, white frocks, white anklet socks to keep her feet germ free – until she'd grown too heavy to reach her feet and pull her white socks on.

The coffin looked so small, like a kid's. She'd asked for white flowers only. At the time it had seemed like the right thing to do. Today, it looked wrong, but everything she'd ever done for that girl had been wrong. I should have let her win that last card game—

'. . . when fire destroyed that grand old heritage home, built by Woody Creek's founding father Richard Hooper.'

Jenny stared at the minister. He hadn't got that from her notes, not the 'founding father', his name, or the 'heritage' bit. She looked at Jim, who was looking at her, each face answering the other's unspoken question, then both glancing in Maisy's direction. She was Margot's grandmother and she liked to talk.

She'd spoken to the *Willama Gazette*.

For days Woody Creek had been headline news in the local and city papers, and on television.

WOMAN DRAGGED FROM INFERNO WHILE SISTER BURNS

TWELVE MEN AND FIVE WOMEN ARRESTED IN DRUG BUST

Three women and nine men had been charged. Most had been released on bail. On the night of the drug bust there must have been forty men, women and kids living out at Monk's hippy commune. All bar a dozen had moved on.

KIDNAPPED INFANT FOUND ALIVE

SECOND VICTIM FOUND IN THE ASHES

'Our prayers are with Margot's family and her greatly loved neighbour Elsie,' the minister said, his words jarring every nerve ending in Jenny's body.

Elsie, a loved neighbour? Elsie was the only one crying for her and the only one likely to cry. She'd been a mother to Margot, and Jenny had told that minister to say so. *Her greatly loved neighbour?* It was worse than meaningless. It was insulting; it was embarrassing, and Jenny cringed in preparation for what the minister might say about Margot's grandmother, who didn't look as if she'd hear what he said anyway. She looked ready to pass out. There was much too much of Maisy, ten or twelve stone too much, and she must have been eighty.

Jenny's fingers counted the years. She knew that Maisy had been ten months older than Amber, that Amber had been . . .

And everyone was standing for a final prayer. Jenny stood, having decided that if Amber was still alive somewhere she'd be seventy-nine turning eighty this year.

I hope they take her home, Jenny thought as Maisy struggled to her feet. I hope they don't take her out to the cemetery. The heat will kill her.

It didn't seem real that Margot was in that coffin. Jim was nudging her to follow. They'd been seated on the chief mourners' pew but Jenny didn't feel like the chief mourner so remained where she was, giving way to Elsie and Harry, then to Maisy and her daughters.

She took Jessica Palmer's arm before they stepped out into the sun. 'Don't take your mum out to the cemetery, Jess,' she said.

'She's determined to go,' Jessica, youngest daughter to Maisy, said. 'Georgie didn't get back for it?'

'Other than the note she left on the kitchen table when she left, I haven't heard a word from her,' Jenny said.

Handkerchiefs wetted beneath the church's garden tap dried fast at the cemetery. Umbrellas and wide-brimmed hats offering the only shade, the minister got it done at breakneck speed, then

Maisy did as she always did, invited the mourners back to her house for a cup of tea.

She was Margot's grandmother by default, or by the fault of her raping mongrel twin sons. She'd told Jenny yesterday that they'd agreed to close their mill down for the day. They hadn't, and had those mill saws not been screaming, Jenny wouldn't have agreed to go to Maisy's for a cup of tea. Macka and Bernie Macdonald had never moved out of their mother's house.

'Do we have to?' Jim asked.

'She'll stand around in the sun talking if we don't,' Jenny said.

*

Entering Maisy's passage was like walking from Hades into an icebox. She owned two big air conditioners, both turned on since morning. As a kid Jenny had loved this house. As a kid, she'd loved Maisy, who'd been more mother to her and Sissy than Amber had ever been.

She drank her tea, ate a slice of Maisy's lemon meringue pie, and mentally composed the letter she had to write to Florence Keating which needed to be in the post by four or it wouldn't get to Queensland in time. If it didn't, Jenny would have to phone that woman, and she was in no mood for a monologue of Florence's guilt; she had enough of her own.

Raelene, also killed in the fire, was being buried next Thursday, not the little Raelie who for seven years had been Jenny's doll-like daughter, but the one Florence Keating and her husband had ruined.

They'd read about Ray's death in the newspaper and got themselves a lawyer to fight for custody of the then seven year old Raelene. Florence had given birth to her and at the time she and her husband had no children.

Jenny, aware that her life wouldn't stand up to a court's scrutiny, hadn't fought for that little girl.

She'd fought to get control of the twelve year old brat Florence had handed back to her, and if Dino Collins hadn't come on the scene with his drugs she might have had a chance. Lost the battle when Raelene started shooting drugs up her arms. Given up. Lost touch with her – until the night Granny's house had burnt when she'd learned that Raelene had given birth to a baby which had somehow ended up in Cara's care. How and why Cara had become involved Jenny didn't know.

She'd never known a lot about Cara. She must have married. She had a son – and the newspapers referred to her as Cara Grenville, foster mother of the kidnapped infant. Raelene and Dino Collins had taken tiny Tracy from her bed, drugged her and taped her into a cardboard carton, and if not for Joe Flanagan's red kelpies, Tracy would have died taped inside that carton.

For days the newspapers and television followed the story – and drove Jenny crazy, but it had been those television cameras which allowed her to see her grandson.

One caught him leaving the children's hospital, a six or seven year old boy, holding on to Cara's hand while looking back at the cameraman – and he might have been Jenny's own son, Jimmy, if not for his spring-coil golden hair, Jenny's hair, Cara's hair, Archie Foote's hair.

'Ready?' Jim asked.

'The car will be like an oven,' Jenny said.

She kissed Maisy, kissed Elsie, accepted kisses from two of Maisy's daughters, then went out to force open the driver's side door of their abused Ford – and to borrow Jim's handkerchief to protect her hands from its red-hot steering wheel.

They'd left their own air conditioner on, and she made a beeline for the sitting room, their only cool room. They would have required half a dozen air conditioners to cool the entire house.

There were six bedrooms in Vern Hooper's old house, and since Trudy had been away at school, all bar one of those bedrooms were rarely used. They had two sitting rooms, the smaller of the two home to an ironing board and bookshelves.

They'd furnished the dining room, a beautiful room, though they rarely ate in there. Jim's typewriter lived on the dining room table. The east-side front room, once Lorna Hooper's library, had become Jenny's sewing room, complete with a large cutting table and two machines.

It was a changed house since the days of Vern Hooper, internally changed. His kitchen, a good-sized room at the west-side rear of the house, had been gutted in the sixties to become a functional kitchen. They'd installed a combustion stove. It was their best room in winter.

They lived in the sitting room come summer, and Jenny fetched writing pad and biro, closed the sitting room doors then, the air conditioner rumbling as it churned out cool air, she sat down to write her letter.

*Dear Florence and Clarrie,*
*We have organised Raelene's funeral for eight thirty on Thursday morning. Ray's insurance account will pay for it, so please don't offer. We've booked a double room for you at the hotel for Wednesday night. If you decide against making the trip down, please cancel it. The phone number is above.*

*There will be no church service. Given the horrific circumstances of her death, we felt that a graveside service was more fitting. The undertaker's phone number is also above, should you wish to alter any of our arrangements.*
*Sincerely,*
*Jen and Jim Hooper*

Six o'clock, Jenny tossing a quick salad together for dinner when she lifted her head to the sound of thunder, a distant rumble.

'The sky is very dark to the west,' Jim said.

'Smoke,' Jenny said.

'Smoke doesn't rumble, Jen.'

'I've lost my belief in rain,' she said.

By seven, the thunder was close, and the sky to the west was a fireworks display of forked lightning.

From a western veranda they watched it come, a grey swathe of it, moving fast towards town.

'It looks like one of those tornadoes they have in America,' Jenny said.

Then it hit, just on nightfall.

Heavy rain on a tin roof is deafening. No rain in this storm. Chunks of ice the size of golf balls thrashed Woody Creek and the noise was horrendous. Voices unable to compete, Jim pointed at their car, a twenty year old two-toned green Ford, dented beyond repair by Raelene when she'd done what she'd deemed necessary to take possession of it. It would wear more dents tomorrow.

Then as fast as it began, the hail was gone and the rain came, wind-blown waves of rain, sheets of it, and the veranda guttering, leaf and hail filled, overflowed and Jen and Jim stood behind their own Niagara Falls.

# Lila

Six nights a week, the Melbourne bus passed through Woody Creek. It was due in at around seven thirty, never early, but rarely more than twenty minutes late. It was late that night. Eight twenty-five when it drove into a town awash with water. Woody Creek's gutters hadn't been built to handle heavy rain.

Blunt's Road was a lake fed by a river of run-off from the tiled roofs of a bunch of brand new houses, built on land once known as O'Brien's acre. South Street's bitumen crown was visible, and the bus clung to what was visible.

It stopped out front of the post office where one passenger stepped down into water – as did the driver. He opened his luggage bay to haul out a large and well-worn case, and with no passenger waiting in the rain to take possession of it, he sloshed through the water to place the case beneath the shelter of the post office's veranda, where its owner had taken cover.

She wasn't dressed for the weather. She'd clad herself that morning in a lolly-pink frock more suitable for the bedroom.

'Trust this bloody town to turn on a flood for me,' Lila Jones/Roberts/Freeman said, then added, 'Ta.'

She'd lived in this godforsaken hole for a few years when she'd been married to her second husband, and every time she'd boarded the bus out since, she'd vowed never to set foot in the place again. Wouldn't have been here tonight if she hadn't been stony motherless broke.

She'd spent the best part of forty years stony motherless broke. Pregnant and disowned by her parents at fifteen, a wife and mother of twins at sixteen, she'd dumped them with her mother-in-law and moved to Sydney where she'd got work at a clothing factory. Got paid on Friday, been broke by Sunday.

Jenny Hooper had worked there. She'd always had money in her purse, smokes in her handbag and an extra sandwich in her lunch bag. She'd shared. Just a pair of kids with kids in '43, their blokes away fighting a war.

A lot of water had run under the bridge since 1943. Jenny's bloke had been rich and Lila's hadn't. Jenny had stayed put. Lila hadn't. She'd crawled in and out of a lot of beds since the forties. Sex is known to be good exercise. Her figure had altered a little, but her hairstyle hadn't, nor her spendthrift habits. Penny-pinching was for pensioners. Age was for others, and if a cruel mirror did at times attempt to point out her wrinkles, she turned her back on it.

From a distance, if sighted from the rear, Lila Jones/Roberts/Freeman could still draw the eye of males. Up close, with her long, dead, flat black hair, her face turned to leather by years of pursuing a good suntan, the males who didn't run when she turned around were becoming few.

She was staring at the river of water flooding down the gutters and wishing that Jenny's bloke owned a house in Melbourne when the lights went out and Woody Creek became a flooded black hole in hell.

'Bloody hell to it,' Lila said, turning to where the driver had placed her case. Her life was in that case.

*

Woody Creek's powerlines had a bad habit of coming down in a storm. Too many trees, too many miles of aging posts and wires that sagged too low. Candles were kept in handy places, as were the old kerosene lamps and lanterns. They came out that night, and within moments of the blackout, that old yellow light glowed again from windows.

The air conditioners died. The televisions died, and with nothing to watch, and cooler outside than in, Woody Creek residents moved their chairs out to verandas to watch their gardens lap up the rain, a more gentle rain now that the storm had moved on.

Jen and Jim were sitting on the veranda when they heard the small gate squeal open. Jenny reached for the torch at her feet and turned its beam towards the bricked path that led to their front steps. Its beam exposed a saturated rag mop of a woman – and her case.

'No,' Jenny said. 'Please God, not tonight.'

'Lovely weather for ducks,' Lila greeted them, and without a word, Jim claimed the torch and went indoors, leaving Jenny to greet her visitor in the dark.

The last time they'd given Lila a bed, they hadn't been able to move her out of it for a month, and these days, one hour of her was too much. They'd ended up buying her a bus ticket and writing her a cheque for fifty dollars, and as the bus had pulled away, they'd sworn there'd be no next time. But what can you do when a drowned rat seeks the shelter of your veranda, and you don't have the heart to hit it with a shovel?

You can lie. Jenny worked on a lie while fetching towels.

'We're leaving for Melbourne at dawn,' she said. 'We would have gone this afternoon if not for the storm. Trudy starts her nurse's training next week.' Or she'd start at the end of the month, and they had been planning a trip, though not until after they'd picked up their new car. The Ford, used by Raelene as a battering ram, might not make the distance, and its boot refused to stay shut unless it was roped down, but whether it got them further than

Willama or not, they were leaving at dawn. Lila had an innate ability to alter Jenny's plans.

'I'll caretake your house for you while you're away,' Lila said.

'Jim prefers to lock up,' Jenny said. 'I'll drive you around to the hotel for the night.'

'If I could afford to pay for a hotel, I wouldn't be up here, would I? The Salvos lent me the fare, and I haven't eaten anything since they fed me breakfast – and I'm going to wee myself in a minute.'

What can you do?

Jim, who'd lit a lamp and found a second torch, returned Jenny's and, its beam lighting the way, she led Lila down to the rear bathroom, unchanged since the days of Vern Hooper, but good enough for an unwanted visitor.

She made a ham and pickle sandwich and, with still no sign of Lila, lit the stove. For five days it hadn't burnt, but if they wanted a cup of tea tonight, the stove was the only way they'd get it. It also heated their hot water service and, familiar with Lila's half-hour showers, Jenny knew that what little warm water remained in the reservoir wouldn't be warm by the time Lila was done with it tonight.

'We swore, Jen,' Jim said.

'We're leaving for Melbourne at dawn. I'll feed her then drive her around to the hotel.'

It was ten o'clock before they offloaded her, Lila clutching a ten-dollar note. Mrs Bowen, the publican's wife, accepted a cheque for two nights' accommodation and an envelope containing another ten dollars to buy Lila a ticket out of town. The Bowens knew her. Everyone in town knew the habits of Lila Jones/Roberts/Freeman.

Jenny did most of the long-distance driving, and in recent years had driven often enough to the city to know the back route through Seymour and Lilydale to Ringwood where Nobby and Rosemary, good friends, always had single beds available. Nobby and Jim had been together through the first three years of the war. Nobby marched each year in the Anzac Day parade, he went to RSL functions. Jim denied the war and his involvement in it.

They couldn't deny Lila. When Jenny phoned the hotel on Wednesday morning, Mrs Bowen told her that Lila Freeman was no longer a guest. She was on the payroll.

Trudy wanted to go down to Frankston. She'd been at Templestowe with her friend Sophie and her family since the school year had ended because Jim, determined to keep her away from Woody Creek until the media's cameras lost interest, had told her not to come home for Christmas. Now, with Lila in town, Trudy was still better off out of it. They moved down to Frankston to Vroni Andrews' guesthouse.

They didn't go to Raelene's funeral. It wasn't much of a funeral. A few brief words spoken at the graveside. Clarrie Keating had flown down alone from Queensland and would fly home that afternoon. Maisy, who attended most funerals, stayed in bed. Raelene had set the fire that killed Margot.

Jenny walked a near deserted beach, forcing herself to remember the little Raelie, who had loved the beach, who, if Florence and Clarrie had stayed out of her life, would have been different. If Florence hadn't got pregnant . . . if Jim hadn't come back into Jenny's life.

'Life is what it is, darlin', and there's only one way to walk it,' Granny used to say, so that morning Jenny walked forward, walked forward for an hour until the funeral was well over, when she turned around and walked back.

In all, they spent ten days in Frankston. They saw Trudy and Sophie in their new uniforms, took too many photographs then left for the long drive to Willama, where they picked up their new car, a white Kingswood Holden, ordered the day Georgie disappeared, which, if not for Lila, they would have been driving a week ago.

Jim, a dyed in the wool Ford man, had been guided by Teddy Hall to the automatic Holden. With no clutch, it required only one foot to drive it. The war had stolen half of Jim's left leg. He could drive a manual, but not confidently. The Ford had been Jenny's car, her first and only car, and, battered or not, the final emptying of its glove box hurt, as did handing over the keys to the salesman.

Jim drove the Kingswood the last fifty kilometres home, and before they were out on the open road, he was in love with it.

The scent of its brand new upholstery was stifling. They wound the windows down, then smelled the heated motor, distrustful yet of its brand newness. It offered a more comfortable ride. There was good support in its bucket seats. The radio worked. For the last fifty kilometres home, their conversation was the car. Lila didn't get a mention.

They parked it in the shed, its white paintwork too perfect to leave out of doors. They unloaded their luggage and many supermarket bags then walked around their new acquisition, admiring its lines.

'You like it,' she said.

'I can drive it,' he said.

The back fence of the hotel was only a narrow street away from their rose hedge; their kitchen chimney must have sent up smoke signals. She arrived, and before the supermarket bags were unpacked, she crept up on them and let herself in via the back door.

'I didn't think you were ever coming home,' she said, then told them how the fates had conspired against them. 'The hotel cook slipped on wet tiles when she ran out to pick up hailstones. Her wrist's broken. I'm cooking for the next few weeks.'

Lila Jones/Roberts/Freeman knew how to cook for a crowd. At various times in her colourful life, between her variety of husbands and men friends, she'd cooked at cafés, for shearers, at roadhouses and at hotels. With the caravan park booked out during the school holiday season and Freddy Bowen's hotel the only place in town to buy a meal, he couldn't afford to be without a cook.

'Free accommodation, he said, and he sticks me in one of their sleep-outs behind the pub with old Shaky Lewis next door,' Lila said. Shaky was the hotel's resident alcoholic handyman.

'Beggars can't afford to be choosy,' Jenny said.

Jim went to bed early to escape her and, at eleven, Jenny walked her across the narrow street.

A too narrow street. She returned, morning, afternoon and evening. She stayed for an hour, or six. Breakfast, lunch and dinner were served at the hotel on Thursdays, Fridays and Saturdays, but only breakfast from Sunday to Wednesday, giving Lila four days and four nights free to spend in Jenny's kitchen – until a delegation of town councillors came by to discuss Georgie's grocery shop, its twin green doors locked since she'd left town.

Robert Fulton owned the hardware store on the corner of South Street and Blunt's Road. Joss Palmer, married to Jessica Macdonald, was Macdonald's mill foreman. Dave Watson, an elderly farmer, had a son, Walter, who'd married Emma Fulton, Robert's sister. He opened the conversation.

'It's about your girl's shop,' he said.

Emma had seen Georgie drive away, had seen the twin green doors of her shop left open. Until the fire, Emma had worked part time for Georgie, and that day she'd closed the doors and fitted the padlock, which had been in place since.

'Is she planning to sell?' Dave asked.

'We haven't heard from her,' Jenny said.

'The town needs that shop,' Joss Palmer said. 'Jessica and her mother have been doing a run down to Willama three or four times a week, shopping for those who can't get down there. If she's not going to open it, it needs to be sold, Jenny.'

'She's not here to sell it, and we can't,' Jenny said.

'If you're prepared to take responsibility for it, Emma said she'd be willing to help out behind the counter,' Robert said.

# The Double Dare

Macka and Bernie Macdonald, joined at the elbow since they'd slid from the womb, spent most nights elbow to elbow at the hotel's bar. They liked watching Lila, who dressed like a woman but drank like a male, drank in the bar like a male where she told bluer jokes than a male, and laughed louder.

She spent little time looking their way. She liked her men younger and better looking. By their fifty-eighth year, Maisy's twins were no-necked, thick-shouldered, broad-chested, pot-bellied, bald-headed old men.

Five days a week they worked side by side at their sawmill, willed jointly to them by George, their father. Seven nights a week they shared a twin room in their mother's house. Maisy fed them; she did their laundry, made their beds, told them what to do and when to do it. On occasion they did it.

She'd told them tonight that one of them would be driving her and Dawn down to the city next Wednesday to see a quack, then told them to make up their minds which one of them was doing it.

Neither twin had become accustomed to a regular supply of sex. What little they got they paid for in Melbourne, and the one who did the driving would have access to a place they knew in Fitzroy, which was what may have got them eyeing off Lila. According to pub rumour, she was a contortionist in bed. The male animal, when segregated in a bar room, has always been prone to exaggeration when it comes to discussions of sexual conquests.

'Ask her what she charges,' Macka said.

'Go to buggery,' Bernie said.

'I dare you!'

'I double dare you, you ugly bastard,' Bernie said.

Neither one took the dare. They had another beer instead, listened to another joke, bluer than the last, then went home for a late dinner.

Dawn was still off her food, and the only member of the family who couldn't afford to go off her food; there wasn't an ounce of fat on her. Maisy was worried about her; Bernie and Macka weren't the worrying kind.

'Whoever is driving us will be driving my car,' Maisy said.

'Drive yourself then,' Macka said.

'I'm too old to battle my way through Melbourne traffic.'

'You're too bloody slow to,' Bernie said.

The twins had a separation complex as kids; Maisy's means of controlling them had been to lock them in separate rooms, or deliver one out to their older sister Patricia's farm – and take his boots so he couldn't walk home. If their father had backed her up, she might have got control of those boys. He hadn't, so she hadn't.

They each drove a ute, a black Holden ute, and those twin utes were a town joke. The last time they'd updated them, Dawn told them they were a joke, not that Macka and Bernie gave a bugger about what anyone said, unless it was said to their faces, and when it was, few said it a second time. The twins fought as one, always had.

They fought each other at times, and to circumvent a twin brawl as to who would be driving a sedate sedan to Melbourne, Dawn tossed a coin. Bernie called heads. He won the right to a night in

Fitzroy. No matter what he called, or whether the decision was made with a coin or a deck of cards, he usually won. At eighteen he'd won the right to marry Jenny Morrison – or to be left standing at the bloody altar by her.

'Eat something and you mightn't need to go to bloody city doctors,' Macka said.

'Stop eating and you mightn't need an undertaker for a year or two more,' Dawn said.

The specialist put Dawn into hospital to do his tests, and a day after he let her out she was back in, a surgeon cutting into her. Instead of a few hours in Fitzroy, Bernie spent those hours with Maisy and Maureen, his eldest sister, sitting in a hospital waiting room.

They read bad news on the surgeon's face before he opened his mouth, and when he opened it, they got worse than they'd read. He told them that Dawny was riddled with cancer, and that there wasn't a bloody thing he could do about it – these weren't his actual words, but what his mess of jargon translated into. Maisy didn't believe him, not until they were allowed in to see Dawny. That's when they knew the quack hadn't been exaggerating.

'Bugger the mill,' he said. Maisy and Maureen left howling at Box Hill, Bernie drove home to get Macka and to tell the rest of them to get down there.

It was after midnight before he hit home. Macka's ute wasn't parked in the drive, and Macka wasn't in his bed. Bernie got rid of Maisy's sedan and in his ute drove the night streets, looking for its twin, which he found parked out the front of the pub. And what the hell was it doing parked out there at that time of night?

It took five minutes of belting on the bar room door to raise a pyjama-clad Freddy Bowen. He told him where he'd find his brother.

The hotel's sleep-out doors would have had some form of locks. Lila's hadn't been utilised. Bernie swung the door wide and flicked on the light switch.

'Get your trousers on, you dim-witted bastard. Dawny's dying,' Bernie said.

Back in the fifties when Billy Roberts had brought his bride to town, the twins had argued Lila's merits. She slept in the raw and as long as you didn't look at her face, she still had merits enough, which she made no attempt to cover up while Macka put his trousers on.

They woke Jess and Joss. Jess rode back to Box Hill with Macka, her two daughters rode with Bernie. By mid-morning the others started arriving and the walls of Maureen's weatherboard sweated with Macdonalds, ex-Macdonalds, offshoots of Macdonald. Maureen had four, Patricia had brought one of her three, Glenys and Joanne arrived in separate cars, Rachael and Rebecca drove down together with Rebecca's twins. No Dawny there to keep the mob under semi control. She lay drugged to the eyeballs in a hospital bed.

Macka spent ten minutes beside it, then drove home to look after the mill, or so he said. Bernie stayed on with the women, taxiing them to and from the hospital, to tram stop or train, taking his turn at sitting with Dawny who, full of morphine, was unaware anyone was there.

'She's never had a day's sickness in her life,' the women said.

'Why didn't she go to the doctor sooner?' they said.

'It would have meant missing work. She never missed a day in her life.'

Daily they expected her to improve, but she got a lung infection, and on the fifth night after the operation her condition was listed as critical. On the sixth night, a call came through to Box Hill before dawn. Maureen phoned home. Macka wasn't answering, so Bernie woke Freddy Bowen again. He raised Macka; Bernie told him to get his arse back down here, then the Macdonalds drove in convoy through the empty streets to sit with Dawny and hold her hand while she died.

Gone by six. They were back at Box Hill before Macka turned up with Lila Jones/Roberts/Freeman in tow. Maisy, who hadn't stopped bawling for a week, stopped bawling to stare at what followed Macka into Maureen's sitting room. Lila had dressed for the occasion, in the only black she owned – a pair of skin-tight leather hot pants, long matching boots and a skimpy black singlet top, stretched to fit her uplifted boobs.

'This is a house of mourning,' Maisy said. 'Take her out, Macka.'

Macka, who had warned Lila to wear something black, thought she looked fine, but he took her out to the kitchen to the food. Like their mother's, Maureen's refrigerator was a gold mine. Lila was eating cake when Bernie picked her up, tossed her over his shoulder and carried her, kicking and scratching, through the house and out to the street where he dumped her into the gutter beside Macka's ute. He'd turned to go back to the house when Macka sucker-punched him in the jaw.

And what was a sucker-punched man expected to do but retaliate, which he did. It wasn't a fair fight with Lila straddling him. She had fingernails an inch long. Sammy, Maureen's copper son, broke them up, and Macka and his Sydney tart took off.

Two o'clock before the convoy of Macdonalds left Box Hill, Bernie, with Maisy at his side, leading the way home, a slow-moving convoy across the city, but once on Sydney Road, Bernie put his foot to the floor.

He thought Macka had come to his senses when he saw his ute parked in the drive. Bernie got his mother out and led her indoors. She was a broken woman, until she saw that well-travelled case in her hall.

Her kitchen was at the rear of the house; she found Macka and his well-worn trollop seated at the table, eating take-away chicken and chips. Maisy, who had never had a bad word to say about anyone, who had never made an enemy in her life, who'd stuck by Amber Morrison through thick and thin – until she'd murdered Norman – picked up the flat iron she used to prop open her kitchen door.

'Get her off my property now, Macka, or by God I'll iron out a few of her wrinkles,' she said.

When a woman like Maisy Macdonald declares war, a man is forced to choose which side he's on. Bernie carried Lila out to a second gutter; there was water in this one and what followed wasn't pretty. The twins had the fighting technique of a pair of rabid gorillas; they drew an audience. Maisy's house was in South Street, right in the centre of town, a stone's throw from most of Woody Creek's scattering of shops. There was a narrow park to the left of the house, then the town hall. The railway paddock was across the road and on the far side of the railway paddock there were a few more shops and the hotel.

They came from all points of the compass – kids came on bikes, over back fences or running through the park, adults came to drag their kids home then changed their minds, passing cars stopped passing and pulled over.

If Dawny hadn't been dead, she would have been out on the street with the hose or the hair broom, breaking them up. If Dawny hadn't been dead, Bernie might have realised that Macka's brains had moved temporally south to his trousers and might have allowed him the last hit. But Dawny was dead, and he'd stood beside her bed watching the life seep out of her, and that useless bastard hadn't been at his side, so today he refused Macka the last hit.

Two overweight males pushing sixty don't have the stamina of youth. They were dead on their feet. They were bruised and bleeding before the local copper and Joss Palmer pulled them apart long enough for Maisy to get between them. Joss and a neighbour tumbled Macka into his ute. His trollop got in with him, and as they were backing out, Bernie pitched the well-travelled case into the tray.

*

A bastard of a week. A bastard of a funeral. Maisy, still not over the last one, was determined that Dawn's would be about Dawn.

She told the girls and Bernie that they were going to get up in the pulpit and say something meaningful about what their sister had been to them.

The girls did as they'd been told. Jess and Rachael's elbows got Bernie to his feet to stand like a fool in his skin-tight suit beside the fancy coffin. In the end, all he could do was put his hand on it.

'I got used to seeing you around, Dawny,' he said. 'I got used to dodging your bloody broom too. You could swing it like a champ, mate. I keep closing the door of your bedroom and the old girl keeps opening the bloody thing up again,' he said, then he took off out the side door and made a beeline for the pub.

They came in later, Macka and his trollop. She was wearing a dress, or wearing most of it. Bernie tried to make his peace. He bought Macka a beer.

'It was a bloody dare, you half-witted bastard,' he said.

'You're jealous, you ugly bastard,' Macka said.

And it was on again.

They broke a few glasses, did a bit of damage before a trio of cops from Willama arrived to assist the local constable. They frog-marched Bernie out to the street and warned him not to return. Macka and Lila were now paying for a refurbished room inside the hotel – and the cook's wrist was still in plaster.

The mill became a war zone. No one got paid on the Friday following Dawn's funeral.

For fifty-eight years they'd been one. Lila Jones/Roberts/Freeman chipped them apart. Dawny had been in her grave two weeks when Macka phoned the Willama mill owner who, six months back, had made an offer for their mill. The Willama bloke wanted all of it, not a half-share. Macka wanted his half-share, so he advertised it for sale.

Maisy paid him out and, in Lila's eyes, that payout made Macka a wealthy man. They left town together.

# Missing

Life wasn't meant to be easy, according to Malcolm Fraser, the dour Liberal man currently occupying the prime minister's lodge. He'd coined that line from a play written by George Bernard Shaw, except Shaw had removed the sting by adding his *take courage; it can be delightful.*

Someone in Sydney hadn't found life or Malcolm's politics delightful. In February, a bomb was placed in a garbage can out the front of the Sydney Hilton Hotel where Fraser and other heads of state were at a meeting to discuss whatever heads of state wasted taxpayers' money discussing. The bomb missed the heads of state but killed three taxpayers.

By March Jenny was finding life a long way from delightful. She couldn't believe that an Australian would make a bomb and place it where it could kill three innocent men. They made bombs in Ireland, not Australia. Australia was the safe country. The war hadn't touched it – or barely touched it. And she couldn't believe what Lila had done. Through the years she'd given that woman a bed, she'd fed her, given her money, bought her bus tickets, and confided in her long ago, had told her how one of the Macdonald twins had fathered Margot.

Jim celebrated the fact that Lila was out of town, that with luck, she wouldn't return. Jenny tried to. But how could someone who for years had claimed to be your friend, who'd made constant claims on that friendship, how could she marry one of her supposed friend's rapists?

She had married him. She'd sent a postcard from the Gold Coast and signed it Lila Macdonald. And how, after what she'd done, had she found the nerve to send that card?

Weeding allowed Jenny to vent her anger, the ripping, the pitching, and the cursing of thistle, nettle and Lila. When that card arrived, she'd thought it was from Georgie – then she'd seen the signature and tossed the thing into the stove and watched it burn.

Nothing was the same without Georgie. Jenny had been able to talk to her about anything. And Elsie, stuck in a bungalow that would have fitted inside Vern Hooper's sitting room, wasn't the same Elsie. She'd been accustomed to the freedom of Granny's fifteen acres, to fruit for the picking, to chooks clucking and a paddock of vegie garden. Now a prisoner of Teddy's bungalow, in the weeks since Margot's death she'd aged ten years. Harry and his kids were worried about her, as was Jenny – when she found time to worry about her. She had no time for anything. She spent her days playing shopkeeper and didn't have a clue how to play the game, and Emma Fulton, now Watson, knew little more.

They had Georgie's invoices. They had the names and phone numbers of the suppliers. There was money in the shop's account to pay for new stock, but it was money Jenny couldn't get at without Georgie's signature, and last week they'd barely made enough to pay the electricity bill, plus Emma's wage.

Those twin green doors closed since Christmas, shoppers had altered their habits – and Willama's two big supermarkets encouraged them by offering weekly specials – and how could Coles supermarket afford to sell large tins of canned fruit for what Jenny paid the supplier for those same cans? Jenny'd sent Jim down to Coles to buy a dozen cans, which saved her ordering them.

She had no time to sew. The material for a bridal gown was still waiting on its roll on the cutting table, and she was running out of time to get that gown done. She had carrots going to seed, onions she couldn't see for the weeds. There was light enough in the evenings to weed by, but by the time she locked those green doors, by the time she tossed something easy on the table for dinner, she was ready to sleep, and usually did, in front of the television – a sign of old age, or exhaustion. Went to bed exhausted. Woke too early, still exhausted.

The inquest into Margot's death was being held in April – not that she wanted to be there, but had she wanted to, who would mind that shop? Jim wouldn't.

Her fingers delving into damp earth, she removed twin foot-high milk thistles and pitched them as far as she could. Why bother? She'd been at it for an hour and had barely made a dent in the carrot patch.

Weeds would be growing on Margot's grave. She had to do something about ordering a stone. Should have done it already. She'd meant to. Couldn't make up her mind what to put on it. She had trouble sticking to any one thought long enough to make up her mind. She'd be thinking about a tombstone and remember what she'd forgotten to order yesterday. She'd be thinking about Georgie and start remembering that last game of cards they'd played with Margot the night she'd died.

Wished she'd let her win that game. That kid had never won much from life, not in the looks department or personality. Georgie had won the lot, as a tiny kid, a teenager and a woman.

When those girls were small, Jenny had tried not to lean towards Georgie. Every item of clothing she'd made for one, she'd made for the other, determined to do the right thing – as Amber had never done with her and Sissy. Shouldn't have bothered. What had looked good on lanky, happy-faced little Georgie, hadn't done a thing for pale, pudgy Margot. Was it any wonder she'd become what she had, growing up in Georgie's shadow?

Should have let her win that game of five hundred. Had Jenny known it was to be her last chance to do something for her, she would have let her win.

You can't know the future. It's a blank page waiting to be written. And you can't alter one day of what has already been written.

She blamed herself – not for Margot's death, but for how she'd grown. She and Jim had spent years attempting to sort out Raelene, but hadn't spent one day trying to do the same for Margot. Back in the forties there'd been no one around to sort out kids' heads. They either grew out of their hang-ups or they didn't – anyway, all of those court-appointed psychologists and social workers hadn't done one scrap of good for Raelene.

Who sorted me out? she thought. Gertrude Foote, midwife, bush psychologist, font of all wisdom and Jenny's beloved granny, that's who – she'd stuck by her through thick and thin.

Missed her. Still missed her so much.

She pulled more weeds, pitching them onto the gravelled path behind her and remembering Armadale and Ray, who hadn't appreciated her untidy style of weeding – or her kids or much else about her. She'd made many mistakes in her life, but marrying Ray had been her greatest.

The only time she'd lived by clocks had been in Armadale, when the kids were at school – and now. Six days a week she opened that shop at nine though only for three hours on Saturday, and thank God today was Saturday. She'd make a start on the bridal gown this afternoon.

She glanced at the new car they no longer parked in the shed. Too much trouble getting it in and out and Jim, celebrating its lack of a clutch, was on the road every day – while she was stuck in the shop. She rarely got a chance to drive it – and when she did, she still looked for its clutch and missing gearstick.

The day they'd ordered it, they'd made big plans. They were going to drive it up to Queensland and stop off in Sydney for a few days to see what thirty years had done to the place. And what had they done since picking that car up? Made one fast Sunday trip down to see Trudy, and by the time they got there, it was time to turn around and come home. Someone had to open that shop.

Jim had written a cheque for the full price of that car. He'd written another to pay for Margot's funeral. He would have written a third for a tombstone – had Jenny known what to put on it. He had no respect for money. Those who grow up with it don't know what it's like to have none.

Vern Hooper, worth a fortune when he died, hadn't left Jim a brass razoo. His mother had. She'd placed her first husband's money into a trust account for him when he'd been a tiny kid.

Jim knew little about his mother's first husband's family, other than that they hadn't been breeders. Norm Nicholas was the only son of Oswald Nicholas, who must have been a gambling man. According to the few details Jim had been able to dig up on him, back in 1885, old Oswald had gambled ten thousand pounds on shares in Broken Hill Proprietary then, before the depression of the 1890s, he'd sold the lot for what must have been a fortune back in those days.

His gamble had set Norm up for life. He'd built the house Jenny now called home – or sometimes called home but more often called Vern Hooper's house. He'd built the sawmill Jenny had known as Hooper's mill. That mill killed Norm, leaving Joanne a forty year old childless widow. She'd married Vern Hooper in 1918, and Jim arrived less than a year after the wedding.

He'd been six years old when his mother died, and worth in excess of a hundred thousand pounds, which he'd had no knowledge of until his twenty-first birthday when letters addressed to him started arriving from his mother's solicitor.

He'd gone off to war in '41 then lost a lot of years in hospitals after the war. Not until '59 had he accessed his money, and as Jenny had discovered with Ray's insurance payout, if you can manage to get enough of the stuff together in one place and leave it untouched, it had a habit of breeding. Jim's hundred thousand pounds had doubled long before Australia changed its pounds to dollars, an event that seemed to double his balance yet again. Jenny found herself looking at figures she'd previously related to the rich and famous, not to Jenny Morrison, who ran her kitchen as she ever had, frugally, who grew her own produce, because she preferred to eat her own produce, who each year made her own jams and preserves the way Granny had taught her to. Until she'd started playing shopkeeper, she made her own money too. Customers travelled from Willama to pay inflated prices for Jenny's dressmaking services and what she earned with her hands felt more real to her than the figures on Jim's bank statements.

She owned two bankbooks, one opened when Ray was killed in a sawmill accident. The mills had insured their workers. On paper, she'd been Ray's widow but she'd always thought of that money as Raelene's and Donny's.

It had paid for Donny's funeral, had bought a stone for his and his father's graves. Jenny had withdrawn more from that account to pay for Raelene's funeral, though not for a stone. Far better that the girl be forgotten in this town.

The second bankbook had been opened for her by Jim when they'd been together in Sydney during the war. It had become Jimmy's blood money account since '47 when Vern Hooper, with Ray's assistance, paid two thousand pounds into it, Vern's idea of compensation when he and his daughters stole Jenny's son. 'No grandson of Vern Hooper would be raised a bastard in this town,' he'd said.

Jenny had never touched that blood money. The book was untouched, except in June when the bank paid in its annual interest; she handed it to a teller then so he might update its balance – which had grown each year since '47 – as had her beautiful boy, somewhere.

Jim never mentioned the son he'd known for that brief week in Sydney when Jimmy had been ten months old. Jenny knew why. He blamed himself for losing him. Had he returned to his family after the war he could have played a role in Jimmy's raising, but he'd chosen Jenny. Jim never mentioned his family – all dead now, other than Lorna. He never mentioned the war. Jenny understood that too – or most of the time she understood. Maisy didn't. Jim dodged Maisy's visits when he could.

John and Amy McPherson had become his friends; Amy, a retired schoolteacher, John, Woody Creek's shy photographer, who had fifty years of photographs and negatives stored in one of his bedrooms. It had only been a matter of time before Jim, Woody Creek's historian, and John had got their heads together. They'd created an incredible book for Woody Creek's centenary, a pictorial history of the town, and the men had worked on other projects since – a hobby, rather than a profession, until Amy came up with an idea for a children's book.

She'd been born with fairy dust in her eyes. She'd turned John's two and a half acres into a fairy land garden, had turned John's talent with a camera into magical wedding albums, then one Sunday morning, she'd come to the house with a batch of photographs and an idea to build a children's book around one of Jenny's rhymes.

Jim, a facts and figures man, had come on board – at first he'd been reluctant, but since posting their fourth children's book, *Butterfly Kingdom*, off to their Sydney publisher, he'd been nagging as hard as Amy for another rhyme.

They were an odd foursome. John was seventeen years Jenny's senior, Amy six or eight years senior to John, but they'd become family to Jenny, close family.

Jenny glanced at her watch. Still plenty of time. She'd dug up Vern Hooper's back lawn to the east of the house and turned it into a vegetable patch, a too large vegetable patch, and this morning she'd come out here to pick the extra produce to sell at the shop, not to weed and dream.

Wished Georgie would call. She didn't wish her back. For the last ten years she'd been telling her to get out of Woody Creek and do something with her life. She had beauty, confidence and brains enough to do anything she wanted, and she'd wasted too many of her years already in this town, in that shop she'd inherited from Charlie White.

Hoped she was well. Feared she wasn't. She'd lost her sister, her home, her possessions, and been lucky not to lose her life. When you lose that much, it might be easy to walk away from the rest.

She'd left a note Jenny had read so many times she could quote it.

*Dear Jen,*
*Ta for the bed. I'm off to get my stitches out and to do something about getting a new licence. The shop is open. Leave it open if you like. I don't want it.*

*We sweep up what's left over after each holocaust and glue it back into something that resembles what we might have been, then we go on. You said it, mate. I've done my sweeping, now I'm off to do the gluing bit.*
*Love ya,*
*Georgie*

Two weeks ago they'd put the shop in the hands of a Willama agent, as a rental property. To date he'd had one nibble from a Bendigo couple, though why any Bendigo couple would consider moving to Woody Creek, Jenny didn't know. She would have moved to Bendigo. She would have moved to Ringwood, to Willama – anywhere. She loathed this town.

And its business centre was dying. Back when she'd been a kid, the shops had been crowded on Fridays and Saturday mornings. There'd been few cars about, but plenty of bikes and horses. They'd had a shoe shop, a barber. Until the thirties, Woody Creek had its own undertaker cum cabinet-maker. These days cabinets were purchased ready-made in Willama, where Woody Creek's dead now queued to be buried. Until the thirties, they'd had a saddler and a bakery, its pastries and fancy cakes set out in the window on pretty paper doilies. Miss Blunt and her father had run a thriving drapery and dressmaking business and Fulton's feed and grain store had done a roaring trade. According to Emma, her brother Robert barely kept his head above water these days.

Reliable transport was killing this town. With doctors, dentists, chemists and most of the big name stores in Willama, there was a stream of cars heading east on Stock Route Road each morning.

The two big supermarkets had killed off a lot of Willama's smaller businesses. At one time there must have been five small grocery shops scattered around. There'd been three butcheries in the main street, at least three bakeries and several small hardware shops. Most had closed their door and reopened as gift shops, hairdressers, clothing boutiques, coffee shops. Coles and Woolworths sold pretty much everything else.

Hearing water sluicing down the pipes, Jenny looked over her shoulder. Jim had arisen. He'd never been an early riser. Granny had, and Jenny had caught her habit and couldn't break it. She spent most of her mornings in the garden, another of Granny's habits.

She'd picked a dozen zucchinis. Prolific breeders, fast growers, she'd picked a dozen only yesterday, but the more she picked the more desperate those plants became to seed the next generation.

She'd shed her seeds before the plant had reached maturity, and at times wasn't certain she'd ever got around to maturing. Four kids she'd given life. Hadn't wanted any of them, not when they'd been conceived. All gone now – not that she'd ever had Cara to lose. She'd walked away from her in '44 and hadn't set eyes on her again until '66 – and couldn't believe her eyes the night she had seen her. Cara looked like her. She'd had her hair, her brow, eyes, hands. Jimmy had looked a little like her, but he'd had Jim's hair and hands. Georgie and Margot looked like their fathers.

Cara had produced seed, that beautiful skinny-necked boy. Raelene had produced little Tracy who, according to the newspapers, she'd signed away to Cara, then changed her mind and stolen her from her bed. Both Jenny and Georgie had jumped to the conclusion that Tracy was Dino Collins' daughter, and were relieved to learn he'd been in jail when that little girl was conceived.

It was Collins who'd masterminded the kidnap, Jenny was certain of that. He'd been on Granny's land that night, had been driving a car registered to Raelene when he'd crashed into a police roadblock on the Mission Bridge – and the doctors shouldn't have wasted taxpayer money on putting that swine back together. They had. She'd followed his story in the newspapers.

Margot had shed her seed, and every day of Jenny's life since, she'd thanked God for Trudy – and thanked him for making her look more Hall than Macdonald.

Did love by proxy count? Did loving Trudy do anything at all to cancel out not loving Margot?

Knew it didn't. From day one, Margot had denied she'd been pregnant. She'd blamed indigestion for her swelling belly. She'd denied Trudy until the day she died. If she'd caught one sight, one sniff of her, she'd throw one of her screaming, foot stamping attacks. Jenny had kept them well apart.

Teddy Hall had fathered Trudy. He'd signed away his parental rights before the adoption but still showed too much interest in her. He'd picked up a good little car for her eighteenth birthday and been determined to give it to her, from him and his parents. Jim could be determined too. He'd paid Teddy for the car.

Jenny picked another zucchini. Two plants would have been enough to feed her, Jim and the McPhersons. She'd planted a dozen.

Jimmy would have had a family by now. He'd married a schoolteacher three or four days before Margaret Hooper's death. Ian Hooper, Jim's cousin, met the wife at Margaret's funeral. Karen, he'd said, or was it Carlene? A pretty girl, he'd said, a teacher.

'Jen? Are you still out there?'

Jenny's mind jarring back to the moment, she turned towards his voice. 'I'm picking vegies for the shop,' she called.

'It's almost nine.'

'My watch says . . .' It still said almost eight o'clock. 'It's stopped,' she said.

'It's had its day, Jen.'

'It keeps perfect time when I find time to wind it. I'll have to run. Can you finish the picking? There's a ton of tomatoes too. Strip off anything that's turning pink.'

# TOMBSTONES

Losing Margot, then Dawn and now Macka, shattered Maisy. Bernie, not the shattering type and once again welcome in Freddy Bowen's bar, spent his evenings there, drinking enough to put him to sleep.

There is little joy in sucking down a skinful alone while bastards who've owed you one since classroom days congregate in flocks like vultures, waiting to rip the flesh off your bones when you fall down.

He was down; he was so far down a nest of worms had started burrowing into his head. He scratched his bald scalp constantly, attempting to rid it of the crawling sensation. In places he'd scratched it raw, then picked the tops off the scabs and named them skin cancer, and blamed Macka for his skin cancers. That brainless bastard was up in Queensland and he didn't have the skin type that stood up to too much sun.

Bernie went to sleep thinking cancer, woke with cancer on his mind. He knew it killed, but it had previously killed others, not Macdonalds.

He went to bed with Macka on his mind and dreamed he was in the room, then he woke and found he wasn't. He missed the ugly bastard. He missed knowing what he was thinking before he thought it. He missed seeing himself wandering around at the mill. Missed him like a man might miss the left arm he'd been attached to since birth.

Then the business with that girl they'd fathered started eating its way through the wormholes and into his head. When Macka had been around, half of the blame for what they'd done to Jenny Morrison had been his to wear. It belonged solely to Bernie now and it crawled with the worms in his brain.

Jenny had been at Dawny's funeral with her lanky, limping Jim. He'd almost met her eyes when he'd been standing beside the coffin trying to find something to say. She'd looked away fast. Always had. For thirty-odd years she'd been crossing over the street when she'd seen him coming.

He should have closed the mill the day of that girl's funeral. Maisy had told them to close it down. She'd told them that for once in their godforsaken lives they were going to do the right thing. They hadn't done it.

He'd stood with Macka watching the fire that killed that girl. An old habit of theirs, following the fire truck. He, Macka and fifty more followed the truck out Forest Road that night, where someone told them that one of the Morrison girls was trapped inside Gertrude Foote's house. Bernie had known which one was trapped. He'd seen the redhead standing with her back against the walnut tree.

No one wants to watch a man, dog or kangaroo burn, but had he or Macka given ten seconds' thought that night to the fact that it was their own flesh and blood that was burning?

Not ten seconds of thought, nor one second. It might have meant no more to them if the redhead had been trapped in that inferno. They'd been buying their smokes from her for twenty years, during which time Bernie had set eyes on her sister just once, on the night of Teddy Hall's engagement to Vonnie Boyle. He'd seen a bit of her when she'd been eight or ten, when for months she'd stayed in town with Maisy – a lisping, whingeing bitch of a girl he'd dodged when he could.

She should have worn his name – or Macka's. At eighteen, they'd both been willing to do the right thing, or maybe just willing to help themselves to legal rights to Jenny Morrison. She'd done a runner the night before the wedding day, had left Bernie standing at the altar, choking in his wedding suit.

For a lot of years, he'd convinced himself that he'd been the one made a fool of. It had worked well enough until he'd got out of the army. During the years since, he'd blamed being young, being drunk, which had worked well enough too when there'd been the two of them, when they'd been drunk. There were no longer two of them and a man couldn't stay drunk twenty-four hours a day – unless he was old Shaky Lewis.

Bernie stopped going to the pub, stopped going to work, lay on his bed dozing, scratching his skin cancers and thinking. Thinking hurts those not accustomed to doing too much of it. He was lying on his back scratching and thinking when Maisy came to the bedroom door to nag him about driving her down to Willama to choose a tombstone for Dawny.

'Drive yourself,' he said.

'If I felt up to driving myself I wouldn't have asked you to drive me, would I?'

Her admission got him out of bed. Until Dawn's death, Maisy had spent more time on the roads than she had at home. She sat watching television and swallowing aspros these days, and she held on to walls when she walked up the passage.

He drove her to Willama. He was tailing her back to the stonemason's office when she went down.

An inflated ball will bounce. Maisy bounced. She lost a bit of skin off her hands and maybe off her backside, but he and the stonemason got her back onto her feet with Maisy still fighting to pay for Dawny's tombstone.

'You're going to see a doctor,' Bernie said.

'I haven't got an appointment.'

'Then you're going to the hospital. You're not dropping dead on me, you old bugger.'

'I'm not going near a hospital. Dawny was all right until they operated on her.'

The stonemason phoned. An Indian doctor fitted her in. Bernie walked her to his office and stayed on to dob about how she bounced off walls and swallowed aspro by the packetful.

The Indian took her blood pressure and told her it was sky high.

'I buried my granddaughter, my daughter and I lost my son to a Sydney trollop. What do you expect my blood pressure to be doing?' Maisy asked.

'On the scales, if you please, Mrs Macdonald.'

'I didn't come in here for you to have a go at my weight.'

'That is your choice, but hiding your face from the figure will not make it less,' he said in the singsong voice of Indian immigrants. 'If you persist in carrying that weight around, your husband will be losing you,' he said, and he started writing scripts.

'Her son,' Bernie corrected, and attempted to suck in his gut.

The doctor eyed him, then asked him to sit down so he might check his blood pressure.

'Be buggered,' Bernie said.

'A man of your height cannot carry the weight you are carrying and expect to live a long life, Mr Macdonald,' the Indian said.

'It's all muscle,' Bernie said, and he returned to the waiting room until Maisy came out with her prescriptions, a diet sheet and a leaflet advertising Weight Watchers.

They had lunch with Rachael. She always put on a good spread. Midway through eating it, he mentioned the Weight Watchers leaflet and Rachael agreed with the Indian that Maisy could afford to lose a few kilos.

Maisy, who ignored kilos, walked away from the conversation to turn on the television. She never missed *Days of Our Lives.*

Bernie left the women watching their soap opera and drove back to give the stonemason a cheque and the words the women had decided they wanted put on Dawny's tombstone. He had his mother's scripts filled at the pharmacy then drove home.

*

There were rich families and poor in Woody Creek. There were families edging their way up to being comfortably off, and others who had once been comfortable sliding closer to the breadline with each generation. The Hoopers had always been rich. The Macdonalds had become rich after the first war.

Between the two great wars, Paul Jenner had started his married life scratching a bare living from dry land. Twenty years ago, he'd scratched up enough money to buy Lonny Bryant's riverfront property, where his labour, along with that of his three sons, had started paying off. Paul Jenner was living proof that if a man is prepared to work his guts out, he'll get to where he wants to be. He now owned the old Hooper farm, and if his bid was successful, he'd own Monk's acres, which would make him the biggest landowner in the district.

There were plenty in town who refused to work at much other than the begetting of a kid every year or two. Breeding had always been a favourite pastime in Woody Creek. Invalid pensioners with crook backs may have done it sitting down, but they did it, as did dole bludgers and their girlfriends. By the late seventies, big families made good economic sense to those who didn't go in for labour, and if the government didn't place a limit soon on the number of bludgers' kids the taxpayer was prepared to feed, in twenty years' time there'd be insufficient taxpayers' kids to keep the bludgers' kids in the style they'd become accustomed to.

Maisy's capital, cut by a third since she'd bought Macka's share of the mill, was, by Woody Creek standards, still enough to make her a rich woman. Few would believe it these days if they'd looked in her fridge, in her cake tins. Bernie couldn't raise a rattle from her biscuit tins, and if he did, all it offered were the slices of fossilised cardboard Maisy had the gall to call biscuits. The freezer, which had once contained a selection of ice-cream and frozen cakes, now froze bread, and not even white bread.

'Just because you're on a bloody diet doesn't mean that I'm supposed to starve,' Bernie complained.

'If it's in the house I'll eat it,' Maisy said. 'And the doctor said you needed to lose weight as much as me.'

She'd always cooked, which may have been why Bernie had never considered leaving home. She sliced lettuce now, grated carrots, served them with tomatoes and onions and paper-thin slices of corned beef. She thawed two lousy slices of frozen bread before each meal, one for her, one for him.

'Stop freezing the bloody stuff.'

'If I don't, I'll eat more than my three slices a day,' Maisy said.

He escaped her on Tuesdays, after dropping her off at her Weight Watchers meeting. The big restaurant in the middle of town served meals all day. He was seated, trying to catch the eye of a waitress, when Jenny and her lanky coot walked in.

Guilt multiplies in an empty gut, and who was looking after the shop while they were eating down here?

He waited until they were seated, then sidled out and bought himself a chocolate-coated ice-cream at a milk bar, which he scoffed in three bites on his way back to the meeting to collect Maisy, who smelled that ice-cream, or saw the melted chocolate on the belly of his shirt.

He didn't mention seeing the Hoopers, but asked a question which had been haunting him for weeks. 'Have they done anything yet about getting that girl a tombstone?'

'I haven't asked them,' Maisy said.

'What's happening with the redhead?'

'They hadn't heard from her the last time I spoke to Jenny.'

*

Maisy never walked if she could drive. Every Sunday since Dawn's funeral, she'd driven around to the cemetery with a bunch of flowers. Weight Watchers suggested their members walk, and that Sunday she set off on foot.

Bernie watched her slow progress through the park, watched her lean on a white post to catch her breath before crossing Park Road, where she was lost to his view. Convinced she'd fallen again, he took off after her.

She was still going, slow but steady. He caught her halfway across the sports oval.

'What's got into you?' she asked.

'Save me sending out a search party for you when you drop dead,' he said.

Maisy, who knew every man, woman and child in town, who went to every Protestant funeral and to a few of the Catholics', knew that cemetery like the back of her hand. He followed her to the raw wound of Dawn's grave where he watched her kiss her flowers before placing half of them on the mound. Assuming the rest were for his father, he hung back to light a smoke. George Macdonald had been gone for a lot of years but Bernie still had bad memories of the day he'd died. He knew where that grave was too, but Maisy was walking the wrong way, so he followed her. Followed her to a not so raw wound in the earth, where she kissed the rest of her flowers then placed them down – and knowing who was under that dirt gave Bernie goose bumps.

'What's wrong with them, leaving it looking like that?'

'They've got the shop to worry about.'

'Not so worried that they can't piss off to Willama.'

'Where did you see them?'

'Going into the restaurant.'

'You went in there eating,' she accused.

'I had a bloody chocolate-coated ice-cream. Lay off me, will you,' he said, and looked towards the Catholic section, and at a second unmarked grave, knowing who was in that hole too, and knowing that his mother wouldn't go within spitting distance of Raelene King's grave.

It wasn't official yet but everyone knew she'd petrol-bombed that house. They'd found Harry Hall's empty petrol can. How she'd got herself caught up in it, no one knew nor ever would. For two days they hadn't known her bones were there. Half of the cops in Melbourne had been up here with their dog squads searching the forest for Raelene King.

'Ask her,' Bernie said.

Maisy's mind far away, she looked at him quizzically. 'Ask who what?'

'Ask Jenny what she's done about marking that girl's grave.'

'Raelene's?'

'Margot's.'

'I will not ask her, and I didn't come over here to have you following me around nagging me about tombstones. It's like an open wound knowing the way Margot must have died, so stop picking at it – and stop picking at your head too – and start wearing that hat I bought you.'

'Offer to buy her one.'

'Go home and let me visit in peace.'

He waited for her, walked home with her, or followed her home, a dozen or so paces behind – followed her home to skinned chicken and zucchini soup. He wanted his Sunday roast, his meat with all the trimmings, swimming in gravy. He wanted butter on thick slices of fresh white bread. She tossed him a slice of chilled brown bread and no butter.

'Use some of that creamed cheese on it,' she suggested.

'It tastes like sh—'

'Stop your swearing at my dinner table.'

'Bloody dinner table? If that was dinner, don't bother feeding me tea.'

Then it happened, on Thursday night. He woke with a pain in his chest and knew he wasn't going to live long enough to die of skin cancer or starvation. He was having a heart attack.

His father's heart had given out on him, though not when he'd been fifty-eight years old. Old George's hadn't missed a beat in ninety years. Bernie's wasn't missing beats, just beating hard and fast. He could hear it pounding in his earhole, thumping against pillow.

He lay on his narrow bed, scratching his hairy chest instead of his head and staring at Macka's empty bed, lit tonight by a full moon, and he blamed his twin for their heart attack too. They'd shared the flu every year or so, shared the measles, mumps, chicken pox and a few attacks of the clap. That bastard didn't have the stamina to satisfy a woman with that Sydney slut's appetites. Wherever Macka was, he was dying – and not doing it alone.

He missed that ugly bastard. He missed his voice from the other bed, missed his snore, and knowing that he was dying on top of his slut – or she on top of him while Bernie died alone, was enough to kill any man.

For an hour he lay there, wondering if he ought to wake his mother, then at around one o'clock his heart attack moved southward to where hard-boiled eggs, a tin of salmon, raw onion and cucumber attempted to unite.

He lay on his back, his gut bubbling, the moonlight tormenting him. He missed Macka more on moonlit nights and, near two, he rolled from his bed determined to cover that window.

As he moved, gas exploded from his rear end, then again while fighting on a pair of trousers, and with no one to blame other than himself, he got out of that room fast, closed his door and went out the back door to blast in the moonlight.

As kids, that moon had called him and Macka out to play and, blasting every eight or ten yards, he followed the pathway they'd used on many a moonlit night, through the park where the bandstand was lit up as bright as day, across Park Street, and across the football oval to the cemetery's six foot high cyclone wire fence, where he stood getting rid of gas beside a peppercorn tree he remembered as being much smaller.

They'd cut a hole in the wire behind that tree, he and Macka, cut it one moonlit night with their father's wire cutters, then used that hole to climb through to the cemetery where they'd decorated tombstones. Denham, the local copper back then, had been hiding behind old Cecelia Morrison's stone one night. They'd scrambled out through that hole and he couldn't.

And not much use looking for it tonight. If he found it he wouldn't be able to squeeze through. Walked on then and in through the small cemetery gate to follow the gravelled paths he'd walked with Maisy until he found the raw wound where the bones of his – or Macka's – only offspring lay.

His sisters had kids, grown-up kids who had kids of their own. He was Uncle Bernie to the multitudes, old Uncle Bernie who owned a sawmill and a black ute and not much else. He should have had a ton more money in the bank. Blown it on new utes, the gee-gees, grog and smokes. Easy come, easy go.

He stood a while beside Margot's grave, blasting rotten egg gas – and maybe it was the wrong place to be doing it, so he backed off and found his way to old Cecelia Morrison *née* Duckworth's stone, feeling no guilt about blasting there. He could just about remember that super superior old bugger.

Poor old Norman was in with his mother now, poor harmless old Norman dead in his bed for three days before they found him – and found crazy Amber, his wife, standing on a chair, cleaning out her bathroom cupboard.

The moon lit the three angels guarding Cecelia's tombstone, as it had on other nights when Bernie and Macka had added a few missing appendages. No chalk in his pockets tonight but a lot of bad memories rolling in his gut.

They'd told Jenny they were going to sacrifice her on that cement slab for a bit of good weather.

*You stink like a pair of pole cats. Let me up.*

A swarm of goose bumps rising thick on Bernie's soul, he stepped back, remembering the night they'd deflowered little Jenny

Morrison on that slab, he and Macka – which most of the time he remembered like something he'd been told that they'd done, or maybe like one of the roles he'd played in the school concerts.

Still real to Jenny. She hated his guts.

They hadn't meant to do it. They hadn't. She'd been like one of their sisters, her and Sissy both. They'd been mucking around, that's all. They'd found her sitting on the oval fence, listening to the band music, and decided to have a bit of fun with her, that's all. Dragged her through the hole in the fence and held her down on that stone.

*I forgot to bring me sacrificial dagger.*

*Have you got something that would do the job, because by the Jesus, I have.*

*I dare you.*

*Don't you dare me, you ugly bastard.*

If Macka hadn't done it first, Bernie wouldn't have – or maybe he would have. Didn't know now if he would have or he wouldn't have. Didn't know if he was coming or going, what he thought or didn't think, or if what he thought he thought was what he thought or what he thought he ought to think, if what he felt was what he thought he ought to feel or if he felt it.

Still erupting from time to time he walked the moonlit paths to the fence and the peppercorn tree, and he found the hole, or found where it had been. Someone had repaired it with twists of wire.

Nothing stayed the same. This place wasn't the playground it had once been – not since they'd carried his father out here. Bernie had found him dead in the mill office, halfway through filling the pay envelopes. No one had been paid that Friday and not one bugger had complained about not being paid. There wasn't a man in town who hadn't respected George Macdonald.

Or Dawny.

She haunted his dreams. Still nagged the hell out of him at times. Eight sisters he had, all older. Seven now. One by one they'd die and be brought out to this bloody place. Maisy would go next – if she was lucky. Then Maureen. She was pushing seventy.

'A man would be better off having a fast heart attack and going first,' he muttered, and he went home to drape a blanket over his curtain rod.

It kept the moon outside where it belonged.

# Odd Couples

Someone may have once told Amber Morrison that cleanliness was next to godliness. She may have taken those words to heart. Experts who studied the workings of the human mind might have diagnosed her obsessive desire to eradicate every speck of dust, every smear of grime from her world as a desire for inner cleanliness, which, to those who knew her history, could suggest she possessed a conscience.

They'd be wrong. Had Amber bothered to self-diagnose she'd have blamed the twenty-two years spent on her mother's fifteen acres, shovelling chook dung from the floors of fowl pens, raking up goat and horse dung, sweeping up the muck her mother tracked into their two-roomed hut on her working boots. Gertrude Foote's idea of cleanliness had differed from that of her daughter.

The hut of Amber's childhood had burnt to the ground five days before Christmas. She'd read every report on the tragedy with relish, had read every news item aloud to Lorna, who had also shown interest.

In April of 1978 Amber read a brief report on the inquest into the death of Margot Macdonald Morrison, disinterested in the one who had died in the fire or in how she'd died. It was the details, the accompanying photograph, that caught her interest. She knew exactly where the cameraman had been standing when he'd taken the photograph, and at what time of day.

She stared at the walnut tree a mite too long, long enough for Lorna to reach out talon-tipped fingers to tap the newspaper. 'Are we reading or dreaming this morning, Duckworth?'

Her teeth exposed in what served Amber as a smile, she turned the page.

Six days a week Elizabeth Duckworth read aloud to her benefactor. Between ten and twelve each morning they sat at the dining room table, the broadsheet newspaper spread between them, the items of interest to Lorna circled by Lorna in red. Given good light and the aid of a magnifying glass, she could read, though her sight, damaged in the accident that had given birth to her Duckworth guide-dog companion, Lorna's sight had continued to deteriorate. Twice each day, Amber fetched eye-drops she dripped into Lorna's eyes, which, when the beetle-brown iris disappeared beneath reptilian eyelids, looked like pickled onions.

Lorna's injured nose produced its own drops. She'd always snorted. Now she sniffed and snorted. In her seventieth year, proud Miss Hooper was a sorry sight. She'd been likened to a totem pole in her youth – a black-draped pole now, short steel wire inserted into its head, its hawk nose mutilated.

Amber was several years her benefactor's senior. Elizabeth Duckworth wasn't. When she'd taken that name, she'd deducted seven years from her own birth date. And why not? If one was taking on a new identity, why not remove a few of the worst years from her past life?

There were days when she cursed her choice of name. Given her situation at the time of its choosing, 'Duckworth' had epitomised respectability and, above all else, Amber Morrison had required that undoubted respectability. Should have chosen Smith, Jones, Brown.

Had she recognised the bandage-swathed woman in the second hospital bed, she would have. She'd seen only the spikes of grey hair, the hospital-issue gown. Had she heard her wardmate's natural voice she may have recognised her haughty tones, but for two weeks, Lorna's mutilated nose had been packed with gauze; the tones she'd emitted were minimal and unfamiliar. Not until much later, until the bandages and gauze packing were removed, had Amber recognised Lorna Hooper's snort of disdain, but by then, left with poor sight in one eye and less in the other, she'd become dependent on Miss Duckworth's excellent vision.

Unsociable was not a word to describe Amber's benefactor. Antisocial, uncharitable, demanding, ill-tempered, an unrelenting enemy may have sufficed. However, to one who had lived for sixteen years with the insane, then for a few years more with the dregs of humanity, cohabiting with a tyrannical, evil-minded hag was, to Amber, next door to paradise – or her staid brick house set in a quiet Kew street was.

Amber delighted in Lorna's wall to wall carpets. She vacuumed them with love. She delighted in the large expanses of outdoor concrete she swept daily, and in her spacious bedroom with its crisp white lace curtains and matching bedcover. Here, in paradise, she was living the clean life she'd craved since childhood.

Joanne Hooper's fine furniture filled Lorna's rooms. Joanne Hooper's delicate ornaments, locked away in a dark sideboard for years, had been removed from their tomb, washed and placed once again on display.

Lorna's obsession with church was the one uncomfortable stone in Amber's comfortable life. Church rubbed her up the wrong way, or the mother and daughter, Alma and Valda Duckworth, who attended Lorna's church did. They'd moved into a house little more than a block and a half from Lorna's locked gates. Since learning they were not the only Duckworths in the area, they'd become determined to link Miss Elizabeth into their clan.

Amber had a place there, on the periphery, through Norman's mother Cecelia Morrison *née* Duckworth. Though considerably younger, Alma had been Norman's first cousin. Amber had met her parents, Uncle Wilber and his wife. She'd met Alma's oldest sister when the Duckworths came in force to Woody Creek to attend Norman's mother's funeral. It was their invasion that killed Amber's second son, or forced him to make his entrance into the world prematurely.

Five times Amber had swollen with child. Only Sissy survived her birth. Amber had loved her girl, if only for living. A love not reciprocated. When Amber was released from the asylum with no place to go, Sissy had refused to see her. *Your daughter has made a new life for herself—*

A new life with the Duckworths. Amber had seen her with Alma and Valda Duckworth at Lorna's church. On the first occasion, she hadn't recognised the draughthorse of a woman who'd pushed ahead of her in the queue to get out of the church door. She'd recognised her later, as had Lorna.

'That obnoxious female,' Lorna named her. A fair description. Sissy had become obnoxious in appearance and manner.

On the second occasion, as she'd walked Lorna down the aisle to their front pew, Amber, recognising Sissy's mammoth back, had warned Lorna who'd led the way out through the side door, then through the shrubbery to the car park.

That was the day Amber decided it was time to move on. She'd accrued funds enough to rent her own small unit – somewhere. She'd looked at advertisements until learning that her pension would be hard-pressed to pay the rent on a single bedroom unit.

And was Sissy likely to recognise her? Amber's once beige-blonde shoulder-length hair was now short silky white curls. Her shoes had once been bought to last, her garments chosen for their lack of colour. In Kew, she'd been able to satisfy her craving for smart expensive shoes, for the pretty hats and the pretty frocks she'd craved in her youth.

Since her release from the asylum she'd been in receipt of a pension. It still arrived each fortnight. Had her benefactor known about it, Amber would have been out on the street. Only last week Lorna had circled a report in the *Age* of the arrest of one hundred and eighty Greek Australians alleged to have been involved in a conspiracy to defraud the Social Security Department. Amber Morrison's private mailbox was in the city. She accessed it monthly on hair-cutting days, when Amber's bankbook had a brief outing before being posted back to Box 282 GPO, MELB.

It amused her to imagine Lorna's expression should she learn of her own involvement in a conspiracy to defraud. She'd been instrumental in securing Miss Elizabeth Duckworth's pension, and thus obtaining at no cost to herself her 'Duckworth'/cleaner/guide-dog/reader/cook.

*

Jenny's mind was on bank accounts – Georgie's bank account in particular. She was opening mail addressed to her daughter, hoping for a statement from the Commonwealth Bank and evidence of another cashed cheque. The last statement had shown three cashed cheques, two for uneven amounts, which suggested payment of bills, but one had been for two hundred dollars.

There was no bank statement amongst today's mail. Bills from suppliers, a three-year term deposit was maturing at a city bank.

'Nothing?' Emma asked.

'Nothing.'

Until circumstances had thrown them together, Jenny and Emma had rarely spoken. Emma, a year or two Jim's senior, had been raising a family before Jenny became the town scandal. They'd spent a couple of uncomfortable days together, but women, forced to spend eight hours a day in close confines, don't remain strangers. They got on well now, and were hopeful that morning. Prospective renters were arriving from Melbourne at eleven, their call the only one received from the agent's city advertisement.

Two weeks ago the Bendigo couple had driven up to look the place over, which had taken them five minutes. The woman sneered at Charlie's old cash drawer and docket book system then, without a word, walked out. Her cocky little bantam husband had at least nodded a form of goodbye.

'Heritage', had since been added to the agent's advertisement. This morning's couple knew what they were driving hours to see – if they understood English. Their name was Con-dappa-doppa-something or other.

Emma, as desperate as Jenny to return to her own life, had lined up a dozen customers to come in at five- or ten-minute intervals – her sisters, her brother's wives, her husband and her eighty-odd year old mother. All is fair in love and war and in the getting rid of unwanted property.

Jenny had done what she could. She'd raided Ray's insurance account to pay for a few improvements since the Bendigo woman's sneer. After the fire Georgie and Teddy Hall had broken into the shop through the storeroom window to retrieve the shop's and the ute's spare keys. There was new glass now in that window, and the smell of fresh paint.

By eleven, the prospective renters hadn't arrived, which necessitated an alteration to Emma's customer roster, but the Con-doppa-somethings eventually came and while Jenny played guide, Emma handled the customers, who rang Charlie White's cow bell at five- and ten-minute intervals.

The Greek couple barely glanced at the bookwork where Jim's neat figures took over from Georgie's larger figures. Jenny showed them the cash drawer, the old docket book system – the heritage bit – then left them to look around. They'd driven a long way and were in no hurry to leave. They walked out the back door and came in the front, then reversed their steps.

Jim called just before one, impatient for a verdict.

'No verdict,' Jenny whispered. 'They've got their measuring tape out now, and we haven't had a customer since the rush of Fultons. Call Amy and Maisy and ask them to come in and buy something.'

He didn't call them, but drove around to buy a packet of cornflakes. Jenny added two packets of cigarettes to his order, two kilos of sugar and a pound of butter. The prospective renters watched Jim hand over his money and receive his change and docket then followed him out to the veranda where the male leaned against a leaning veranda post. A passing dog approached, wanting that post, but the woman flung a stream of Greek at it and the dog moved on.

'Trudy would have understood that,' Jenny said. 'Her girlfriend's grandmother can't speak a word of English.'

For half an hour more the Con-doppas stood in the shade of Charlie's veranda, eyeing the few customers who entered and left, the woman commenting on each in her own tongue, Jenny and Emma coming up with possible translations by means of her expression, his tone and the length of his reply.

Then a black car with dark tinted windows pulled into the gutter out front and the Greek couple got into it.

'It looks like a mafia hit man's car,' Emma said.

'Drug baron,' Jenny said. 'They're looking for a replacement for Monk's cellar.'

On the night of the kidnap, the police searching for Tracy had found a crop of marijuana growing beneath artificial light in Monk's old root cellar.

'You could fit a good few plants in here,' Emma said. 'Plenty of lighting.'

Then the prospective renters were gone, and all Jenny could do was wait.

For two hours she watched the phone, willing the agent to call. He didn't, so she called him and, no, he hadn't heard from the Greek couple, however, the Wallis couple from Bendigo had phoned again this morning and made an offer. They wanted a month by month lease, with an option to buy written into the contract, along with a purchase price well below the value of the building, business and stock. They also wanted a no fault escape clause added to the lease.

The agent called the following day. The Wallis couple were interested in another property in Mortlake. Their offer was only good until tomorrow at ten.

'Tell them to buy in Mortlake,' Jenny said. She couldn't inflict that Wallis woman or her bantam rooster mate on Woody Creek.

# Rest In Peace

Bernie had given up going to work, and with no porridge and cream, no eggs and bacon to get out of bed for, he was rarely out before *Days of Our Lives.* Joss Palmer, his brother-in-law foreman, ran the mill, and one Friday in April, he phoned Maisy, who shook Bernie awake at ten.

'Who's dead?'

'No one. Sam O'Brien cut half of his fingers off,' she said.

'Shit!' Bernie replied.

The saws were silent when he got down there. Old Sam was sitting on a log nursing his towel-wrapped hand, but otherwise looking happy enough. Bernie wasn't. Macdonald's had a good record; their equipment was modern and accidents rare.

'How the bloody hell did it happen?'

A few had seen those fingers fly. A few told what they'd seen. A few stood back smoking, maybe thinking what Bernie was thinking, that a bloke, three months away from retirement, might donate a couple of knuckles from his left hand for a decent compo payout.

And there was no money being made with a dozen and a half

men standing around blowing smoke and expecting to be paid today. He wrote a cheque for the wages bill, then drove the victim and two of his three missing knuckles down to the hospital.

It was seven o'clock before they returned to town, and neither Bernie nor his passenger sober. They hadn't spent the entire day at the Farmer's Arms. After dropping Sam off at the hospital, Bernie had driven down to the Holden place to test-drive a new ute. He'd taken it for a spin out to the tombstone place to find out how much longer Dawny's grave would be without a stone, and while waiting for an answer, he picked up a brochure – because it was there.

He could have gone home. He should have gone home. Old Sam could have caught the bus. Instead Bernie went to the hotel for a beer and a counter lunch – a beautiful wedge of meat pie and a pile of mashed potatoes – where, after a second beer, he'd decided to order a new ute, white – and let the bastards laugh about that.

If old Sam hadn't needed a painkiller when the hospital turned him loose, Bernie might have driven home sober, but by four, Sam was suffering for his compo payout, so they'd called into the Farmer's Arms where Bernie ordered two whiskies. One never being enough for old Sam, he'd paid for two more. Bernie paid for the next two, pleased to have a drinker at his side. Sometime later they'd started looking at the pictures in that brochure then old Sam, as he was apt to do after a few whiskies, started offering a bit of good advice.

Maisy waited dinner. Bernie couldn't rightly say what it was – nor could anyone else. He tested a forkful – and it tasted as bad as it looked.

Maisy wanted to know where he'd been till this time of night.

'I ordered a tombstone,' he said.

'For old Sam? Jessica told me it was only his hand.'

'He'll be able to afford to pay for his own bloody tombstone,' Bernie said. 'I'm having my name put on it.'

'You're not dead yet,' Maisy said.

'It's for your granddaughter,' he said.

Maisy stopped shovelling whatever it was they were shovelling. 'It's too late to put your name on anything to do with her, and Jenny will already have ordered one.'

'Then you'd better tell her or she'll end up with one at each end.'

'You tell her. You ordered it.'

'She'd spit in my bloody eye and blind me.'

'If she does, you deserve it.'

'I'll drive you around there.'

'As if I'd get into a car with you tonight – and I thought that you'd given up the drink.'

'Ring her up then?'

'You did it, you ring her up. I've told you before that I'm not interfering in their private business.'

Bernie had known better days. The pie and mashed potato lunch still swimming nicely in whisky, he chose to leave it unpolluted by macaroni and slimy greens and he walked outside to his ute. Drove by Hooper's corner, turned right at King Street, right into Blunt's Road and right again into Hooper Street, this time slowing as he passed their driveway. He didn't turn in, or stop. Drove by, then turned right onto Three Pines Road where he braked directly opposite their house and sat staring at it, scratching his skin cancers.

There was no sign of movement in the garden, so he got out and crossed over the road to hide behind their rosebush hedge. By summer's end it was tall enough to hide a man of his height. He didn't have much of it. He was peering between the thorns and the few remaining blooms when a door slammed. He ducked low, knowing they must have seen him, or his ute. Half a dozen of their windows looked west, and everyone and their dog knew his ute.

Lanky Jim came limping around the corner to the west-side veranda, looking for him, probably thinking that Maisy had dropped dead, so Bernie showed himself, or showed his head between the roses, then without preamble, let rip.

'Me and Mum thought we'd like to take care of young Margot's tombstone – that's if Jenny's got no objections.' And too bloody late if she had. He'd already written the cheque.

'I'll speak to her,' Jim said, turning, limping back indoors, leaving his rose hedge thorns to punish the rapist.

Bernie didn't go home. He drove on down Three Pines Road to where it forked. He took the right fork, out Forest Road.

Gertrude Foote's boundary gate was closed. If he hadn't been drunk, he might not have opened it, but he was, so he did, and drove on down to the walnut tree.

'Shit,' he said.

He hadn't been near the place since the night of the fire and nor had anyone else as far as he could see. Blackened stumps, blackened piles of junk and silver-white ash were all that remained of the house he and his working bee had built around Gertrude Foote's two-roomed hut, back in '58. Maybe he'd been thinking of his kid at the time – his or Macka's. He hoped he had. He no longer knew why he'd done it, and the whys and wherefores didn't matter much now. That girl was dead and the house was rubble, all bar the sitting room chimney and fireplace that old Jorge, the Albanian, had built.

Is there anything more lonely than a chimney left standing amid a pile of blackened junk? Maybe there is. Beer was Bernie's choice of drink. Beer gave him a lift. Whisky made him lonely.

He sat in his ute, staring at the site for a while, then he got out to walk, and later to lean against the chimney, commiserating with it while attempting to identify items.

He could make out the blackened, twisted frame of a bed's springs, set up like a piece of modern art to be photographed by a city cameraman. He'd seen it in one of the newspapers at the time. That was where they'd found the girl's body, or what had been left of it – in her bed – or on what had been left of her bed.

He stared for minutes at the bedsprings, then walked across ash and twisted corrugated iron, dragged the bedsprings free and loaded them onto his ute. He'd have a new ute next week. May as well get some use out of the old one.

A heavy man full of whisky doesn't move fast, not on a pair of bandy legs never designed to support his mass of weight, but they kept him going. He transferred eight or ten sheets of corrugated iron to the ute's tray while his mind travelled back to the war. Join the navy and see the world, they used to say. He and Macka had joined the army to escape rape charges. They'd seen a bit of the world, a bombed, burnt out world. They'd seen a lot of burnt houses and their burnt owners, seen so much death close up it had no longer meant much to either of them.

They'd always wished themselves taller, had envied the kids who had outstripped them at fifteen, sixteen. They'd grown an inch or so taller than their old man, could look down on Maisy and the sisters, all runts. Not that lack of height had mattered much when there'd been the two of them. They'd fought as one, aware that no youth or man could do them much harm while they'd watched each other's backs. It had worked during five years of war. They'd come home without a scratch. A lot hadn't. Three they'd taunted in the schoolyard hadn't come home. They'd taunted Jim Hooper. He'd come home with half of one leg and a decent section of his mind missing – or for a time his mind had gone missing, and maybe still was.

He made kids' fairy books, he and Jenny and the McPhersons. He refused to march on Anzac Day. Men who had lost two legs marched on Anzac Day. Bernie and Macka marched every year, side by side in their uniforms – until they'd grown out of their uniforms and had to march in suits, their medals pinned to their breast pockets.

Bernie would march alone this year – or he wouldn't.

'You bastard of a year,' he muttered.

The light was gone before he got an old iron bedstead apart, the redhead's bed. He tossed the bits of it onto his ute and called his load enough. Too late to unload it – the tip closed its gates at six – so he took it home to spend the night in the driveway, then went to the bathroom to shower off a bit of the dirt.

Too much of him to wash, places he couldn't reach easily – and too much of that dirt beneath his skin. He could feel it crawling there tonight. Whisky had always got him crawling with termites from the past.

Maisy was making tea when he came out. She offered two slabs of her fossilised cardboard smeared with cottage cheese, a slice of tomato on each. He pushed them back to her side of the table. She offered him one of her blood pressure pills, with a glass of water.

'Take it,' she ordered. 'You look ready to have a stroke.'

'You take it,' he said and pushed it back to her side.

'Do as you're told for once in your life, Bernie. I'm not losing another one of you. Did you tell Jenny about your tombstone?'

'I told her lanky coot,' he said.

'What did he say?'

'That he'd bloody tell her.'

'What did you say?'

'That we'd put up a bloody stone.'

'You didn't tell him you'd already ordered it.'

'He didn't tell me that they'd already ordered one either.'

'What if she says no?'

'You can use it as a garden ornament, now for Christ's sake leave me alone. I've got a bastard of a headache.'

'Strokes start with a headache. Take that pill!'

He took it to shut her up. He tried a bit of her cardboard later. A man has to eat something.

*

Bernie was out of the house before eight the following morning, aware he had to get rid of the load on his ute before Maisy saw it and wanted to know what he'd been up to. He was embarrassed about what he'd been up to, and when the tip man arrived to open the gate at nine, Bernie was at the head of the queue.

A potpourri of stinks greeted him – rotten fruit, dead cat, fish heads – a melding of odours that intoxicates the common house fly. They swarmed like bees, dive-bombing Bernie's eyes, aiming for his nostrils as he added his load to a pile of the unnameable.

As kids he and Macka had done a lot of poking around out here; they hadn't noticed the stink or the flies. Not a lot of rotten food got tossed out when they'd been kids. Families had eaten it. Old Sam O'Brien was on about the bad years of the Great Depression yesterday. Get a bit of grog into a few of the older blokes and they'd talk for hours about the struggle to keep food in the mouths of their kids through those years. Bernie hadn't noticed them. He'd never known hunger, not back then he hadn't.

With a length of masonite he scraped what ash he could from the ute's loading area then got out of the place and drove home, or was driving towards home until he passed the fish and chip shop where his rumbling belly ordered a spring roll and a bag of chips. The door was closed and a sign on it told him it would be closed until midday.

The service station out on Stock Route Road would be open. They sold a bit of take-away tucker – though not at this time of morning. He bought two chocolate-coated ice-creams then, needing privacy in which to eat them, drove again to Gertrude Foote's land.

*

His second and third loads to the tip that morning consisted of corrugated iron and blackened stumps. He'd found a cache of tools in a corner of the old shed, an axe or two, a selection of rakes, picks and umpteen shovels. He'd found no wheelbarrow, and when he returned with his fourth load, Maisy's wood barrow rode back out Forest Road with him. He'd filled it with bits of blackened shoes and books, bits of smashed crockery and twisted cutlery before realising he should have thought to pick up a plank while in town. He'd need something to use as a ramp to run that barrow up to the ute's loading area.

Back in the shade of the shed, he was searching for a plank when he found an old straw hat. Summer may have been over according to the calendar but wasn't according to today's weather, and his scab-covered dome didn't need a dose of sunburn. He shook off the dust and when the hat didn't fall apart, checked it, internally and externally, for red-backs before trying it on for size. It got a grip on his head and had a strap of elastic to keep it on – perished elastic, but he tied a knot in it then continued his search for something strong enough, long enough, to use as a ramp.

And some bugger crept up on him. 'What's lost?'

Bernie turned around faster than he'd turned in a good while and found Harry Hall standing in the doorway, lighting a smoke.

'I need a ramp,' Bernie said, feeling his blood pressure rising up to his face.

'You'll find something under my house,' Harry said as he walked by his boss to a half-full wheat bag where he started scooping chook food into a basin.

'I thought you'd moved into town.'

'The chooks haven't,' Harry said.

He'd been driving logging trucks for Macdonald's since the thirties, and Bernie, feeling like a comic figure in a woman's straw hat with elastic under his chin, headed off through bum-high dry grass towards the house recently vacated by that lanky, redheaded, pug-nosed bugger and his part darkie wife.

He found what he needed, found a solid old door which might make a more stable ramp then a plank. Hoisting it onto his shoulder, he returned to his ute and to cackling, squabbling chooks pecking at those lower down the chook hierarchy. They tried out their wings when he dropped the door in their yard, but returned to watch, heads to the side while he scooped out a trench with the heel of his boot, then rammed the end of the door into it. It felt stable enough. He was testing it with his weight when Harry came from behind a clump of saplings, his chook food basin now full of eggs.

'It might last longer if you fill 'em up and I run 'em up,' he said.

There was length in that coot, string and bone length, and not much else. 'Sounds logical to me,' Bernie said.

They worked together then, one raking, one shovelling, two shadows moving across the ash, the long and the lean, the short and fat in the hat, until the load threatened to spill over the sides of the ute, at which point Bernie tossed shovel and barrow on top, then opened his door.

'Hang on for a tick,' Harry said. 'I'll bring my ute around.'

Bernie lit a smoke and leaned in the shade of the walnut tree until the second ute, older, with more rattles, backed over the fallen chicken wire fence and across the now raked ash of what had once been Gertrude Foote's bedroom, to the site of the kitchen Bernie and Shaky Lewis had designed and built. It halted beside an old iron chimney, lying flat on its back.

Bernie remembered its weight from the days of the working bee. 'It took ten men to put the big bastard up,' he said.

'It's been the bane of my life,' Harry said. 'I must have crawled around the roof fifty times trying to plug its leak. It's going today if I have to take to it with the axe.'

They tested its weight. Harry found a crowbar and, with a bit of leverage, they got it standing on edge. A lot of heaving got half of it loaded. They tossed the metal frame of Gertrude's treadle sewing machine on top to keep it stable, then Bernie walked to the stove, unmarked by the inferno.

Harry rolled a smoke as he watched him lift one side of it.

'Leave it,' he said. 'It seems somehow sacrilegious for it to end its life at the tip. Let her rest in peace.'

Or rust in peace.

# Shock Therapy

Bob Menzies died in May, and to Jenny it was like losing a family member. He'd been around for as long as she'd been voting. Prince Charles flew over to attend the funeral, and seeing him on the television screen made Jenny feel so old. She'd watched him grow from baby to boy, from boy to a man. Hadn't been allowed to watch her own son grow into a man.

Thought of Jimmy that week. Walked the house at night thinking about him, wondering where he was, what he was doing, whether he had sons who looked like him. She tried to talk about him to Jim, but there were things Jim preferred not to remember.

A bad, bad week that one.

Then winter hit a week before it should have, and on a day when the wind blew sleety rain in from the South Pole, Emma came to work with the news that her husband wanted to take the caravan up to Queensland, that they'd be leaving the first week of June.

'I can't do it alone, Jim.'

She didn't want to do it, alone or otherwise. Jim's interest in the shop extended no further than the bookwork. She rang the agent the following morning and told him that if the Wallis woman was still interested in renting, to give her whatever she wanted.

'I want out,' Jenny said.

They moved in with a cash register which spat out strips of paper, *N. and B. Wallis's Supermarket* printed at the top, and within a week, a wet and muddy week, they were complaining about a minor drip in the storeroom Georgie had handled with a strategically placed bucket. N. and B. Wallis weren't interested in strategically placed buckets. They wanted the roof repaired. They wanted two leaning veranda posts replaced.

Jenny wanted a briquette heater installed in the sitting room. She didn't get it, and N. and B. Wallis didn't get their repairs. Amy wanted a goblin and witch rhyme. She didn't get it either. Jenny's teeth wouldn't stop chattering long enough to find a rhyme for witch – other than the obvious, which she now reserved for the Wallis woman.

'I want a caravan, Jim. I want to go somewhere warm.'

'All things pass, Jen,' he said.

'My life included,' she said.

*

Maisy had developed a habit of calling in for a cup of tea on Tuesdays, on her way home from her Weight Watchers meeting. They sat in the kitchen. It was warm. On a Tuesday in July, she arrived with a purple brocade suit Jenny had sewn for her several years ago.

'I've got Donna's wedding next weekend. It hasn't gone around me for a while, but I've lost a bit of weight so I got it out to try it on, and the skirt slid down to my hips. I was wondering if you could run the side seams in a bit for me, love, before next Saturday.'

Jenny knew she'd been dieting, but with so much to lose, her weight loss hadn't been obvious, or it hadn't until she tried on that skirt.

'You've lost inches, Maisy.'

'I must have.'

Gough Whitlam resigned from federal parliament before July ended. He'd been given some figurehead job at a university. Politicians, once they'd served their stint, had it made for life. The taxpayers supported them, supplied them with secretaries and chauffeurs, picked up the bills for their world tours – and if it was acceptable for them to gourmandise on the taxpayer teat, then who could blame the bludgers for sucking up the leftovers?

Back in the old days, the peasants had slaved in the fields to keep the rich in their palaces, and as far as Jenny could see, not a lot had changed – apart from the workhouses for the poor. Maybe a bread and water subsistence diet had encouraged a few back to work – or at least slowed down their breeding. Every time she turned around she saw a new Duffy baby in a pram – and wanted to sterilise its mother.

Not a good year, not from day one. She missed Georgie, missed Trudy, worried about Elsie, who was refusing now to leave that bungalow, which at least was warm. Jenny escaped there too often to get away from the annoyance of Jim's typewriter now rattling all day on her kitchen table. He did a lot of typing for a Willama chap who wrote textbooks.

The Wallis couple were a permanent annoyance. In August, that shop sucked more money from Ray's insurance account when their minor drip became major, and Jenny was certain the bantam had been up in the roof with a chisel. They'd get a bargain if that sale ever went through. She didn't want them to get a bargain, but by August they were pushing to buy and Jenny was damn near ready to forge Georgie's signature to get rid of that shop and its problems.

Elsie and Harry wanted to report Georgie as a missing person, but she'd cashed another cheque in June, which, unless someone else was cashing her cheques, proved to Jenny that she was okay.

On a sunny day in September she ran into Jack Thompson and his widowed mother in Willama. He was Sergeant Thompson now, but in '58–59, Jenny had known him as Woody Creek's constable and Georgie's first and only serious boyfriend. He'd been down at the old place drinking coffee with them the night Joe Flanagan came bellowing across the orchard paddock. Joe – or his red kelpies – had found Tracy taped into a cardboard carton and dumped beside his front fence.

'How's Georgie?' Jack asked, always his first question.

'We haven't heard from her. Harry wants to report her missing.'

'Was she well when she left?'

'She was quiet. We know she had her stiches removed, that she's got her chequebook with her. She cashed one in June.'

Jack's mother lived in Molliston, fifty-odd kilometres east of Willama. An only son, most of his days off were spent on the road, and twice in the past months he'd continued on to Woody Creek. He'd read Georgie's note.

'She's got a good head on her shoulders and an independent streak a mile wide,' he said. 'I wouldn't be too concerned about her while she's cashing cheques.'

'I've been wondering if, on the strength of that note, I could sell her shop.'

'She told you to do what you like with it,' he said. 'She signed that note – and she's not likely to sue you, Jen. Have a chat to your solicitor . . . speaking of which, you could be hearing from one in the next weeks. Collins is going to trial. It's more than likely that you and Georgie will be called.'

'I spoke to a chap a few months ago and told him I'd do backward somersaults off a thirty-foot springboard if it would get that swine convicted,' Jenny said.

She'd seen Dino Collins running towards Joe Flanagan's land that night. She'd heard Raelene call his name.

'From what I've heard recently, the prosecution will need all the help they can get. He's got himself a damn good story and a top solicitor.'

'They found his fingerprints on the masking tape used to seal Tracy into that carton,' Jenny said.

'A partial. They got good prints off the shifting spanner King used on Georgie's eyebrow. He's not denying that the spanner and tape belonged to him, but claims that King lived with him off and on for years and that she'd picked up the tape and spanner from his cabin.'

'He was driving her car when he crashed.'

'He's got a story to cover that too and two blokes who'll swear in court that they gave him a lift up to Woody Creek the previous day, that he'd been drinking with them out at the commune the night the infant was taken. Collins claims that King turned up at his door at dawn, begging him to give her another chance. Did Georgie see him at the house?'

'She heard Raelene call his name. Dino. Raelene always called him Dino.'

'You know he broke a couple of bones in his neck?' Jack said.

'The papers said he had spinal injuries.'

'He's in a wheelchair. They say he could be in it for life – which will get him the sympathy vote with the jury.'

'They won't let him off, will they?'

'It depends on who gets picked on the day – and I'd better get going. Mum has got a doctor's appointment.'

That day, Jenny made her own appointment with Jim's solicitors, and the following Monday morning she and Jim drove together to Willama where Jenny told a condensed tale of the fire, the shop, then offered Georgie's note.

The solicitor glanced at it, glanced at the rental agreement, asked his receptionist to make photocopies of both then asked if they'd reported their daughter missing.

'She's not missing while she's still cashing cheques,' Jenny said.

He said he'd get back to them. Jenny told him she hoped it would be soon, then they walked down to the Commonwealth Bank to ask for Georgie's current bank statement. The teller couldn't give them a statement, nor could the manager, but he told them one would be posted.

In October, *Butterfly Kingdom* was released. They found half a dozen copies of it in one of the bookshops and one each of their earlier books. *Butterfly Kingdom* was as magical as the rest.

Amy had become the face behind their fairytales, the others more than content to hide behind her. Jim and John walked out to the street, Jenny wandered down to the adult fiction shelves where she chose a book, because the redhead on the cover reminded her of Georgie. *Rusty*, by C.J. Langhall.

*Rusty.* The first time Georgie had crawled over to investigate Charlie White's bootlaces, he'd named her Rusty, and in the years she'd worked for him, he'd never called her anything else – except in his will. He'd named her as his major beneficiary and no one in town had wondered why. She'd mothered him during his final years, along with managing his shop.

*C.J. Langhall.* Jenny mouthed the name, which for some reason sounded familiar, and it couldn't have been familiar. *Rusty* was the author's debut novel. She glanced at the rear cover, which occasionally gave you an idea of what you'd find in the book.

> *Archie Fleet, a gambling man, lives a subsistence life in a crumbling farmhouse with Rusty, his sixteen-year-old granddaughter. When Archie's daughter, who for fifteen years he's believed dead, is arrested for the murder of her in-laws, Archie learns he has two younger granddaughters, one raised by the wealthy in-laws, and one by her drug addict mother.*

Archie Fleet reminded Jenny of Archie Foote, and she wanted to read about him and his granddaughters. She bought the book, Amy stopped talking, and they drove home to a letterbox half full of mail, one letter informing Jennifer Hooper that she'd be required to give evidence at the trial of James Collins, due to commence in the final week of November.

She'd argued about attending court the last time a similar letter had arrived. She'd had a good excuse. Trudy, maybe thirteen at the time, had been home from school with hepatitis. As if courts gave a damn. They'd sent her another letter, a subpoena which had forced her to present herself at a given time, at a given place. She'd left Jim at home with Trudy and driven alone to Melbourne, returning the following day on the bus, with a sore head, thanks to Raelene. The one good thing to come of that trip was the night she'd spent with Cara – and Raelene's subsequent arrest.

Cara would be at Collins' trial. Jenny wanted to see her. She'd give the court no argument this time.

*

They left Woody Creek on a warm November morning, Jim behind the wheel. He'd taken to the new car like a duck to water and was a more confident driver than she. When they'd owned the old manual Ford, she'd been the main driver, and she wasn't yet accustomed to the passenger seat. It gave her too much time to look around, gave her time to look at Jim's face in profile, at his big hands on the wheel.

As a kid she'd ridden a few times in Vern Hooper's passenger seat, back when Vern had been as slim as Jim. Though she attempted to deny it, Jim did resemble his father. He had the same steel-grey hair, the same long jaw, the same hands. Different eyes and mouth.

After Vern's stroke, he'd walked with a leg-throwing limp, but by then he'd been older and overweight. Jim's limp was more habit than handicap. Like everything else, artificial limbs had been improved by technology.

He didn't dress like his father. Might have, had Jenny not chosen his clothing, had she not chosen the wool for his sweaters and knitted every one he owned. He'd inherited every inch of his father's height, and, like Vern, he couldn't buy a sweater long enough in the body and sleeve.

They lost their fine day before they reached Kilmore, and were both looking for sweaters when they arrived in Ringwood.

Nobby was at work. He owned a timberyard. When Jenny had met up again with Jim in '58, he'd been working for Nobby in the timberyard office and living in a caravan behind his house. Nobby and Rosemary were good friends who they saw too little of – though not too little of their beds, single, one on either side of the spare room. They sagged, complained when their occupant rolled over.

For three nights they slept in them, each day Jenny expecting the call that didn't come. They were still waiting when five hundred free-loving Americans – husbands, wives, sons, daughters and babies – drank a vat of cyanide so they might follow their leader to his version of paradise. And how could a mother squirt poison into her baby's mouth, and how could one maniac demand obedience from a community almost as large as Woody Creek's?

'What was going on in those mothers' heads?' Jenny asked.

'Religion is a drug to some,' Nobby said. 'They get hooked on it.'

Until the night of the kidnap there must have been twelve or fifteen families living out at the commune on Monk's land, worshipping marijuana – or hooked on it. A few had followed their leader to jail since the drug bust.

Tony Bell and his wife's names on the deeds to that land, they'd pleaded guilty and been sentenced, he to five years and his wife to fifteen months. Most in Woody Creek knew the Bells were not the front men, that they'd been paid plenty to plead guilty. Tony Bell couldn't have found two pennies to rub together when he'd moved to Woody Creek in the early sixties. A few in town swore that Dino Collins had been one of the Bells' backers. He'd never been short of money and had been hanging around Woody Creek long before the Monk property changed hands. He'd built a cabin out there. The truth might come out at his trial.

On their fourth night in Ringwood, Jenny was sound asleep and dreaming of a younger Margot when she heard Jim yell, 'Get down, you crazy bastard!' Then crash!

He was a sleep talker, a walker too, and in his dreams he had two legs. At home they slept in a wide double bed pushed in hard against the wall, Jim boxed in by Jenny. Nobby's twin beds had a chest of drawers between them; she knew what had happened before she turned on the light. Found him on the floor between the beds, and when she couldn't rouse him, she called Nobby.

He came, Rosemary came, Jim came around. They got him back onto the bed, and he'd damn near knocked his eye out on the corner of those drawers. They fetched cotton wool and sticking plaster. Jenny wanted to take him to the hospital, but Jim would refuse to see a doctor even if he was dying of the plague. They patched him up, moved the chest of drawers, moved Jenny's bed in hard against his, and by five were back in their beds.

She couldn't sleep. She blamed the Jonestown poisonings for Jim's nightmare, the dead babies, the pictures of the dead – or being with Nobby. Jim might deny all memory of the war by day, but it came back to haunt him by night.

What little she knew of his war years had come to her via Nobby. He'd been with Jim until a bullet shattered his kneecap and bought him a ticket home. From Nobby, who'd contacted Ian Hooper, Jim's cousin, she'd learnt that Jim had spent the years between '47 and '51 in private sanatoriums, and in one of those places he'd had shock therapy, which Nobby claimed could wipe the memory clean.

Jim wasn't in court to hear Jenny give her evidence. Rosemary went in with her, on the train, and it became a day Jenny would have liked shock therapy to wipe from her memory. That night she packed their case, and before dawn they left for home, she behind the wheel. Jim's right eye was blood red and closed, his artificial leg travelled home in the boot. He'd jarred his knee, or the stump beneath his knee, when he'd fallen.

For three more days they followed the trial in the newspapers and on television and when the jury was sent off to deliberate, Jenny expected a fast decision. Two days later they were still deliberating.

'Jack Thomson said it would depend on the jury they picked,' Jenny said. 'His solicitor picked a mob of bleeding hearts. They'll let him off.'

She'd seen the pathetic shape of Dino Collins strapped into a wheelchair, complete with oxygen bottles and a businesslike nursing sister, and the swine had stared at her for the hours they'd kept her in the witness box, his barrister calling her a liar – or damn near.

She'd kept repeating herself. It was all she could do. She'd said she'd seen enough of Dino Collins in the past ten years to recognise his shape on a pitch dark night, and that the night hadn't been dark. She told the jury there'd been a slice of moon and that every light, inside and outside the house, had been turned on. She'd told them that she'd parked her car with its nose to the fence, that the fence was four feet from the house. Told them too that she'd heard Raelene scream 'Dino', and that as a fifteen year old kid, Raelene had introduced Collins to her as Dino.

She didn't get to see Cara, who'd done her time in the witness box the day before Jenny. The newspapers printed a bad photograph of the woman they referred to as Mrs Grenville and printed a transcript of her evidence. She'd spoken of 'Dino' Collins, of how, twenty years ago, he'd boasted to her and her school friend about taping the family cat into a cardboard carton when his elderly aunt had been hospitalised. She'd spoken of his years of harassment. *He waited until I had something precious to lose, then he took it*, she'd said.

He'd given evidence and he wrote good fiction, or his barrister wrote it for him. Jenny read every word of Collins' story, and that of the two fishermen who swore he'd been with them the night Tracy was taken.

'He'll get off,' Jim said. He was back on his crutches, one leg of his trousers flapping in the breeze – and still refusing to see a doctor.

'He had drugs in his system when he crashed the car, the same drugs they found in Tracy – and you've probably damaged your knee. You need to have it x-rayed,' Jenny nagged.

'It will heal,' he said.

'You're as pig-headed as your father!' she said, frustrated by him, and by that jury who'd seen the pathetic shell of the swine, his scarred jaw, one side of it sunken, half of his teeth missing. He'd been a good-looking boy when she'd met him – a boy to her, but years older than Raelene.

One more day she waited, then after all of the effort, after all of that money wasted on judge, lawyer and jurists, the headlines in the morning newspaper screamed COLLINS JURY DISMISSED. UNABLE TO REACH VERDICT.

She pitched the newspaper at the wall. She'd seen him! The car he'd crashed on Mission Bridge had been registered to Raelene King, and he'd been the one who had shot those drugs into little Tracy. Raelene, never an intellectual giant, wouldn't have had brains enough to know how much heroin would kill a four year old girl. Lies or not, wheelchair or not, he was as guilty as sin.

'The brainless, bleeding heart fools,' Jenny ranted.

'They saw a man crippled for his love of a pretty girl, a man accidently caught up in a crime he hadn't known she'd committed, Jen,' Jim said.

'Stop being so damn logical. And he's got a record as long as his arm.'

'And he's strapped into that wheelchair for life. Let it go.'

'You let everything go, and I can't. He was there, and he damn near killed a little girl and probably screwed up her head for life – if she didn't come out of it with brain damage.'

She was ranting when the phone rang, and if it was someone wanting her dressmaking services they'd chosen the wrong day to call.

'Hello,' she said, her tone saying a lot more.

'So what happens to the mongrel now?' the caller asked.

'Georgie?' Jenny screamed down the phone line, the dumb jury and Collins forgotten.

'Deafen me, why don't you.'

'Where are you?'

'Up where the diamonds grow.' For an instant Jenny visualised a diamond ring on her finger, then Georgie killed the image. 'I'm working at a roadhouse. Won't be for much longer. It's as hot as hell up here.'

'Up where?'

'The top of Western Australia.'

'What are you doing up there?'

'Slinging hamburgers, and stop wasting my coins and tell me what's going to happen with Collins.'

'Nothing, and that's why I'm screaming.'

'What's happening with the shop?'

'I've sold it, but it won't be legal until your signature is on the papers. When are you coming home?'

'Send me what you want me to sign, care of the Perth GPO. I should be down there in a week or two.'

'I've been worried sick about you. What have you been doing?'

'Seeing the country.'

'Where?'

'Across the Top End, halfway down the middle. You name it.'

'You could have sent us a card.'

'You've been nagging me for twenty years to get out of town and do something. You're never happy, mate.'

'Are you all right?'

'Sparking on all six cylinders.' Jenny heard a match strike, almost heard the exhalation of smoke, and she reached for her own packet. 'My ute's temporarily out of action,' Georgie said. 'I put a rock through the sump out near Wittenoom.'

'Where?'

'Up here. It ran out of oil and fried the motor. The roads up this end are worse than Woody Creek's.'

'Are you coming home?'

'Not today – and this thing swallows coins faster than Shaky can—'

And no more. Jenny stood listening to a dead line, willing Georgie back. The line remained dead. She placed the phone down and, for an hour, waited for her to call back. She didn't.

On Monday morning, Jenny posted a manila envelope containing a five-page letter, Georgie's replacement driving licence, notification that her three-year term deposit had matured, also a batch of papers from the solicitor, a pencilled X marking the places requiring Georgie's and a witness's signature.

Two days before Christmas, the signed papers were returned, with a Christmas card covered front, back and inside with Georgie's large script.

# A Forging Soul

In January of '79, N. and B. Wallis brought in the wreckers to get rid of Charlie's veranda. It raised a minor dust storm and a lot of talk, though not on Charlie's corner. Few could believe that the new owners had got rid of that corner veranda. Through the years a lot of information had been passed on there. The Duffys' dogs, grown accustomed to watering the many veranda posts as they wandered by, missed it. They walked with heads and tails down, mourning the loss of those leaning posts.

Then the painters came to town. They were followed by shop-fitters. Then Charlie's twin green doors gave way to one sliding glass door, and in place of his rusting cow bell's familiar clang, an eardrum-blasting electronic buzzer now informed the town that a customer had walked into Charlie's.

Old men keeping an eye on the destruction of a landmark, as old men are apt to do, had that door rumble open for them as they walked by, and even the stone deaf amongst them jumped when the electronic buzzer went off.

With the newly painted west wall now taking the full brunt of February's afternoon sun, the Wallises and their new refrigerated cabinets sweated. Two weeks after the automatic door went in, a blast of cool air started coming out each time the door beeped. Cool air dies fast on sunbaked pavements.

Their green doors stolen along with their veranda posts, the Duffys' dogs lifted their legs to introduce themselves to the glass door, and the unfriendly bastard beeped and disappeared. One of the more elderly, his bladder weak, hopped on three legs to the doorframe, and the sneaky glass bastard attacked him from the rear. What was a dog expected to do other than fight back? Duffy dogs, who fought in packs, attacked that door, the door beeped in dismay and the barkers, aware they had it on the run, urged the fighters on, while Duffy kids, dodging around and over dogs, got in and out with what they could. It was a self-service supermarket, wasn't it? A full-page spread in the *Willama Gazette* had advertised its grand opening specials.

Given time and enough phone calls, the Willama dog catcher arrived to deal with the dogs. The local constable dealt with the kids – or didn't deal with them. His predecessors may have manhandled them, controlled them with threats of dire punishment. Back in the old days, police had been expected to keep the peace. Let them draw their batons these days and screams of police brutality rang in the ears of television viewers for days. Kids thumbed their noses at police now. They called them Pig.

Until March that glass door rumbled open for every man, woman, kid, dog and magpie in Woody Creek, then the chap who had installed the thing came back to have another go at it. Thereafter, the door didn't open as readily. He didn't tone down its beep, but ears accustomed to screaming mill saws five days a week became accustomed to one more noise.

New paint, new door, new freezer cabinets and glass counter wouldn't wipe Charlie White's name from the collective memory of the town, nor could a cash register that spat out curled slips of paper with every purchase.

'Nick up to Charlie's for me, love, and get me a packet of Rinso,' the women said.

Maisy drove to Willama twice each week but never shopped there. She attended the Weight Watchers meeting on Tuesdays, had lunch with Rachael, watched *Days of Our Lives*, then drove back to Woody Creek for afternoon tea with Jenny. On Fridays, she had lunch with Rebecca and watched *Days of Our Lives* there. On the other days, she walked down to Blunt's crossing, then down North Street to the butcher's, the newsagent's, then continued on to White's Street, over Charlie's crossing and back to South Street where she picked up a few items from the supermarket, then walked home in time for *Days of Our Lives*.

Or that had been her habit until the B half of the Wallis duo called her an interfering old biddy and told her to mind her own business, and Maisy told her that she'd never darken her door again, and that unless she changed her attitude, no one else would either.

'All I tried to explain to her was how none of the businesses tried to cut the throats of the other businesses,' Maisy explained – to everyone.

The altercation didn't alter her habits, or only one of them. She took great pleasure now in walking by that beeping door, her nose in the air.

There'd never been a skerrick of harm in Maisy Macdonald. She talked too much, but rarely had a bad word to say about anyone. For sixty of her eighty years she'd congregated with the women beneath Charlie's veranda, catching up with the news, or passing it on.

They congregated now beneath the smaller veranda of the post office where a self-sown tree, growing for years between that veranda and the house Norman and Amber Morrison had once called home, offered an extra pool of shade where the women compared notes and tut-tutted about B. Wallis's poor attitude. The police station cum residence was on the corner directly opposite that tree, and on the other corner, the town hall, the park, then Maisy's house.

She loved her house. She'd watched it grow from the ground up – sixty-eight years ago. At the time she'd been sharing a bed with a miserable old bugger of an aunty, and if anyone had ever wondered why a sixteen year old kid had married near forty year old, bald-headed George Macdonald, they need look no further than Maisy's miserable old bugger of an aunty who had taught her how to dodge a broomstick and not much more. Maisy hadn't been searching for love when she'd married, only kindness. George had been kind.

He'd been sex starved too. He'd given her ten kids in little more than ten years. He'd also given her the second best house in town in which to raise those kids and, in it, everything that opened and shut. Given space to grow, she'd grown up with her kids, and grown to love their father.

There were better houses being built in town, modern houses, but not in the centre of town. Two lovely homes had gone up recently in Slaughter Yard Lane, a new street built to give access to the Bowling Club. Melbourne retirees liked a game of bowls. Maisy had given their bowling balls a try the day the club opened. They weren't her cup of tea. There was a cluster of new brick homes where Stock Route Road ran into Blunt's Street, and fifty per cent of their owners were Melbourne retirees. Maisy and a few of her cronies welcomed each new arrival to town. A few returned the visit. A lot more didn't. A few shopped locally. A lot more didn't.

Maisy wasn't the only woman who kept an eye on the time while she chatted, nor was she the only one who never missed *Days of Our Lives*. She was home with time to spare, time to make a cup of tea and take her pre-prepared salad from the refrigerator. She'd learnt that trick at Weight Watchers, to pre-prepare. If you knew it was waiting for you in the fridge, it stopped you from grabbing something easy.

She'd been watching that show since episode one, and it was like visiting with friends now. The credits were still playing when the phone rang. She'd trained her girls never to phone for the half-hour her show was on, and whichever one it was now had timed her call to the second. Without rising, Maisy reached for the telephone.

The long-distance STD beeps suggested it was Maureen, her only city daughter, though Maureen usually called after seven when phone calls were cheaper.

'What is it, love?'

'Is that you, Maisy?' a stranger's voice enquired.

A not so strange stranger's voice. For an instant, Maisy remained silent, her mind sifting stored information for the name that went with that voice. Some eighty year old minds grow dim, even wander off to the fairies. Not Maisy's. She'd had her finger on the pulse of this town since she'd stopped sucking it.

'That's not you, is it, Sissy?' she asked.

'How did you pick me?'

'They tell me I've got a good ear for voices,' Maisy said. All seven of her daughters sounded much the same, but she could pick each one of them on the phone. She could pick the voices of most of her cronies, and how could she ever forget Sissy Morrison's? For twenty-odd years she'd heard a lot of it. 'What a lovely surprise,' she said.

'You wouldn't happen to be in touch with my mother, would you?' Sissy asked.

'Amber?' Maisy asked, confused by the question. 'Why on earth would I be in touch with her?'

'I couldn't think of anyone else who might be,' Sissy admitted.

'I haven't heard a word about your mother since she went missing from that place in Brunswick. Someone contacted me about her then, but that was years ago. She's probably dead, love.'

'She's not. I'll swear that I saw her at church last Sunday with Lorna Hooper,' Sissy said.

And Maisy laughed. 'That would be a day I'd like to see. From what I remember, Lorna used to cross over the road if she saw your mother coming, and that was before your father died.'

'She wouldn't recognise her. Lorna didn't recognise me at first.'

Or didn't want to, Maisy thought, but if you can't say something nice or helpful, it's better to keep your mouth shut and listen.

'Alma Duckworth, one of my cousins, has been going to the Kew church for years. We go with them sometimes, and last Sunday I heard this woman talking to the minister and she sounded exactly the same as Mum used to sound when she was putting on the jam for the Hoopers. And she walks like her too.'

'Does she look like her?'

'She's as old as you are. She looks like Methuselah.'

'He had whiskers, love,' Maisy said, wondering what Sissy might look like. As a girl, she'd been the living image of old Cecelia, Norman's mother.

'There's more to it,' Sissy said. 'She calls herself Elizabeth Duckworth, and Alma and her daughter have been trying for years to connect her up to the family, and they can't. She's the only Duckworth that Alma has come across that she hasn't been able to connect up to one of their dead relatives.'

'I still say that if she was with Lorna Hooper it's not your mother.'

'Lorna wouldn't know who she's living with. Alma reckons she's as blind as a bat.'

'Someone is having you on about that,' Maisy said. 'Lorna Hooper drove herself up here a few years ago in one of those tiny little Morris Minor cars. When we watched her folding herself into the driver's seat, Jenny said she—'

'Don't mention that little slut's name to me, Maisy.'

'—looked like a praying mantis folding its legs into a matchbox,' Maisy finished, or not quite finished. 'Lorna was seeing well enough to drive that day.'

'Why would she be visiting *her*?'

Maisy scratched her neck and eyed the phone, aware that whatever she said would be the wrong thing to say. Sissy had been engaged to Jim Hooper at one time and had damn near gone off her head when he'd broken the engagement six weeks before the wedding.

'Are you there?' Sissy asked.

'Yes, love.' Then she said it. 'Lorna was visiting her brother. He and . . . and your sister got married.' Silence at the other end of the line, a painful silence, until Maisy killed it. 'They've got a daughter, a lovely kid who's training to be a nurse in Melbourne.'

'As if I care,' Sissy snapped. 'And if you'd seen Amber, you'd know her like I did.'

'They say that everyone's got a double.'

'It's her, not her double. And there's more. Alma's old minister's wife told Alma that Lorna ran over Elizabeth Duckworth near Brunswick, and that they ended up in the same hospital, and when they let them out, Lorna brought her Miss Duckworth home with her. And,' Sissy said, 'and – one of the Duckworth cousins is a journalist, and he found out that Amber Morrison went missing from that place in Brunswick at around the same time that Lorna ran down her Miss Duckworth. He said that the accident was in the newspapers, and that they didn't know who the other woman was for three days – and if that's too much of a coincidence for you then it's not for me, or Alma – and if you heard her talking, you'd know I was right about it being Mum. Do you ever get down to Melbourne?'

'I used to drive down when George was alive but the traffic is too mad for my liking these days.'

'Is Maureen still living down here?'

'She's still in the same house at Box Hill, love.'

'Would she recognise Mum?'

'I doubt it. She left town when you and . . . when you were only a bit of a kid.'

Beeps on the line warned them that Telecom's allocated three minutes were up.

'I'll have to go,' Sissy said. 'It costs a fortune ringing the country during the day. If you've got a pencil handy I'll give you my number and you can give me a call if you're ever down here.'

Maisy had a pencil tied to her telephone pad. She noted Sissy's number, then the line went dead.

And it wasn't going to end like that – Maisy had never looked at a phone bill in her life. She dialled the new number.

An hour later, the phone back in its cradle, Maisy picked up her car keys and drove around to Jenny's.

'You'll never guess who I've been on the phone with!'

'Who?'

'Your sister, and she swears that your mother is living with Lorna Hooper in Kew and calling herself Miss Elizabeth Duckworth.' It was all out before the front door closed behind her. Her news continuing to spill, she followed Jenny through the entrance hall and into a short passage leading to the kitchen, where she claimed her chair at the western end of the table. Handbag and car keys placed down, she continued with her tale.

'Remember that day I told you how I almost bumped into Amber in Willama, in Woolworths?' Jenny nodded and went about making a pot of tea. 'Well,' Maisy said.

'Well what?'

'Well, who just happened to be in your sitting room talking to Jim when I came running in to tell you I'd seen your mother?'

'Come off the grass, Maisy. As if Lorna would have Amber within spitting distance.'

'That's what I said – at first, that's what I said, but there's more to it, and the more I heard the more convinced I was. Sissy swears she recognised your mother's voice while her back was turned to her. She said that when she turned around and saw who that voice was coming from, she almost fell over. She said she looked old, that her hair was white and curly and that she was dressed like a toff. The woman I saw in Woolworths that day was dressed up to the nines and she had short curly white hair underneath her hat.'

'Ten thousand people live in and around Willama and a good percentage of them are old – and wear hats,' Jenny said.

'Okay, now you tell me why two people who hadn't sighted some woman for thirty-odd years – and who hadn't sighted each other either – could come up with the exact same description of a woman they thought was your mother – if it wasn't?'

Jenny offered a biscuit with the cup of tea. Maisy broke it in half then ate the small half while giving a rundown of its calorie content.

'You're looking good,' Jenny said.

'I'm feeling better than I've felt in ten years. I'm off all but one of my blood pressure pills.'

'Jim,' Jenny called. He came from the dining room, his typewriter's summertime residence – he came as far as the doorway. 'Maisy just had a phone call from Sissy, and she swears that Amber is housekeeping for your sister.'

'I can think of no two people who deserve each other more,' Jim said, then returned to his typewriter.

*

It took a month for Maisy to talk Bernie into making the trip down to Melbourne. He hadn't been back since Dawny's death, and had no desire to.

'I'll take you down on Saturday night if you'll ride in the ute.'

'I'll ride in the ute if you promise to keep your speed down, but it's not worth going just for one night. We'll leave Friday night and come home on Monday.'

'I need to be at the mill on Monday or another one of the old buggers will go me for compo.'

They left on Saturday morning, in the ute. Maisy phoned Sissy five minutes after they arrived and arranged to meet her out the front of the Kew church at ten thirty on Sunday. Then Bernie refused to drive her to the church.

'Mandy will drive us,' Maureen said.

Mandy also refused. 'If she's who you think she is, Nan, then she's not someone to go messing about with. Let sleeping dogs lie.'

Six of Maisy's girls had their driving licences. Maureen wasn't one of them. She had no desire to disturb murdering Amber, but she'd known Sissy well as a kid, and she wanted to get a look at her.

'We'll get a taxi, and ask him to wait,' Maureen said.

'No good will come of it, Mum,' Mandy warned.

They should have listened to her. The taxi arrived late, and they were late getting to the address. Three women and a male stood at the kerb, one of the women glowering. Maisy recognised that glower, and that's about all she recognised.

'Oh my God,' Maureen said, cowering back low in the rear seat as Maisy opened the door.

'You're coming with me?'

'I'm not,' Maureen said.

Maisy crossed the road alone to greet a giant of a woman clad in a maroon frock straining to fit and not quite managing it. It hugged her swollen stomach, clutched her broad backside, revealed the backs of bare dimpled knees and legs the size of tree stumps. She was her grandmother, old Cecelia Morrison, on a bad day. Taller though, broader, different hair. Old Cecelia's had been sparse, grey/white and pinned into a bun. Sissy's was a shoulder-length salt and pepper, sprayed to hold its bouffant style.

There were two women with her, shorter, one not a lot slimmer, and a male who looked like death warmed up – and not warmed up enough. He was skin stretched over bone, and hairless; his oversized skull appeared to be contracting around his eye sockets, attempting to force his eyeballs out.

The introductions were made while Maisy stood gaping, the names going in one ear and out the other as she followed the trio to the cemented area close to the church door. Maisy, stunned silent, stood at Sissy's side. She wasn't silent, or not until the organist stopped playing and a chubby, middle-aged parson emerged, his shrinking congregation behind him.

'That's them,' Sissy said.

As if she needed to point out Lorna Hooper's elongated black-clad bones, or her man-sized lace-up shoes. She was gripping the arm of a fluffy-headed little woman clad in dusty pink.

'Oh my God,' Maisy breathed.

'Is it her?' Sissy hissed.

'Oh my God.' Maisy hadn't set eyes on Amber Morrison in forty years the day she'd seen her in Woolworths, but she'd known her. She knew her today. 'Oh my God.'

'Is it her?' Sissy demanded, louder.

Maisy nodded and stepped back.

Sissy wanted her to step forward. 'Get up close and listen,' she hissed.

There was no need to listen. She knew that stretched-lip smile, which someone had once described as a chimp's grimace, the smile Amber was offering to the minister as she shook his hand, the smile Maisy had known since the classroom. They'd started school on the same day. Had been girls together, young wives, mothers, close neighbours. She'd seen that smile the day Amber had turned up late at little Barbie Dobson's funeral, had seen it the day the police took her away from Woody Creek, poor Norman rotting in his bed, his face caved in by a cast iron frying pan, a carving knife jammed between his ribs.

A forgiving soul, Maisy, she'd forgiven Amber a thousand unforgivable sins, and as many stings, but poor, pompous Norman hadn't deserved to end his life like he had.

*Memories are long in Woody Creek*, she'd written to Amber when the Salvation Army people contacted her to let her know Amber was being released from the asylum. Maisy's memory was as long. She wouldn't have been game to turn her back if she'd given Amber a bed.

She stepped back again as the emaciated Duckworth male began to offer his opinion.

'She appears . . . to . . . to have made a . . . a new . . .' His sentence commenced with no expectation of completion, or of anyone listening even if he had bothered to complete it. Maisy didn't. She turned tail and hotfooted it back to the taxi.

'Get me out of here,' she said.

'Wait,' Maureen said.

Sissy and the Duckworth women had approached Amber.

'Who do you think you're fooling, Mum?' Sissy said.

Rarely in her sixty years of life had she considered the likely repercussions of any action. She'd given no thought as to what might come after Amber's unveiling.

The minister stopped shaking hands. His congregation stood staring. Lorna Hooper froze, the blood draining from her chin and brow to what the accident had left of her battle-scarred nose.

Sissy hadn't expected Lorna's response. The pink-clad arm she'd been clutching might have been a striking snake. She flung it from her, and the little woman attached to it teetered, then, blind as a bat or not, Lorna made a beeline for home.

Sissy should have expected Alma Duckworth's response. For the greater part of her life, Sissy had lived comfortably enough on Duckworth charity. Alma, well positioned to catch Amber, caught her, then she and Valda, her daughter, supported her back into the church. Sissy followed them. She'd been invited to lunch today at Alma's, and it was almost lunchtime.

She stood in that quiet place staring at her mother, who hadn't said a word, who sat on a rear pew, her mouth open, panting like Alma's white poodle.

And she shouldn't have been in that church. She'd committed murder and Alma knew it, yet there she was fanning a murderess's face with her hat – and calling her dear. And Valda knew it too, and there she was patting her shoulder. The minister didn't know who his church was sheltering. He fetched her a sip of communion wine.

Sissy stood well back, her arms folded across her breasts, the thinnest part of her. She was considering enlightening the parson as to whom he was offering his communion wine to – except a church didn't seem like the right place to talk about murders and insane asylums.

She watched her mother sip that wine, listened to the minister suggest they drive Miss Duckworth home, where any misunderstanding between the elderly companions could surely be sorted out over a cup of tea. Valda agreed with him. She wasn't married and nor was he. She'd had her eye on him for six months.

And as if Lorna Hooper would take Amber back. In what now seemed like another lifetime, Sissy had been overly familiar with Lorna.

Maisy had let Sissy down. If Sissy had given a split second of thought as to what might come later, Maisy had been heavily involved in that later, but she'd taken off like a scalded cat and left Sissy holding the bag – which having so recently claimed she was now eager to be rid of.

*

At Box Hill, Maisy was urging Bernie to take her home. She'd packed her case. It was waiting at the front door, but Bernie had seen a leg of lamb slid into the oven before Maureen called the taxi, and he wanted some of it.

Sissy's need for lunch got her into Reg's car. They followed Valda and her mother and the minister to Lorna's street – and got there in time to see a suitcase follow a bundle of clothing onto the nature strip, to watch a hat escaping merrily down the road, to witness Lorna clip a padlock to the chain locking the tall black gates before her back disappeared into her hard-faced red clinker brick house.

Valda retrieved the hat. The minister and Alma collected the scattered clothing and a shoe. They forced what they could into the case then loaded the lot into Reg's boot.

The Duckworth clan had always looked after their orphans, their widows and fallen women – and their alcoholic sons. Would Jesus have done less? Like Jesus, the Duckworth clan possessed a wizardry with food, and that Sunday, Alma and Valda stretched a midday luncheon for four to feed the six seated around their dining room table.

The sixth guest wasted her share. Amber stared at her plate of cold roast mutton, potato salad and greens, and she cursed her stupidity. How many times had she decided she must move on, then changed her mind? She'd been lucky on the night of the accident, and for too long had trusted her luck to hold. As any gambler knew, luck can swing in an instant.

She dared a glance at Sissy, revolted by what the years had done to her. A bulging hump of rounded shoulders, of ballooning belly, of mud-green eyes sunk deep into a tub of well-used lard. A black bush of mono eyebrows, a mastiff jaw, working on cold mutton and greens.

She dared a glance in Cousin Reginald's direction. Wouldn't have recognised him in a million years. Should have. She'd known him for a month or two – in the biblical sense.

In '26 she'd been a young married woman, mourning the loss of four day old Leonora April. Cousin Reginald had been sympathetic. A pleasant-faced, overeducated but inexperienced youth, studying the word of God and preparing to follow Charles, his parson father, into the ministry, he'd driven Amber to doctors' appointments in his little green roadster, had driven her later to theatres, and one night he hadn't driven her directly back to the manse.

She'd initiated young Cousin Reg into the joys of sin. An eager student, too eager. Parson Charles had smelt a rat and put an end to their association. Packed Reginald off to the tropics to re-find his commitment to God, and sent Amber home to Norman, her sin growing in her belly.

Some months later, another name had been added to *CLARENCE*, *SIMON* and *LEONORA APRIL*'s tombstone. Norman had chosen the name. *REGINALD*, the letters cut larger, deeper. From that day to this, Amber had not given Cousin Reginald a second's thought.

Her mind reassembling, rearranging, she sat staring at her plate, attempting to resurrect her old escape plans. Impossible to concentrate. A thousand memories buried beneath the dust of yesterday kept pushing through, mean memories, cheap memories, ugly – though not her memories of Reg. She'd dared to live a while, to feel, to laugh with him.

Dared a second glance in his direction – and caught him staring at her. His eyes shuddered and he looked down at his hands, shaking hands, spilling lettuce from his fork. Strong, inventive hands in his youth. A greedy youth's mouth.

Tried to force her eyes up to the mound of female at his side. Remembered only the pain of her bones being ripped apart so she might birth that mound of female. Remembered the heavy months of carrying her weight. She'd carried it willingly, so certain her womb had been creating the most beautiful of babies. And why not, its mother had been the prettiest girl in town. For hours she'd pushed, screamed to free her beautiful Ruby Rose into life, and when she'd seen what she'd created, she'd been inconsolable. Her mother had handed her a swaddled, snuffling pig of an infant. A glutton at her breast. A glutton still.

Norman had named her, named her Cecelia Louise, for his mother, while somewhere out there in the stratosphere Amber's beautiful Ruby Rose had remained forever unborn.

She glanced at the glutton's plate, scraped clean. Couldn't look higher. Knew too well what she'd see. That glutton's eyes would be on Amber's untouched meal. Minutely, Amber's chin lifted, minutely her lids lifted, only to prove herself right. No joy in that proof. Anger, that mind-blurring, red haze of anger she dared not breathe into her lungs. Held her breath against it until her need for air was overwhelming, squealed the legs of her chair back, and the chair, too abruptly vacated, crashed to the floor.

'The bathroom is the second door on the left, dear,' Alma directed.

Amber opened the second door on the left and locked it behind her. She placed her handbag on a small vanity unit then wet her hands, soaped them, rinsed then soaped them again. Washed her face, her throat; for minutes she stood, the tap running, until she could look that staring mirror face in the eye.

Elizabeth Duckworth's face. The frock she wore, the small hat that matched it so well, were Elizabeth's. The handbag over her shoulder was Elizabeth's.

Sissy had murdered Elizabeth.

All ten of the eaters' eyes had followed Amber's hasty exit. Only Reginald's watched for her return. The minister studied his watch. Alma and Valda cleared the table. Sissy, who'd claimed Amber's untouched meal, was tucking into the meat and potato salad when Valda served a cream-filled sponge.

The minister forgot his watch long enough to eat a slice, to drink a small cup of tea, to compliment the cook before claiming a pressing engagement. Valda saw him to the door.

No similar escape for Reginald. He ate his sponge and remembered his Aunt Cecelia's funeral, the slow train trip to Woody Creek with his parents, cousins, aunts and uncles. He remembered Norman's railway house, and the dead infant born to Cousin Amber. He remembered the grunting stray Amber had put to a milk-swollen breast, and at nineteen he'd become obsessed by where that tiny mouth had sucked.

*Thou must not covet thy neighbour's wife* – or your cousins. He'd coveted pretty Amber and for months after that trip had spent his nights with his Bible, attempting to wipe the vision of that pale beauty and the sucking infant from his head.

*Repent ye sinner.*

Then came that night when he'd walked pale sad Amber in the Fitzroy Gardens and she'd asked him to hold her. He'd done more than hold her. A rambling rose, pretty Amber, as vital when supported against the woodshed wall as in his narrow bed.

They'd sent him off to an outpost in hell where he'd spent his days attempting to speak of God to fuzzy-haired blacks who'd had as much interest in God as he. He'd discovered gin and tonic in the tropics. Later, he'd discovered compliant native girls and their black breasts. They'd faded the image of Amber's white.

The Japanese ruined his party. He was no fighter. They'd evacuated him from Port Moresby with the women and children, and he would have preferred to take his chances with the Japs than with his widowed father, but in true Duckworth spirit, Charles had forgiven his erring son – and emptied his gin bottles down the sink.

Charles had offered a fatherly hand to Sissy when she'd been orphaned by Norman's murder and Amber's subsequent incarceration. Two men living alone had required a housekeeper and for years the church paid Sissy's small stipend. She'd learnt to sniff out gin bottles.

Until '57, Reg had laboured in a back office at David Jones, snatching time to moisten his throat at lunchtime and after work; Sissy's kitchen skills had not encouraged him home.

Charles eventually succumbed to Sissy's brand of housekeeping. The church buried him.

The dead require no church-supplied house or housekeeper; 'the family' took Reg and Sissy in. 'The family' found Sissy employment at a child care centre – and God save the children – but only for a day or two. A variety of other positions had been found for her before the Duckworths gave up and she'd returned to her preferred position of permanent house guest. Guests sat while others laboured.

Reginald recalled a few glorious years at David Jones where he'd spent most of his days in an alcoholic haze, but those glorious years ended in a hospital ward where he'd been diagnosed with advanced liver disease. The family stepped in to save one who had no desire to be saved. They'd packed him off to a teetotaller Duckworth who owned a farm, fifteen miles from the nearest town. House guests are only tolerable for a month or two. The Duckworth clan shuttled him and Sissy between relatives for years – until an elderly Duckworth recalled an earlier problematic duo. By the securing and furnishing of a flat, earlier relatives had rid themselves of the ongoing problem of the young Norman Morrison and his mother, Cecelia – *née* Duckworth.

The proposal had first been put to Sissy, not in Reginald's presence, though his newly acquired invalid pension was mentioned.

'Cousin Reginald is in desperate need of your care, Cecelia. You alone managed to keep him sober during your years of housekeeping at the manse. As the wife and carer of an invalid pensioner you would secure, for your own personal use, your own pension.'

'You're stark raving mad,' Sissy said.

She'd lived off her broken heart since '41. Her unworn wedding dress, still packed into its box, had travelled with her since her father's demise, its life spent beneath a variety of beds. The Duckworths moved that box again – moved it and Sissy to Bendigo, to a house filled with children. Sissy's patience with 'brats' known to be nonexistent, the Duckworths left her there for three months, and when they finally came to move her to her new lodging, they'd started again.

'As a married couple, you and Reginald would be eligible for government housing, dear. Your carer's pension would be paid to you each fortnight.'

'How much?'

They had the figure at their fingertips, and it wasn't enough.

They moved her and her wedding dress into Aunt Bessy's spare room in Hawthorn. Bessy, in her dotage, had lost a few of her marbles and control of her bladder. After a month of this, Reg, government housing and a carer's pension became a carrot dangled before a donkey.

'All right then!' the donkey brayed.

And thus it was arranged. Sissy, a Duckworth in all but name, took that name at a small service in Hawthorn.

Reginald took Sissy as an exit light in the impenetrable tunnel of Duckworth watchdogs. He made no attempt to consummate the union, nor had he been given the opportunity. After the service, he was returned to his Portsea cousin. Sissy spent her wedding night in Hawthorn.

It took a month or two more for the necessary departmental strings to be pulled, but if a string required pulling there was a Duckworth available to pull it. A unit on the fourth floor of one of the multilevel Housing Commission red brick monoliths, built in sight of the city, was allocated to the bride and groom, a two-bedroom unit the family furnished with their collective discards. A five year old Falcon sedan was provided for Reginald, its registration and insurance paid for twelve months, and he was threatened with the loss of that vehicle should one sip of alcohol pass his lips. Then the family drove away to collectively wash their hands of the matter.

Sissy had washed little since.

*

Alma and Valda washed the dishes that day. Amber, who had found a chair beside the parlour window, hadn't moved from it all afternoon. Sissy sat in the kitchen. Reginald paced between parlour and kitchen doorways.

'I've told you a dozen times that I'm not having anything to do with her,' Sissy said.

'We'll make other arrangements for her tomorrow, Cecelia. Nothing can be done on a Sunday.'

'I told you to let her minister look after her, and you brought her here, so you can keep her.'

'She's your mother, dear.'

'Don't you blame me for that. And you two wanted to prove who she was as much as me anyway.'

'She's an elderly woman, tossed out of house and home—'

'Serve her right for lying to everyone.'

# The Balcony

During the afternoon more Duckworths, summoned via phone, arrived to lend weight to the argument, and come evening, Alma and Valda again working their wizardry, the multitudes were fed.

Amber didn't join them at the table. From time to time one or another of the Duckworth entourage attempted to speak to her, but Amber, empty of words, remained mute.

Come nightfall, Reginald removed himself from the scene of battle to await the outcome in his car, leaving Sissy to fight alone until nine, when, manipulated by Duckworths, expert in the art of manipulation, she capitulated. Amber was assisted out to the car by Alma and her daughter.

'It's just for tonight, dear. I'll phone Miss Hooper first thing in the morning. I'm sure it can all be sorted out.'

They seated Amber in the rear of the vehicle, which ten minutes later tilted dramatically to the left when Sissy took her place in the front passenger seat. The door closed after two worthy slams, the motor fired, and the flock of Duckworths was left quacking on the footpath.

A drive then through night streets. Amber, who had been Lorna's eyes, who had spent the past twelve years watching the road when in a vehicle, sat head down, eyes closed, unaware as to where she was being carried.

She made no attempt to open the door when the motor died. Sissy's door opened, the vehicle shuddering upright as she stepped out and stomped towards the brick monolith. Reginald walked around to the boot, opened it and removed the case. He opened the rear door and Amber stepped out of the car to stare at her case, then follow it and Reg into the Housing Commission block – as a sheep being led to its slaughter.

She knew those buildings. They reminded her of Lorna's eight-drawer filing cabinet which stored a conglomeration of papers in individually labelled files, just as those buildings stored a conglomerate of humanity. She followed her case to a lift where Sissy waited for the doors to open, and when they did, Reg, the case and Sissy stepped into it. Amber remained in the passage.

'Get in!' Sissy demanded.

Memories of hell in that voice. Amber stepped into the lift, the doors interlocked, closing her in. She stood unbreathing until they opened, when the voice from hell commanded: 'Get out!'

Down a long corridor of many doors to one which opened to Sissy's key. And the air wafting out of that hole in the wall, flavoured with burned grease, stinking shoes and sweating humanity, sucked the marrow from Amber's bones. Her life, her world upended, she had ascended up to hell. But her case was carried in through that hole in the wall and tonight all she was was her case and the handbag she'd been gripping since the confrontation out the front of the church. Elizabeth Duckworth's bankbook was in her handbag, the key to Amber Morrison's private mailbox was in that handbag, and their gold mesh purse.

'If you're coming in, then get in and shut that rotten door!'

So bidden, Amber entered, mouth dry, throat parched, soul desiccated, eyes attempting not to see – but seeing a glass door which no doubt led out to one of the balconies – and a faster solution to her predicament than becoming Mrs Brown, or Smith, or Jones. High-stepping over an unwashed plate, around a loaded chair, between the chaos of two undisciplined lives, she walked towards salvation.

'Locked,' Reginald said sadly as he turned on the television. It bellowed. Sissy bellowed, and in the confined area of a small sitting room, the noise reverberated against Amber's eardrums. She'd become accustomed to the silence of Kew.

Kew gone. Elizabeth Duckworth gone and Amber Morrison too old to rise again from the ashes.

Watched Sissy flop down onto a cleared area of the couch. It flinched. Two magazines on it flinched. A packet of toffee flinched and shed its colourfully wrapped sweets.

'It's ridiculous, and so are your brainless relatives,' Sissy said, scooping up spilled sweets, unwrapping one and popping it into her mouth. 'It's straight out rotten, stinking ridiculous,' she said, her massive jaw working that toffee.

Amber stared past her to the case, placed down in a clearing where the passage fed into the sitting room, weighing it in her mind as a tool for the breakage of glass. Again she turned to the balcony door to peer through glass to a railing, a high railing. If she could break the glass, the case's inches might provide a step of sufficient height for her to climb over it, or to lean far enough over it.

She glanced at Reginald, his gaze fixed on the screen where actors cavorted in an immaculate mansion, and Amber, who hadn't shed a tear since four day old Leonora April had died, shed one for Lorna's near-silent television, for her house, her bathroom, which Amber needed desperately. When the world ends and all else seizes, bladders don't. Amber's, unrelieved in hours, was threatening to release its load.

Her nose following the scent of burnt grease she found a small walk-through kitchen. The odour of public urinal directed her to a bathroom where she emptied her bladder while keeping her backside well clear of a facility uncleaned since first installed. Rinsed her hands beneath a tap trickling into a filthy basin. Didn't touch the tap, basin or the slime of bewhiskered soap swimming in a pool of filth.

A second door led out of the bathroom. She opened it. The stench of body odour and cheap shoes suggested she close it, but she pushed on, high-stepping across scattered clothing, to another door. It led her back to the passage, back to her case.

'Stop wandering around and sit down!'

Amber remained standing, with her case, while surveying the immense pair of spread thighs utilising the greater percentage of a three-seater couch. No space to sit down. She turned to the closed front door. Only a lift out there. She didn't like lifts. Didn't like enclosed spaces. Had spent too much time locked into enclosed spaces. There'd be stairs. She reached for her case but it was heavy and with no strength to carry it and her legs threatening to let her down, she dragged it out to the kitchen. She'd be stronger in the morning. She'd get through this night and tomorrow . . . tomorrow, perhaps Mrs Brown would ride a train to . . .

To someplace.

With the kitchen table buried beneath its load of the miscellaneous and no space to place her handbag down, she sat, her case at her knee, her handbag on her lap.

Televised voices, ear-splitting music coming in waves through the open door, crashing, hammering Amber's eardrums. Couldn't think for noise, and she had to think, to plan, had to grasp hold of her mind and direct it.

Nightmares have no direction. She was trapped in her worst nightmare, back with the filth, the stink, the noise, the lifts and locks – and that nightmare shape of mammoth female who was her daughter.

Her daughter. And him?

Couldn't think, not beyond her, beyond him, beyond how, beyond why.

Sat staring at the shape of a window that she didn't recognise as a window until he came to turn on the kitchen light. Closed her eyes against its glare, against him, against the loaded sink beneath the window, the loaded benchtops. Sat, eyes closed, until roused by the voice from hell.

'There's a pillow and blanket on the couch.' Amber looked at the table, at a space between an open envelope and the salt and pepper. A pattern in the table's laminated surface, a cluster of what resembled clumps of folded grey umbrellas. Shelter from the storm.

'Don't think that you're staying here after tonight.'

Stay here? Had there been an iota of strength left in Amber's body, she might have laughed at the suggestion. No strength, no hope, no reply, so she counted that clump of grey umbrellas. She'd got through many bad times by counting, through endless days and nights. She'd counted her steps, counted the cracks in the ceiling, the stars in the sky, the hairs on her arm when there'd been nothing else to count.

'If you think you're fooling anyone with your deaf and dumb act, you're wrong,' Sissy ranted.

'Tomorrow . . . is . . . is perhaps time . . . time enough . . .' Reginald began.

'Don't you take her side, you useless mongrel. You didn't take my side against your brainless rotten relatives, did you? She murdered my father, and you know it, and so do they, and they expect me to spend the night with her in my house.'

Reginald escaped towards the bathroom, Sissy in pursuit. 'She's putting on an act, that's what's she's doing, and I've seen enough of her acts in my life to last until I'm a hundred.'

He returned to the kitchen, to pick up and place down an item or two, until the slam of a door. It was as a signal to the disjointed skin and bones of Reginald. They regrouped as one to move towards the refrigerator, to fling it open, snatch a bottle of lemon cordial, half-fill a glass with it, add water then, at a tottering run, he was gone.

The television silenced. The sitting room light died and a hush descended, a hush allowing alien sounds to seep through the walls, secret muted mutters.

*Tomorrow. Tomorrow. Tomorrow.*

There would be no tomorrow for Amber. Lorna would not allow it. Amber knew how her mind worked. For twelve years she'd made a close study of her benefactor, and during those years had watched her in action many times. An unrelenting enemy, Lorna Hooper would see Amber's exposure only as it applied to herself: Miss Lorna Hooper had been duped. She'd been played for a fool. Proud Miss Hooper was nobody's fool.

She'd approved of the old minister and his wife, had invited them to take afternoon tea with her. She'd taken a dislike to their replacements, a modern-thinking young minister and his fashion-plate wife. Lorna had begun a year-long campaign to be rid of them – a hard-fought campaign. She'd won it.

Her own sister, her own nephew, had felt the sting of Lorna's ire. Elizabeth Duckworth had felt her scorn before she'd learnt to circumvent it.

Tonight Lorna would be planning her new campaign. She'd be stalking the house, selecting her weapons, her papers, phone numbers, magnifying glass. Only when armed to the teeth would she sleep the sleep of the just.

Amber glanced again at the kitchen window, which would surely open. Was a fourth-floor window high enough? Was there an afterlife where man was placed on trial for his every earthly sin? There was a hell. She was already in it.

She glanced at the bench beneath the window. She'd need to clear space there, would need to stand on a chair to climb onto the bench – or find a direction which didn't begin and end with her end.

There was no direction. On the dot of nine Lorna's war of attrition would begin. She had unwittingly become a party to the defrauding of the Social Security Department. She'd obtained the forms, filled in the boxes, lodged Miss Elizabeth Duckworth's application for the old age pension – as a means of obtaining a housekeeper at no cost to herself – and at nine tomorrow morning, her housekeeper would receive her just punishment.

Always pay back the sum you borrowed, Amber thought. Little Amber Foote had never liked that concept and had difficulty learning it. If the ten you borrowed was only a phantom ten, then why bother giving that phantom ten back? Had to, or the answer to her sum had been incorrect.

Elizabeth Duckworth couldn't pay back her borrowed thousands. She'd spent most of them on her back.

Amber Morrison had spent nothing of her pension, or not since moving to Kew. Each month she'd squirrelled her portions away in a city bank. The world may have forgotten her but since the asylum doors had swung open, the pension department had never forgotten to post her fortnightly cheque. For a time after Amber's disappearance, she'd unlocked her GPO mailbox with trepidation, fearing the hand of the law on her shoulder, fearing the mailbox's contents – or its emptiness. Not once had she received a *Please Explain* letter, nor had it ever been empty.

A near full moon had found its way to the patch of sky outside the window. As a child, she'd loved moonlit nights. She'd walked for miles with her mother when the moon had been full. As a wife she'd walked alone on moonlit nights. At the asylum she'd walked in circles.

She'd walked by day at Kew. Each morning, summer, winter, autumn and spring, Lorna's hand gripping her arm, they'd walked their measured mile, and by nightfall Amber's eighty year old feet had been content to rest on their footstool while her fingers had done the walking. Lorna had been sufficiently impressed by one piece of Miss Duckworth's embroidery to fetch her magnifying glass so she might study it more closely for the imperfections she'd surely find there. A woman of few feminine skills, Lorna, but an efficient businesswoman, a keeper of papers and of telephone numbers, and tomorrow, at nine o'clock precisely, in some government department, a telephone would ring and Lorna would link Elizabeth Duckworth's name to Amber Morrison's. Then the police would come. Though perhaps not in the morning. It might take a day, maybe two, for the information to be passed on to the relevant department.

For the twelve years Elizabeth Duckworth had sat at Lorna's side in church, mouthing prayers, hymns, she'd never thought to ask God's forgiveness of her sins. Elizabeth, the kindly spinster daughter of a clergyman had been born sinless – and in hindsight, born too swiftly, in a hospital bed, with a broken leg and a fractured skull.

Maryanne Brown could be born as fast. She'd known a Maryanne Brown a long time ago. She'd died young. Tomorrow morning she'd go early to the GPO, collect Amber's last cheque and her bankbook, empty her account, and then Maryanne Brown would catch a train, then another, then another. Plenty of Browns in the telephone book.

Amber stood and her aging joints, unmoving for hours, complained. She leaned, palms on the table, her eyes watching the moon moving away from the window, until her legs were strong enough to hold her, when she stepped to the right, so she might keep the moon in view a while longer. Envied its freedom. She'd known too little freedom.

Elizabeth had her own bank account. That saintly lady had squirrelled away a small pile of nuts for the winter, and if Lorna was on the phone at nine, she wouldn't be at the Kew bank. Perhaps Kew first to empty Elizabeth's account, then into the city, empty Amber's, then the train.

She lifted her case, a far too heavy case to haul around on trams. She'd need to call a taxi – or leave it here and return for it in a taxi.

And ride that lift down, then up, then down again?

She was walking now, walking the small area around the table, around the metal and vinyl chairs, listening to the tap-tap rhythm of her heels on vinyl. They'd tapped in the asylum, in Norman's house, in her mother's house – had stopped tapping in Lorna's house. All she'd required to achieve content had been given there.

As she reached down to remove her shoes so she might walk silently, she heard muffled snoring from behind a wall. Lifted her head to listen, to remember.

*She murdered my father—*

Murdered? Norman had been dead for years before Amber had silenced his snore on a night when the moon had been full and that red mist of anger had come down to engulf her mind. And like the fool she'd been in Woody Creek, she'd returned to her bed to sleep in blissful silence.

She hadn't returned to her bed the next time she'd done it. Had no access to money in Brunswick. Lived a hand to mouth existence there. She'd been on her way to no place that night, with nothing other than her hessian shopping bag.

The devil looks after his own, her mother used to say. That night he'd sent his handmaiden to look after Amber.

She had no recollection of the accident that gave birth to Elizabeth. She'd been escaping through dark streets, her few possessions in her shopping bag, then no more, nothing, until she'd opened her eyes three days later in a hospital bed.

Hadn't given her wardmate a second thought. Had been concerned about the contents of that shopping bag, her photograph, Maisy's letter.

*Memories are long in Woody Creek, Amb.*

They hadn't found her hessian bag, no doubt strewn to the four winds along with its contents.

Amber cleared a space at one end of the table, then in two stages, lifted her case to the space. With its clean surface to work on, she opened her handbag. There was little in it. Elizabeth Duckworth's bankbook; the keys to Lorna's house and gate; the gold mesh purse she'd found at an opportunity shop, used but not worn out. She'd always wanted such a purse. Born with a craving for pretty things, expensive things, and no way to get them – until Lorna.

Pretty is as pretty does, her mother used to say. A penny saved is a penny earned. Old bitch, overflowing with her isms. Gone now, long gone, along with her penny-pinching poverty.

Maryanne Brown would bring poverty back.

Amber sighed and opened Elizabeth's bankbook. Its total was worth collecting. Amber had accrued thousands. She'd empty both in the morning, then get a taxi and ask the driver to ride up with her in the lift to fetch her case. Tip him in advance if necessary.

It was a plan, and good enough for now. Her handbag repacked, she zipped and hung it by its shoulder strap over the back of a chair while she opened her case. A jumble of pinks, maroons, lilac and blue, like a box of dried rose petals. White underwear, a black cardigan, a flattened blue hat. She reshaped the hat, brushed grit from it, then placed it on a chair.

Removed each frock, each item, shook, brushed and draped it over the back of a chair, her hand searching deeper for her pair of Royal Doulton vases, for her Waterford crystal bowl. The case had felt heavy enough to contain them. They weren't in it. And one shoe was missing, not her best shoes, but comfortable for walking. And grass stains on her undergarments, and her lilac floral frock.

No blue overcoat. Perhaps it was in the car. Lorna would have rid her house of that familiar coat, left hanging beside the black coat on hooks behind the front door. How many miles had those blue and black overcoats walked side by side?

Her maroon jacket was in the case, and it had filth on its sleeve – which it had transferred to the grey and maroon floral print. Dog's filth. She could smell it. Anger rose, but she killed it. Tonight was no time for concern over filth. She was surrounded by it. Had to think 'tomorrow', think 'nine o'clock tomorrow' and the birth of Maryanne Brown. She had to keep her focus on tomorrow morning. It was all she had.

She squinted at the too small face of her watch, a pretty thing but not easy to read at night. It told her that her tomorrow morning had already begun. It told her that she had eight and a half hours left before Lorna dialled the pension department's number.

Did the Kew bank open its door at nine or nine thirty? Perhaps the latter. Elizabeth would be waiting at its door at nine to take her final curtain call.

She looked at the sink, at the tap. Her mouth dry for hours, wanting what that tap contained. She walked around the table to stand before a sink loaded with plates, mugs, bowls and saucepan lids all swimming together in greasy grey water. Turned on a bare heel to a stove, fitted in between the far door and the kitchen bench. A lidless saucepan on one hotplate, a small kettle on another. The kettle suggested that tea might be found in this hell in the sky. She wanted tea and reached to test the kettle's weight of water. Empty, and the sink full, and it was too much, the stink, the filth they lived in. It nauseated her, exhausted her. But two modern taps over the sink suggested that one would deliver hot water. In her mother's hut, she'd boiled the kettle for hot water. No tap in her kitchen, no sink. She'd washed-up in a tin dish on the kitchen table. Since leaving her mother's hut, Amber had measured all labour by her labour there. When you have known worse, the bad is never as bad.

One sleeve pushed high, she reached a hand into greasy water to feel for and remove the plug. Filth burped and gurgled through the pipes to the dirt far below. The tap to the right supplied hot water. She filled the kettle, found the correct switch for a rear hotplate, then while it boiled, she filled the sink with near scalding water to which she added a dash of Rinso, found amid the chaos of the bench.

The plates, mugs, cutlery and miscellaneous items left to soak clean, she searched that bench for tea, for a teapot. Not there. She extended her search to unexpected places. Found an open packet of tea in the refrigerator, beside four cans of condensed milk. Found the door shelves and the lower shelf of the refrigerator loaded with large bottles of lemon cordial. Found tiers of canned tuna. Small cans. Amber counted thirteen.

Found a large tub of ice-cream in the freezer section, iced into the freezer section, meat pies clinging to the ice-cream tub's side. No teapot, or not until she closed the refrigerator door and looked higher. Teapot on top of the refrigerator, beside a bowl containing two mouldy lemons, a long dead banana and a cockroach, not dead. She mashed it with a mouldy lemon.

No bin in Sissy's kitchen, no rear door where she might empty tea leaves, or toss out mouldy fruit. She considered the window, then emptied the teapot into the bowl where the mashed cockroach, his insides seeping, attempted to swim for his life.

Amber worked hard for her cup of tea. She opened a can of condensed milk with a pair of scissors and the heel of her shoe when her search of drawers failed to locate a can opener. She washed the dishes, washed the sink with a fossil of sponge found in a drawer she'd searched for a can opener. She washed filth from the tiles behind the sink, then began on the benchtop, moving massed items to random cupboards.

She cleared the table of salt and pepper, sauce and scissors, bills and pills, and placed them neatly on the benchtop, then used the fossil and more Rinso to wash the laminated table top clean, and when it was done to her satisfaction she made tea and sat down at a clean table to sip – and a cup of tea had never tasted so good.

One step at a time. That's all it had ever taken. When she'd cleaned up after Norman, when she'd cleaned at Kew, just one step at a time, one small corner, then the next and the next until there were no more corners to clean.

By dawn Amber had found a modern stove she'd scrubbed white with Rinso and a nail brush, found on her second trip to the bathroom. She'd found a very modern refrigerator, which by seven was as clean inside as it was out. Found a can opener when she dried the dishes, found a nice set of cutlery, which justified her lining of a cutlery drawer with pages ripped from a magazine.

Each knife, fork, spoon and the miscellaneous placed into its own pigeonhole. She'd lined two wall cupboards with more pages from that same magazine and in one she'd placed the plates and bowls; in the other, the mugs and glasses.

An organised kitchen leads to an organised mind. Her mind was functioning well when Reginald emerged before eight, clad in a moth-eaten dressing gown. He caught her drinking tea. If he noticed the cleared table, the empty sink, the white stove as he brushed by it, it was not obvious.

Amber sipped until she heard a cistern flush, at which point she rose, washed and dried her cup, slid her feet into her shoes, tidied her short curls and set her hat on them.

He didn't return. Water was gurgling again down the pipes. She carried her case back to the door, placed her handbag strap over her shoulder, then stood with her case, waiting for him.

He came but only as far as the kitchen. From the sitting room, she watched him take a bottle of lemon cordial from the refrigerator then seek a receptacle. He settled for her cup, half-filled it, added water, then sighting her watching, he emptied the cup and placed it down.

'Are there stairs, Reginald?' His chin lifted, or the place where his chin should have been, and in a family where heavy chins dominated, how he'd been born chinless, Amber didn't know. 'Stairs,' she repeated.

'A lift,' he said, his eyes shuddering in a last ditch attempt to escape their bony confines. Red and scaly lids reined them in. He blinked, twice, three times, cleared his throat again, and tried once more. 'We are . . . on the . . . on the fourth . . .'

He'd had little to say as a youth. Charles had done the sermonising, leaving few spaces for the other occupants of his house to find their voices. Amber had once allowed Cousin Reg time to express his dreams. This morning she had no time to waste. 'There must be a staircase?'

He nodded.

'Where?'

'To the . . .' He raised his left hand.

'Stairs to the left?' He nodded. 'Is there a tram nearby?'

Again he raised his left hand.

'I'll need to leave my case here for an hour or two. Do you have a spare key?'

He went to his room, returning moments later clad in an abominable rag of a tracksuit and bedroom slippers, but offering a key. She zipped it into her handbag as he led the way along the passage to a stairwell.

And Amber descended into heaven, counting the steps as she circled down.

Fifty-three.

# Nose Job

'You should have seen Lorna Hooper's face,' Maisy said. She'd been talking since she'd sat down, and Jenny listening, wide eyed.

'I don't think either of them saw me. I hope they didn't. I was standing well back with Reg. But, my God, you should have seen the way Lorna looked at Amber. She'd been hanging on to her arm, and when she realised who she was hanging on to, she gave Amber an almighty shove. She would have gone down if not for Alma Duckworth. She caught her, then Lorna gave her a look that should have smote her dead on the spot.'

They were sampling the morning tea menu at Woody Creek's new tea room – three tables and twelve chairs set up beneath the veranda of Blunt's drapery store. Two years ago, Miss Blunt had sold her business to John and Pauline Taylor, a city couple who, since N. and B. Wallis had moved into Charlie's, had become disillusioned by drapery and were in the process of diversifying. Enough of the locals, loyal to Miss Blunt, had paid her exorbitant prices but didn't feel the same loyalty towards the Taylors, not when they could buy similar items for a third of the price at Charlie's.

N. and B. Wallis now stocked pantihose, underwear and various items of cheap children's clothing. They were go-getters, and that's about all Jenny had to say for the pair who'd bought Georgie's shop.

Maisy no longer entered that beeping door, not since she'd been called an old biddy, when all she'd attempted to do was explain to the B half of the Wallis duo how Woody Creek businesses had never attempted to cut the throats of the other businesses, that there was room for all in Woody Creek as long as everyone stuck to selling what they'd always sold. Her advice hadn't gone down well, and since that day, Maisy had taken the Taylors under her wing.

'They did well last Friday,' she said. 'Me and Patricia had one of their ham and cheese omelettes for lunch and these chairs were full.'

The farmers and their wives still came to town on Fridays, or the few who chose not to make the longer drive to Willama came in to do their shopping, though the streets, once crowded on Fridays, were no longer crowded.

'They'll get no one sitting out here come winter,' Jenny said.

'If it takes off, Pauline said they'll move things around inside and set their tables up in there.'

The male Taylor was a retired baker. He baked in the room Miss Blunt had used as a fitting room, and when he was working at his old trade the shop smelled of baking. On the days he didn't bake, a whiff of the past still clung to the rear corners of Blunt's drapery, but the days he didn't bake were becoming rare. He supplied cakes and pies to the hotel. He'd made and decorated a beautiful wedding cake for the Jenner wedding. A couple like the Taylors would survive, though maybe not as drapers. In the time Jenny had been drinking tea out front of the shop, not one customer had walked in through the door.

'How did she look?' Jenny asked.

'A damn sight happier before she saw Sissy—'

'I meant Sissy,' Jenny said.

'The same,' Maisy said. 'Basically the same. Bigger, of course, older, her hair's half-grey but still hanging around her shoulders, and she had so much hairspray on it, it almost cracked when she turned her head. She was wearing one of those stretchy material dresses that hug every bulge. She's got a stomach on her as big as I had when I was nine months pregnant with the twins, but otherwise much the same.' Maisy's fork bit into a slice of lemon meringue pie. Her tongue tasted. 'Their filling is more gluey than mine. The lemon isn't supposed to be gluey.'

'Did Lorna speak to her?'

'Lorna didn't say anything to anybody. Not a syllable. I thought she was going to have a stroke. She turned purple, or her nose did. Did she have a nose job or something?'

Some people never change. Maisy hadn't, or not in personality. She took up a lot less space these days, ate only a portion of the lemon filling, all of the meringue, but didn't touch the pastry. Egg whites were full of protein, she explained. Dieters required plenty of protein and as she no longer used sugar in her tea, the body needed a certain amount of it to supply energy.

She'd been the best cook in town for sixty-odd years, had won first prize at the CWA's cooking competitions every year until she'd started counting calories.

'You know how people say, "She went as white as a ghost"? They do, or Lorna went yellow – except for her nose – and all I was going to say about it was that whoever did the work ought to be sued for malpractice. She used to at least have a nose that matched the rest of her hatchet face. It's a scarred blob of a thing now.'

'I've seen it. Go on.'

'There's nothing to go on with. I hotfooted it back to the taxi and told the driver to go. I wouldn't have seen as much as I did if Maureen hadn't told him to wait.' She hunted a fly eager to taste her pie, then ate a little more of the lemon filling. 'That day I ran into Amber in Woolworths, I should have twigged. I mean, seeing her, and then Lorna on the same day, and sort of in the same place, should have got me wondering, but I didn't even think about them in the same breath. I mean, it would have been too ridiculous. And it is – or it was.'

'Did Amber say anything to Sissy?'

'Not while I was watching. She was watching Lorna, not Sissy.' Maisy pushed the plate from her reach and sat back in her chair. 'Remember that Reginald cousin of your father's?'

'Charles the parson's son?'

Maisy nodded. 'That's who she's married to.'

'Who who is married to?' Jenny asked.

'Sissy.'

Jenny's jaw dropped. 'You're kidding me?'

'I'm not.'

'He's old,' Jenny said.

'He's ten years younger than me. I remember thinking what a nice sort of boy he was when he came up here that time to bury Norman's mother. He looks like a walking skeleton and I could smell the drink oozing out of his pores, and at eleven o'clock on a Sunday morning out front of a church.'

'What the hell possessed her to marry him?'

'God knows, but she's married to him. Did your father ever talk about a cousin Alma?'

'He had a million cousins, Maisy.'

'She seems a nice enough woman. Sissy told me on the phone that Alma was engaged to a bloke during the war and he didn't come back to do the right thing by her. She's got a daughter. They lived with Alma's father until he died, then the sisters and brothers – there's about ten of them – anyway, they all put in money and bought them a house near Lorna's.'

'Dad told me once that his mother was one of thirteen.'

'An army of them came up here to bury her. We had trouble finding enough beds. I squeezed in three of your father's male cousins. Vern took two or three couples, Lonny and Nancy Bryant had five staying out at their farm the night you turned up.'

'Fifty-five years ago,' Jenny said.

'You can't be fifty-five!' Maisy said, then shrugged. 'I suppose you must be. Which reminds me – Alma was saying when we were out front of the church that her sister saw your mother – that Juliana woman – or what she said was that her sister Clarice saw the foreign woman who was found dead up here that night – saw her while she was alive and pregnant – on the train up here – which seems like yesterday, not fifty-five years ago,' Maisy said.

'Did the Duckworths buy Reginald a house?'

'They got them a Commission flat in one of those big blocks of units they've built in Collingwood, or near Collingwood.'

'That's miles from Kew. Why go to church at Kew?' Jenny asked.

'The Duckworths take turns at having them out for Sunday dinner,' Maisy said. 'Sissy told me she'd spoken to Lorna at the church before and that they'd seen your mother before but didn't recognise her until she heard her voice – while Sissy had her back turned. It's funny that. I used to be able to pick Bernie and Macka by their voices if my back was turned, but face to face I never could. We never hear from Macka, you know. Not once, not that I'd expect him to write; neither one of them wrote more than half a dozen lines all the time they were away in the war, but he could have phoned. I thought he'd have the brains to see through that woman in a week and come running home.'

Disinterested in talk of the twins, Jenny ate the last of her vanilla slice then pushed the plate to the edge of table where a beady-eyed sparrow might steal the crumbs. He wanted them. He flew in to perch on the back of a spare chair but failed to find the necessary nerve to fly to the plate.

Norman used to feed the sparrows at the station; they'd pecked around his shoes for crumbs. She stole a corner of Maisy's discarded pastry and tossed it towards the gutter, and a flock emerged from somewhere for a free meal.

'You'll have every sparrow in town coming here to eat,' Maisy said.

'They might keep the flies away.'

The birds left as fast as they'd arrived, apart from that one bright-eyed hopeful who returned to his perch to eye Jenny's plate. She stole another piece of pastry, this time offering it on her palm, prepared to sit with her hand extended until greed got the better of that cheeky little coot. Norman had sat with crusts on his palm until temptation had got the better of the station's birds. My bright-eyed friends, he'd named them.

*My Bright-Eyed Friend*, Jenny thought. Amy and Jim had been at her for months to come up with a rhyme. Amy had suggested a witch and goblin rhyme, only because she'd found half a dozen tiny goblins in a box of junk she'd bid on at an auction.

They were magical books. They reminded Jenny of the fairy book Jim had brought one morning to Norman's station where four year old Jenny had fallen in love with it, then up in Sydney, at a secondhand book stall, she'd found an identical copy and bought it for herself more than for Jimmy. She still had it, and it was still intact. They'd designed their first book, *The Lady's Garden*, along the lines of Jenny's old fairy book.

She'd written that rhyme to explain to six year old Trudy how she'd grown in another lady's tummy garden. Their second book they'd built around one of Jenny's reworked childhood rhymes. The butterfly book rhyme had been conjured up one night after she'd seen Joey Hall, Elsie's son, who Jenny had grown with. They'd spoken about chasing butterflies on Granny's land, spoken until dawn. He lived in Queensland and rarely came home, but when he did, the years slipped away.

*Little family going places, Daddy sparrow has the cases . . .*

The female half of Taylors' drapery frightened Jenny's rhyme and her bright-eyed friend away when she came with her teapot to refill their cups. She was a pleasant woman who had the right personality to make a place for herself in this town. The B half of the Wallis duo had been given the right initial.

Jenny turned to look at the shop she had known all her life. Same window, same veranda, though not quite the same. Concrete had been laid beneath it; a concrete footpath now led to it and away, or away as far as North Street. The once open drain out front was now concrete and the road was sealed, or its centre was sealed.

The last time she'd seen Sissy she'd been standing at Miss Blunt's counter. They'd had words. After Margot's birth they'd rarely met, but when they had, they'd always had words. May have had a few more that day had Ray King not parked his motorbike out front, had Jimmy not wanted to take a closer look at that bike. Jenny had gone one way, Sissy the other. Sisters? They'd never been sisters. From that day to this they hadn't set eyes on each other. How many years ago? The war was over; the boys had started coming home.

Sissy and Cousin Reginald. My God. The one and only time Jenny had set eyes on Reginald had been the day of Norman's funeral. He'd eyed her. She'd been the town scandal and no doubt the family scandal, an unwed mother of three – though apparently not the only scandal. Alma Duckworth had also produced a daughter out of wedlock and raised her.

'Sissy used to send me a Christmas card until around eight years ago,' Maisy said. 'She didn't say, but that could have been when she married Reg. She probably didn't want me to know. By the way she talks about him on the phone, she can't stand the sight of him.'

'God help him.'

'She wouldn't be easy to live with. She was a bugger of a kid,' Maisy said.

'I lived with her, Maisy, and she couldn't stand the sight of me, either.'

'Your mother was much the same as her when she was young. She led your gran a terrible dance. I was down there the day she tried to talk Amber out of marrying your father.'

Granny had tried to talk Jenny out of marrying Ray. She hadn't listened either, nor had she when Ray had come back to town with his two babies. Should have told him to go. Instead she'd spent years caring for Donny and Raelene. Wasted twelve years of her life—

Maisy was talking, and when she mentioned Norman, Jenny reined her mind back from its wandering. 'I always had a soft spot for him, and the things they wrote about your father in the paper that time when they were trying to get your mother released from the asylum. They should have been sued. Your dad worshipped the ground Amber walked on. He came to life when she walked into the room. She could be charming when she felt like it, and some nights she'd play up to your dad and he'd almost wriggle like a pup with pleasure. I remember one day she came over to my place in hysterics. Norman had got down on his knee and asked her to marry him. She'd had no intention of marrying him then.

'It was later,' Maisy said. 'I was pregnant again, and she asked me what it was like having kids to a man I didn't love. She knew I'd married George for his house. I remember telling her that I loved his kids and they loved him, so I loved him too. Then the next thing I knew, she and your father had set the date.'

'He didn't own a house?' Jenny said.

'He lived in one in the centre of town, and it was furnished better than most. You'd remember the parlour and the crystal cabinet. Amber and your gran used to eat off tin plates and drink out of enamel mugs – not that I'd ever say a word against your gran. I loved her and her cosy little hut. I spent half my life running down there when I was a kid. Anyway, six months after the wedding your mother told me she'd made the biggest mistake of her life. "And don't you dare tell Mum I said that," she said to me. She hated your gran for being proved right.'

'Why would she call herself Miss Duckworth?' Jenny asked.

'That's got me beat. It led to her downfall. And telling them that her father Charles had been an Anglican minister. For a while, Alma thought she might have been their Parson Charles' illegitimate daughter, except Miss Duckworth had said she'd lived with her father in Launceston until his death. It was the Tasmanian branch of Duckworths who found out there'd never been a Charles Duckworth parson in Launceston, which is what got them suspicious.'

A mill hooter let the town know it was midday. Maisy stood. 'I've got to go, love, but to cut a long story short, Alma found out that Lorna skittled her Miss Duckworth around the same time as Amber went missing from that Brunswick place, which wasn't far from where Lorna skittled her – and I'll have to go. That pretty little blonde one is pregnant and they're going to tell us today who she's pregnant to.'

*

*Days of Our Lives* followers knew who the little blonde was pregnant to before Amber ascended those fifty-three steps back up to hell. She let herself in with the loaned key, smelling tinned fish before sighting Reginald, who was seated before the television, forking tuna out of the can. No sign of Sissy.

She carried her shopping bags through to the kitchen table, cleared when she'd left this morning, now filling but not full. She cleared it again, delved into one of her shopping bags for a packet of her favourite kitchen sponges. She removed one, wet it and wiped the table before unpacking her shopping bags.

She'd bought fresh milk, butter, cheese, bread, a writing pad, biro, envelopes, a scrubbing brush, rubber gloves, a bottle of Handy Andy and a bottle of bleach. Large bottles were more economical but heavy. The small bottle had grown heavy before she'd climbed a dozen of those steps, but she'd done it.

With no sign or sound of Sissy, she assumed she'd gone out, and set about boiling the kettle and making tea. She was eating a cheese sandwich, her writing pad open beside her plate, when a sneeze penetrated a wall and closed doors. Amber closed her pad and looked towards the doors as the first sneeze was followed by half a dozen more. Then the cistern flushed and water began burping down the pipes behind the wall. The pad again opened, the sandwich placed down, Amber returned to the letter she'd been composing in her mind since riding the Kew tram back to the city.

During the years she'd spent with Lorna, Amber had become adept at . . . at covering her tracks.

*My dear Miss Hooper,*
*How can I ever repay you for your kindness to a stranger in her time of great need? I fully understand your response on Sunday. Your shock was no doubt as great as my own. Had the deception been a conscious ploy for your sympathy, I would not beg your forgiveness now, but until yesterday I was unaware of my cruel deception.*

Never a writer, nor a reader, or not until Lorna had required her sight, practice over her twelve-year close association with an over-intelligent tyrant had polished Amber's seventh-grade skills.

*I learned yesterday that my daughter's married name is Duckworth and that her father-in-law was a minister of the church.*

Those of a devious nature, when obliged to bend to a tyrant's will, will become more devious.

Then Sissy emerged, wet hair hanging. Amber closed her pad.

'You told Reg that you were coming back to get your case.'

'Good afternoon, Mrs Duckworth,' Amber said.

'Don't you "Mrs Duckworth" me. You know who I am,' Sissy snarled and stomped out.

Amber returned to her letter.

*When roused from my stupor at the hospital, no doubt I grasped at the few pleasant memories I had retained . . .*

Not so pleasant memories. Sissy was back and two slices of fresh bread hit the table opposite the pad. Amber closed it to watch a knife spread butter – as a bricklayer might spread mortar on a brick – to watch her block of cheese attacked, thick slices gouged from it to be buried in butter. Watched the second slice of bread slapped on the first, flattened with a palm then, uncut, the sandwich lifted and a massive jaw clamped while with one hand Sissy tested the weight of the teapot. Judging it full enough, she found a mug, judged it clean enough, poured tea, then the dressing-gown-clad humps and lumps of Sissy flopped down onto a chair to add milk and sugar.

Reginald came to place his empty can of tuna on the table. The smell of dead fish overpowering, Amber picked up the can with finger and thumb, placed it into one of the empty supermarket bags, sealed it, then again sat.

They were watching her, he blinking, Sissy staring. Unable to write her letter, Amber opened her handbag and removed the borrowed key. She'd had four duplicate keys cut this morning, one each of Lorna's three and one of the borrowed unit key. An expensive exercise, but necessary to her plan, which she'd altered since counting those fifty-three steps down, since the tram she'd caught this morning at a very conveniently positioned tram stop, which she'd catch again when her letter was done.

Reginald returned to the sitting room to eat his cheese sandwich and to flick channels. Sissy set about the construction of a second sandwich, and Amber, pressed for time, returned to her letter.

*I have spent this morning attempting to sort out the confusion my loss of memory has created. As you, my dear, are aware, I have no personal income, and although I know you have been hurt deeply by my unconscious deception, it would be greatly appreciated if you could hold my mail at Kew until I find alternative accommodation.*

*The gentleman I spoke to this morning at the Social Security Department told me it could take some weeks before the confusion is sorted out and his office can issue me with a pension in my own name . . .*

Sissy's stomach bulges moulding themselves around the table, she leaned forward to better see what was being written, and again Amber closed the pad.

'As if I'm interested, and what's the use of writing to her? She's supposed to be blind.'

'Miss Hooper's loss of sight is severe but not complete, Mrs Duckworth.'

'I told you my name. I told you yesterday. I told you last night. I'm not telling you again.'

Her raised voice brought Reginald back to the door, and Sissy turned to face him. 'I lived with her acts for twenty years – except when she was selling herself on the streets down here, and if she thinks I don't remember that, I do, and everything else she ever did too.'

Amber lowered her head and again took up her pen. She had today and half of today was already gone. She now had money in her handbag, and Elizabeth Duckworth had none – or little. It would have taken more time to close the account. She left two dollars ten in the book which was now swimming in the pipes that ran beneath the city. Dropped it onto a street grating, edged it through with a shoe and – goodbye, Elizabeth.

Though not quite goodbye. The twin vases, found at an opportunity shop, paid for and carried home to Kew by Elizabeth, decorated Lorna's sitting room mantelpiece, and Elizabeth's delightful crystal bowl lived on Lorna's blackwood sideboard.

*As you are aware, my Royal Doulton vases have great sentimental value to me. I thank you for not placing them at risk with my other belongings. I can only assume that one of the young street louts vandalised my case's contents. As to my Waterford crystal bowl, I am sure it and my vases will be safe in your care until I can arrange to collect the last of my belongings.*

*This morning when I awakened, back again in the bosom of my family, my first thoughts were for you and of how you will manage alone, my dear. I beg you not to drive your vehicle without me at your side, and feel sure that Mrs Duckworth and her daughter would be more than willing to take you shopping.*

*In closing, I bless you for your kindness to me when we met as strangers and I hope that one day you can find it within your heart to forgive my accidental deception. Should you need me, you need only to call.*

*My very best regards to you always,*
*Elizabeth*

'I told you that your name is Amber Morrison!'

'Yes, dear, you did.'

'Then why sign that letter *Elizabeth*?'

'It is who I have been for some time.'

'And *My dear Miss Hooper.* No one writes "my dear" anyone these days, and crawling to her after what she did to you yesterday – you make me sick.'

Sissy, never a reader, could now apparently do it quite well upside down. Amber looked into those sunken mud eyes for a moment, then back to her pad to carefully remove her page and fold it. She'd bought a packet of twenty envelopes, and on one she wrote the familiar Kew address. She'd bought no stamps.

'You're not staying here tonight.'

'I have nowhere to go, Mrs—'

'Don't you dare.'

'—Cecelia,' Amber said, her lips grimacing on that name. She slipped her letter into the envelope, adding Lorna's keys then, with a lick, sealed it.

'You can't put something like that in a letterbox. And if you think for one second that she'll take you back, then you're stark raving mad. If she'd had any spit left in her, she would have spat in your face outside that church – and if you think it wasn't her who tossed your clothes everywhere, then you're dumb along with being a stark raving mad crawler,' Sissy said, snatching more bread from the packet.

Amber, unwilling to watch the last of her cheese disappear, placed the envelope into her handbag and left the kitchen, left the unit to again descend those fifty-three steps to heaven, where she still had much to do.

*

In each life there are highs, lows and the flat spaces in between. Amber had survived the ultra lows, had lived the highs in Kew. This was neither a high nor a low. This was her one day. She now had sufficient funds in her handbag for Maryanne to escape to Perth – or to Tasmania – to rent a small flat, furnish it. Or should she stay a while in this place, well camouflaged by the mixed and matched mass of humanity she'd passed on those fifty-three steps?

Since childhood, when stressed by a life she could not control, her feet had been unable to remain still. In adulthood, when life in Norman's house had returned more punishment than reward, she'd walked from dusk to dawn. This morning the circling descent had been mind-cleansing and therapeutic – as had been her freedom to ride the tram with the city's masses. She rode with them again, rode the familiar tram to Kew where she deposited her letter in the familiar letterbox. No sign of Lorna.

By three thirty Amber was in Richmond, at her favourite opportunity shop. She'd found her vases there, but this morning she ignored the folderols and made a beeline for the frock racks. The dusty pink worn since Sunday morning was no longer fresh, nor was the clothing picked up from Lorna's gutter. She found two frocks, not as smart as Elizabeth's pink, but quite suitable for Mrs Maryanne Brown. Later she chose new underwear, two new towels. Her plans had altered since this morning. Elizabeth was not required to die, but to go into hiding.

*

It was six o'clock before she commenced her slow circling ascent, a new key pinned to the lining of her handbag: Elizabeth

Duckworth's. Having decided not to kill herself, she'd rented a private mailbox at Richmond, which would require another letter to be written, though not tonight. Amber was near dead on her feet when almost knocked from them by a herd of running louts – who might have intentionally knocked her down had they been aware of the contents of her handbag. She'd emptied both Amber's and Elizabeth's accounts. Amber's bankbook had joined Elizabeth's in the drains below Melbourne.

Television blaring when she unlocked the door, Reginald sleeping on his chair and no sign of Sissy, she crept across the chaos to the sitting room to turn the volume low before continuing through to the kitchen, where she armed herself with a beige-toned floral frock, new underwear, towel, a scrubbing brush, sponge, her bottles of Handy Andy and bleach, the rubber gloves, a sealed cake of perfumed soap and her handbag. She required a bath.

And found Sissy standing before the toothpaste-splattered, soap-greased mirror, grimacing as she unwound plastic rollers from her hair.

Something moved within Amber's exhausted breast, the merest flicker of something. The protest of a weary heart perhaps? Something. In another lifetime, she had loved that plain as mud ox of a girl. Always she'd done her best for Sissy. She'd bought her pretty frocks, spent hours styling her heavy hair. For a moment, Amber stood with her load in the doorway, watching her daughter struggle.

She sighed and turned towards the kitchen. She yawned, sighed again, then: 'Bring your comb and pins out to the light, Cecelia. I will do what I can for you.'

# The Party

Elsie Hall couldn't tell you with any certainty the day or the year of her birth. She had vague recollections of a father who had dropped her and her sister Lucy off at the Aboriginal mission but had retained no image of him. She had no similar memory of a mother.

She remembered horses, barking dogs, a canvas-covered wagon and Lucy, who told her Daddy was coming back. He hadn't come.

There was little doubt that he'd been a white man. Elsie's skin tones had never been quite white but her features were European. She'd been raised white by Gertrude Foote, or, rather, from the age of eleven or twelve she'd been raised white.

Harry Hall, a lanky, freckle-faced redhead, might have been seventeen when Gertrude took him under her wing. At eighteen he'd married Elsie, who was four or five years his senior, and already the mother of ten year old Joseph Richard Foote, or Joey.

Joey, also not quite white, raised as Gertrude's grandson, had celebrated his eighteenth birthday then left home to fight a war. He'd met Annette, a nurse and the daughter of a Queensland cane farmer, who he married when the war was over when he became

Joe Foote, a Bundaberg cane farmer of Spanish descent. In Woody Creek he'd been Darkie Hall, son of Elsie and Dingo Wadi. His visits home were brief.

Lenny Hall had been raised as the son of Elsie and Harry, but by birth was Elsie's nephew, a big blond-headed, blue-eyed chap, a top footballer in his day, now wed to a Willama girl and living in a modern brick house out Cemetery Road. His full sister, Joany, and Tony, her Italian immigrant husband, grew tomatoes on a property fifteen kilometres west of Woody Creek.

Harry and Elsie had produced five of their own: Ronnie, a redhead and a dead ringer for his father; Maudie, born with Elsie's dark hair, Harry's freckles and blue eyes; sandy-headed and blue-eyed Brian, an accountant at a city bank; redheaded Josie, a theatre nurse at the Alfred Hospital; and Teddy, the middle man. Born with Elsie's dark hair and eyes, her darker than average skin tones, Teddy had always known he was the odd man out. He'd started leaving home as a three year old, started stealing his father's tobacco as a ten year old. Man sized by the age of fourteen, he'd discovered that a bottle of beer could make his dark complexion go away.

He'd left home at twenty. He might have gone further than Willama had he not been arrested and charged with the purchasing of known stolen property, two cartons of Charlie White's cigarettes. Harry and Lenny bailed him out and took him home to do the right thing by Margot, who had been five months pregnant at the time. She'd refused to marry a 'blackfeller', though after Trudy's birth, the odd relationship had continued for seven more years. Teddy's one saving grace during those years had been his skill with motors. Show him a piston and, hungover or not, he'd name the car or truck it had come out of. Take a dying motor to him and, drunk or not, an hour or two later he'd have it purring.

He was twenty-eight the year Roy, the garage owner, retired, which, had Roy been able to find a buyer for his rundown house and tin shed garage, his umpteen years of accumulated greasy bits of vehicles long dead, might have been the end of Teddy.

Few prospective buyers bothered to get out of their cars, so Roy had made Teddy an offer too good to refuse. He'd had money in the bank. Harry had put it there. For years he'd been confiscating Teddy's wages, his only means of keeping his son off the grog. He gave up that bankbook. Teddy put down a deposit on Roy's house and business and the bank gave him a loan for the rest.

That's when Vonnie Boyle, a not quite eighteen year old kid, had wormed her way into Teddy's life. She'd sorted out his bookwork first, then his tin shed, and later his life, and in doing so had ruined Margot's. Young Vonnie knew almost as much about motors and gearboxes as her husband. That girl could do anything other than carry a baby beyond five months.

In November of '78, the original loan paid off, Vonnie spoke to the bank about a new loan to build a new garage, and while the site was being cleared, she booked a two-week holiday at Veronica Andrews' Frankston guesthouse, where she'd be waited on and could lie around all day. She was pregnant again.

She started bleeding in Frankston.

Since the late forties, Veronica and her retired doctor partner had done a few hundred abortions in the rooms behind their guesthouse. That night they did what they could to prevent one. Vonnie was moved by ambulance to the Royal Women's Hospital where she got by the five-month marker before Teddy drove home alone. He spent his weekends on the road through January and February, hope growing in his eyes, and in Elsie's.

And in Jenny's. Her reasons were selfish. Teddy showed too much interest in Trudy. If they were in the same room, his eyes rarely left her. He'd never mentioned her birth, and probably never would, which didn't alter the fact that he was her blood father. Since his wedding day, Jenny had been willing Vonnie pregnant, preferably with triplets.

She was only having one, and on a Sunday night in late March, Teddy popped his head inside the bungalow to relay the latest news. Jim and Jen were there, playing cards.

'The quack said today that if Vonnie can hang on until the week after next, he'll operate. She's a determined little bugger. She'll hang on.'

Hope made his eyes glisten that night, made him smile, and it was Trudy's smile, and Jenny's heart lurched.

'I heard its ticker this morning. It's beating away in there like a steady little motor,' he said, and he sniffed and left them to their game.

On the morning of the tenth of April 1979, Michael John Hall was delivered, all five pound eight ounces of him, and within an hour of his birth, the news that he was alive and well, that Vonnie and Teddy were over the moon, had travelled from Bundaberg to Mildura, to Melbourne and back to Molliston. Vonnie's parents made their own few phone calls. Their son, Michael John, had died at twenty-one in a car accident. Vonnie was their only daughter, and her son their only grandchild.

Harry had lost count of his. Elsie could tell you the birth dates of every one, including Trudy, but this one's arrival deserved celebrating. They baptised Michael John in early June, and Halls and Boyles came from every direction to be a part of that miracle. Jen and Jim offered their house for the party. Harry booked half a dozen onsite caravans and cabins, but no Hall went to bed that night, not the adults, the teenagers or the kids – nor did Jenny.

Joey had flown down from Bundaberg for the day and would return tomorrow. He'd flown alone. His children believed they'd inherited their dark eyes and hair from their Grandmother Foote's Spanish pirate ancestor. Jenny's fault. When Joey had grown a moustache at fifteen, she'd told him he looked like a Spanish pirate. Or maybe it was the town's fault. The five year old boy in Joey had never forgotten, or forgiven, the constable who'd pointed out the fact that he had the wrong-coloured skin.

Near daylight, Joey and a minor herd of yawning Halls drove down to have a look at the house they'd been raised in, the land they'd played on. The light, though poor, was just sufficient to see the colour of a utility parked in their old driveway.

'That's Georgie's ute,' Teddy said, and he and Josie crept inside.

Found her dead to the world, on the kitchen floor, zipped into a sleeping bag.

Josie wanted to wake her.

'Let her sleep,' Teddy said.

Before the Halls went their separate ways, they told Jenny. She crept in at nine and found Georgie still curled up in her sleeping bag, so crept out to walk around Elsie's crumbling house, to peer beneath the termite-riddled structure, then walk across the goat paddock to stare at the blackened site and to shake her head again. The shed was still standing. She had a poke around inside it, picked up a little spade she could use at home. She carried it back to the car, had a smoke then, with still no sound of movement from within, she decided she'd waited long enough.

Cocooned in the green sleeping bag, Georgie looked like a giant caterpillar, and how anyone could sleep so heavily on a hard board floor, Jenny didn't know. She reached out a hand to the small portion of her that was visible, that dark copper hair – or what was left of it.

'What the hell have you done to your hair?' she said. Hadn't meant to wake her like that. She'd planned to do it gently.

Georgie opened her eyes and rolled onto her back. 'What the hell are you nagging about at this time of day?'

'It's after ten, and your hair's gone.'

More of Georgie emerged. A hand appeared and ran fingers through her inch-long crew-cut. 'You're right,' she said. 'Damn those termites.'

'Why would you go and do a thing like that?'

'Bore water,' Georgie said as more of her was revealed, clad in a sweater and baggy jeans, heavy socks.

'There's nothing of you.'

'Nice to see you too, mate.'

'That goes without saying – if there was enough of you to see. You're skin and bone and why would you let anyone do *that* to your beautiful hair?'

'Birdsville,' Georgie said. 'Their water is fifty per cent tar. What's happening with Dino Collins?'

'He was supposed to go to trial again two months ago but they carted him off to a psychiatric hospital. As far as I know, he's still there.'

'He's playing possum,' Georgie said.

'That's what I said. What time did you get here?'

'Late – or early. I lost my watch.'

'Why didn't you come in?'

'I wasn't dressed for a party, Jen.'

'You look like someone's rag bag.'

'Ta.'

Jenny considered Elsie's old table as a chair. She tested it, wiped away a little dust and grime, then sat, swinging her legs. 'I saw Collins at the first trial. There's less of him than you – though he had more hair.'

'I hoped you might have been celebrating his demise last night,' Georgie said.

'Vonnie and Teddy had a baby and Joey flew down. You should have come in. You haven't seen him in years.'

'I saw him at the Centenary, and I barely knew your Joey.'

'I barely knew him this time. His hair is almost white and his face is as lined as Elsie's.' She studied Georgie's face while watching her pull on a pair of working boots then reach into her sleeping bag for a navy windcheater jacket she pulled on over her sweater. 'That looks as if it came out of a rag bag too.'

'It was hanging behind the door of a cabin I spent a night in. Any more insults, or are you all done for this morning?' Georgie said, then turned her attention to Elsie's old wood stove, barely visible beneath its layer of dust and possum droppings.

'You'll catch a disease down here – if you don't die of pneumonia first – if the roof doesn't fall in on you before you have time to catch it.'

'I've paid out good money to camp in worse, mate.'

Elsie had left her old fridge behind, her old kitchen table, no chair, no hearth brush, no wood on the hearth, a sink with a tap offering no water.

'We disconnected the hose,' Jenny said as Georgie tried the tap. 'It dripped. Harry needs what's in the tank for the chooks.'

'Disconnected the power too,' Georgie said. 'I could have used a bit of light last night. Does the fridge still work?'

'It was barely working when they moved,' Jenny said, eyeing the antique standing at an acute angle in the corner. The kitchen floor had run downhill for years. 'We've had three different mobs squatting down here in the past twelve months. I'm thinking of selling to Joe Flanagan. He wants my access to the creek for his cows.'

'Over my dead body.'

'If you stay down here, that won't take long. Get your things and come home.'

'I'm home, or as close as it gets, or I would be if I had some power.'

'If electricity is put through white ant riddled wiring, this place will burn.'

'White ants don't eat wire,' Georgie said, then walked through to Elsie's parlour, through a sleep-out to the rear door. Jenny went as far as the parlour, its floor a clutter of bottles, strewn paper, unidentifiable clothing left behind by Elsie or the squatters. She looked at a hole in the floorboards where a squatter may have fallen through. Peered through it to the junk below. No sign of a body down there.

'The whole place is being held together by white ant nests, Georgie.'

'They're doing an all right job,' Georgie said, giving the doorframe a shake.

Termites had partied on the stumps supporting the front veranda. Its roof had fallen a month ago, blocking the front door – which hadn't opened in years anyway. Jenny sighed and walked out to stand on the rear steps, watching Georgie searching Harry's old wood heap for chips.

'Come home, love.'

'I'll be forty next year, Jen. I reckon that might just about make me old enough to know where I need to be right now,' Georgie said.

Harry drove down at five to feed the chooks. Georgie had found the remains of a broom beneath the house. She'd swept the kitchen and parlour floors. She'd found an empty oil drum to sit on. The stove was burning, her billy was boiling.

He leaned against the kitchen's doorframe while telling her the roof wouldn't stand up to the next wind. She asked him if his old fridge had still been working when they'd cut off the power. He told her it had. He told her that the rafters and wall supports in his old bedroom were paper thin, told her that every movement in the rafters put an added strain on old power wires.

'If she burns, she burns, Harry.'

'I pulled you out of one fire, Georgie.'

'Which sort of proved to me that I wasn't written down to die young, Harry.'

# The Hair

With the stove burning, the kitchen was warmer than the back of her ute. Georgie had paid to have a canvas canopy fitted to it in Townsville and had spent a few nights beneath that tarp, comfortable enough on her inflatable mattress. She'd seen a lot of country, crossed a lot of mountains, walked a lot of beaches, watched the burning of a crop of sugarcane somewhere north of Brisbane, hoping its controlled burning might wipe out the uncontrolled burning of her dreams.

It hadn't, and so what? She'd eaten ripe pineapples in Queensland, slurped mangoes by the dozen, tried a custard apple too. Had always wanted to try one. One had been enough.

She'd worked for a time in Townsville before taking off for Mount Isa. Had worked in a few places, slept in a few caravans and cabins, then driven on, turning when she'd felt like turning, stopping when she'd felt like stopping, working when she'd needed the company and writing a cheque when she hadn't.

She'd spent three months in Darwin working as a pub waitress, interested in a city blown away in the cyclone of '74 but thriving by '78. She'd seen an eight-foot crocodile outside of Darwin, its jaws open, ready to eat her.

For six weeks she'd worked at a roadhouse up near Karratha while her ute had been out of action. Without her wheels, she'd had to do something to fill her time. Waited ten days for her ute's reconditioned motor to arrive, waited another week for it to be fitted then waited a month more because the roadhouse bloke had begged her to stay on until he could replace her. She'd liked him, so she'd stayed.

Met a lot of people. A few she'd liked, a lot she hadn't. Sold petrol at a service station on the outskirts of Perth. Cooked and sold hamburgers and chips in Albany. Hadn't liked that owner. Had slapped him in the eye with a lump of hamburger meat one night and walked out without her pay.

She'd been selling ice-creams and mixing milkshakes in Coolgardie, sleeping at night in a crumbling caravan, when she'd read that a date had been fixed for Dino Collins' second trial. This time, she'd be there to convict that mongrel and, desperate to get there, she'd driven from Norseman to Ceduna – across the Nullarbor in a day, a very long day, but the road was straight and the traffic minimal, so she'd kept on driving.

She'd been driving since before her nineteenth birthday. Jack Thompson had given her a licence in October of '58. He'd kissed her around the same time. Maybe everyone remembers the bloke who first kissed them. A few had kissed her since, though not in recent years. Women were few and far between in some of the places she'd been. She'd talked a few blokes out of pursuing her, had belted one with a lump of firewood. The crew-cut had helped, as had the scar through her eyebrow, her rag bag clothes and ute, unwashed since she'd left Woody Creek.

She loved driving. Always had. It released her mind to roam, and to wonder what her life might have been had she married Jack Thompson at nineteen and had a kid or two. He'd spent a year nagging her. She wasn't sure why she hadn't married him.

Old Charlie maybe – or Granny. 'I'm footloose and fancy free, me darlin',' she used to say. At fourteen, fifteen, Ray King a constant in her life, footloose and man-free had seemed like a good way to live. And it had been during her eighteen months on the road. She'd woken when she'd felt like waking, no clocks to watch, or not since she'd left her watch in a washroom in Queensland after trying to remove two frogs from a toilet she'd needed to use. Could have replaced it but had got to enjoy her timeless state.

She had no fear for the life she should have lost in the fire that killed Margot. Being dragged from that smoke-filled bedroom to gasp in life's air had been like a second birth, as had losing everything she'd spent her life working to gain. Or almost everything – she'd saved the contents of her top drawer, a small drawer. She glanced now at a battered cardboard carton, her only travelling companion. Jack's nautilus shell was in it, her reason for grabbing that drawer. They'd picked it up on a Frankston beach.

She hadn't lost her money in the fire. She couldn't have done what she'd done without money, which she couldn't have accessed as readily if not for fate. The day she'd unlocked the shop for an irate retiree, she'd found half a dozen letters on the floor. The postie, accustomed to tossing shop mail onto Charlie's long counter, must have shoved it beneath the green doors. She hadn't opened the envelopes, not then. Tossed the lot into the ute's glove box then drove back to Jen's to empty the contents of that top drawer into her carton, to toss in a handful of borrowed clothing. Left then, no plan in her mind other than to put a few miles between her and this town before they buried Margot.

She'd opened her mail in Willama while waiting for her eyebrow stitches to be removed and she'd found a new chequebook. She'd found two accounts from suppliers too. Her first purchases, a biro and a packet of envelopes, she'd paid for from the shop's canvas change bag. Had always left coins and a few notes in that bag at night when she'd emptied the cash drawer. Written two cheques, posted them, then walked down to the bank. The bloke there knew her, and so he ought to. She'd seen a movie with him once, had supper with him. He'd cashed her cheque. She'd cashed all bar one since. Had saved it for an emergency. No more emergencies. She was home.

She would have been here months ago if not for her need of a shower. She'd slept in the ute in Ceduna, then pushed on to Adelaide where, in need of a shower, she'd booked into a caravan park. Five minutes after parking her ute beside an onsite van, the trio of males she'd named the 'three disciples' had come belting on her door.

'Stop following us around,' the John of the group had greeted her.

'You again,' she'd said.

They'd given her a long beep when their F100 half-truck had passed her somewhere between Alice Springs and Darwin, her Victorian number plate and their own the only two on that road. Then three or so weeks later, they'd walked into the Darwin hotel where she'd been waitressing. Simon, the youngest of the trio, tried to pick her up. She'd told him she was old enough to be his mother – might have been, had she started breeding at twelve. He'd called her Mum thereafter so she'd called them the disciples. The third member of their group was a Paul.

The next time she'd seen them she'd called them saviours. She'd been stuck out in the middle of nowhere, up near the top of Western Australia, her ute dead on the side of an unmade road, a hole through its sump, and she almost ready to get down on her knees in the dust and start praying for salvation. Then out of the haze, like knights in rusty armour, they came to tow her to Karratha where they'd offered floor space in their tent for her sleeping bag. She'd camped with them until they'd moved on and she'd taken that job at the roadhouse, for its accommodation, a crumbling caravan out back.

That night in Adelaide she'd eaten with them, she supplying the bread, baked beans and beetroot, they, the sausages and beer. At midnight, after one too many beers, she'd decided to go grape picking. John's credit card had reached its limit, the F100's gearbox was buggered and they were broke.

She'd shared their tent for two weeks, had picked a lot of grapes by day and drunk a lot of beer by night, and maybe had the best weeks of her life. Someone wrote a song about people who needed people being the luckiest people in the world. Maybe they were when they had the right people around them.

With the disciples' truck back on the road, they'd gone their separate ways, the boys heading home across country to Melbourne, she heading for the same place, but via the scenic route. A swine of a road, the coastal road, narrow, winding, too much traffic on it, and most of the number plates Victorian. A pretty drive, had she been able to take her eyes off the road to look at the scenery. She'd seen little of it.

She'd seen a sign pointing to Geelong, a city she'd visited as a peanut in fifteen year old Jenny's belly, the city where the cops had finally arrested the redheaded water-pistol bandit who'd created the peanut.

How had a fifteen year old kid survived that? How had she got herself home? Made of tough stuff, Jenny, or having three kids before her eighteenth birthday had toughened her up. She'd handled Margot's death. She'd handled the police, the reporters, and no doubt the funeral. The thought of putting what the fire had left of Margot into a coffin was what had given Georgie the impetus to run. Desire to see the mongrel responsible for Margot's death hanged had turned her nose towards home.

Dino Collins hadn't lit that fire. He'd had the best alibi in the world for that one. It had taken the cops an hour to cut him out of the car wreck and for the next two weeks he'd been more dead than alive. Raelene lit that fire, but it was Collins who had turned a fifteen year old brat of a kid into someone capable of setting fire to a house while its occupants were sleeping, and whether he'd denied it or not at his first trial, he'd been the one who had broken into Cara's house and kidnapped Tracy, and if they ever got him back into court, Georgie would do her damnedest to convict him.

The Paul disciple had said his older brother lived at Ferntree Gully, not far from where the little girl had been kidnapped. He'd said that one of his brother's sons had gone to school with Tracy's brother. Georgie hadn't mentioned her own involvement. She'd never been into gut spilling, which must have been a genetic trait. For years, she'd been in contact with Cara, from '67 to '74 they'd spoken for hours on the phone, written long letters, and not once had Cara mentioned that she was pregnant.

She'd been engaged for a time to a big name solicitor, Chris Marino. In '69 she'd asked Georgie to be her bridesmaid, then the wedding had been called off. The boy Georgie had seen on television had looked to be around the right age to have been born in '69 or '70. He'd looked like Cara – like Jimmy too, other than his hair.

Georgie believed she could put a date to when Cara had become involved with Raelene and Tracy. It would have been around Easter of '74. That's when Cara had left her job at the school, moved out of her Windsor unit, stopped writing, stopped phoning. Not a word had Georgie heard from her in four years, then on the night of the kidnap, she'd turned up at the old place in a brand new Holden station wagon looking like an exhausted ghost, turned up as Cara Grenville, foster mother of Tracy King, according to the newspapers. When had she married? How had she become involved in the mess of Raelene's life? Who had fathered her son? Georgie had no answers, so she poked a few sticks of wood into the open firebox which provided both light and warmth tonight.

She'd been over the road a few times today to fetch fallen wood. Plenty of it over there, though an axe would have been handy. She knew she'd find one in Granny's shed, or would unless someone had helped himself to the tools. She'd check it out when she was ready. Wasn't yet. Turning her eyes in the direction of the space where Granny's house once stood gave her goose bumps and the urge to get back into her ute and go.

Granny's husband, the man Jenny called Itchy-foot, had spent his life travelling – running away from himself, according to

Granny. Georgie liked to believe she'd run away from the self she'd been before the fire and was between selves at the moment.

She'd accumulated little, a good pair of boots, a pair of jeans. They'd fitted when she'd bought them. Baggy now. She'd found the windcheater jacket. It was warm. She'd bought an Akubra hat and two pairs of khaki long shorts. She'd bought a couple of books from a secondhand bookshop in Geelong. Hadn't been looking for a read at the time, just a feed. The smell of fish and chips frying had turned her into that side street. She'd been eating hot chips through a hole poked through the paper wrapping when she'd walked into one of the biggest secondhand bookshops she'd seen, and the well-dressed white-headed bloke behind the counter eyed her travelling outfit and hot chips as he might have a Neanderthal pulled fresh from the bogs. She'd lost a shelf full of books in the fire, lost thirty pairs of shoes, lost correspondence college certificates she'd wasted years of her life in chasing, lost her comfortable kitchen, and Granny's stove and doors that closed.

No door on Elsie's kitchen. Harry had removed it when his brood had outgrown the kitchen, his brood and Margot. She'd eaten most of her meals at that lopsided table – and tonight wasn't the time to start thinking about her. Georgie lit a cigarette and moved her oil drum closer to the stove and, in the light from the fire, she looked at the hand holding the cigarette.

'You've got big hands for a woman,' the Paul disciple had said.

They were bigger than Jenny's. As a twelve year old her hands had been bigger than Jenny's, the same shape though – as were Cara's, and hers closer in size and skin tone to Jenny's. That's how Georgie had recognised her that day in Charlie's, by Jenny's hands, Jenny's hair, Jenny's eyes. All Jenny – as Margot had been all Macdonald. The Macdonald twins may have stretched to five six or seven. Margot had stopped growing at five foot. Jimmy would have grown tall. As a six year old, though two and a half years younger than Margot, he'd been her height.

Georgie had got over losing him. She'd got over losing Granny. She'd get over Margot, though it wasn't the loss of her so much as how she'd lost her. Couldn't think of that night without flinching, so pushed her mind back from the fire to Cara.

They'd run together to Joe Flanagan's back door, Georgie more familiar with the land, holding on to Cara's hand, and Cara gripping it when they'd been led through to the bathroom where that tiny kid, who might have been Raelene at four, lay in the bathtub, on a blanket, old Joe's missus on her knees beside the bath, washing what had appeared to Georgie to be a dead kid's face.

Then the ambulance had arrived to take Cara and Tracy, and Jack Thompson had driven Georgie down to the hospital to have her eyebrow stitched. She'd expected Tracy to be taken there, had expected to find Cara there, but learnt after she'd been stitched that they'd been flown to Melbourne by air ambulance.

Georgie blew three smoke rings towards the firebox and forced her mind to the roads, to Simon, sitting beside her in the dust beside their campfire, she attempting to teach him how to blow smoke rings. Memories of laughter around that campfire.

No laughter that day in the secondhand bookshop. The white-headed owner had asked a fortune for half a dozen second or sixth-hand books.

'I don't want to buy your shop,' she'd said.

'Two are new releases.'

'Two years ago,' she'd said, handing over a ten-dollar note. He'd taken it then stood with his hand out for the coins. She'd counted them onto his palm.

'Do you need a bag?'

'And a receipt, thanks,' she'd said.

'My register is out of paper.'

'If I'm spending the family fortune I'd like a record of what I'm spending it on,' she'd said.

His expression telling her she was a pain in the arse, he'd reached beneath his counter for a receipt book, then taken his time writing an itemised account. Wasted more finding and inking a rubber stamp, then stamping his receipt. *Pre Loved Books.*

She'd planned to sleep in Melbourne that night, then spend a few days in closing her 'mouse money' accounts before heading home, but she'd gone to a supermarket for smokes and seen the newspaper headlines: SECOND TRIAL DELAYED. COLLINS ADMITTED TO HOSPITAL.

She'd found a caravan park where she'd rented a cabin, cheaper by the week than by the night. It had its own bathroom, its own fridge, a bed and a good light to read by. Booked it for a week and ended up staying in Geelong for two months. She got a job at a supermarket, as a checkout chick.

The first book she'd opened, *Papillon*, hit the cabin wall an hour after she'd opened it. She'd read to page twenty, had started reading the next page – and it hadn't made sense. Found out why. There were twenty-odd pages of it missing, and she'd been enjoying it, or had been interested in the character they'd just found guilty. Tossed it into the supplied kitchen waste bin, on top of most of the meat pie she'd bought for her dinner, and opened *Kane and Abel.* It filled three nights. She'd found space for it in her carton of possessions.

Number three book hit the rubbish bin. Number four's first chapter was okay, but deteriorated into romantic bulldust. She binned it too. Not *Marnie*. She'd wanted to be that girl, robbing her employers then changing her name and appearance and moving on. Marnie epitomised footloose and fancy free – until she'd been caught.

As had Laurence George Morgan, Jenny's water-pistol bandit, Georgie's accidental father. He'd robbed banks, jewellers, stolen cars and spent his ill-gotten gains on classy hotels, guesthouses and Jenny – until the cops had run him down. His mug shot had travelled Australia in her carton. A survivor, Laurie Morgan, he'd somehow managed to worm his way into that top drawer, as had Itchy-foot's diaries, and the green top Cara had given her for her twenty-seventh birthday, which she'd used to wrap Jack's nautilus shell. Her seven 'mouse money' bankbooks had been in the drawer, and the pendant Jack had given her for her nineteenth birthday. Apart from Itchy-foot's diaries, those few items made up the base layer in her carton. The diaries she'd left with Jenny – Itchy-foot's will had stipulated that they be sent to her.

*Marnie* found a place in the carton before she'd started on book number six, which had been about to join its mates in the bin when she'd found the bookshop bloke's receipt in the plastic bag she'd been using for her soiled laundry. He'd sold her faulty merchandise and charged top prices for it, so she'd emptied her overflowing kitchen bin. The cover of the first book was somewhat meat pie and sauce smeared, but a damp cloth wiped it clean enough. One book's close association with an apple core had stained it for life, but even brand new it wouldn't have been fit to read. She'd placed the discards into the bag and the following day returned to the bookshop, clad in her checkout chick uniform, her eyebrow scar camouflaged for work. Practice had taught her how to feather in the missing hairs, when she could be bothered. Most of the time she couldn't. It could have been worse. Raelene could have knocked her eye out with that spanner.

The white-headed coot recognised his receipt, so she'd opened *Papillon* to display its missing pages.

'Were they missing when you bought it?'

'Had I required loo paper, I would have used one of the others,' she'd said, then emptied the bag onto his counter.

'I don't give refunds,' he'd said, pointing to a sign on the wall behind his register stating *NO REFUNDS* in large black print.

'Which doesn't apply to faulty merchandise,' Georgie said.

It took time. It took a second customer waiting for service before he'd refunded her one dollar eighty, and she'd left – left the books and bag on his counter.

'I'm not responsible for my customers' poor taste, sweetheart,' he'd called after her.

She'd spent her Mondays, her days off from the supermarket, on trains to Melbourne where she'd applied for a copy of her birth certificate, aware she'd need identification when she attempted to access her seven bank accounts opened back in '67, a few days after Charlie's funeral – opened with the black money he'd secreted away in an antique biscuit tin beneath his storeroom bed.

Had his daughter deserved it, Georgie may have given it up, but she hadn't. She hadn't bothered to say goodbye to her father, though the poor old bloke had hung around for a week, waiting for her and his granddaughter to come.

A few generations of mice had nested in that money, which Georgie had laundered, literally laundered it, in the kitchen sink, with Rinso and Dettol – then ironed those notes dry, ironed them flat.

With Australia in the process of changing over to decimal currency, she'd had to get rid of the old notes fast, which had led to the best weekend of her life. She'd caught the bus to Melbourne and stayed the weekend with Cara. Bought her red ute off the showroom floor and paid cash for it. She'd taken Cara and a handbag full of 'mouse money' to the racetrack, where they'd cashed big notes to place fifty-cent bets then, on the Monday, with Cara back in the schoolroom, Georgie had done the rounds of city banks, opening accounts in a variety of versions of her name. For twelve months Cara had added leftover 'mouse money' to each account. They'd got rid of it.

Half-sisters and best friends for a time. The rot had set in when Raelene and Dino Collins broke into Cara's unit and stripped it. Georgie's fault. They'd found Cara's address on a letter in her handbag. Georgie's concern had been for Cara's possessions. She hadn't known of her history with Dino Collins. Not until she'd read the reports on Collins' first trial had she known of Collins' youthful threat made to a schoolgirl.

The night of the kidnap Cara had hinted at a history. 'This is his payback, Georgie,' she'd said. 'He bided his time until I had something to lose, then he took it.'

Should have questioned her that night. Hadn't. Had believed there'd be time, that there'd be phone calls and chubby letters.

Nothing. Not a note.

Each Monday for weeks, Georgie had caught the train from Geelong to Melbourne and with her driver's licence, birth certificate and chequebook for identification, she'd accessed her bank accounts. Gina Morgan's and Georgina Morrison King's balances had been transferred into Georgina Morgan Morrison's account. She'd filled in forms to apply for a credit card. John the disciple's card had given him access to money, until he'd accessed it too often. She thought about the trio in Melbourne, about their bank bill. Interest rates on credit were high. She could have helped them out with her 'mouse money', which had never been quite real to her anyway. Didn't know where they lived. Didn't have a clue what their family names were, other than one of them being a Dunn, which had reminded her of the chook dung she'd dodged for most of her life.

One Monday she'd found the correspondence college she'd posted her assignments to. She'd gone in and spoken to a woman about her lost certificates. It would be possible to obtain replacement certificates if she filled in a form and lodged it along with a statutory declaration, the woman had said. Maybe she'd do it. The 'statutory declaration' suggested those certificates might have been worth more than the paper they'd been printed on. She'd sat her first exams with a bunch of schoolkids. Had sat her accountancy exams with a bunch of the mixed and matched. Should have kept them in her safety deposit box with her share certificates. Could have put them in her top drawer instead of Itchy-foot's diaries.

The quintessential survivor, Archie Foote, he'd wriggled his way in, as had her seven bankbooks. What did that make her? The quintessential money-making machine?

She had a ton of money. The money from the sale of Charlie's would need to be invested. The rent she received from Charlie's old house would have ballooned while she'd been away.

She'd get her finances organised while she was home and maybe buy a new ute. Her red ute had taken a battering and had half of Australia clinging to it. A good old ute though, it had carried her safely around Australia and brought her home.

Home?

Woody Creek was her only address. The bank had it. The correspondence college knew her Woody Creek address.

Amy McPherson was a Justice of the Peace. She'd witness a statutory declaration.

See what tomorrow brings, Georgie thought.

# Fog

When two days of nagging didn't convince Georgie to move into town, Harry, Teddy and Lenny came to pull down and carry away the front veranda. They exposed the meter box. It looked intact. Teddy crawled into the roof cavity to look at the wires. He reported them intact.

Harry had taken charge of Georgie's chainsaw. He and his sons felled three saplings, grown round enough in Georgie's absence to qualify as trees. They used them as props beneath the kitchen floor, which did nothing to alter its lean but might prevent the lean from becoming more acute. The junk beneath Elsie's house supplied a slab of solid timber. They used it to prop up the rear legs of Elsie's old refrigerator.

It took four days more for the electricity company to reconnect the power, but by the sixth day of Georgie's occupation, while Harry held the hose, Georgie flicked the light switch and a globe lit up in Elsie's kitchen. Once satisfied the house wasn't going to burn, Harry reconnected his hose to the pipe feeding into the kitchen tap. They had little faith when Georgie pushed the refrigerator plug into its socket and turned it on but, like Frankenstein, the antique shuddered into life.

Georgie hadn't been into town. A traveller accrues survival supplies and Jenny had been coming by daily with fresh bread, soups, stew and smokes. Georgie had been home for eight days before she ran out of coffee.

She parked her ute where she'd always parked it, at the kerb out front of Charlie's – of what had once been Charlie's. An alien now stood on that windy corner, a long white characterless barn.

Without its verandas, its roof looked taller, or maybe it was the green paint on that previously rusty roof that made it appear taller. She walked down its western side, then back, walked by its glass door then on to the post office where she collected her mail. A share dividend and an envelope containing her bank card. She slid both into her handbag then walked back to the barn, to the glass door that blasted her eardrums when it rumbled open. Glanced up to where Charlie's cow bell had hung. Gone, as was his long counter. A row of white cabinet fridges stood where it had been, self-service fridges, self-service aisles too, narrow by necessity.

No sign of a shop assistant, but half a dozen trolleys. She helped herself to one then served herself a pound of butter, a block of tasty cheese, a large jar of coffee. Stood staring at Charlie's storeroom door for minutes. It was open, so she peered in, expecting cartons but seeing saucepans, garden hoses, crockery – and grog!

Elsie's tank water wasn't drinkable. She loaded a carton of Victoria Bitter into her trolley then picked up a small saucepan. She'd been boiling eggs in her travelling billy, heating beans and soups and stew in it then boiling water for coffee. She tossed the saucepan in.

The new owner, now waiting behind a small glass counter to take her money, looked to be somewhere between fifty and sixty, and didn't look happy to see her. She knew how to use a modern register, as did Georgie these days.

'How's business?' Georgie asked.

'Slow,' the woman said. 'You're not a local.'

'No. I'll have a carton of Marlboro too, thanks.'

Smokes and beer swelled the register's total, though not enough to lift the corners of the woman's mouth.

'Have a good day,' Georgie said.

'They're few and far between up here,' the woman said.

That afternoon, she was seated on the back steps, smoking and staring beyond the space where the house had stood to old Joe Flanagan's wood paddock, when she heard a car motor die out the front, heard a car door close. Not Jenny's car door. Not Jenny's quick footsteps on the gravel either.

She turned as Jack Thompson walked around the corner, then smiled and raised her hands high.

'Don't shoot, officer. I'm unarmed,' she said.

'I come in peace.' He smiled. Then, 'What happened to your hair?'

'I blame the white ants,' she said. 'What do you blame?'

'Genes,' he said.

'What are you doing up here?'

'We're at Mum's for the night. Mick Murphy told me you were back.' Mick Murphy, married to Maudy Hall and raising a second family with her.

'My question still stands,' she said.

'Mick said that your mother is worried about you.'

'Maudy always liked a bit of drama in her day.'

'You don't look like you should.'

'I don't need a comb,' she said, running her fingers through her crew-cut. 'Have you heard anything recently about the little girl?'

He'd been the first cop on the scene at Flanagan's that night, but for Jack a lot of water had flowed under the bridge since, a lot of little girls had been lost, abused, murdered. He waited for more information.

'Tracy King.'

'Oh. I saw her foster mother at Collins' trial. I saw your mother too, and you'd swear they were sisters.'

'Cousins,' Georgie said. 'The papers at the time said Tracy could have suffered permanent brain damage.'

'Like your Maudy, the media like a bit of drama in their day. She was kept in hospital for four or five days – which doesn't suggest brain damage to me. They've moved interstate, I think. I know Mrs Grenville had to fly in for Collins' trial.'

'Did the police ever speak to Tracy?'

Jack nodded. 'They got nothing. She was four years old. All she'd been interested in was who had driven her to the hospital and when she was going home. The mother refused to allow those doing the interview to wake up memories of bad men and boxes.'

'She looked dead that night.'

'Had there been more heat in the day she would have been.'

'Is Collins playing possum, Jack?'

'They say not. He's in a wheelchair and having trouble coming to terms with the fact. The psych treating him says he's having flashbacks. His parents drowned when he was a kid. He's supposed to have dived for an hour attempting to drag them out of their submerged car.'

'*Collins is a man to be pitied, not punished*,' Georgie quoted. 'I've read it all. There's not a word been printed about the mongrel I haven't read.' She drew on her cigarette then pitched the butt. 'And I still guarantee that he's playing possum.'

'The last time I saw him he was drugged to the eyeballs and had one of those oxygen tube things under his nose.'

'If it was to his benefit, he could play dead and you'd believe him,' Georgie said. 'Want a beer?'

'I wouldn't say no to a coffee.'

'A beer might be faster.'

'When did you start drinking?'

'Since I tasted some of the stuff they call water in the outback – and what's in Elsie's tank tastes worse,' she said, leading the way through to the kitchen.

He tested the floor as he entered and followed as far as the sitting room, where he stood looking down the hole to the junk below.

'What's this?'

'A modern innovation,' Georgie said. 'All houses will have them in a year or two. It saves picking up what you sweep. Do you want beer now or coffee later?'

'You're a mad woman,' he said. 'This place will fall on your head one night.'

'So they keep telling me.' She removed a bottle from the refrigerator, used the edge of the table to knock the top off, rinsed an enamel mug with beer then filled it while he tested the floorboards as he entered the kitchen. 'Mug or bottle?' she asked, offering both.

'Have you spoken to anyone since that night?' he asked.

'You get to speak to a few in eighteen months, Jack.'

He chose the mug. 'I meant a professional.'

'I had a few words with a professional road builder—'

'You lost a sister. You were damn near burned in your bed. You're living in conditions a vagrant wouldn't call home – and drinking. You need to talk it out, Gina.'

'I closed Gina's account before I left Melbourne. I was going to close Georgina's too but she's now the proud new owner of a birth certificate and a bank card.'

'Are you all right for money?'

'Want a loan?' She gestured to her upturned oil drum, her sleeping bag on it, folded as a cushion. 'The guest gets the chair,' she said.

He drank but didn't sit, so she sat.

'What's going on in your head, love?'

'It's too short for lice.'

'You had beautiful hair.'

'You didn't have a bad crop yourself.'

'At least you remember what I used to have.'

'I remember everything,' she said. 'I see everything. Raelene opened up a third eye in my eyebrow that night and through it I can see ants crawling around the moon's craters. Someone should have hit me with a shifting spanner twenty years ago.'

'I considered clubbing you and dragging you off to my cave.'

'How many kids did you end up with?'

'Just the two boys. The youngest is still in school, the oldest is still trying to do what his mother wants him to do.'

'What's that?'

'Become a businessman instead of a copper. He wants to be a copper.'

'You're still living in Melbourne?'

'We built a new house a few years back. Where have you been?'

'Like the old song says, *I've been everywhere, man*.'

'How long are you here for?'

'As long as it takes.'

'As long as it takes to do what?'

'I'll let you know when I find out,' Georgie said.

'If you don't want to stay with your mum, get a cabin out at the caravan park.'

'Been there, done that. This house mightn't be home but the land is. I've got a stove, an unlimited wood yard.'

'And you're sitting on an oil drum, freezing your arse off.'

'While confronting my past, reviewing it with my third eye. Isn't that what we're supposed to do after a catastrophe?' she said.

'Your sister has been dead for near on two years. It's time to start getting on with your life.'

'That, my friend, is a supremely ridiculous statement. While one lives and breathes, one is getting on with one's life. I had a birthday in March, and the March before that, and next year I'll have another one. Drink your beer and go. You're disturbing my third eye.'

'You're disturbing me, or this place is, and that bloody haircut is.'

Again she ran her fingers through her hair. 'Cutting it off was a part of the great erasure of self, the rubbing out of she who had been me. Whoever she was should have died in that fire, and would have if Raelene hadn't knocked down the chicken wire fence. Had it been standing, there's no way Harry and those two cops could have got close enough to my bedroom window to break it. I'll guarantee that she was heading for my bedroom to toss another one of her petrol bombs when she tripped and bombed herself. She didn't give a damn one way or the other about Margot. It was me she wanted dead, me and Cara, but Cara was gone, and Raelene inadvertently saved me by knocking down that fence. Try to work that one out, Jack, because I can't.'

'Some might say God was watching over you?'

'Good one. Why me and not Margot?'

'I've got no answers for you, love,' he said.

'And some paid professional does? A priest, maybe? Can he tell me why Raelene's body was found four metres from my bed and I didn't even hear her screams?'

'You were zonked out on painkillers when I left at two.'

'Do you dream much?'

'If I do, I forget them,' Jack said.

Georgie stood to look out of the lone kitchen window, to wipe with her hand at its dust and cobweb curtain. 'I used to forget them. Now I dream in technicolour and they stay, every one of them stays. I was dreaming about Raelene the night of the fire. I was chasing her through a maze of tunnels beneath Charlie's shop. She'd pinched my handbag,' she said, then wiped the window again. 'I thought so,' she said. 'There's a pea souper of a fog coming down out there. You'd better go while you can still see to go.'

Jack remembered Woody Creek's pea soup fogs. He emptied his mug, kissed her cheek, told her to look after herself, and he left.

# The Cast Iron Frying Pan

The fog-shrouded land kept morning at bay; no sunrise for the rooster to crow about so he didn't crow. Georgie had set her inflatable mattress close to the stove's hearth, a cosy enough bed last night. Only cold ash in the firebox this morning. She'd stockpiled wood in the rear sleep-out, had found newspapers aplenty, and within minutes twigs were crackling and flames offering the suggestion of heat to her blackened billy.

She wanted a coffee, wanted a smoke but refused to light a cigarette until the steaming mug was in her hand. Wished she had an electric jug. Wished she was someplace warm. Fed the fire larger pieces of wood and thought of warmer places, a few she'd wished cooler – but whichever direction she'd driven, she'd ended up in towns that were much the same, had ended up dealing with people who were much the same.

She had no idea of the time. It could have been seven or eleven when she walked out to the back steps to look towards Joe Flanagan's land. There was nothing there. No fence, no trees, even the goat paddock had gone – and the blackened square of earth behind it. Knew it was still there – she could smell the dank ash stink of it riding the swirling fog banks. Turned her back on it and returned to stand before the stove, to dip a finger into the billy. The water hadn't warmed – and whether she was staying or going, a small electric Birko wouldn't take up much space. The three disciples had carried one to heat soup, beans, boil eggs and water – when they'd had power to plug into. She didn't have much but she had power.

Robert Fulton always opened his doors at nine. He might have a Birko in stock. She glanced at her wrist, missing her watch this morning, then dipped a finger in again. There was barely warmth enough in the stove to heat its own metal. She glanced out at her ute. It would be warmer, or would warm up faster.

The decision made, she added more water to her billy, fitted its dented lid, then closed up the flue and walked out to her ute.

The motor started. It always started. It stalled too as she backed out to the road. Knowing it well, she gave it a bit more choke, got it going again, then drove off into the fog, the only proof she was on the road being the occasional passing white post.

Stock Route Road had gone missing, but it was wider and had a broken white line painted down its centre. Keeping to the left of the line, she drove on, seeing little other than a truck or two rising out of the fog ahead then disappearing back into it. Mission Bridge was still there, looking eerie as it rose out of a fog bank, but she crossed over and continued on towards Willama.

Too many houses in that town for the fog to cancel their presence, the roads wide, well kept and tree lined. A clean town, she knew it well.

The emptiness of Coles supermarket's car park told her that the hour was early; she parked close to the entrance and walked in. Its wide aisles were warm and she wandered them, tossing items into a trolley – a bag of potatoes to bake on her oven tray, two apples, two bananas, a loaf of crusty bread still hot from the baker's oven, two tins of preserved peaches, on special this week – and they reminded her of Charlie.

No Birko to be found on Coles' shelves, but a choice of three electric jugs. She chose the smallest of them, and a toaster. Picked up a pack of three glasses, just in case Jack came back again to share her beer. Looked at a set of screwdrivers then, with a shrug, tossed them into her trolley, aware they were too cheap to be much good but that they might well do what she had in mind for them to do. No one queuing at the checkout, she emptied her trolley and, just for the hell of it, offered her brand new credit card to the assistant, and was surprised when it worked.

It paid for a watch later, then a pair of shoes, a pair of stretch jeans that looked as if they'd fit. It paid for two sweaters, woollen and warm. The bank charged no interest if the bill was paid on time.

By eleven thirty the sun was out in Willama. Woody Creek fogs had a bad habit of hanging around all day, so she drove around to the Holden showroom to look at the new ute, a beauty and she wanted it, then, feeling guilty for wanting it, she shouted her old ute two new rear tyres, or her card shouted. It could prove itself the best invention since the wheel should she decide to hit the roads again. Maybe she would. Maybe she'd buy that new ute and a small caravan and keep on driving around Australia until she ran out of money.

By one, the sun was strong enough to follow her home, strong enough to shine heat on Elsie's west-facing window. The kitchen felt warm.

Her shopping dumped on the table, she ripped her way into her screwdriver set, determined that the kitchen remain warm. An hour later, a door removed from the east-side bedroom now swung in the kitchen doorway. It didn't swing well, but it closed.

For dinner that night she ate two baked potatoes swimming in butter, with cheese and black pepper – and, thanks to the door, she slept warm, though became aware that her new door might well have been the only support for that bedroom wall when she heard new creaks in the house, but not a breath of wind. She slept like a log and dreamed of Jimmy. They were playing hidey beneath Elsie's house.

Woody Creek's fogs had a habit of coming down day after day once they started. She expected to wake to fog, but instead woke to blue sky. Her old habit when waking had been to look first at her watch. She slid back into old habits that morning. The time was eight fifteen.

Elsie's outdoor lavatory, built well away from the house, necessitated a walk through grass to reach it, icy crackling grass, every blade of it a spear of white that morning. The drip puddle beneath the tank's tap wore a coating of ice; the ute's windscreen wore a layer, the hose feeding the kitchen tap had frozen solid but the tank gave up its water, and it felt warm.

She stood, full billy in hand, looking at Granny's land, its wintry green turned white. The rooster, no more impressed by frost than fog, crowed out his protest from the burnt-out site. She watched him stepping from foot to foot on something that had survived that fire. She hadn't been across the goat paddock yet. Hadn't walked that blackened area. Looked for it this morning but saw only white.

Her coffee made, strong coffee, she lit her first smoke of the day then returned to the back door to look again for the black. Not a sign of it, so with coffee mug in one hand and cigarette in the other, she walked the track across the goat paddock. Margot had kept it well worn. With no Margot to walk it, the grass was encroaching.

She went no further than the small wooden gate to Granny's home paddock where she leaned, seeking the rooster who no longer crowed on his perch but pecked at the earth with his harem where Granny's house had stood. With the chicken wire fence on the ground, the chooks had the run of Granny's home paddock. She counted fifteen hens. There must have been forty in '77. She could see only one rooster, a Red Orpington, who might have been a chick the last time she'd seen him. A big, bad-tempered White Leghorn had ruled the roost eighteen months ago.

She sucked the last from her butt, tossed it onto the icy grass, emptied her mug, set it down on a gatepost, then walked through the gate and across to the shed seeking wheat to bribe the chooks back to their own yard. They remembered her, or recognised the feed basin, and ran to her feet to curtsy for wheat. Bugs and grubs might go down well enough, a bit of grass might help with the digestion, but nothing settled so easily in the crop as familiar grain.

*Glad-to-see-you-back*, the rooster crowed. *Hope-you-stay-a-while.*

She saw Granny's stove standing where it had fallen, saw the big tank lying on its side. Walked by the site to the chicken wire gate and out to the fowl yard where she tossed wheat beneath the walnut tree. They came squawking behind her, through the gate, across the fallen fence, and when she'd rid the home yard of chooks, she walked across the fallen fence wire to stand staring at fresh dung on the stove's hotplate.

There was a load of dung inside the big tank, evidence that many hens had found shelter there. If they wanted its shelter, they could have it, but in their own yard, not in Granny's. She rolled it across new grass. It jibbed at the chicken wire but she repositioned it and rolled it again until its thunderous momentum was halted by the walnut tree where she propped it with chunks of wood and broken brick.

The weak sun creeping higher twinkled on icy fenceposts, those standing and their fallen mates. She looked at the fallen as she crossed back to the other side to stand a while staring at the rectangle of cement floor where Raelene had died. With the sun shining on its coating of ice it looked like a granite slab marking a grave. Crazed granite, the cement laid by Bernie Macdonald's working bee, that had little depth to it. Its first crack had appeared two months after Georgie and Margot moved back home.

Someone had knocked down the brick chimney and carted the bricks away. She walked to where it had stood, then turned to look at the place where Margot died, a brief glance, then fast away to that slab of concrete. She could look at it without flinching.

It covered the area of what had once been Granny's kitchen floor. She remembered that room as a roaring wind tunnel of fire.

Could still hear it in her head but shook it away and walked back to the stove.

Its old iron chimney was gone. Granny had told her once that her father had bought that chimney from old man Monk, that it had replaced the original timber and mud chimney. Always a too massive thing for that little hut, Georgie had expected to see it lying where it had fallen. She hadn't expected to see Granny's stove.

How many times had she dreamt of walking here? The night after the disciples had given her a tow into Karratha, the first night she'd shared their tent, she'd had a nightmare about walking the burnt-out rooms where Margot's hands had reached up through the ash to grasp her and drag her down. Never a sleep-walker, she'd attempted to take off in her sleeping bag and landed on top of Simon.

'I'm ready, willing and able, Mum,' he'd said and, having got a grip on her, he'd hung on. She'd almost loved those boys and sighed now for their loss, or maybe for the loss of their laughter.

She'd delayed coming over here, expecting . . . expecting to feel more. There was nothing left to feel much about, apart from the stove, the slab of concrete—

And the prongs of a fork reaching up through ash and ice, twisted prongs, like the clawed fingers of her dream—

She stepped back from it, then stepped forward, reaching down to give it a hand out of the dirt. It was blackened, but intact. With her thumb she rubbed soil from its handle and saw that old familiar pattern Granny's cutlery had worn, like someone fanning a bare bottom, the Hall kids used to say. She placed it on the stove then squatted to see if the oven door still opened.

It opened. And Granny's cast iron frying pan was on its bottom shelf! She snatched its handle, disbelieving what her eyes were seeing, what her hand was holding. How did it get into that oven? Who would have put it in there? Harry, maybe. Someone had cleaned up the site. Shook her head then, knowing that if Harry had found that frying pan he would have taken it home to Elsie.

Had it been in the oven the night of the fire? Margot had done that with saucepans she'd used when she'd heated up a tin of something and couldn't be bothered washing the saucepan. She'd melted a plastic bowl she couldn't be bothered washing one day.

For minutes Georgie stood feeling the familiar weight of that pan in her hand and, for the first time since the fire, forced her mind back, back beyond the fire, back to when she'd returned from Monk's with Cara and found Jenny, Jim, Harry, Elsie and Margot in the kitchen. That was the last time she'd spoken to Margot. An hour later, with the search for Raelene called off for the night, Teddy and Lenny had turned up, and Margot had swallowed her sleeping pills and gone to bed. Georgie could still see her standing in the bathroom doorway washing those pills down and accusing Georgie with her pale purple/grey eyes.

Shook that image away and forced her mind further back, back to breakfast that morning. She'd fried eggs. Most mornings she'd fried eggs. Like Granny, she'd wiped the pan clean with newspaper and hung it on its nail. Had Margot cooked an egg for breakfast? Had she put her teeth in and eaten eggs on toast that final morning?

Georgie looked at the handle, cast iron like the pan, wanting to believe Margot had hidden the pan and its congealed grease in the oven, needing to believe her hand had been the last to touch that handle, that her desire for the eggs on toast she'd loved had inadvertently saved that pan. Eighteen months of rust had done what it could, which wasn't a lot. Being sealed in the oven, its layer of fat and baked-on grease had protected it.

'Steak and eggs for dinner,' she told it, then, clutching her pan and fork, she walked to the shed to find a hammer to straighten the fork's clawed prongs, and an axe. She'd need to restock her woodpile today.

The hens returned to peck and scratch at forbidden ground. Georgie drove into town to buy a slab of steak and a newspaper, and to use Jenny's shower. Slowly the frost backed away to where only the shadows lurked.

It was after one before she walked back across the goat paddock to study the fallen section of fence. One post had been snapped off at the base, one midway up and a third had been scorched sufficiently to release its grip on the wire. A good six or eight metres of chicken wire lay on the earth, weeds growing over and through it as old mother-nature attempted to heal what Raelene had destroyed. Weeds can't compete with determination, Granny used to say. They had no hope that day. Georgie found an edge to the wire netting then heaved on it until wire and weed lifted.

It took the afternoon, but a sunny afternoon. It took the axe and sweat enough for her to remove her windcheater, but the trunks of a few more well-grown saplings turned into fenceposts, and once the clean red dirt was tamped down firmly around them, a roll of thin wire from the shed bound that bulging chicken wire to each sapling post. Rusting chicken wire, a twisted fence when she was done, but strong enough to hold back hens. It took the last hour of daylight and more wheat to bribe the hens back to their own yard.

An icy chill was creeping up from the earth before she had hammered in the final garden stake, hoping it would assist that sagging wire to stand tall. The stake hit something hard and would go no further. She moved it a little to the right and hammered again. Same result. Moved it to the left, where her hammering lifted a circular lump of earth. And when the earth was scraped away, out came the plaque which for most of Georgie's life had hung on a nail over Granny's front door: *Ejected 2. 8. 1869*, the letters and figures formed by small nail holes patiently hammered into one of Granny's aluminium dinner plates by Jenny. Gertrude Maria Foote had been born on the second day of August in 1869.

Georgie squatted there, smiling while scraping dirt from it, rich dirt veined by charcoal. She didn't see what the plaque had been sheltering, not immediately. About to continue her hammering, her stake disturbed a pale white/green sprout. It didn't look like a weed. A sucker from Granny's climbing rose maybe? Or the wisteria, or even that nameless yellow flowering thing with the overpowering perfume? Georgie didn't care which one of the three it might be, only that something else had survived the fire. The stake and fence forgotten, she squatted to clear weeds from around the shoot to keep it safe until longer, stronger sunshine told it to grow.

Her days passed more easily then. She'd found a focus. There must have been two dozen garden stakes leaning in the eastern corner of the shed with Granny's variety of shovels and spades, crowbar, rakes and the old three-pronged weeder, Granny's favourite tool. Its handle had grown splintery. Every year she'd sharpened her tools and oiled the handles. The tin of linseed oil she'd used was still on the shelf in the shed beside her oilstone.

Why the tools hadn't been stolen along with a good fifty per cent of the hens Georgie didn't know. Thieves preferred to eat than to labour, she decided. An elderly pick, a crowbar, may have been worth a bob or two as scrap metal, but dead hens were easier to carry away.

She found Granny's earth-turning shovel and, after sharpening it and giving the handle a good soaking of oil, she started turning the blackened earth, burying it, and leaving in its place a patch of clean brown soil.

# Alice In Wonderland

Jenny used to say the town stood to attention and saluted when Trudy stepped down from the bus in her ladies' college uniform, her lisle stockings and school hat. Most of the old brigade had been familiar with Vern Hooper's daughters who'd stepped down from the train clad in similar garb. That uniform wasn't all that marked Trudy as a Hooper. She had the dark eyes, the dark hair and height enough to be the granddaughter of the great Vern Hooper. She wasn't, but there were few who knew it. She'd inherited her colouring and height from Teddy Hall.

She didn't arrive on the bus that Saturday in August. She drove a white Torana sedan into the yard and parked it behind Georgie's ute. No ladies' college uniform that day. Georgie recognised the Torana but raised her eyebrows as a sneaker and jeans-clad Trudy stepped out. Jen and Jim waited to greet her. Georgie suffered her kiss on the veranda. She suffered a replay of the hair thing, and was pleased she'd wriggled into her new jeans, that she'd worn her new sweater, patched in her missing segment of eyebrow and decided to tolerate the pinch of new shoes.

Later, at dinner, she watched Jim's eyes adore his daughter, watched Jenny fuss over her, and felt a minor twinge of envy. Trudy had it all – two parents, a beautiful old home, an education, and she'd have a career in a year or two.

'Remember when Margot used to say she wanted to be a nurse?' Georgie said. Jim stopped eating. Jenny stood to move the kettle over the central hotplate. Just a memory, a kinder memory of Margot as a fifteen year old, just an innocent remark. Georgie said no more.

By seven thirty, her duty visit done, Georgie was urging Trudy to move her car when Elsie, Harry, Teddy, Vonnie and their baby arrived, further blocking the ute in. She gave up – parried the hair thing again then, for Teddy's benefit, relayed the tale of the rock through the sump thing, the three guys driving an F100 who had given her a tow to the nearest town, a hundred-odd kilometres away.

The grunter was in Teddy's arms, which to Georgie looked highly ridiculous. Trudy did the required amount of worshipping of Michael John Hall, which enabled Georgie to keep her distance – watched her coo at its smiling face, listened to her speak of assisting at a few deliveries – and how in God's name anyone could stand around watching that, Georgie didn't know.

Granny had. She'd delivered a few generations of this town. She'd delivered Georgie, and Elsie's six.

'I'd like two or three more,' Vonnie said, which turned the conversation to pregnancies and caesareans – time for Georgie to excuse herself, to walk outside for a smoke and wonder if there was something queer about her. Dino Collins and Raelene had called her the red dyke. In one of the places she'd been where women were thin on the ground, she'd told a stockman she was queer.

Cigarettes don't burn long and a smoker gets rid of one faster when the air outside is frosty. The conversation had turned to Trudy's ten-day holiday in America when the smoker returned, and the new Hall god was in Elsie's arms.

'Of all the places you could go, why America?' Jenny asked.

'Sophie's got an uncle and aunty over there and half a dozen cousins she's never met.'

Georgie knew why Jenny didn't like America. Trudy, Jim and the Halls didn't know. Georgie knew that the miniature grunter in Elsie's arms was Trudy's half-brother. Trudy didn't know. She didn't know that the earth where her natural mother had died had been turned over this morning, that turning it had been Georgie's private burial service for Margot.

Years ago, Jenny and Elsie wanted to tell Trudy the facts of her birth. Jim and Harry hadn't, so she'd never been told.

The male and the female animal were two different species. Their brains functioned in a different way. How could a marriage between the two have any hope of working? Some did. Evidence of that was in this kitchen. A lot didn't. The Paul disciple had been married until his wife caught the seven-year itch and took off for Queensland with a workmate.

'Any boyfriends, Tru?' Vonnie asked.

'A few,' Trudy said, and everyone laughed. Georgie wanted another smoke – or wanted to ask Teddy to move his car. What time did babies go to bed?

Harry, who must have been feeling the pinch, rolled a smoke while Trudy gave him a lecture on the hazards of smoking.

She was a nice kid, a totally together kid who'd decided early on her trade and never wavered – and she was no kid now. Still seemed like a kid to Georgie – a kid with Teddy's eyes, big and brown and expressive, with Teddy's dark hair, held back from her face tonight by a stretchy blue headband. Looked like *Alice in Wonderland* – after she'd eaten the grow tall biscuit. Harry and Teddy's height had somehow been enough to cancel Margot's and the Macdonalds' lack of it.

On paper, she was Jenny and Jim's daughter and Georgie's half-sister. By blood she was Georgie's niece. She called Elsie and Harry Nan and Pa. Always had. Had she ever questioned why? Would she ever question why? Knowing Trudy, probably not, and tonight, Georgie envied her disinterest in where she'd come from.

The Hall kids had been born knowing who they were. As a twelve year old, Teddy had known what he'd been born to do. At seventeen, Vonnie had known she'd wanted Teddy. She'd set her sights on him and chased him until he'd stopped running. And he looked happy to have stopped his running, looked content, his son back in his arms.

Did I ever want anything enough to go after it? Georgie asked herself. She'd gone after her bits of paper, had studied hard to pass the accountancy exams, though not because she had any desire to become an accountant. Her only reason for doing it had been to prove to herself that she could – and she had to do something about replacing that piece of paper, had to speak to Amy McPherson tomorrow.

She'd once envied kids their fathers. She'd envied the Hall kids, who'd called Harry Dad. As a four year old she'd envied Margot's two fathers. She'd put on such a turn one day in town, Jenny had produced Laurie Morgan's photograph, cut from a newspaper, glued around a bit of cardboard cut from a cereal packet. For a lot of years – or three years, which is a lot when you're a kid – Georgie had believed her daddy to be a famous movie star.

She was seven years old that day in Armadale when she'd removed famous daddy from his frame and read the few available lines of print glued around his cardboard mounting. *Redheaded water-pistol bandit* . . . she'd read. *Arrested in Geelong* . . .

Could still see those words. She'd almost tossed him that day. A few times since, she'd almost tossed him, but that newspaper cutting was half of who she was and, watching Trudy and Teddy, she knew how large that half might be, and how *do* you throw away the only contact you've ever had with half of yourself?

Harry went out the back door to light his smoke. Georgie went the other way, through the large and frosty entrance hall to the sitting room where a log fire smouldered in the grate, warming maybe a foot of air around it. A cold room, but pretty with its deep blue velvet drapes and fancy pelmets, its semi modern couch and chairs upholstered to match the drapes. She lit a smoke and stood smouldering with the fire, hoping her smoke would join the logs' and go up the chimney.

This room had been well built in its day, with wide decorative cornices, a fancy mantelpiece and a beautiful old fireplace, a fancy light fitting which shed too little light hanging from the ridiculously high ceiling. She toed a smouldering log into a blaze then returned to the warmth of the kitchen.

The grunter ate at ten. The Halls went home so he might dine on breast and Georgie picked up her handbag to follow them out to the car. Watched Trudy give Elsie and Harry hugs, and again wondered if she'd ever questioned why she gave them hugs.

'See you next time, darlin',' Elsie said.

'Love you, Nan and Pa.'

Maybe you grow up not caring too much about where you came from when you live with two parents in the biggest house in town. Georgie copped another Trudy kiss before she moved her Torana, freeing Georgie to drive home to her draughty squat.

*

The removal of that bedroom door had caused its wall to buckle, and by mid-August the house was creaking and groaning like an old bloke with arthritis, but with every inch of that blackened earth turned, Georgie had started on the removal of the concrete slab. She was making a lot of noise but little impression when Jack Thompson crept up on her one Sunday morning.

'What are you doing?'

'Not a lot,' she said. 'Do you know anything about breaking up concrete?'

'Have you got a sledgehammer?' he asked.

'I've tried that.'

'A crowbar?'

She'd tried that too, but she fetched the tools he'd ask for from the shed and he gave her a practical demonstration on how to break up a slab of concrete. It was a two-man job. While one shoved the crowbar beneath a corner and heaved, the other one gave the cement a decent whack with the sledgehammer. Their first whack broke away a good-sized chunk which required four hands to move it.

'You're not just a pretty face,' she said.

'I've got a lot of hidden qualities,' he said.

They worked side by side then, taking turns on hammer and crowbar. Always good mates, Georgie and Jack – becoming more than best mates had ruined a good friendship. They worked all morning and when backs and hands complained, they stacked the broken-off lumps of concrete along the fenceline as an added deterrent to the hens.

They worked together until the sun disappeared behind the treetops, and like an old and weary married couple crossed over the goat paddock, he to open the beer and pour it into glasses while she stoked up the stove and set Granny's frying pan on to heat.

They ate eggs and toast for dinner, emptied the bottle of beer then drank coffee, he seated on the south side of the table on an upturned packing crate, she seated on the north side, on her oil drum chair.

He turned the conversation to Collins. 'I saw him a week ago. He was like a zombie.'

'Still in his wheelchair?'

'Yeah. He's got the use of his arms, and I'll almost swear I saw his knee twitch. He didn't open his mouth while I was there, just sat picking at that tattoo he's got on his knuckles.'

'A Willama bloke broke his neck diving into the creek a few years ago. His foot doesn't twitch – or his hands. He'll lull everyone into a false sense of security then do a runner.'

'Not the bloke I saw last week.'

'Will he go to trial again?'

'And have every bleeding-heart in the country up in arms?'

'So he gets away with it?'

'He's not going anywhere, love.'

She made more coffee, and lit a smoke. He lit his own and was counting what he had left in his packet when she asked how to go about finding someone she'd lost track of.

'Electoral rolls,' he said.

'Been there, done that. Can a cop track them down through their rego numbers?'

'Who do you want to track down?'

'Cara Norris – Grenville.'

'I thought you said she was your cousin. Oh,' he said. 'I almost forgot why I came up here. Are you still interested in locating your water-pistol bandit?'

'You arrested him?'

His hair might have receded, he might have added a few stone, but his smile hadn't altered.

'I put Dad onto tracking him down – after our trip to Frankston,' he said.

She'd told him about Laurie Morgan the night they'd driven Margot home, Trudy unnamed, unwanted, in the city in a humidicrib. He'd suggested asking his retired policeman father to see what he could do about locating Laurence Morgan, and she'd told him very definitely not to tell his father.

'What did he find out?'

'Plenty, by the feel of the envelope.'

'Why didn't you tell me back then?'

'It wasn't through lack of trying. I must have phoned you a dozen times and had the phone slammed down in my ear as many,' he said.

She played with her packet of cigarettes. 'You disturbed my equilibrium.'

'You did your own disturbing of mine. Still do for that matter. Anyway, Mum found it a few weeks back when she was clearing out Dad's desk.'

'What's in it?'

'It's sealed and it's got your name on it, but from what I recall, there were photographs, newspaper cuttings and pages of Dad's notes.'

'Mug shot photographs?'

'I seem to recall him in uniform in one of them.'

'Prison uniform?'

'Army. He was standing with two other chaps. They were wearing slouch hats.'

'He was jailed for three years in '39. The army wouldn't take crims.'

'It will be in the envelope,' he said. 'And once the Japs came into the war I think they were taking every able-bodied man they could get.' He reached out a hand to ruffle her elongated crew-cut. 'It's growing,' he said. 'You're starting to look a bit more like yourself.'

'Jenny threatened to murder me if I shear it,' she said.

'How come you never married, love?'

'I'm queer,' she said.

'That outfit will do it for you, though I reckon I know better,' he said. She drew smoke and blew three perfect smoke rings at him, and he smiled. 'How do you do that?'

'Practice.'

'You didn't smoke when I knew you.'

'I was nineteen in '59, Jacko. A lot can happen in twenty years.'

'Mum told me once that you never get over your first love. There's a part of me that won't let go of you,' he said. She directed three more perfect rings at him. 'If that's your usual response when a bloke declares his lifelong love, it could be what's holding you back.'

'Back from what?'

'Getting married. Having a few kids.'

'I'm footloose and fancy free, and that's the way I like it.'

'There's no future in it, no eternity.'

'I thought eternity was what came later – if you don't end up in hell.'

'It comes with your kids,' he said. 'I look at Johnny and Ronny and I see my dad and myself in them, and I know that if I live long enough, I'll see my dad and myself in their sons. That's my eternity – and I'd better get back. I told Mum I'd be a couple of hours.'

'Idiot. She'll be worrying about you.'

'She knew where I was going,' he said.

'Can you post that envelope up to me?'

'I can do better than that. It's in my glove box.'

She was out the door before him. She was trying his door handle when he came with his keys, and when he handed her a large manila envelope, she held it to her breast, her arms crossed over it. She expected him to get into the car. Not yet ready to go, he kissed her and she didn't have a hand, or the heart, or maybe the desire, to belt him. Should have belted him. He drew her close and kissed her again.

'I've been wanting to do that for twenty years,' he said, his mouth close to her own, then he went back for more, and maybe she wasn't queer. She remembered his kiss. Didn't fight him until he came up for air, when she held him off with a palm on his chest.

'We look at the past through rose-tinted glasses, Jack, and see some utopian place where kids played. It was never what we thought it was.'

'It was for me,' he said, reaching again to hold her. She gave him a light tap on the cheek with the envelope then stepped back.

'Thanks for this. Tell your mum thanks for not tossing it out.'

'I loved you back then and I love you now. I think I get it under control, then I see you and I know that nothing has changed for me, nor ever will.'

'Your marital status has,' she said. 'The past was crap, Jack. Ta for the cement, but don't come back.'

'I'll come back,' he said.

'Then I won't be here.'

She watched his tail-lights disappear into the bush, knowing she could have had a different life with him, that she could have shared his eternity – or messed it up. His kids would have been redheads, would have looked like the water-pistol bandit and not like their father.

Back in the kitchen, she ripped her way into the envelope and emptied its contents on the table. There must have been twenty-odd pages of Laurence George Morgan, copies of old newspaper reports, handwritten pages. Afraid to look closer, to discover that Tom Thompson had found the wrong Laurie Morgan, she lit a cigarette and made another coffee before sitting down on the upturned crate.

In 1959, when Tom had done his search, Laurence George Morgan had been living in Essendon, Melbourne, with his wife, two small sons and infant daughter. He'd been employed in the menswear department of Myers. And of course it wasn't Georgie's Laurence Morgan. He'd been a bank robber. He'd held up a jeweller with his water pistol. He'd stolen cars.

Her fingers delving deeper found a photograph, in sepia tones. Three men wearing slouch hats and army trousers, one wearing a singlet, one a shirt and one's chest bare. They were standing over an unexploded bomb, and the bloke baring his chest looked like a young Clark Gable wearing his slouch hat at a cocky angle.

And she breathed. She breathed and touched her father's face with an index finger. It was him.

'My God.'

Fingers delving deeper still until she found a pristine newspaper photograph, identical to the mug shot she'd been carrying around since she was four years old.

'My God.'

As a kid, she'd seen Laurie Morgan as a man. He was a boy, and a nice-looking boy in 1939. If he was still alive, he'd be an old man now. Jenny would turn fifty-six in December, and her water pistol-bandit had been years her senior – not as old as John McPherson. Younger than Amy.

She read of his parents' and sister's death, read of his every escapade, then found the date of his release from prison – not from Long Bay but from a prison farm. For twenty years she'd seen him as an old lag, locked up in Long Bay.

He'd been honourably discharged from the army in 1945.

'My God.'

She'd slept with the framed image of her father beneath her pillow until Jenny had moved them to Ray King's rooms in Armadale, where he'd spent a few months on the windowsill, beside Jimmy's photograph of his father.

The day she'd removed him from his frame, she'd considered a burial, in the garden where Jenny had buried Ray's sheep livers. She'd dug the hole, had found an empty custard powder packet for a coffin. Couldn't put him in the dirt, so she'd buried him in one of Jenny's kitchen dresser drawers, beneath the fancy tablecloths she'd never used.

The contents of that manila envelope again altered Georgie's image of Laurence George Morgan. The old lag with the flattened nose and cauliflower ears was gone and in his place had risen the Myers salesman, the married man, the father of three.

Then it hit her. His kids were as much her siblings as had been Margot and Jimmy and Cara – though closer in age to Trudy. And she had to tell Jenny, had to show her what Jack's father had found. She didn't look at her watch. Knew it was late but also knew that Jenny never went to bed early.

The papers shovelled back into their envelope, she picked up her keys and handbag and drove into town.

# TIME

Archie Foote, a sprightly eighty-odd, may have made his century if not for old man kangaroo's decision to cross over the road as Archie had driven by too fast to swerve. Archibald Gerald Foote had died as he'd lived, in a hurry to get to somewhere else fast.

The date of Gertrude Foote's birth, hidden behind her crazy tombstone, was considered by many to be a joke in very poor taste. It would have made her twelve months away from ninety when she'd waved her final goodbye from the goat paddock. Gertrude Foote had ridden her horse into town not six weeks before she'd died and hadn't looked a day over seventy.

Amber Morrison's eightieth birthday well behind her, she'd believed the fifty-three step climb up to Sissy's unit would kill her. It hadn't, and as the old saying goes, what doesn't kill us makes us stronger. By spring, her ascensions were faster.

The letter she'd hand delivered to Lorna's box on the morning after her unveiling had been returned to Elizabeth Duckworth's private mailbox, in an envelope addressed by Lorna's hand. Every letter since had returned in its original envelope, *Return to sender*, written in red, front and rear, and seemingly unopened.

The minister had responded to Elizabeth's letter which had expressed her deep concern for her poor dear Miss Hooper: . . . *She has relied on my sight for many years, during which time, I have pleaded with her on many occasions not to drive her vehicle. For her own sake and the sake of those who share the roads, I beg you to do what you can to have her licence revoked.* He'd responded – but done nothing. Each week Amber rode an early tram to Kew where she walked by her old address, taking note of the vehicle's position, and condition. There was a new dent in the passenger side fender, a new scrape along the driver's side rear door.

Mrs Maryanne Brown, the woman Amber might yet become, had written a letter to the transport department, suggesting that her daughter had been forced to brake suddenly to avoid an accident with near blind Miss Lorna Hooper. Mrs Maryanne Brown's letter had been acknowledged, but government departments move slowly – and God bless them for that.

The pension department had moved slowly, but it had moved. Amber Morrison's pension cheques were now delivered fortnightly to Sissy's mailbox. Two of Miss Elizabeth Duckworth's pension cheques had gone astray, or been shredded by Lorna, but the third had found its way to Box 122, Richmond Post Office.

Last week, Maryanne Brown's birth certificate had been delivered to Box 122. Amber hadn't been certain of her date of birth and had sweated for three weeks before the certificate arrived. And a vast relief it was. Coexisting with Sissy and Reginald was proving expensive. Roast a leg of lamb on Sunday night and it was gone by Monday. Expecting to boil a lump of corned beef on Monday and have it supply cold meat for the week was foolhardy. A loaf of bread disappeared in a day; a pound of butter in two.

She'd had other expenses. A week of Sissy's couch had sent her to a furniture store. For a fee, they'd delivered a single bed, a lightweight easy chair and a standard reading lamp. With Sissy's double bed pushed in hard against the wall and her dressing table moved to stand beside it, Amber had made space enough for her bed at

Sissy's feet. Supermarkets sold deodorant spray; pharmacies sold earplugs, which in recent weeks Amber had taken to wearing for much of the day. They didn't cancel the noise of the blaring television, but muffled it. Sissy's explosions penetrated, though they were not as frequent, nor were her demands for Amber to move on. She'd realised during the early weeks of Amber's occupancy that three could live more cheaply than two. The rent, electricity and phone bills had not increased with one extra in residence, but those bills, when divided by three, became much less.

The car registration, insurance and telephone bill arriving in the same batch of mail had shaken the multilevel building to its foundations, or shaken Sissy into a screaming, door-slamming tantrum, until Amber had gone to the bathroom, removed sufficient notes from one of the long narrow pockets she'd stitched inside her elasticised corselets and placed it on the table. It bought Sissy's silence and Reginald's fealty for life. Amber's pocket accounts earned no interest but should the need arise, they'd offer Maryanne Brown a ready means of escape, though preferably not before Maryanne was in receipt of her own pension.

Amber had found a life of absolute freedom once she'd descended those fifty-three steps and on pension days and Sundays she had her freedom in the unit.

*Chaos bows to your hands, Mrs Morrison,* Norman had once said. Chaos, though not yet bowing, had backed away. The bathroom, small, was modern, and now smelled of bleach and disinfectant. The kitchen was immaculate and very functional. She cooked there. She served. Reginald still snacked on tuna, but she'd trained him to wash his empty cans before disposing of them into a lidded kitchen bin she'd carried up those stairs.

She did her heavy-duty cleaning on pension day when the duo left the unit sometime after ten thirty, rarely returning until four. On Sundays Reginald shaved, a major production, as was the styling of Sissy's hair, then the stiffening of her style with hairspray, but once out that door they were gone for the day.

Amber wrote her letters on Sundays, and on a very pleasant Sunday in late September, all signs of Sissy and Reginald removed from both sitting room and kitchen, Amber poured a long glass of lemon cordial and began her letter.

*My dear Miss Hooper,*
*I hope this letter finds you as it leaves me . . .*

And she heard a key turn in the lock. It takes time to stand, to empty a long glass – to almost identify a forgotten taste which didn't belong in cordial. Then Sissy entered the kitchen to accuse. 'Who were you writing to?'

Big, loud, emerald green-clad this morning, sweating emerald green-clad, petticoat hanging below her skirt but not a hair out of place. Too big to tangle with, Amber didn't fight for possession of her pad.

'You're still writing to her, you old idiot!'

Still writing, and Lorna still returning those seemingly unopened envelopes, though Amber knew better. For twelve months she'd watched her benefactor steam open and read her sister Margaret's letters, then carefully reseal them, write, in red, *Return to sender* on both the front and rear of the envelope then drop them, with a smirk, into the post box.

'When are you going to get it through your senile old head that she wants nothing to do with you?' Sissy bellowed.

'The Bible tells us to pity those not as fortunate as us, Cecelia.'

'Don't you talk to me about the Bible! I'm the one who just sat for an hour in the same church as that miserable old hag, and you should have seen the way she sneered at me when I spoke to her.'

'Was she alone?' Amber asked, her hand out, waiting for her pad. Sissy tossed it. It flapped its pages as it fell.

'You'd go running back to her if she as much as crooked her little finger,' Sissy accused, which perhaps told Amber that her presence in the unit was appreciated, that Sissy had no desire to lose her housekeeper cum cook cum hairdresser, that those who live in squalor, who sleep between filthy sheets, usually prefer not to.

The pad retrieved, Amber took it to her shared bedroom, drew her case from beneath her bed and placed her pad and writing equipment into it before sliding the case back into the dark.

Would she return to Kew if Lorna called? Perhaps she would. She missed the serenity, missed the planning of meals a week ahead, missed her Royal Doulton vases. There was nothing of beauty the eyes might rest upon in Sissy's unit.

She served a salad lunch and, while they ate, Amber learned why the duo was not eating lunch with Alma and Valda Duckworth.

'Alma has been . . . hospitalised . . .' Reginald began.

'Valda took her to the hospital early this morning and couldn't even be bothered picking up a phone to let us know,' Sissy added.

'Gallstone . . .' Reginald said.

'They're operating in the morning,' Sissy said, spooning mayonnaise over her meal. She enjoyed a little salad with her mayonnaise.

*

An anomalous household, three aliens coexisting within a too small membrane, surrounded by rampaging natives who passed them without acknowledgment in the corridors. Their young ruled those fifty-three steps, and on many occasions, Amber evaded packs of them. There were nights when Sissy turned the television off so she might better hear the natives' tribal wars, but the three lived safe enough within their oxygenated membrane – three until October, when Reginald's lemon cordial soaked system gave up the struggle. Amber dialled triple zero. Sissy told him to die and be done with it.

Two uniformed men carried Reginald from the unit. Sissy spent the remainder of her day and evening on the telephone, informing a variety of Duckworths. Amber spent her day and evening cleaning Reginald's room, turning his mattress and remaking his bed with clean sheets, not in preparation for his return but for his demise. When the ambulance men had carried him away, his shuddering eyeballs had been canary yellow.

He didn't die, not that day, nor on Saturday, and come evening, Sissy found the key to the balcony door and unlocked it.

'He tried to jump,' she said when Amber followed her outside. 'He got halfway over the rail and I dragged the useless sod back. You can't manage on a single pension and if you're single, they move you into a one-bedroom place.'

Amber listened. Sissy rarely spoke to her. She never instigated conversation.

'The Duckworths will have to pay for his funeral,' she said. 'We haven't got any money.'

The phone rang early on Sunday morning, not to inform them of Reginald's demise as Sissy had surmised, but a Duckworth, offering her lunch, then a lift to the hospital.

'If you pick me up,' Sissy said. They picked her up at the door.

Her social life improved during the weeks of Reginald's illness. There were many charitable Duckworths prepared to take their turn waiting at Cousin Reg's bedside for his torment to be eased by God. Amber, who now slept in Reginald's bed, free of earplugs, expected him to die. She tossed half a dozen small cans of his tuna into the kitchen tidy. She drank his lemon cordial, though not too much of it in a day. She'd identified its odd flavour.

Then Reginald's condition began to improve. A liver will regenerate if given half a chance. Twenty-two days after he was carried out of the unit, a male-dominated bunch of Duckworth farmers collected him from the hospital and took him home to their farm to recuperate. Then the following Sunday, three Duckworths knocked on Sissy's door. An improved version of Sissy opened it. Her greying hair had been transformed to raven brown, her eyebrows no longer associated and she was clad in a loose-fitting black frock, purchased by Amber, prematurely, in anticipation of a funeral. It was a vast improvement on the emerald green, the puce, the vibrant floral which, one by one, had made the trip down to the laundromat but not returned.

Amber offered tea. The Duckworths were not interested in tea. They made it clear that they were there only to sniff out Reginald's supply of alcohol and to explain to Sissy how one more sniff of alcohol would kill her husband.

'If I've told you all once I've told you a dozen times, he wasn't drinking at home,' Sissy said.

They questioned Amber, who chose not to mention Reginald's lemon cordial, which she missed. She opened cupboards for the Duckworths, opened wardrobes so they might satisfy themselves that there was no hidden alcohol in the unit, and not one bottle did they find, not one empty bottle.

They confiscated Reginald's car keys before they left, convinced he'd been drinking outside of the unit, and thus could no longer be trusted to drive.

'We need that car,' Sissy's voice pursued them down to the lifts. 'He can't walk a hundred yards.' Nor could she.

Two weeks later, Amber lost her bedroom to an improved version of Reginald – well dressed, shaven, a hat covering his over-sized bald dome.

*

In October, Bob Hawke, president of the ACTU, won pre-selection in the safe Labor seat of Wills. There was little doubt he'd get into parliament, and when he did, God save Malcolm Fraser and his Liberal Party. Bob was well known, and a man of the people.

Georgie saw the writing on the wall. Two nights later, she heard Elsie's bedroom wall buckle. She was out of her sleeping bag in time to watch it fall. It took a portion of the roof down with it, raising a cloud of dust before putting out her light.

By torchlight she turned the power off at the main. She didn't crawl back into her sleeping bag. Fate had told her it was time to leave.

She'd completed her planting weeks ago, had settled two dozen punnets of seedlings in rows she'd drawn in the ash-laden soil where

Granny's house had stood, then for good measure, she'd scattered three packets of assorted flower seeds between the rows. She'd guided those first tendrils of Granny's climbing rose towards the chicken wire fence, had dug up three wisteria suckers from beside the shed and transplanted them at intervals alongside the chicken wire. Perhaps they and her seedlings would fight the weeds for their space in life, as she was now ready to fight for her own space.

Jenny's sewing machine had been busy this past month, not for paying customers but for Georgie, who by torchlight packed her case, brand new, shiny and large. The replacement copies of the correspondence college's certificates were already in it, along with the manila envelope containing Laurie Morgan's mug shot in its battered frame.

Her worn-out working boots she tossed down the hole in Elsie's parlour floor, with Trudy's well-worn shoes, the washed-out windcheater and baggy jeans. She packed her khaki shorts, tossed her oilskin coat into a new cardboard carton with her electric jug and toaster, her saucepan, billy and Granny's cast iron frying pan. Jack's nautilus shell, wrapped again in Cara's green top, went into a corner of her case.

She drove away an hour before sunrise, her bare arms feeling the morning chill, but the forecast was for heat today, and she hadn't wanted to pack a pretty black and white top Jenny had stitched for her. It crushed. Her new sandals weren't as comfortable as her old working boots. They'd wear into shape, as would she.

She had three inches of hair to comb. Long hair she could cope with, or short. She couldn't handle that in-between stage, but she was between lives, so maybe an in-between hairstyle was right for this day. Maybe she'd let it grow. Maybe she'd have it shorn when she got to where she was going. South to Melbourne, north-east to Sydney. Somewhere.

She didn't say goodbye to Jenny but gave her an elongated blast of the horn as she turned the corner into Hooper Street. It fed out onto Blunt's Road, which fed into Stock Route Road. She'd make up her mind which way to go once she reached Willama.

*

On Melbourne Cup Day, the day the city stood still for a horse race, Valda Duckworth had the day off, and at two o'clock, she and Alma popped into Sissy's unit for a cup of tea. Amber served them on one of her embroidered cloths, served the tea in her new bone china cups, very old new, picked up at the opportunity shop in Richmond when she'd collected Elizabeth and Maryanne's pension cheques. The television was on, but quietly. Valda had turned the volume down. Hyperno won the Melbourne Cup that year.

Amber was drying her cups lovingly when Alma came into the kitchen to thank her for afternoon tea and to praise her light hand with scones.

'Bless you for what you've done for them, my dear,' she said. 'You will join us for dinner on Christmas Day?'

'She's not coming with us,' Sissy said.

'She's your mother, Cecelia. Have a little Christian charity,' Valda said, then made a point of kissing Amber's cheek.

Pleasant people. Each time Amber had dealings with them they raised in her the desire to be Maryanne Brown, who might be surrounded by pleasant people. When Reginald had reclaimed his room, she'd spoken again to an estate agent. He'd driven her around to see a small unit. She had a bed, a chair, a lamp. The Salvation Army would provide a kitchen table and chairs. She'd wanted that unit with its built-in wardrobe where her garments would be safe from the stink of sweat-soaked fabric. She'd told the agent she'd think about it, then arrived home to find a neighbour, from the unit opposite Sissy's, moving out.

'They're giving us a three-bedroom house,' one of the children told a friend. 'It's got a backyard,' she said. 'We can get a puppy, Mummy said.'

A house with three bedrooms. No stairs, on a tramline. Perhaps a clothes line, a shop on the corner. To Amber it sounded utopian. That night she changed her mind about a small second-floor unit in a box of similar units.

Sissy's script was appalling, but not difficult to copy. Amber stole her shopping lists. She found her signature one Sunday and spent the day perfecting it. The following Sunday, she penned her first brief letter to the Housing Department.

*Dear Sir, or Madam,*
*I am currently renting a two-bedroom fourth-floor unit, where I care for my elderly mother and my husband, who was recently hospitalised with severe liver damage. I am in desperate need of a three bedroomed house, preferably on the Camberwell line.*
*Yours sincerely,*
*Cecelia L. Duckworth*

Ten days it took them to acknowledge receipt of her letter, and their acknowledgment came not on a Tuesday, while Sissy was at bingo, or on pension day, but on a Monday. Reginald retrieved it. It was addressed to Cecelia L. Duckworth so Sissy opened the letter, glanced at it, put its contents down to more Duckworth interference and tossed it at Reginald, still sober. Amber later claimed the letter and filed it.

In December she wrote a longer and more desperate page.

*Dear Sir, or Madam,*
*Further to my previous letter, re the rehousing issue. My mother and husband are incapable of using the stairs when the lifts are out of order, which happened twice this week. I have my own health issues, of my own making, I admit. I am severely overweight, which makes the fifty-three step climb while loaded like a pack mule, physical abuse of the elderly.*

*Please find the name and phone number of my husband's doctor below.*
*Yours faithfully,*
*Cecelia L. Duckworth*

She included a Christmas card, wishing the department season's greetings and a more comfortable Christmas than she was likely to enjoy. Elizabeth signed a second Christmas card, purchased specifically for Lorna, a Christmas tree with a jolly Santa placing his gifts beneath it. It included a cheery seasonal greeting, to which Amber added a few words.

*My dear Lorna,*
*I will be dining on Christmas Day with Alma Duckworth, who has kindly offered to collect the last of my belongings. Aware as I am of your attitude to dust-collecting ornaments, I feel certain that you will be pleased to see the last of my vases and crystal bowl.*
*My very best Christmas wishes,*
*Elizabeth*

The card was returned promptly to Box 122, Richmond.

*

Georgie, who'd been selling shoes in Hornsby and spending her Sundays sightseeing, having ascertained that Amberley, once a boarding house, was now a block of four units, owned by a John Summerhill, not Robert Norris or a Cara Grenville, packed her case and drove away from Sydney.

She spent a week in Woody Creek, because Jenny wanted to have a family Christmas. She watched a bride walk from the Catholic church in her virginal white, because Jenny wanted her to see the fairytale gown she'd created. A few brides still vowed before God to obey their husbands. Many were forgoing the old vows and the aisle to seal their unions in gardens. Marriage, multiple children, a mother at home to raise the kids belonged to an era now kicking its last. Large families and stay at home mothers had become the prerogative of the unemployable and the unwed.

The Duffy clan, always breeders, had been raised to new heights by Gough Whitlam's single mother's pension. Two Duffys, their many offspring, current boyfriends and umpteen dogs now rented the old Roberts house in King Street, and God help Bobby Dobson and his wife, who'd built a new house behind the old Roberts place and worked their guts out in Willama to pay for it.

Woody Creek's new post office opened its doors for business that Christmas. Built on land that had once been Charlie White's backyard, it was a small box of a building. The afternoon sun in its face, few loitered there. It might be a pleasant place to work come winter.

The decorations and lights purchased for the Centenary celebrations had been dragged out from beneath the town hall's stage and strung again from light pole, shop and veranda. The butcher did a roaring trade with his pre-ordered hams and pickled pork and legs of lamb. Christmas puddings were boiled. Heavy fruitcakes were baked early to mature in tins, spare beds aired before being made up with clean sheets for Christmas guests.

Then Macdonald's mills closed down, as the town mills had always closed down between Christmas and New Year. It wasn't the tatty decorations, the lights, hams, pork or puddings that meant Christmas in Woody Creek, but the silencing of those screaming saws and the roads empty of logging trucks.

Maisy's house, already half-full on Christmas Eve, would squeeze in more tomorrow. Her cake and biscuit tins were full and, determined to keep them full, she was making more mince pies. Bernie was walking the house sniffing the almost forgotten aroma of plentiful food when the phone rang.

'Grab it for me, Bernie,' Maisy said. 'I'm covered in flour.'

He stopped its jangling.

The call was from Brisbane, a brief call, and when Bernie returned to the kitchen his face was as white as the flour on Maisy's hands.

Cecil George Macdonald, known locally as Macka, had passed away in Brisbane three days ago. To date, the hospital had been unable to locate his wife.

# A Very Bad Year

Men don't cry. They tremble. Bernie trembled when he shook the hands offered along with the condolences. He trembled at the thought of driving to Melbourne, of catching a plane to Brisbane so he might bring his twin home, his twin, his left arm, the second half of who he'd been.

Dead?

His fork trembled at the dinner table. His razor trembled while he shaved. His other half may have been a brainless bastard, unheard from since early '78, but Bernie, as with the rest of the family, had known Macka would wake up to himself one day and come home.

He was dead. He wasn't coming home. He was locked into a freezer like a slab of beef and Bernie had to bring that slab of beef home and bury it.

Maisy couldn't stop howling. Mothers weren't supposed to outlive their children and she'd now outlived two.

They were all there, the daughters, the in-laws, the grandchildren and great-grandchildren, no longer there to celebrate Christ's birth but to mourn Macka's death.

And later to accuse. And what use was it to accuse the hospital that had let him die, to accuse those faceless doctors. Lila Jones/Roberts/Freeman/Macdonald had a face. It was she who had dumped Macka at the hospital two weeks ago and who hadn't been sighted since.

'She poisoned him, that's why no one has heard from her,' Macka's sisters and a few of his nieces said. 'She murdered him like she murdered that Freeman kid she married that time.'

'Macka never had kidney trouble,' Maisy howled. 'He never had a day's sickness in his life that Bernie didn't have.'

'She poisoned him, that's why. She got him up there away from his family and she poisoned him,' Jess said.

The howling and the accusations kept coming. Bernie and a few brothers-in-law escaped to the hotel to do their own accusing.

'She wore the bastard out in bed,' they said, and they filled Bernie's glass and the glass trembled on its way to his trembling mouth.

A nephew flew to Brisbane with him to bring Macka home. They brought him back to Melbourne where an undertaker took charge of the box, and when 1980 was still brand new, the Macdonalds buried Macka.

On that same day old Joe Flanagan buried his missus and the town was shocked to hear that Rosie Flanagan was dead. The last time anyone had set eyes on her she'd been out in the paddock with the cows and she'd looked twenty years younger than old Joe. Not a soul in town had known she'd gone down to the city. Not a soul had known she had cancer, not until her funeral notice came out in the *Willama Gazette*, above Cecil George (Macka) Macdonald's column and a half of notices. Joe had always counted his pennies, a habit none of the Macdonalds had learnt.

And how could anyone have known Rosie Flanagan was dying? There wasn't a woman in town who'd knocked on her door. Let a Jehovah's Witness, a salesman or a kid wanting to sell five-cent raffle tickets approach old Joe's front gate and he or his red kelpies changed their minds about opening it.

A handful attended Rosie's service at the Catholic church. Jenny and Jim put in an appearance. If not for the Flanagans – or their dogs – little Tracy would have been found dead in that carton, and they had to put in an appearance at Macka's funeral, not for him or his twin, but for Maisy and her daughters, and if they were putting on their funeral suits for one, they may as well attend the two.

Shouldn't have bothered fronting up at the Catholic church. When Jim approached the sons to offer his hand, both of the ferret-faced swine eyed Jenny as if they expected her to drop her knickers out the front of the church. Joe's sons had been twelve or thirteen year old neighbours when she'd been an unwed mother of three living on Granny's land.

In the car before Jim, Jenny claimed the driver's seat, and with an hour to fill before the next funeral, she drove out to Mission Bridge where she parked in the shade.

'I want out, Jim.'

'Out of what?'

'Out of that town, out of the obligation to go to funerals I don't want to go to. Out of your father's house. It's too big for two people and I miss the girls.'

'They were home for Christmas.'

'Trudy was home for a day and Georgie for five. It's not enough – and that town is too much. Sell up and move.'

'I don't want to move, Jen.'

'What about what I want?'

She didn't want to be at the Anglican church, which was packed solid with every Macdonald – every Macdonald offspring, every Macdonald mill worker, driver, tree-feller and retired mill worker was there. Harry Hall got a foot inside the door. Jen and Jim stood at his side.

The mills had been silenced for Macka. The mill workers weren't silent when his coffin was carried out. They formed the old guard of honour, axes over the shoulder, and gave him the last hooray, Harry lining up with them. Men appreciate a bit of ceremony.

Jenny waited long enough outside the church to kiss Maisy, then she got away. Drove home to smoke in the garden so Jim couldn't count her butts.

Five o'clock; they were in the sitting room, the air conditioner pumping out cool air while they sorted through a pile of photographs Jim was fitting between slices of Jenny's *My Bright-Eyed Friend* rhyme. John had taken a photograph of Norman's station and somehow managed to slot in a train and a family of sparrows – or Amy had slotted them in. Jenny's mind was back with Norman at that station when she heard the rumble of a car motor, then heard it die. It sounded close, and she rose to lift a curtain.

'Who owns a yellow sports car?' she asked, then dropped the curtain fast. 'On your feet, Jim. Check the back locks and get the case down. We're going to Melbourne.'

He didn't argue. He didn't ask why. He knew why.

The photographs returned to the dining room table, Jenny's high heels back on her feet, she snatched her handbag up from the hall table before opening the front door where she stood barring Lila's entrance.

'We're just leaving,' she said.

'Where are you off to?'

'Melbourne.'

'I'll look after the house for you while you're gone,' Lila said.

'It's locked. Are you coming, Jim?' Jenny called.

'I slept in the car on the way down,' Lila said. 'I've got three dollars to my name and I'm damn near out of petrol. Can I borrow twenty?'

'We need what we've got on us,' Jenny said, which was no lie. It was too late to get to a bank today.

Jim came with the case. He deadlocked the front door, the security door.

'What am I supposed to do?' Lila asked.

'Move your car so we can get out,' Jenny said. 'The girls are expecting us.' They weren't, nor were Nobby and Rosemary, but they'd have house guests tonight.

*

Given a week Jim might pack a case. Give him five minutes and you were asking for trouble. He'd packed no change of socks, had forgotten to toss in Jenny's nightgown. She slept in her petticoat the first night then went shopping the following day.

They saw the girls. They had breakfast with Trudy. She worked nights. They had an early dinner with Georgie, who sold shoes in the city until five thirty and processed data in St Kilda from seven to midnight.

'What data?' Jenny asked.

'A bank's. You write a cheque to pay a bill. I tell a computer to transfer money from your account to the account of whoever you paid.'

'How do you tell a computer?'

'By punching holes into the cards.'

'How?'

'With a keyboard.'

It sounded like science fiction to Jenny. 'Why two jobs? You don't need the money.'

'I'll be giving up my shoe shop job in February. I'm starting another course,' Georgie said.

'What are you doing this time?'

'I'll tell you if I make it through the first week, Jen.'

'Where are you living?'

'I'm moving into a shared house at the weekend. I'll call you when I get settled.'

And that was that.

They took the long route home, out through Lilydale, but Jenny didn't want to go home, so they booked into a motel in Benalla.

'If you don't want to live in Melbourne, we could buy a house here. It's a nice town.'

Jim wasn't interested in buying or selling, he didn't like the motel bed and he wasn't fond of eating out. He wrote a cheque for the room then turned the car's nose towards home.

'She'll still be there,' Jenny said.

'She'll be long gone,' he said.

No sign of her or her fancy car that night, but the following morning, Jenny was in the shower, and with Jim having just popped up to the newsagent's to pick up a week's worth of newspapers the back door was not locked. Hearing movement in the kitchen, Jenny assumed he'd returned. She came from the shower in her dressing gown, her hair towel wrapped, and found Lila buttering four slices of toast in the kitchen.

'I thought you were never coming back,' she said, her knife dipping into homemade apricot jam. 'I haven't eaten today. The caravan park bloke couldn't get any money off my card and when I went over to the loo the bastard put a padlock on my van.'

'Take your toast and go, Lila.'

'He locked my case in the van, and where am I supposed to go without money?'

'Find yourself another loaded rapist,' Jenny said.

'That's what you're niggly about, me and Macka? You're still friendly with his mother, aren't you?'

'She didn't hold me down on a tombstone and get me pregnant at fourteen.'

'I didn't either, and it's not my fault who I fall in love with.'

'The only person you've ever been in love with is yourself, now get out of my kitchen before I say worse.'

'Can you lend me enough money to get my case – and for a bit of petrol?'

'Go.'

'I'll pay you back every penny I owe you when I get Macka's money.'

'Let me know when and I'll post you an account for the last twenty years.'

Lila hadn't moved from her chair. She was eating toast, drinking tea, and when she placed her cup down, Jenny snatched it and poured it down the sink.

'Take your toast or it goes in the rubbish bin.'

'We've been friends for thirty years.'

'You've got a nerve to pull that after what you did!' Jenny said, but Jim was back. She snatched her cigarettes from the table and walked out as he attempted to walk in. 'You knew I was in the shower. Why didn't you lock that door?'

He followed her out to the east-side veranda where she lit a cigarette, blowing the smoke towards the yellow car blocking him out of the drive.

'Have you got any money on you?'

'Not much,' he said.

'Is the chequebook still in the glove box?'

'I didn't take it out.'

'Drive out and pay the caravan bloke what she owes him, and get her case. It's the only way I'll get rid of her.'

For the half-hour it took him to drive out to the park, pay the man and drive back, Jenny stood on the veranda smoking, her hair drying wild. She took the case from his hand at the gate, tossed it onto Lila's passenger seat, then told him to drive around to Teddy's garage and buy her a packet of smokes. He didn't approve of her smoking but he was scared of Lila. He went, and Jenny returned to the kitchen to rid herself of the 'friend' who had plagued her life for thirty years.

'The case is in your car. Go.'

'It's out of petrol,' Lila said.

Jenny opened her handbag, found two dollars eighty in coins and threw them on the table. Coins roll. Lila rose to retrieve then count them.

'That won't get me far, and who helped you out when you got yourself up the duff in Sydney?'

'Get out of my house and my life, and stay out of it,' Jenny said.

'I came up here for my husband's funeral, expecting to get a bit of sympathy, and everyone is treating me like poison.'

'If they'd been able to find you when he died, you might have got a bit of sympathy. If you'd let his mother know he was dying she might have got up there to say goodbye.'

'How was I to know he was dying?'

Jenny was a pacifist at heart. Blame Norman for that. She walked away from confrontations, most confrontations. She'd doused Lorna Hooper with a dish of pan fat and water one night. She'd smashed Vern Hooper's windscreen one day. There was fire in her belly when she allowed it to burn. It took a lot of bad words to move Lila Jones/Roberts/Freeman/Macdonald from her kitchen, and more to get her into her two-seater car, and before it roared out of town, Jenny was shaking.

By midday, she had a migraine, which might have been the reason why she walked away from confrontations. She swallowed a handful of aspros, and when they refused to hit the spot, she tried to walk it off. Walked out Forest Road, walked on towards Granny's land, needing the peace of that land today, and Granny. Still caught glimpses of her moving around in the orchard. Still heard her voice in the call of a bird. But not that day. She wandered those fifteen acres cursing the fool of a girl she'd once been.

But she hadn't been a fool in Sydney. She'd been Jenny Hooper, the young mother of a beautiful boy with a husband away fighting a war. When he'd been listed as missing she'd found work, doing the only thing she'd known how to do, sewing at a clothing factory while Myrtle, her landlady, had looked after Jimmy.

She'd worked hard, had saved her money so she and Jimmy could stay safe with Myrtle until Jim was found and brought home. Didn't know how she'd become involved with Lila, but there'd been no real harm in her, not in those days. She'd been a beautiful, brainless kid with twin sons, a mother-in-law in Newcastle and a nineteen year old husband in the army. Then everything turned bad.

Jenny had been six months pregnant with Cara when she'd been forced to leave the factory, then a week or so later she'd cut her ties with Lila and hidden for three months in Myrtle's private rooms. Three weeks after that Yankee baby was out of her, she'd gone home to Granny.

Had never told her about Cara. Had never told Jim, and she was scared stiff of Lila's mouth. She didn't know there'd been a baby. Years ago Jenny had lied to her about having a late abortion, but she still knew too much.

'I have to get out of this town, Granny.'

*

On the following Tuesday afternoon Jenny learned from Maisy how far her two dollars eighty had taken Lila.

'That Scott solicitor rang me up yesterday demanding that I give Lila access to her husband's money,' Maisy said. 'Macka had nothing left to give her access to. They'd been living high on the pig's back, renting a fancy apartment, where they haven't paid their rent for the last month – and they owe two payments on that car she's driving around in. The finance company tried to repossess it up there, a bloke told Bernie, which I told Scott. If you're looking after the widow's affairs, I said, then we'll post down their bills to you. You should see their credit card bills.'

Jenny had no interest in Lila's bills, only her whereabouts. 'Is she living in Willama?'

'She's working at the big restaurant in the centre of town and living with one of the waitresses, five houses down from Rebecca. I won't be eating there again,' Maisy said.

'She won't be there long. She's never liked work.'

'Sissy was saying last Sunday that your mother hasn't changed.'

'Still murdering, you mean?'

'She can't remember anything about Norman, Sissy said, and I meant her cleaning. By the sound of things, they're getting on better. She was telling me too that your mother can't even remember my name,' Maisy said.

'She's not my mother. If you have to talk about her, call her Amber,' Jenny said.

'Anyway, she reckons that Amber's brain injuries from the accident wiped out everything that happened to her before the accident, that her memories start from when she woke up in hospital, which is why she didn't know her own name and why she didn't recognise Lorna,' Maisy said. 'I saw a movie once about a woman who lost her memory after an accident, then she got another hit on the head and it all came back to her.'

'If they're looking for a volunteer to swing the hammer, I'll put my hand up,' Jenny said.

'You're all talk and no action,' Maisy said. 'Anyway, she's still writing to Lorna, who keeps posting her letters back. She even posted back her Christmas card, Sissy said. She's got it into her head lately that your mother and Lorna must have been on together.'

Jenny hadn't laughed in weeks, but the visual image of Amber and Lorna 'on together' broke her up. She laughed until she coughed, coughed until she choked, until Maisy told her that she'd need to give up smoking.

At four, Jenny started chopping onions for a stew, and Maisy took the hint and left. The stew boiling, Jenny moved it to the hob to simmer then went to her sewing room where a half-finished ballgown lay across the cutting table. It was supposed to be ready for a final fitting tomorrow morning at eleven. She'd have to work tonight, and her sight was no longer good enough for night sewing. It might have been if she'd given in to reading glasses. Jim lived in glasses. He reached for them before he reached for his leg in the mornings. She didn't want to become dependent on glasses and swore she'd give up sewing before she did.

Age was in her head lately, the big SIXTY out there on the horizon, flashing its neon sign. The older she grew the faster the years flew.

Trudy would turn twenty-one in April and she'd said the last time she rang that she didn't want a Woody Creek party. And who could blame her for that? She had a lot of friends, Melbourne friends, and other than hiring one of the reception places down there and having the party catered, there was no way and no place Jenny could organise a twenty-first party. Leave it to her to organise it. Give her a limit and tell her to do whatever she liked within that limit.

The big machine humming, Jenny sat before it, feeding a pretty green crepe beneath its foot while her mind travelled. Sewing was therapy for the hands, not the mind. She thought of Lila's fancy car, which Jim said would have cost a fortune. She thought of the mill, of the money Maisy had paid Macka for his half-share of it. How long ago? Not long after Margot's funeral.

*Living high on the pig's back* – Lila must have revelled in that. When she'd moved to Woody Creek as Mrs Billy Roberts, she'd lived in an old house and driven an old car. She'd lived well with the Freeman chap, the semi invalid son of rich parents, and Lila closer to his mother's age than to his. Of her four husbands, two had divorced her. The Freeman chap had suffered a heart attack fourteen months after the wedding. Macka hadn't lasted much longer. Who would the next fool be?

Jenny shook her mind back to Trudy. She was a gem of a kid, a gem Jenny had failed to recognise twenty-one years ago. Back in '59 she'd seen Margot's underdone infant as another problem to overcome. It wasn't until she and Vroni Andrews had picked up that tiny baby from the hospital, until Jenny had smelt the familiar Georgie and Jimmy scent of new life, that she'd recognised Trudy as her own – her own granddaughter – and Trudy didn't know it. Wished she knew it.

*What would you say if I said I wanted to raise her, Jim?*

*That you were giving me a second chance to do something worthwhile.*

Trudy had given him his one chance at fatherhood and he'd jumped into it feet first. She'd offered Jenny motherhood at an age when she'd been ready for it. They'd had three perfect years before Raelene had come into their perfect lives to shake them up. Dead.

Margot dead. Jimmy gone. Only Georgie and Trudy now. Georgie would turn forty on 26 March. Trudy's birthday was on 11 April.

She didn't look twenty-one, or not to Jenny. She'd grown into her face and height as a thirteen year old and had altered little since. Same slightly turned-up nose, same wide innocent eyes, though not so innocent. Living with Raelene had opened them – and nursing had done the rest. A fine mixture, Trudy Juliana Hooper. She had Teddy's mouth, his teeth. She had a smidgen of Harry around the nose. Her hands and eyes were Elsie's. There wasn't a smidgen of Jenny in her and there should have been. There was more of Jim – she had his calrh good sense, his logic, his attitude to cigarettes, too – but not one drop of his blood.

She hadn't inherited his hang-up about eating out at hotels. On 11 April, she booked a table for fourteen at the White Horse Hotel, not too far from Ringwood or Box Hill, where she and Sophie lived and worked. Only one of Trudy's mates being a smoker, there were no ashtrays on the table. Georgie and Jenny and the young male smoking friend made frequent trips out to a large ashtray in the foyer.

Jim drank two glasses of wine. He sat until nine, yawned until nine thirty, then handed the chequebook to Jenny and drove alone to Ringwood. It was after midnight when the waiter refused Jenny's cheque. Georgie handed over her bank card and Jenny ripped up one cheque and wrote another, payable to Georgie, who taxied her out to Ringwood.

Three days later they drove home to Woody Creek to an uproar. Old Joe Flanagan had bought a brand new Toyota, a Jap car, and in Woody Creek, Jap was still a dirty word – and this two weeks before Anzac Day! It was sufficient to convince many that old Joe Flanagan had lost his marbles along with his missus.

He was missing her. He'd been advertising in the *Willama Gazette* for months for a cleaner/cook but got no takers in Woody Creek. And he wouldn't only be missing Rosie in his kitchen. She'd spent half her life working like a slave in his milking shed.

A hated man, Joe Flanagan, but he had pups for sale, a litter of seven, and he bred the best dogs in the district, dogs the farmers wanted. John and Amy McPherson looked at Joe's pups but changed their minds when he told them his price.

His nature was imprinted on his face, a mean, miserable ferret of a face – like his sons, with an added greasy grey goatee beard and moustache. He had a full head of greasy grey hair which hadn't seen a pair of scissors since poor Rosie had died. He dressed like a pensioner down on his luck and the mean old coot had money coming out of his ears.

Jenny wasn't concerned about Joe Flanagan, his Toyota, his advertisement or his pups. Since the night of the party, since Trudy had kissed her and told her it was like kissing an ashtray, she'd given up smoking. Yes, the Olympic Games were being held in Russia this year and, yes, their troops were causing havoc in Afghanistan and, yes, half a dozen countries were boycotting the Games in protest. And who cared? Jenny wanted a smoke.

Then it was Anzac Day and Jim sat as he always sat on Anzac Day, and if she turned the television on to watch the march, he turned it off. She walked off in a huff to watch the meagre Woody Creek parade, stood alone watching men form up on Charlie's corner, then march down to the town hall for the service. Every Anzac Day since '59 she'd stood alone while Jim withdrew to his silent place. She'd asked him years ago why he denied that day. He'd told her it was a public holiday in celebration of massacre.

Giving up smoking was supposed to be easier if you got through the first week. She'd got through two weeks and this past week had been harder than the first. It wasn't as if there was a time limit on weeks. It was for life, and when Jim was in one of his withdrawn moods, smoking saved her sanity.

All things pass, as did Anzac Day, and by May, seven farmers forgave Joe Flanagan and his Toyota long enough to buy a pup.

In May, Malcolm Fraser, Australia's prime minister, appealed to Australian athletes to boycott the Moscow games, but the Olympic

Committee decided to send half of the team. They'd probably end up in gulags, but they probably issued cigarettes in gulags. Jenny had never smoked a Russian cigarette. Someone had given her a Turkish cigarette once. If a Russian offered her one today, she'd smoke it. If Joe Flanagan offered her his pipe, she'd smoke it.

Maisy, who did her supermarket shopping in Willama after her Weight Watchers meeting on Tuesdays, called in for a cup of tea on the way home. She filled Jenny in on the latest anti Wallis woman news, but without a smoke in her hand Jenny couldn't sit still to listen.

'Betty Dobson sent young Steven in to get a bottle of tomato sauce she'd forgotten to pick up in Willama, and that Wallis woman told him to go elsewhere,' Maisy said. 'There's those who move up here and make an effort to fit in, then there's those like her who'd have trouble fitting in anywhere.'

Jenny nodded and peeled a carrot.

Maisy was half the woman she'd been. She used to fill that chair and hang over its edges, had never walked if she could drive. She walked four mornings a week now, walked around the central block and by the supermarket corner, walked close enough to the glass door to make it beep and rumble open, and if it failed to do so, she waved her hand or basket at it until it did. Most had seen her doing it.

Bernie didn't go to the Weight Watchers meetings, but was also half the man he'd been in '77. Jenny had seen him march by in the parade, and he'd been wearing his old army uniform, his medals and Macka's pinned to it. Half the man, but maybe twice the man, a few in town said. He was a good son to Maisy. Jenny couldn't deny that.

She denied the tombstone he'd bought for Margot. She hadn't been out to the cemetery since it had gone up. Most in town had seen it. Most who visited the cemetery would have had trouble not seeing it, according to Amy. She saw it the day of Miss Blunt's funeral.

Jenny sang at the service and said her goodbye there. Goose bumps still rose on her soul when she thought of Margot's funeral – goose bumps of guilt, multiplied by lack of a smoke. Jim had followed the hearse to the cemetery. He'd seen Margot's stone. 'Big,' he'd said. 'Very fancy. White.'

And fancy tombstone or not, and half the man or twice the man, Jenny would never forgive Bernie Macdonald. She hadn't spoken one word to him since the night she'd felt obligated to toss a 'thank you' in his direction when he'd given her a lift down to the Willama hospital with Donny, back in '58 – twenty-two years ago.

It's human nature to forgive. There were plenty in town who'd forgiven him his youthful sins – or perhaps with Macka dead and in his grave, it became easier to lay old blame at a dead man's feet. Jenny couldn't.

She couldn't forget cigarettes either. She'd smelt the wafting smoke from Bernie's cigarette when he'd walked out of the newsagent's this morning just as she'd walked in, and he'd had the gall to hold the door open for her. She hadn't felt obligated to thank him – had wanted to knock him over and snatch the smoke from his hand.

Vern's old rosebush hedge, always pruned in June and July, was a hell of a job. This year she'd suggested Harry's chainsaw and a faster, more brutal pruning. You can't kill a rosebush – Granny's climbing rose was testament to that – but Vern Hooper had pruned his own rosebushes each June and July, Jim at his side once he'd been old enough to hold a pair of secateurs. He knew when and how it was supposed to be done and he liked to do things the right way.

They were pruning when they heard that old Dave Watson, one of the town councillors for umpteen years, had died. It was expected, but it meant that he'd have to be replaced on the council.

They were pruning along the south fence when Joss Palmer, Walter Watson, who was Dave's son, and Robert Fulton, all councillors, came to the fence to tell Jim that Brian Fogarty, a blow-in councillor, had suggested the male Wallis to take old Dave's place. Jim's secateurs continued snipping. Jenny's stilled.

'How about joining us, Jim?' Walter said.

'Not my cup of tea,' Jim said.

'Your old man was on the council for years,' Joss said. 'You'd get in.'

'I'm not my old man, Joss,' Jim said, easing a thorny twig from his gardening glove.

'If we can't get a local bloke to stand against him, Wallis will get in unopposed. His wife runs him and will end up running the town,' Robert Fulton said.

Jim suggested they try John McPherson.

The councillors had no luck there, and that night five men met in Robert Fulton's sitting room, all local councillors.

'Who else is there?' They'd tried three out of town farmers. They'd tried two Dobsons. Hadn't tried Weasel Lewis, but old Shaky Lewis would have had a better chance of getting votes than Weasel.

'How about sounding out Bernie Macdonald?' Joss said.

'I wouldn't touch him with a ten-foot pole,' Robert said.

'His old man sat on the council for fifty years. He's off the grog. He employs more than any other bugger in town. Who's got more right?' Joss asked.

'He wouldn't do it.'

'If we don't put it to him we won't know if he will or not.'

'He's a mongrel. He's always been a mongrel, and he'll die one,' Robert said.

'Better him than that henpecked Wallis bastard and his missus,' Walter said.

'Who's for sounding him out?' Joss asked.

'I'll give you ten to one that he won't do it,' Robert said.

'Tell his mother the Wallis coot will be elected unopposed, and she'll make him do it,' Walter said, and the men laughed. Maisy's waving of her basket at that beeping door was a town joke.

Joss mentioned it at the dinner table on Sunday night.

'No bloody way,' Bernie said.

'You will so do it,' Maisy said, and Jessica seconded the motion.

'You've got the gift of the bloody gab. You do it,' Bernie said.

'If Joss will nominate me, I will,' Maisy said.

Joss didn't bite.

Maureen always phoned on Sunday night. She got around Bernie on the phone.

'Dad would be so proud to think that one of his sons was taking his place on the council,' she said.

Poor old George; his sons had never given him a lot to be proud of. Maureen said more, but Bernie wasn't listening. He was thinking about making a bloody fool of himself in front of the whole town.

Joe Flanagan's kelpies would have got more votes than Wallis. Bernie Macdonald got in with a massive majority and, two weeks later, all but half a dozen roses pruned, the Wallis duo placed their store on the market.

It was big news in Woody Creek. It was the best news, the only news, until Saturday afternoon when Joe Flanagan's Jap car pulled into Jenny's driveway and Joe wasn't driving it.

# Tobacco Smoke

Shock can paralyse. Jim had his secateurs in hand, he could have fought her off. Instead, too late, he attempted to dodge claret lips. The lawn edge was six inches higher than the surrounding brick path and it didn't take a lot to upset Jim's balance when his artificial leg was doing the supporting of his near six and a half foot height, so when his foot hit the edge he landed on his backside on the lawn. She got him while he was down, planted her kiss on his mouth and told him to congratulate her.

Jenny came with her own secateurs. She'd seen the car and noticed its colour but maroon was becoming a popular shade for cars, there were a lot of similarly shaped cars on the road and Jenny was unable to tell the difference between any of the imported models. She wiped at Jim's lipstick-smeared mouth with a gardening glove, her back turned to Lila and her vehicle.

Jim, born in the horse and cart era, had never trusted horses but given his trust early to his father's motorised vehicles, and as a twelve year old had learnt to drive a big black Hudson. He could still put a model name and year to every car in town.

'That's Joe Flanagan's car,' he said, wiping his own mouth with the handkerchief he never failed to carry.

'Nice to see you too,' Lila said.

Jenny was walking away when Jim repeated his words. 'It's Joe Flanagan's car, Jen.'

'You wouldn't give me a bed,' Lila said, and Jenny turned, ripped off her gardening gloves and tossed them at her visitor, not because she'd taken old Joe's advertised job but because she'd lit a cigarette.

'Put that out,' Jim said. 'Jen has given up.'

'That's why she's got a bee up her arse,' Lila said.

Tobacco smoke wafting on the air of a winter afternoon – is there a smell like it in the world? That old desire slowed Jenny's footsteps and, halfway across the lawn, she turned to face her nemesis.

'He's had three housekeepers we know of. One lasted for two hours, one for two days,' Jenny said. 'I wish you joy of him – and how come he lent you his car?'

Lila's reply was a gush of smoke then the flash of her left hand, and be it new or one of her vast selection, there was a wedding ring on it. Jim stared at the hand, decided he'd done sufficient pruning for the day and escaped towards the shed. Jenny turned towards the house, then back, her legs refusing to walk her away from that sweet scent of burning tobacco.

'You didn't marry him?'

'He's got money coming out of his ears,' Lila said.

'You bloody fool! How do you think he got his money?'

'Cows. You should see the size of the cheques the butter factory gives him for his cream,' Lila said.

'He buried his wife in a suit I made for her twenty years ago. That's how he got his money—'

'Some women don't know how to handle men,' Lila said. 'Are you going to invite me in, or make me stand out here with everyone gawping?'

'Go home to your groom.'

'I can't. His sons are there. I'll toss my fag,' Lila said, and so saying she tossed it onto the lawn, a long butt, a good half of a cigarette, and every muscle in Jenny's body wanting to run and snatch it, she turned her back on it and opened the front door, Lila on her heels.

'I told you the last time you were here that you're not welcome, Lila.'

'Yeah, yeah, yeah,' Lila said.

'You've lost your marbles – and so has he.'

'All the better to roll 'em, my dear,' Lila said. She followed Jenny in through the front door where she veered right into the sitting room to turn on the television.

Jenny stood in the hall, watching her flick the channel selector around the dial. It was Murphy's law that, no matter when you turned on that box, you'd catch it in the middle of a commercial, but by her third circle of available channels, she found a movie, an old black and white tear-jerker from the thirties. She sat then, and Jenny walked to the doorway.

'I was halfway through watching it when they turned up,' Lila said. 'Remember *Forever Amber*?'

Jenny remembered it. It had been a 'must see' movie in its day. Like a woman's breasts, few old movies stand the test of time.

'Why?' Jenny asked.

'You wouldn't give me a bed,' Lila repeated. 'He was advertising for a live-in housekeeper when I went back to the dole mob after I lost my job. They gave me his number so I phoned him. He got a bit more than he expected.'

'You're no better than a prostitute, Lila.'

'And you've got a filthy mind. I was talking about my cooking.' Lila turned to the screen, then back to the doorway. 'It was like doing it with a sex-starved chimp – if you're interested. He's covered in hair from the neck down.'

Unable to take any more, Jenny closed the door and went out to the kitchen to vomit, but Jim was in there stoking the stove.

'His sons will have him committed,' he said.

'She doesn't know what she's in for – and I can't live in this town if she's in it, Jim. If you want me to stay off the smokes, for God's sake, sell up and get me out of here.'

For ten years, she'd been urging him to sell. The year they'd sent Trudy to boarding school, she'd almost talked him around.

'Going by her past record, she won't stay long,' Jim said.

'Today is too long,' Jenny moaned.

The movie ended at four. Lila found them in the kitchen. 'Your sitting room is like a tomb,' she accused.

'You weren't invited to sit in it,' Jenny said.

They rarely used the sitting room during the worst of winter when a two-log fire did little to remove the chill. The room was too big. The house was too big, and the garden – and this town was too small.

'Where do your guests sit?' Lila asked.

'We don't have guests. Go home.'

During winter, two easy chairs lived in their cosy kitchen where they ate, read, worked beneath powerful fluorescent lighting. Jim's typewriter spent most of its winters on the south side of the kitchen table.

Lila moved a kitchen chair close to the stove; she took out her cigarettes.

'No.' A chorus of two.

'The smoke will go up the chimney,' Lila argued.

'No,' they chorused. 'If you want to smoke, you smoke outside.' Watched her, willing her out that back door so they could lock her out, but she put her cigarettes away.

'I told him not to tell his sons what he'd done, but the silly old bugger phoned them.'

'You'll learn,' Jenny said.

'What?'

'What most gave up attempting to do fifty years ago.'

'What?'

'Trying to tell old Joe Flanagan what to do.'

Jim turned on the television, a small portable which used up too much space on the kitchen bench but offered a clear picture of footballers rolling around in the mud. He followed Collingwood. They were playing someone. Jenny had no interest in a mob of men rolling around in the mud, but the mass of males held Lila's interest until the game ended and the news came on.

Someone had shot a judge at his own front door. A while ago, there'd been a shooting outside a family court. Australia was catching America's disease. Australia's first test tube baby had been born intact and healthy. Jenny sat forward to listen to that.

'When you think of the trouble we went to to dodge getting pregnant and now the buggers have found a way to inject them into us with syringes,' Lila said.

'You're well past worrying about it and we're trying to listen,' Jenny said.

Jim gave up and left the room. Lila changed the channel and Jenny rose to serve two bowls of soup which she carried into the sitting room, where Jim had lit the open fire. They pulled chairs close to it and sat to watch the ABC news, then the show that followed the news.

They sat until ten, when Jenny stoked the kitchen stove, closed it down for the night and told Lila to go home.

'His sons are staying until tomorrow. Toss me a blanket, will you?'

Jenny tossed her an elderly quilt and a pillow, aware she'd find her in one of the spare beds come morning. Lila had spent enough time in this house to familiarise herself with every room, though the chill might confine her to the kitchen.

She was there come morning, sound asleep on the two easy chairs she'd moved seat to seat. She'd no doubt slept on worst.

*

News had travelled fast in Woody Creek before the telephone. It travelled faster via phone. Joe Flanagan's Jap car parked overnight in Jim Hooper's driveway started a trail of early morning walkers.

Women who didn't require bread for breakfast chose to walk by Hooper's corner on their way to Blunt's drapery cum tea room cum Sunday morning bakery. Pauline and John Taylor had found their niche in Woody Creek. There'd been no hot crusty bread sold in town since a few years after the war ended.

One of his sons dropped Joe Flanagan off at ten, and he didn't look much like old Joe. He was a clean-shaven ferret, his hair clipped to the scalp, a scalp glowing flame red beneath the winter sun. Jenny watched him through a front window. He had spare keys to his Toyota and was in it before Lila joined her, still wrapped in her borrowed quilt.

'The silly old bugger,' she said. 'I gave him a red rinse before the wedding and he looked ten years younger.' She tossed the quilt at Jenny, let herself out via the front door and walked down to her groom, or his car.

Gone then. Gone, but for how long?

'I'm phoning the estate agent,' Jenny said.

*

On Monday night money changed hands at the hotel where a pool had been running as to how long Lila would remain a widow. Freddy Bowen opened a new page to take down names and their guess at the number of days it might take Joe's sons to have him declared insane, or for Lila to wear the old coot out in bed.

There wasn't a lot of wear and tear going on at weekends, though Joe's committal to an asylum looked hopeful. Through July Joe's sons arrived on Friday nights and didn't leave until Sunday morning. Jenny and Jim passed them on the road to Melbourne. They saw a lot of the girls through July.

On the last Saturday in July Lila, having tried Jenny's door, walked down to the bend to see if her car was at the McPhersons'. It wasn't. Lila didn't knock on their door. The McPhersons spied on her, Amy through her birdwatching binoculars and John through his camera's zoom lens.

A vibrant auburn-headed girl of nineteen when she'd moved to Woody Creek after the First World War, Amy had become bird-like and near crippled by arthritis. John, eight years her junior, had altered less. His hair, always snowy, was now white. He'd never been a muscular man, but he was a walker who, during his seventy-three years, had never been without a dog. The couple had walked the dogs night and morning. John walked them alone now.

He owned a car, an old green Morris Oxford. It made a weekly trip to Willama but sat idle for six days out of seven. He owned three cameras and a darkroom where he developed his own film. He was tinkering with the internals of a camera when Jen and Jim called in on Monday afternoon. Amy had phoned. She had something she wanted them to see. She offered twenty colour photographs of her evil-faced goblins – and Lila, one goblin clinging to her windblown hair.

'She's our witch,' Amy said. She'd been at Jenny for two years to come up with a witch and goblin rhyme. Those photographs, shot in a hurry though a window, trimmed by Amy's hands then photographed again, were superb, and sad.

'When did you see her?'

'Saturday afternoon,' Amy said. 'She walked down the drive, stood looking at the house for a while, then left.'

Poor desperate Lila. There wasn't a house in town where she'd be welcome. A beautiful girl when she'd worked at the Sydney factory, an attractive woman twenty years ago, but aging too fast now – and desperate enough to marry Joe Flanagan. That desperation had been trapped by John. The wicked little goblin clinging to her hair didn't make Jenny smile but raised a wave of pity and sadness for the girl Lila had been.

Jim wanted that book. 'If we paid her, she'd agree to sit for the photographs.'

'She has such perfect hair,' Amy said.

At sixteen, she'd *had* perfect hair, dark and wavy and long enough to sit on.

'Clad her in a floating black gown,' John said.

'We've been sorting through the photographs left over from *Butterfly Kingdom.* There were so many delightful shots we couldn't use. And our sparrows from *My Bright-Eyed Friend.* We need a rhyme, Jennifer.'

'I don't think I could do it to her,' Jenny said.

They took half a dozen of the better prints with them when they left, but there was no sign of Lila that weekend. With the weather unfit for man, beast or fowl, Joe's sons must have stayed in Melbourne. Not until August was near done did Lila come again, on foot, clad in the first Mrs Flanagan's tweed overcoat and her fur-lined boots.

'Off to the snow?' Jenny asked.

'I may as well as come here.'

'I don't recall posting an invitation.'

'Any port in a storm,' Lila said.

And that was about it; that was the way she'd lived her life, why she'd married Macka, why she'd married old Joe – any port in a storm. There'd been no safe harbour for Lila, not since she'd deserted her husband and three sons in '46 – and before that. Her parents had disowned her when she'd got herself pregnant at fifteen. Norma, her cousin, had kept an eye on her in Sydney. Norma was dead. Jenny was all she had now, and Barbara, another factory worker, in Sydney, and three adult sons she wouldn't have recognised if she'd fallen over them on a city street.

'The hotel is warmer,' Jenny said.

'So is the North Pole,' Lila said. 'Lend me the fare and I'll go there.' She was wearing a woollen beanie which she removed once indoors. 'Look at my roots,' she said. 'They're half an inch long and the mean old bastard won't give me the money to have them done. I gave up the dole for him.'

'Want to make a few bob?' Jenny asked.

'Doing what?'

'Modelling. John and Amy McPherson want to know how much you'd charge to sit for some photographs.'

'They're into porno, the up-themselves old buggers!' Lila squealed.

'We need a witch for one of our kids' books,' Jenny said.

'You bitch,' Lila said. 'I thought you were being serious.' She moved the kettle over the central hotplate, removed her coat and turned on the television.

Jim, currently up to his ears in a solo project, loaded his finished pages onto his typewriter, picked the lot up and left the warmth of the kitchen, Jenny following him to the bathroom. She opened the door for him, turned on the wall-mounted radiator. The vanity unit was long enough, though barely high enough, to double as a writing desk, but the room was warm. He'd always used the bathroom as a temporary winter study when Maisy visited.

Jenny went to the small sitting room where she picked up copies of their kids' books and took them back to the kitchen.

'That's what we do,' she said. She offered John and Amy's photographs. Lila glanced at them.

'He ought to take another photograph then shoot himself,' she said. 'I don't look like that.'

'He took it through a window, with his zoom lens. It distorts things,' Jenny said. 'But we'd want to make you look worse, stick warts on your nose, turn your hair into a bird's nest—'

'If they shout me a dye job I'll pose nude for the old buggers,' Lila said, and Jenny shrugged.

'Make your appointment,' she said.

'How am I going to get down there?'

'If it's not costing Joe, he'll drive you.'

'He told me he'd cut it for me.'

'Make your appointment for next Friday and I'll drive you down,' Jenny said.

Amy and Jim would be jubilant. John, a man of few words, showed few emotions. He communicated through a camera lens, but he had a smile that spoke volumes, or it did to Jenny, and he could usually find a word or two when she joined him on a dog walk.

She drove Lila home at five after telling a small lie, saying that Harry and Elsie were coming around for dinner and a game of cards. Lila liked them no more than they liked her, and they were coming to play cards, though not for dinner.

Jenny watched Lila light up a smoke, stayed long enough to suck in a whiff of it, then drove home, attempting to find a rhyme for goblin, considered a cobbling goblin, considered a witch with an itch, then admitted that sucking on nicotine is what had greased her rhyming cogs.

She'd smoked a packet a day at fifteen when she'd been with Laurie Morgan. She'd added her own smoke to the blue haze at the Sydney club when she'd sung with Wilfred Whitehead. Smoked at the jazz club in Melbourne. Smoked with Ray. Smoking had always been a part of who she was, and without it, a major part of her was missing. Cigarettes had turned off the switch to a barricaded doorway to her past, and without that nicotine hit, she spent too much time opening that door.

She was looking for her new canasta cards when she found the watch an old dog had chewed on at a beach in Sydney the morning after five American sailors had pack raped her. She looked again at the inscription on the rear of the watch. *Billy Bob from Mom and Dad, 7/18/43.* It brought back memories of Myrtle Norris, memories of a swollen belly, of the night she'd shown Myrtle that watch as proof of the pack rape. It hadn't proved a thing.

*What do you know about the father, Jenny?* she'd asked a few weeks later.

She'd died years ago, but Jenny could still hear her plum-in-the-mouth voice. Myrtle had never said that she'd doubted Jenny's tale of the five sailors – not outright.

Norma, Barbara and Lila had doubted the rape story. To them, her unwanted pregnancy had been like the passing of some initiation rite. *Come clean, kiddo. Who was he?*

One of them had been Billy Bob. Who other than a Yank would inscribe a watch with that name? He and his pack had used her on that beach like dogs at a bitch in heat, and yet she'd worn that watch for years. She'd worn it until Jim had come back into her life, until Trudy had become their own, until Jim had bought her a new watch to measure the hours and days of their new life.

*Billy Bob from Mom and Dad, 7/18/43.* Hoped the Japs had killed him and his friends. Should have pitched his watch away that morning. She'd kept it as evidence to show the police, then decided not to report them to the police. Should have pitched it in the incinerator with the taffeta dress. She'd thought about it, but it was gold, and how could anyone throw away gold?

She should have sold it to the jeweller the day she sold him Ray's wedding ring, but she'd needed the watch in Armadale. It had got the kids to school on time, had told her when to pick them up.

For twenty years it had lived in a box in the kitchen drawer and when the melted remains of her pearl in a cage pendant had been returned to her, she'd placed it in the box with the watch, promising herself that one day she'd use the gold in that watch to remake the pendant. And why not? Why not spend the money she would have wasted on cigarettes on something she wanted?

She stood a while juggling the watch and pendant remains on her palms while August's wind moaned around Vern Hooper's chimney and Jim's typewriter zinged and clunked as he readied it to start a new line.

'How much longer are you going to be rattling that thing?'

'I told Jack I'd have it done by next weekend,' he said, and rattled on.

*

She left him typing in the kitchen on Friday, tolerated half an hour of unrelenting Lila on the trip to Willama, and the more she talked the heavier Jenny's foot became on the accelerator.

And God save the hairdresser, but with an hour or more to fill, Jenny drove down to the big jeweller's on the corner of Main and Carter streets where she placed Billy Bob's watch and the melted pendant on the jeweller's counter. The wife looked at both then fetched her husband from his back room.

'We don't see many of these around,' he said of the watch.

'I was wondering if you could melt it down and replicate my earrings in a pendant.' She'd worn her pearl in a cage earrings this morning, and showed him an ear. 'The pendant was about twice the size of the earring.'

The jeweller wound the watch then took off its rear plate to peer into its internals, which hadn't moved in over twenty years. They moved that morning.

'It could be worth more to you intact than its gold content,' he said, then asked to take a closer look at her earring. She removed one. He studied it through his eyeglass.

'It's old,' he said.

'I inherited them from my grandfather. Is it doable?'

'Anything is doable,' he said.

She left one earring with him. Maybe he'd lose it. Maybe he'd make a mess of the pendant. Maybe she'd never wear it if he didn't make a mess of it, but having got rid of the watch and Lila, she wandered down to a big fabric store to smell the new scents of bulk fabric, to handle silks and brocades and dream up a fairytale wedding gown for Trudy, who hadn't even brought a boyfriend to her party. She'd meet someone one day, and when she did, Jenny would bring her to this shop to choose the most beautiful fabric and from it she'd make her a magical wedding gown.

# More Than She Can Chew

The phone rang at seven on Saturday morning, and Jenny flew from her bed, certain that one of the girls had been in an accident.

'Hooper residence,' she said.

'Get your husband,' a male said. No STD beeps. It was a local call, and that voice was remotely familiar.

'Who's calling?'

'Flanagan. Get your husband.'

'He's in bed. Call back at a reasonable time,' Jenny said, then wondered if he'd murdered his new wife who he expected to milk cows. Lila? She didn't even know what the milk she used in her tea came out of.

Jim, also concerned, had followed her out on one leg and the crutch he used if he had to get out of bed at night.

'Flanagan,' Jenny said, giving up the phone. Jim listened, Jenny shivering beside him until she heard Lila's laugh. She wasn't dead. Jenny had been seeing her dead and, relieved that she wasn't, ran to the bedroom for shoes and dressing gown then returned to listen secondhand to old Joe's ranting.

'It was an advance,' Jim repeated. 'She agreed to sit for some photographs.'

A long silence followed, or Jim was silent. Jenny could hear the tinny overtones of old Joe's ranting escaping from the phone to warm the frosty entrance hall air.

'No,' Jim said. 'No. No. No. They are to be used in a children's book . . . Yes . . . Yes. We produce books for children . . . Children's fairytales . . . Yes . . . No . . . Yes. The character requires her hair to be black . . . Yes . . . She will receive further payment after the photographs have been taken . . . That will depend on the . . . on the publisher. Of course . . . Certainly.'

Then Joe hung up but Jim was unable to put the handset down. He stood on his one leg and a crutch in the hall, laughing like a madman, laughing so hard that Jenny had to hang up the phone then lend him support.

'She told him . . .' And he erupted again.

'What?'

'She told him she'd agreed to star in John and Amy McPherson's pornographic movie,' he said. The crutch fell and he grabbed at the wall. Jenny moved a chair closer then ran to fetch his other leg.

They laughed through breakfast, and when it was late enough, they called John and Amy, and there was laughter at both ends of the line.

'He's bitten off more than he can chew with that lady,' Amy said.

'She's bitten off more than she can chew,' Jenny said, and she told them how Joe expected her to milk cows.

There was too much laughter that day, that week too. Oh to be a fly on the wall in Joe's kitchen. Jenny had sighted him often during the years she'd lived with Granny. They'd shared a back fence. She'd considered him old then, old and bad tempered. He was older now, but no doubt still capable of putting his boot into a dog or cow, and maybe Lila, who had been around for so long, she'd almost become family – not favourite family, but a member she did care about.

The following Thursday, the kitchen warm and their bedroom

freezing; they sat watching the late news and Jenny saw Ayers Rock. A dingo had somehow got into one of the campers' tents and taken a small baby from her crib.

'Georgie climbed that rock,' she said. Jenny wanted to see it. She wanted to sell up and move, wanted a briquette heater installed in the sitting room, wanted a smoke too, and when did that wanting stop?

Over the next days the Chamberlain couple were big news in the newspapers and on television, as was the red land and that rock. It looked hot there. Jenny craved heat.

Lila just wanted her money. They clad her in her witch's outfits, designed by Amy, stitched by Jenny. They stuck hairy warts on her chin, her nose. They teased and pinned her hair into a high bird's nest and sat two goblins in it, then, with Jenny carrying the props and Amy directing the shots, John's camera snapped and, say what you like about Lila, she played the role well – and talked nonstop.

'They reckon that woman sacrificed her baby,' she said between shots.

'It's rumour, Mrs Flanagan,' Amy said.

'Call me Lila. I change the married bit too often to keep up with it, and I'll be changing it again soon. That crazy old cow threatened to cut my hair off last night.' And she laughed, and John's camera clicked.

He used three rolls of film on her, trapped her in a variety of poses and floating gowns, and when she dressed to leave, Amy wanted him to take a few more shots of her in her black leather hot pants and long matching boots, so John used another roll of film. Classics of their era, those boots and leather pants, an era long past, but when John developed that final roll, Amy was determined to use them, so demanded another rhyme.

'*Her name was Lila, the blokes all feel her . . .*' Jenny sang.

'You're making my John blush,' Amy said. 'What we require is our witch, clad for the city – stocking up on oil of toad . . .'

'*The witch had an itch, in a city ditch,*' Jenny said.

*

By the eighties, grief had to be advertised if you expected it to sell. Sympathy for the Chamberlain couple, who refused to spill their grief on camera, had evaporated, but Jenny found herself relating to Lindy, found herself comparing the media vultures to the great and all-powerful Vern Hooper. He'd been sympathetic when she'd howled and hidden the swelling of Margot in Granny's lean-to. His sympathy had fast turned to contempt when she'd come home from Melbourne pregnant with Georgie and found the nerve to look him in the eye.

The media had been sympathetic to the Chamberlains for a day or two. Now they squeezed their story for blood. Experts on the native dog and its habits were interviewed. One so-called expert said he was doubtful that a native dog would creep into a tent, doubtful that a dingo would be capable of carrying away a ten week old infant.

*

September came with ice-cream days, those sweater off, arms bared to the sun days when the scent of the earth drew Jenny outside to dig, to plant. Lila, who neither reaped nor sowed, followed Jenny around the garden on those days.

'I've had them all in this town,' Lila said, blowing smoke.

'You've had a good few of them,' Jenny agreed.

'Joe says that dingoes wouldn't go anywhere near a tent that smelled of humans,' Lila said.

'He's old enough to remember when there were dingoes up here. Granny's generation shot them on sight.'

'That mob killed anything that moved. They shot all of the Tasmanian devils.'

'Tigers,' Jenny corrected.

'We don't have tigers.'

'Tasmanian tigers, not devils.'

'Whatever,' Lila said. 'They reckon she used to dress that kid in black.'

'Who?'

'Lindy Chamberlain.'

'Bulldust.'

'How do you know?'

'Go home, Lila.'

'I can't. His sons brought their wives with them.'

'They're your daughters-in-law,' Jenny said.

'They're up-themselves bitches. I told them I was going to be in a kids' book, and they smirked at each other, like they knew what sort of a book I'd be in.'

On and on it went, like the yark-yark-yark of an alien bird eating the blossom in the garden.

'They're jealous of me, that's what's wrong with them . . .'

'Mmmm.'

'Joe said a tame dog wouldn't even go into a stranger's tent.'

'Mmmm.'

'When you do that I know you're not listening.'

'It means I can't be bothered arguing against irrational bulldust,' Jenny said, settling a tomato seedling into the earth.

'Dingoes are wild dogs. They might attack you in the bush but they wouldn't creep into your tent.'

'According to Joe,' Jenny said.

'And a bloke on the television. And as if one could drag a three month old baby out of its bed while that other kid was sleeping right beside it. You can't tell me that he wouldn't have woken up and yelled.'

'Have you ever watched a kid sleep?' Jenny asked.

'I had kids.'

'Weren't around much while they were sleeping.' She planted another seedling.

'Joe said that dingoes are no bigger than his dogs.'

'Mmmm,' Jenny said. Jaws on them like a vice, unpredictable, Granny used to say of the wild dog. Untameable too. She'd told a story one night about her father's attempt to turn one of their pups into a house dog. Granny had never owned another dog. Her generation had named the town's untrustworthy 'dingo'. Old Dingo Wadi. Old Dingo Duffy.

That was back in the sane old days when smoking had been a social habit not a death sentence, back in the days when the truth had been expected and, more often than not, spoken. These days, truth, sanity and chastity were out of vogue and every other day new age experts, given their moment on television, brainwashed the masses into believing the latest theory on breastfeeding, dog or child training – with frequent breaks for commercials singing their praise to birdseed paste, better than butter, and toothpaste which would keep your teeth sparkling clean and prevent cavities. Even the six o'clock news was interrupted for a commercial.

Jenny had been brainwashed into giving up butter only because margarine was spreadable from the fridge. She'd been brainwashed into giving up cigarettes – to satisfy Trudy, who rarely came home to smell if the house was smoke free or not.

'Well?' Lila asked.

'Well what?'

'If dingoes creep into tents to get a white's baby, how come we don't hear about them eating the blacks'?' Lila asked.

'Collateral damage,' Jenny said, standing, stretching her back.

'What?'

'Their kids die like flies. Georgie and a dozen more saw a tiny black baby lying beside the coals of a campfire with half a dozen dogs fighting over and around it. Did that baby live out the day? Did it die? If it died, did anyone report its parents for child abuse?'

'A few years ago, one of the whites would have picked it up and taken it, like your grandmother took Elsie Hall.'

'Is that so?'

'Joe says she did.'

'It's a great pity that ghosts can't sue for slander,' Jenny said.

'Joe told me that Elsie's father came over there trying to get her back one day and your grandmother fired off a rifle at him.'

'Elsie's rapist, not her father. She was around twelve at the time. Tell your groom to get his facts right.'

'Whatever. She thinks she's white, you know. We saw her at the butcher's the other day with that kid of the mechanic's in a pusher, and she was dressed up like the Queen Mother.'

'When were you elected to head up Woody Creek's dress-code bureau?' Jenny asked.

'You're just jealous because my legs still look good in shorts, and because John wanted to photograph me in my hot pants.'

'John and Amy have a fine sense of the ridiculous – incidentally, they worked out why Joe married you.'

'Why?'

'He would have been paying enough tax to pay your dole and, on top of that, he had to pay someone to clean and cook. By marrying you, he got himself a housekeeper and a dependant to claim on his tax – and I'm going out.'

'I'll come with you.'

'I'm walking.'

'I already walked in here.'

'Try your luck with Jim. He's in the bathroom.'

Light rain had begun to fall. Jenny stood looking at the car, wanting to get into it and drive, but Lila would be in the passenger seat before Jenny could lock the door, so she fetched her overcoat and Trudy's Collingwood beanie, then walked out into the rain. It wasn't heavy – maybe just a passing shower.

John's Morris wasn't in the drive and the dog was, which meant that neither Amy nor John was at home. They had been Jenny's sanctuary, her place to run since Granny went.

The dog, a black and white gent, greeted her at the gate, and she stopped to talk to him for a while. Walked around the long bend then to the bridge, which was not a good place to dawdle these days. Back in the late sixties, half a dozen mission families had been moved into neat little houses on the far side of the creek. The best of those families had moved on; the worst had remained to turn those homes into a derelict enclave the town wits named Woody Creek West. Drunks, both male and female, took a short cut home from the hotel through Amy and John's garden on pension night. They fought there, a few fell down and slept there, while their kids raised themselves.

A few years ago, the whites would have stepped in and taken those kids, would have given them a chance at life. These days they didn't dare, so they gave the parents money to spend on grog and they closed their eyes to what was happening to the kids.

There was much spoken of racism and Australia's colour bar. Acceptance of a race had nothing to do with colour. There was a dirt bar, a drunken violence bar, a neglected kids bar. Handouts and the right to vote won't inject self-respect into black or white. Respect is purchased with sobriety, soap and water, a day's work for a day's pay.

Norman had leant on that bridge railing watching the birds. He could name every one. No birds today. A few rag-tail kids wandering aimlessly, a few youths staring. They didn't like sightseers, and she turned away and walked back to Forest Road.

During the years she'd lived with Granny she'd grown accustomed to walking that road and had come to love the scent of the forest after a shower, a bouquet of eucalyptus and damp mulch and wild mint. The smell of exhaust fumes was added during holiday season when the caravan park filled. No holidaymakers today. The road and the forest were her own.

She saw the colour before she opened the boundary gate. Georgie had turned and seeded the earth where Granny's house had stood; there'd been a patch of colour amid the weeds last year, but the wind had been at work since, and the rains. Granny's land was blooming. Her climbing rose had flourished. Last year it had produced a few stunted flowers but this year it was a hedge, grown along the chicken wire fence, a hedge of pink and green today.

Jenny walked there for half an hour, finding colour in the goat paddock, a cluster of marigolds, finding a lone snapdragon, not as tall as it may have grown in a cultivated garden, but adding colour to the green of the grass and looking fresh after the rain.

White ants had done for Elsie's house. She stood well back from it, looking at its sagging roof, its broken windows, its chimney. It wouldn't have looked out of place in Woody Creek West.

# The Ring

Television had murdered respect for politicians. If viewers took a dislike to a PM's visage, they not only changed the channel, but their vote. Dour-faced Malcolm Fraser, who sounded more Pom than Australian, didn't perform well on camera. Andrew Peacock had the looks and charm of a movie star, or so he believed. Bob Hawke, a down to earth Aussie to his booze-soaked bootlaces, was everyone's mate, his face well known for years on the box as the ACTU trade union man. Bob bulldozed his way into parliament.

There were dozens of elected politicians who sat around on the backbenches for years, faceless when they arrived and nameless when they were gone. Bob wasn't the type to sit quietly on anyone's backbench. Give him a year or two and he'd weasel his way up to the top of the pile, then God help well-heeled Malcolm – if Andrew Peacock didn't do him in first. He had his eye on the top job, and the in-fighting amongst the Liberals was destabilising the party – or softening them up for another Labor attack.

There had been no television cameramen, no flashing box in the corner of sitting rooms during Bob Menzies' long reign. Filmgoers had seen him on newsreels, the quintessential statesman, standing beside king or queen and appearing to be in his rightful place. While Menzies had been at the helm, Australia had known stability and, without thought, Jenny had cast her vote for him, but she had little respect for the current Liberal Party and not much less for the opposition. By November, she didn't know if the problem was in Canberra, in Woody Creek or in her own head. There were days when, had a livestock train been passing through town, she might have stowed away with the sheep.

She'd always loved trains, or maybe just their railway lines leading away from Woody Creek. She'd been born beside the railway lines, then lived beside them. For years, Norman had carried her to work with him, and all day she'd played at his station. Loved watching the trains pull in then pull out, taking their lucky passengers down those twin ruled lines to the east, or to the west.

At fifteen she'd stowed away in a goods van, escaping from newborn Margot and marriage to one of her rapists. Four months later those lines and a Salvation Army couple had brought her back to town, pregnant with Georgie. At eighteen, Margot and Georgie left behind, she'd ridden trains for two days with ten month old Jimmy, running that time from Vern Hooper's threats of court. She'd run to Sydney, to Jim, to a room in a classy boarding house where for the week of his leave, they'd played mummies and daddies and happily ever after.

Jimmy had been a three year old when those lines brought her back, Cara, a three week old baby, left in Sydney with Myrtle, the childless landlady. In '46, Jenny had caught the train with Ray King and all three of her kids, escaping that time from who she was – or wasn't. Jimmy had been going on six when she'd come running home again. A week later he was gone, stolen from Granny's kitchen by Lorna Hooper.

The railway lines were still in reasonable repair. Goods trains used them during the wheat harvest, but Melbourne was no longer the city Jenny had known. There were streets down there today where you could play 'spot the Aussie', and have trouble spotting one. Migrants of every race and religious persuasion had swelled Melbourne's population and the amount of traffic on the roads. Vietnamese had set up their own do-it-yourself migration policy in the late seventies, arriving at Australia's northern boundaries in leaky boats. Migration wasn't new to Australia. Whether they'd come on the First Fleet in chains, as free settlers like the first James Hooper, or with gold fever, they'd come on boats from other lands. In the years after the war, countless thousands of immigrants, displaced by that five-year massacre, had been shipped in, sent to camps for a few weeks, given a few words of English, then packed off in manageable batches to work in country towns where they'd been expected to fit into the community. Australia had absorbed them into her mix and match of humanity. They'd intermarried with the locals and thirty years on it was difficult to pick them from the old Aussie – and impossible to pick their kids. No doubt they'd had their own cultures, though back in Bob Menzies' era, no one had mentioned the word – unless they were discussing the making of cheese. A cheesy word, culture.

Multiculturalism was the parliamentarians' latest fad. Very cheesy people, today's politicians, with cheesy smiles and policies, one of which had given immigrants their own multicultural, multilingual television channel. They could tune into it and forget they'd left their homeland. There were days when Jenny tuned into their channel to forget she was in Woody Creek.

In November, she was informed, in Vietnamese, that America had elected a third-rate movie star as their new president. She laughed. In December, when a gun-toting maniac murdered John Lennon, she changed channels fast, distrusting the foreign-speaking announcer, and when an English-speaking reporter offered her the same news, she howled. She was still howling when she set up the Christmas tree, still sniffing while she stuffed chickens, peeled pumpkin and potatoes. Her tears curdled the custard for the Christmas pudding. It went lumpy.

And the girls, supposed to arrive at twelve, didn't arrive until half past one, by which time the chickens were falling apart, the vegetables were overdone, the pudding boiled dry and the lumpy custard was cold.

'Still off the smokes?' Georgie asked.

'I'm off all round,' Jenny said.

'You look ten years younger, Mummy,' Trudy said.

'I raised you to be honest, Trudy,' Jenny said.

They left at three thirty. Trudy was on duty tonight. The dishes washed and put away, Jenny began pulling the plastic tree apart, fitting its plastic pieces back into their box to remain dust free until next Christmas. It looked like plastic, smelled like plastic, felt like plastic – as did the whole bloody world and ninety per cent of those inhabiting it.

Jim gave her an eternity ring for her birthday, a beautiful ring she'd admired the day they picked up her pearl in a cage pendant, and she hadn't admired it because she'd wanted to own it, but because it was beautiful. And what did a woman of damn near sixty need with a beautiful ring? She had too many already to take off when she stitched expensive fabrics. And why the hell was a woman three years away from sixty still stitching beautiful gowns for others and buying her own clothing from Target?

She dripped tears for most of the day. She dripped on Juliana Conti's antique brooch, which was worth thousands, which made it too precious to wear, as was that ring. How do you weed a garden with eight hundred dollars wrapped around your finger?

She howled too because if she willed Juliana's brooch to Georgie, Jim would want to know why she hadn't willed it to Trudy, and because if she gave Trudy the pearl in a cage pendant and earrings, they'd never see the light of day again. Trudy wasn't into decoration. She rarely bothered with lipstick.

Imagine that there'd been no Florence Keating. Imagine she'd never hired a solicitor to get Raelene back. *Imagine if I'd been waiting down at Granny's for Jim when they brought him home from the Jap camp, Jimmy would have been . . .*

Would have been. Could have been. Might have been. They were like that Christmas tree, made of non-biodegradable plastic. Bury a could-have-been one year and the next time she started digging in the past, up it came, still in pristine condition. Just give it a rinse off with tears and it was ready again to decorate her psyche.

She didn't want to see 1981 so went to bed to howl for all of her buried might-have-beens, and he came in to ask why she was howling, and how did she know why she was howling? She was, that's all.

He kissed her blubbering mouth and his kiss, his touch, had never changed. Up in Sydney, when she'd promised Granny she wouldn't let him come within a foot of her, he'd only needed to reach out a hand and she'd forgotten her promise.

# What Will Be Will Be

A bare week ago Cara had phoned Cathy to ask if she and Gerry might like to be witnesses at a brief marriage service in the city.

'If you're going to bother doing it, then you're not doing it hole in the wall again,' Cathy had said. 'And why do it now when I'm eight months pregnant?'

Because the reason why they hadn't done it sooner was no longer around to disapprove, Cara thought, though didn't say.

'You are allowed to say no, Cath.'

'Of course I'm not. Of course we want to be your witnesses, but you'll have to do it up here. I can't travel. We can have a bit of a party afterwards if you do it up here,' Cathy said.

'I just buried Dad, Cath. We don't want a party.'

'You buried him ten days ago and he's been dead for two months,' Cathy said.

He'd died in England, over two months ago, at a time when Cara couldn't get away. Then it had taken time to arrange the flight and the funeral. They'd opened Myrtle's grave – ghoulish, but what Robert had wanted – and he no doubt a happier man back with his beloved Myrtle than he'd been in England.

'You'll order the celebrant, Cath, or do we bring him with us?'

'Leave it to me,' Cathy said.

'I'm in your hands,' Cara had said.

Should have known better. They'd been friends since their college days, and back then, if given five minute's notice, Cathy had been able to raise a party of fifty. In Ballarat she had parents, a mother-in-law, two sets of grandparents, Gerry, her doctor husband, four sons, friends she'd known since kindergarten. If there was anyone in town she didn't know, Gerry knew them.

There'd been no sign of a party when Cara and Morrie and the children arrived at three, no sign of Cathy's rowdy boys – no sign of Gerry, Morrie and Robin by the time Cara exited the bathroom.

'What are you up to, Cath?'

She'd borrowed frocks. Tracy was a froth of pink. 'It's like a princess dress, Mummy,' Tracy said.

It was, and how many seven year old girls won't melt at the sight of pink frills and ballet shoes? How many can resist a long mirror when a coronet of rosebuds and ribbons is pinned into her hair?

Thank God Cathy had been unable to borrow a frilly bridal gown. The frock she'd chosen for Cara was white, but more Queen Lizzy garden party than bridal. She'd borrowed white sandals, gorgeous sandals, and a white broad-brimmed hat. The bouquets were new.

'I didn't go overboard,' Cathy said.

'No. You torpedoed the boat, you control freak,' Cara said.

'You're the control freak, now get dressed, or we'll be late.'

'What time is he coming?' He, the marriage celebrant.

'I told you that you weren't doing it hole in the corner. Our minster squeezed you in at four, as a favour to me, and he has to be at a dinner in Melbourne by seven, so we can't keep him waiting.'

'You . . .'

'Your daughter is listening. Now get dressed.'

'Did Morrie know what you were up to?'

'As if I'd tell him so that you could start blaming him again,' Cathy said.

Cara had never blamed Morrie for the fiasco of their first marriage. She'd blamed his mother for allowing him to believe that Jenny and his sisters were dead. In '69, they'd made their first vows beside her bed and three days later, Margaret Hooper Grenville-Langdon had died – never knowing what her lie had done to their lives.

'I'm sort of adopted,' Cara had confessed to Morrie on their wedding night.

'How can you be sort of adopted?'

'You can if your mother and the biological mother pull a swiftie.'

Their marriage had been eight hours old when they found out that they'd shared that biological mother, Jenny.

Nothing had changed during the years since – or no new laws had been written into the constitution allowing unions between half-brother and -sister. Cara's profession, her life, her outlook on life had changed, and she could put her finger on the exact instant it had changed.

She'd been standing with Morrie in the hospital corridor, Tracy a wall away and as close to death as she'd been to life. That was the moment. She'd looked at Morrie and known that nothing mattered in this life but living it, and if she'd walked away from him that night, she'd be sentencing both of them to half-lives.

She loved him, had loved him since she'd turned nineteen, when he'd been introduced to her as Gerry's pommy mate. She'd loved him for five years before that disastrous wedding night.

Blamed him for his carelessness when she'd realised she was pregnant with Robin, but that had been as much her own fault as his.

Robert had never forgiven him for deserting his pregnant daughter. Poor Robert. He'd believed what he'd been told. The truth of why her marriage had failed, the truth of what she'd been carrying would have killed him and Myrtle, so she'd lied, told them about the English cad who'd married her only to get his hands on his grandfather's estate.

She'd never expected to produce a living baby. Not for one minute had she considered raising it. Her only thought during the months she'd carried Robin had been the getting out of him, the getting rid of him – and the guilt of his conception.

Myrtle and Robert obtained a court order preventing her from signing their grandson away. She'd left them holding the baby in Sydney and had gone home to Melbourne. But babies grow; they become little boys who look at you with big blue trusting eyes. Robin had smiled at her with Morrie's mouth and she'd fallen in love for the second time.

Robert had loved him. He'd loved Tracy too and done his utmost to talk Cara out of moving to England. He'd had months to work on her. On that nightmare day when Tracy had been taken from her bed, Cara had learnt that *Rusty*, a novel she'd worked on for years, had been accepted for publication. Once upon a time she'd believed that the publisher's acceptance of a manuscript was the end of the process for the author. It wasn't. She'd been forced to stay in Australia, to see it through the editing process, then forced to stay longer for Dino Collins' trial.

Flew away gladly when it was done, she, Robert and the children, Robin looking forward to seeing the little red MG he'd considered his own for seven years which had made the trip across the ocean months before them. Robin and Morrie's mutual love of that car had given them a foundation on which to build a relationship. They were father and son now and they looked like father and son.

Robert had never built a relationship with the English cad. He'd flown with them for her sake and the children's, certain that the cad would let his daughter down again.

Morrie would never let her down. Right or wrong, he loved her, and once back behind the stone walls of Langdon Hall where they'd been living as Mr and Mrs Grenville-Langdon since '78, they'd *be* Mr and Mrs Grenville-Langdon.

The white frock was a firm fit at the waist, but Cathy got the zipper zipped. The sandal heels were ultra high, and shoes worn by another never feel quite right, but Cara walked out to the car in them, and Cathy got them to the church with five minutes to spare.

And it wasn't empty. And she should have known. Somehow, Cathy had got the entire Sydney mob down here – Uncle John, Beth, the six cousins, their partners and a dozen of the cousin's kids.

'Cathy!' Cara moaned.

'Just walk when the organ starts playing,' Cathy said. 'Walk, don't gallop,' and she waddled down the aisle to Gerry and her boys, and the rest of her mob.

'Why are they all here, Mummy?' Tracy asked.

'Shush, pet. Cathy's having a party, and we have to do this bit first,' Cara whispered.

'Where's Robbie?'

'He's standing with Daddy right at the front. We have to walk down to them now.'

They walked the long aisle holding hands, down to Morrie, to Robin who stood at his father's side, a very serious, if undersized, best man, his big eyes agog at the transformation of his pixie sister, but the minister, eager to get this done and get down to Melbourne, got down to business.

'Dearly beloved, we are gathered here . . .'

With little interest in long-winded ministers and no previous knowledge of church, Tracy turned to stare at the silent crowd.

'Why is the party in this place, Robbie?' Young voices always sound loud in a church.

'You have to be quiet,' Robin warned.

Cara had expected trauma, nightmares, when Tracy was released from hospital, but she had no memory of her twenty-four hour ordeal in that carton. The police and their psychologist had spoken to her. She'd told them that she went to sleep in her bed with Bunny Long Ears and when she woke up she was in the sick children's place and Bunny Long Ears was there too, and who brought him and her there?

Cara had told them more – told them everything. She'd relived her fifteenth year when she'd broken handsome Dino Collins' nose and knocked out one of his teeth out with the spine of *Mansfield Park.* That's when his harassment had begun.

She'd stood in the witness box at his trial, willing the jury to believe her, to find him guilty and lock him away forever, and when they hadn't, she'd howled and wished him dead.

Hated him and, in a wheelchair or not, hospitalised or not, she feared him and wanted those oceans back between her children and him. Only four more days and they'd fly home. Only four more sleeps.

And this was her wedding day and she shouldn't have been thinking about Dino Collins.

She glanced up as Tracy pointed to where the afternoon sun hit claret glass and shot a ray of red light towards the altar – just as the minister reached the bit about impediments, of anyone knowing just cause as to why this union should not take place, to speak now.

If Myrtle and Robert had found their way to paradise where all questions were answered, they knew of just cause. Were they aiming that shaft of red?

Stop!

Their aim was too high, and it was done and their daughter's sinful union blessed by God.

*

By seven, Tracy, worn out by her day, was ready for bed. They'd booked a room at a motel, but Robin was watching a television movie with Cathy's boys and he didn't want to leave.

Cara took a copy of *Angel at My Door* from her case and placed it on Cathy's pillow. It had been published in England six weeks ago and was not yet available in Australia. Cathy had been there at its beginning; she'd read a very early draft of it. *Balancing Act* would be ready for its final edit when they got home. There'd be more. With Morrie at her side, all things were possible.

Not all things. They could never have another baby – but they could adopt, and would, very soon. Morrie could never meet the sister he remembered – Georgie, the big girl with hair the colour of new-minted pennies. Cara could have no more contact with Georgie.

Morrie remembered his father, the man with one leg he'd visited in a hospital ward, the man who'd held a six year old boy too tightly and cried. Years ago he'd spoken about meeting his father. He could never meet him now.

Cara had met him, first in the dark of that awful night, then again in Georgie's kitchen. An excessively tall man, he was a little like his son, but there was more of Jenny in Morrie's face and personality.

He remembered her too, but had no desire to meet the woman who'd sold him like so much livestock. The aging paper he referred to as his bill of sale was still in his wallet.

But all else was possible.

Cara tucked her sleepy girl into one of Cathy's son's beds, kissed her and told her to go to sleep.

'Where's Daddy?'

'He's talking to all of the people,' Cara said.

She changed out of her borrowed frock then and looked at its label. Someone had spent big money on it. Loved the sandals, but her feet were relieved to shed them, and the pantihose.

She'd lived in pantihose during her years of teaching. Rarely rolled on a pair these days. Lived in jeans, in comfortable tops and comfortable sandals, and tonight her feet sighed as she slid them into their own sandals.

There was a drip of something on the skirt of the frock. She hadn't noticed it until she slipped it onto the hanger. It would wash. The label said so. *Hand wash. Drip dry.*

Tomorrow.

The frock hung, she returned to Cathy's party.

The oldies had taken over the comfortable chairs in the lounge room. Cara crept by them and out to the yard to look for Pete, always her favourite cousin. Instead she found Cathy, seated beside her mother on the back veranda.

'You look worn out, Cath.'

'Why did you take your dress off?' Cathy said.

'I needed to breathe, oh mighty one,' Cara said.

Cathy patted her mighty belly. 'It's on its way,' she said.

'She's been having pains for the last hour,' her mother said.

'It's not due,' Cara said.

'It is in ten days, which means it's a girl. Our boys were all born late.'

'You're big enough to be having quintuplets,' Cara said. 'One ought to be a girl.'

# Jim's Obsession

Years come and go. Few cast reflections more lasting than our reflection in a shop window as we walk by. Yesterday's melodies linger, but the big news of the day leaves little impression.

Not so the disappearance of the Chamberlain baby. If there was a man or woman in Australia who didn't follow the inquest into the death of that tiny baby, then he owned no television set, couldn't read a paper and chose not to speak to his neighbour. Everyone had an opinion.

The inquest claimed the end of one year and the beginning of the next, when because of public interest, the coroner's findings were televised.

And it was official. A dingo had taken the baby from the couple's tent. Person or persons unknown had taken the remains from the dingo and disposed of it.

A long hot summer the summer of '81. The airconditioner, fitted into a sitting room window, battled on as Jenny sweated that summer to a close. Leaves were changing colour before the last of the heat left town. It had taken its toll on the old Hooper house. The constant vibration of the air conditioner had opened up a crack where the ornate cornice met the wall above that window.

There was seventy years of dust trapped above the ceiling. Daily it fell. Cobwebs did what they could to catch it. Last year, Jenny would have climbed a ladder to chase those cobwebs, but Jim, a foot taller, a foot closer to those ridiculously high ceilings, didn't notice crack or cobweb, so Jenny closed the sitting room doors and allowed the spiders privacy in which to spin. It wasn't the only crack. There was too much house, too many rooms never used. It needed a plasterer, a painter, and most of its floors complained when she walked on them. Harry said the house needed restumping.

In April, *The Witch Queen* left Woody Creek to commence the second part of the process, and Jim agreed to Jenny booking seats on a bus tour to Ayers Rock, but before she could book them, he became obsessed by Molly Squire.

He and John had put a book together for Jack Thompson's mother's hundredth birthday and they'd come upon a handwritten rhyme, titled *Squire Molly*, used as a bookmark in an old hotel guest book, one of several in the carton of photographs, letters and miscellaneous junk that Jack had delivered to Jenny's dining room. The town of Molliston was named for Molly Squire, its first settler.

By June, Jim, deep into his research, wouldn't take time off for a trip to Melbourne, or to Willama. By June, his new project had moved from the dining room to Jenny's warm kitchen. And she'd had her fill of Molly – and of Jim's rattletrap typewriter – and Jim. Left him sitting one bitter day and drove alone to Willama.

If he'd been with her he would have been driving and she wouldn't have seen the green disposable lighter when she stepped from the car in Coles' car park. If that lighter hadn't flicked into a flame, she would have tossed it into a bin. Maybe if it had been red, she would have tossed it anyway. Had it been amber, she may have stopped long enough to consider her actions, but green meant go, so she walked into Coles and bought a packet of cigarettes. Smoked one before she unlocked the boot to load her supermarket bags. Smoked another before she left for home. Washed her hands well. Bought a bag of mints which she sucked all the way home.

Jim didn't notice the smell. If she'd smoked the entire packet he wouldn't have noticed. He probably hadn't noticed she'd been missing for four hours – and wouldn't miss her in bed either. She rugged herself up in her overcoat and beanie and went outside to the veranda for a smoke and to write a rhyme about a witch with an itch, and oil of a bat, and tail of a rat. Freezing cold out there but she lit a third cigarette and started a second rhyme, this one titled 'Confession to Jim'.

*If this paper holds a sniff of ashtray – a minor whiff*
*do not call me weak. It's brain retrieval*
*The conditions cause the stink – just be pleased that I don't drink*
*and see my weakness as the lesser of two evils.*

*Smoking smites a man stone dead, but it's damn good for his head*
*Future doctors will prescribe smokes for all ills*
*With instruction, Don't exceed more than twenty of the weed*
*per day. And do remember please that smoking kills*

Two o'clock when she placed both rhymes with Jim's notes on the kitchen table. He was working when she opened the kitchen door at eleven. He actually looked up from his documents.

'Why, Jen?'

'Too much Molly and no Alice Springs,' she said. 'And Woody Creek, and this bloody cold mausoleum and that mouldy old junk all over my kitchen table.'

*

Trudy phoned on Sunday night. Jim had typed up both rhymes, the witch for Amy, the confession he'd posted to Trudy.

'How could you, Mum, after all of this time?'

'Easy.'

'You admitted to me on Christmas Day that your breathing was better. Why would you do that to yourself?' Trudy said.

'It's not much use having a good set of lungs if you're suffering from brain rot, Tru – and your father is doing enough nagging so I can do without yours.'

*

In late June, Jim took time off to drive to Molliston. John and Amy went with them. The car was warm. The old-folks' home they visited was warm. Jim had arranged to go there to interview the elderly, hopeful of unearthing a few factual details on the life and times of Molly Squire. Amy ended up playing the piano while Jenny sang the old songs, and the old folk applauded and wanted more.

John aimed his lens at Molly's monastery later, which according to the locals was haunted, not by Molly, but by the ghost of her murdered great-granddaughter. Jenny and Amy liked the idea of a ghostly theme. They tossed ideas at Jim on the drive home.

In July, Lady Di married her Prince Charming, to the accompaniment of the rattle and zing of Jim's typewriter. Jenny watched the spectacle while hemming a wedding gown and a half-acre of train. Di's gown was more spectacular, her train longer, but the maker should have chosen a non-crushable fabric.

'Can you stop that noise for five minutes? I can't hear a word, Jim.'

'It's been going for hours,' he said. As had he – and both would continue a few hours more.

'Who taught you to touch-type?'

'I picked it up somewhere,' he said without glancing up from his copy.

In one of the rehabilitation hospitals he'd spent years in, or from his sisters? Both taboo subjects. Jenny had never 'picked it up', though long and close association with his rattling relic had taught her the basics. She used it to type out her accounts – used the old hunt-and-peck method. Each of his fingers had its own eye. He could look at his handwritten notes while his fingers flew those worn keys.

She turned the television volume higher and stitched on. She had another wedding gown and three bridesmaids' frocks coming in next week. Shouldn't have agreed to do that wedding, not in winter. Her sewing room was a tomb in winter.

*

Through August she spent her days in that tomb where a small electric heater did little to mitigate the chill while Jim rattled in her warm kitchen.

Then September, and the Chamberlains back on the front page of newspapers. Forensic experts in England had found evidence of a small bloody handprint, a woman's handprint, on the back of the baby's jumpsuit.

In September, Jenny's latest wedding gown made the society page of the *Willama Gazette*.

*The bride's fairytale gown, created by Mrs Jennifer Hooper . . .*

Fame at last for old mother Hooper, Jenny thought, a clever lady with a needle and thread. She'd never wanted that fame. She'd wanted to be a famous singer. She could still do it, still did it – at funerals and old-folks' homes.

She'd never wanted to live in Vern Hooper's house. That had been Jim's decision. Most decisions were.

'You have a lovely home,' the mother of the society bride had said.

Was it lovely? The sitting room may have looked lovely to one who didn't have to freeze in it, look up at the cracks and at the globe in the fancy light fitting that had blown. Last year, Jenny would have carried the stepladder in from the shed and replaced the globe. Jim was no good on ladders.

He was good at pruning, but hadn't touched a pair of secateurs this winter. She did what she could once the sun came back, a smoke in one hand, secateurs in the other. She was pruning when Jim emerged from hibernation.

'Done,' he said.

'Thank God,' she said.

'I'm going around to John's. He said he'd have the photographs ready today. I've left the manuscript on the table. Give it a glance if you get time.'

She tossed her smoke, washed her hands and went inside to read. She liked the anonymous rhyme, had read it many times, but read it again.

*She'd led a life of ill repute had pretty Moll, the prostitute.*
*Sent in chains from her homeland. Cast upon a foreign sand . . .*
*Where she met young Wal, a common thief, who brought her little more than grief.*
*And o'r two states they were pursued until the night Wal's past he rued.*
*The trappers close upon their trail, when from the dark they heard a wail*
*And on that cold and frosty dawn they found them in a den forlorn,*
*An infant on Wal's lap, at rest, another held to Molly's breast.*
*They left her there to take her chance while young Wal did the scaffold dance.*
*And many a tale was told of Moll, but never a sight was seen*
*And many a rumour spoken, of the beauty Moll had been,*
*And many a year gone by before she was sighted with her daughters,*
*Clad in naught but the skin they wore, a-frolicking in the waters.*
*She'd led a life of disrepute, had Moll, the aging prostitute.*
*And all of ye who've heard folk say that a life of crime will never pay,*
*I'm here to tell you it's a folly. Just take a look at Squire Molly.*

Jenny turned to page two. *No record exists of Molly or Walter Squire's transportation to Australia.*

'What?' Jenny asked. He may as well have written *The end*. She knew no record existed. He'd searched for months. He'd found a few Squires, a few Walters and many Mollys transported for prostitution, but without the year of her transportation or her family name, she could have been any one of those Mollys, or none of them. They'd found no record of a marriage, nor of the birth of her two daughters. All they knew of Molly Squire was that she and her adult daughters had been found by Molliston's first settlers, squatting on two thousand acres of prime river land and ready to spear anyone who attempted to move them off their land.

Jenny persevered through page two, through page three, which was more than enough for her to decide she didn't want to read Jim's book – and that few would. It was well written. He could string big words together – blocks of big words.

Page four had space for a photograph, and beneath that space was a paragraph about James Murphy. Who was he? She scanned the next page, and the next, looking for Molly and her daughters but finding more names, a glut of names and dates she had no interest in reading. She turned back to the anonymous rhyme.

If there was no record of Molly Squire's existence, if there were no relatives to upset, why stick to known facts? That rhyme set the scene for a fabulous story, the baby on Wal's lap, the baby at Molly's breast, then the husband hanged and a young woman left alone, miles from civilisation. How had she managed to raise two infant daughters? How had she come by money enough to build her mansion?

Blame that unknown poet, blame Jim for staying out all afternoon, blame his opening sentence, or too much overgrown garden. Blame what you will, but she sat down at Jim's typewriter to find the youthful Molly, a girl who'd had nothing to sell but herself.

Mid-page, she gave her an excuse for becoming a prostitute. She set her up with six orphaned siblings, starving to death in a wretched hut in Ireland – and if it resembled Granny's hut, too bad. Then, because a woman with two babies wouldn't have survived alone in the bush, and because Molly and her daughters had defended their land with spears, Jenny allowed them to meet up and live with a tribe of blacks – at a camp which looked much like Elsie's description of old Wadi's.

More pages rolled in, rolled out, very messy pages, words cancelled with x's; entire lines cancelled with x's, but somewhere between the x's and the blacks' camp, Molly developed a voice much like Lila's. And too bad about that too. Molly was telling Jenny's seeking fingers where to go.

*He could put his boots under my bed – if I had one . . . if he owned a pair of boots, Molly thought.*

Molly and a handsome young black that Jenny named Wadimulla were just about to get down to business when Jim came home expecting to eat. She'd been cooking up fiction instead of the stew she'd planned for tonight.

'I forgot the time,' she said.

He counted her butts. 'What have you been doing – other than smoking?'

'Typing,' she said.

'The rattle as I came in the door was self-explanatory, Jen,' he said. 'Did you get time to look at the book?'

'You lost me on page two,' she said.

'What's wrong with it?'

'Lack of Molly. The poem told me what the book was going to be about, then Molly disappeared and you introduced umpteen people I don't give a damn about.'

'She's in it later,' he defended.

'I want her youth! Who's interested in an elderly squatter?' She wound a half-finished page from the typewriter and handed it to him, then eight messy pages more.

He glanced at them and followed her out to the kitchen where the wood in the firebox had turned to ash. She added newspaper and a few sticks of kindling. She opened the flue. He sat down to be served, and to glance at her pages while waiting.

She was whipping up an omelette when he started laughing. She loved his laugh. He didn't do it often and when he did, he cried and had to take his glasses off to wipe his eyes. He wiped them, then read on, but couldn't read for laughing.

'What's so funny?'

'This is,' he said.

'I've never professed to be a writer. It's just an idea of what I wanted to read on the first pages.'

'You've turned her into Lila.'

'From what we know of her she probably was a Lila. One of those old blokes said that she'd paid her builders in bed.'

'Where did you find Wadimulla?'

'He seemed logical.'

'You can't mix fact and fiction, Jen.'

'Who says you can't and who's alive to argue?' she said, claiming her pages.

She showed them to Amy, who also recognised Lila. She chuckled silently, as only Amy could, and when she was done with her reading, she circled three paragraphs and told Jim he had to include them – and told Jenny later to stay on Molly's trail.

She tried, but pencil and paper failed to raise her. Something had happened in her head while her blind fingers had been busy searching out the right keys. The logical side of her brain being up to its ears in concentration had given the creative side freedom to run amok.

A week later she dreamed of Molly/Lila and her daughters. They were living in a dark hut on Granny's land, and the dream was so real, she rose from her bed to write it down. And out they came to play, Molly and her nine and ten year old girls, the younger of them running wild in the bush with the Aboriginal kids, the older, a brat of a kid, refusing to eat a lump of blackened goanna.

*'It'th poithonous,' Hilda whined.*

*'Starve then,' Molly replied.*

Jenny wrote of the forest, the creek, the fish in the creek, of the naked Wadimulla, spearing dinner. She wrote of the bark canoe he cut from a large gum tree. There were canoe trees scattered throughout Woody Creek's forest where it ran down to the creek. Molliston had forests and a river. She hadn't seen a canoe tree there, but they'd be there.

She was clothing Molly and her girls in possum skins, cobbled together with animal sinews, when Jim wandered out to see what she was doing at that time of morning.

'I had a dream,' she said and handed him six more pages.

He accepted her description of the bush and a paragraph of Molly's girls, who may have eaten goanna, but refused Wadimulla and his fish. Amy was in love with Wadimulla, she said he epitomised the tall and noble black savage.

Then the first inquest into the Chamberlain baby's death was quashed and a new inquest announced. A Sydney forensic biologist had found baby blood beneath the dashboard of the couple's car.

'Why would they murder a tiny baby?' Jenny asked.

'Murderers rarely look like murderers,' Jim said.

Lindy Chamberlain appeared to have the staying power of a champion racehorse, and by the look of things she'd need it.

*The Witch Queen* was released in time for Christmas sales. Six free copies arrived in Woody Creek. Jenny gave a copy to Lila.

'What am I going to do with a kids' book?' she asked.

'Sign it,' Jenny said. 'You're all over it.'

'I won't be signing Flanagan much longer. How much money do you get for doing them?'

'Not much, once it's split four ways,' Jenny said.

'Do I get any more?'

'Not unless we use more of the photos.'

'Use them all,' Lila said. 'If I ever get my hands on enough money, you won't see my heels for dust.'

Amy and John wanted to do a follow-up. They had photographs enough and the rhyme. Jim was playing again with Molly, as was Jenny – when Jim wasn't around. He was no longer amused.

Then Trudy, now a qualified nursing sister, came home for a week before leaving for Africa, where she'd spend twelve months with a mob of volunteers who'd attempt to do what Granny and Itchy-foot had attempted to do ninety-odd years ago, what missionary groups and volunteers had been attempting to do forever. And what had they achieved? It was the black African's culture to breed too many kids then watch half of them die of disease and starvation.

Jenny left her with her father and went for a walk down to the old place to rest her eyes.

Granny hands had been busy in the earth. Her climbing rose and the lilac wisteria had intertwined along the chicken wire fence, though there was not a chook left to appreciate the beautification of their yard. Harry had taken the last of them into town. Unguarded, the hens had made too easy meals for foxes, of both the four- and two-legged variety.

The shell of Elsie's house was still standing, and the old shed holding together. No barn owl snoozed in its rafters. A smell in there, not of mice, but of long abandonment.

The front fence to the west of Elsie's house was down, saplings encroaching. Nothing now to warn the forest that this was Gertrude Foote's land. Lives had been lived here, good lives with no handouts. Days had begun with hard labour and ended the same way.

Jenny sighed and walked back to where the old lean-to had once leaned, where Margot had been born, and Georgie. Not Jimmy, though she'd tried for hours to scream him out.

She walked north to where Granny's front door had been, the door Granny and Maisy had carried her through that day. They'd carried her out to the car where she'd screamed all the way to Willama, while Granny, who'd spent hours telling her to push, now begged her not to push. God, how she'd sucked on that chloroform mask, sucked it in and died, and come back from the dead vomiting her heart out, and howling because her belly hadn't been cut, because she knew they'd pulled Jim's baby out of her in pieces.

They hadn't. They'd got him out alive. Battered and bruised, scratched and bung-eyed, but a week later he'd been her most beautiful baby.

Three kids, born to her before she'd been old enough to have kids, each one an accidental seed, pollinated by accident. Georgie, her tall strong sapling; Margot, too long in Georgie's shade, had grown stunted; little sapling Jimmy, his roots transplanted early to grow in strange soil.

According to Lorna, he now called himself James Langdon. Jenny had written twice to James Langdon at his Thames Ditton box number but received no reply. Perhaps Lorna had lied. Jim said not. Jim said she never bothered to lie. The logical side of Jenny's head knew that Jimmy had received her letters and chosen not to reply. The other side didn't, nor did her bones, nor her womb where he'd grown. Down there, she knew that one day, somewhere, sometime, she'd see him again, and she'd recognise him too.

She wandered the land for an hour, finding flowers in hidden places, wandered until a bunch of dark-complexioned males with a flagon came from behind Elsie's house. No Wadimulla amongst them. They looked dangerous and, the hairs on the back of her neck rising, she walked fast towards the rear fence where she climbed between the wires and into Joe Flanagan's land, the safer option today.

He'd always owned a pair or two of red kelpies, which for forty years had appeared to be the same red kelpies. For as long as Jenny and her kids had used Joe's land as a short cut to town, those red kelpies had come on their bellies to warn them off the property. She was midway through the heavily timbered wood paddock before one came from behind a tree to show his teeth, and not in a neighbourly smile.

*Back up, lady.*

Jenny didn't back up. She got her back to a tree then looked for his red mate – or for old Joe, or even Lila.

He barked half-heartedly, glanced over his shoulder. No keeper, no companion watching to dob on him, so he sat and offered Jenny a conspiratorial wink before scratching his fleas.

'Where's your mate today?' Jenny asked.

*She's got eight new kids to feed, lady. Where do you think she be?* he said in that conversational voice of all dogs.

'Tell her – and your pups – that I'm going to build down here one day.'

*Joe's bitch'll'ave that fence down in a week, lady.*

# The Dog Affair

Amber was usually out and about before the roar of traffic claimed Melbourne, before the stink of car and truck fumes killed that barely perceivable perfume of a lost city.

She dressed carefully for her early morning jaunts, camouflaging her pretty frocks beneath a black overcoat, concealing her white curls beneath the black headscarf worn by many elderly European immigrants. No one spoke to her. Tram drivers on the Kew line were familiar with that old dame in black who once a week rode the early morning tram to that same stop in Kew.

A conveniently placed stop, and on an October morning, Amber used her walking stick as she stepped down to the road then made the turn into Lorna's street. A newspaper boy on his cycle passed her. She watched him stop before the tall metal gates where he jammed two rolled newspapers between its rails before riding on.

Lorna must have been watching for him. She came to retrieve her papers, and Amber crossed over to the far side of the road, slowly, a stooped old European lady leaning heavily on her stick. She watched Lorna from behind the trunk of a tree, smiled as taloned hands felt the gate rails for her newspapers. Watched her locate the newspapers, snatch them – as a black rat might snatch a lump of mouldy cheese from a trap.

Does your cheese grow mouldy without your Duckworth? Amber thought. Do you sit where the light comes in through the window with your magnifying glass, struggling to read of Lindy and her pastor? They'd been judged guilty of the murder of baby Azaria, though he not as guilty as she. Men never were. Eve had tempted pure-hearted Adam, and for that, all women would eternally pay. The pastor had been allowed to go home to his children; Lindy was sentenced to life, a pregnant Lindy.

Amber had once sacrificed a baby. She'd tried to bury it. Dug a grave in the moonlight beneath the oleander tree, and he'd come huffing and blowing in his nightshirt to ruin everything. Some are born to ruin.

Lorna stood a while in her driveway, reading the headlines, no magnifying glass necessary, proof enough to Amber that she could still see, though no proof was necessary. Months ago, she'd included a wisp of her hair inside one of her letters to Lorna, then a sliver of newsprint. The letters returned, seemingly unopened – but there was no wisp of white curl or sliver of newsprint in those envelopes.

She watched Lorna walk back to her house, watched until she was inside, then retraced her footsteps to the tram stop.

The minister replied to Elizabeth Duckworth's letters. The Housing Department acknowledged receipt of Mrs Cecelia L. Duckworth's frequent letters. Amber opened them, unless Sissy got to them first. She had last month. She'd read it, tossed it at Reginald and again accused his family of interference.

'They're only doing it because she's stuck here.'

She, her, even *it* on Sundays when Maisy phoned, when Sissy spent an hour speaking in code. Never Mum, never Amber. Never told her to leave, not now. Sissy enjoyed the meals served up to her each night.

Never a thank you offered, neither for the meals nor the nut-brown dye Amber combed through Sissy's weight of hair each month. She offered a snarl during the plucking of new growth from between and around her now well-shaped eyebrows. A mother's care had always improved that mud-eyed ox of a girl, though not enough.

Since the loss of Reginald's car, each Sunday morning a Duckworth came to the unit door to sniff for alcohol before collecting the duo for church and lunch. They found no alcohol. A few of the drivers ignored Amber, a few offered a nod, others asked if she wished to accompany Sissy and Reginald to church. Amber declined all invitations. Sundays were her days.

*Dear Sir or Madam,*
*Three years ago I was advised by your department that I was on the waiting list to be moved into a three-bedroom house. We are still waiting and our situation has now reached the hopeless stage.*

*My mother is eighty-three, and senile. My husband, in his seventies, has liver damage. As mentioned in my previous letters, there are fifty-three steps leading down to the ground floor. No doubt I am not the only resident who has complained about the deplorable condition of the lifts.*

*Please find enclosed letters from my husband's, my own and my mother's doctors, stating that in our poor physical condition it is imperative that we be moved to more appropriate accommodation without delay.*
*Yours sincerely*
*Cecelia L. Duckworth*

Amber didn't have a doctor. *Archibald G. Foote, Physician* signed his name on the bottom of a brief note, mentioning his patient's weakened state and her growing senility. Sissy and Reginald shared their doctor, an Asian chap who was unaware he'd written two very fine letters.

Amber now owned a selection of writing pads, small and large, cheap and expensive. She owned a blue biro, a black and a red, also a bottle of black ink and a pen. *Archibald G. Foote, Physician* had used pen and ink on unlined heavy cream paper, his script closely resembling Lorna's cursive copperplate. Sissy and Reginald's doctor, a Dr Nguyen, had used a small white pad and blue biro. Lorna's letters were penned on the common, larger pad. More expansive when she wrote to Lorna, Amber could fill two pages and still have more to say.

Like Lorna, Amber now had her own labelled files, not in a cabinet's drawers but a concertina file.

It was a Tuesday in January '83 when Amber received a letter from the Housing Department informing Mrs Cecelia L. Duckworth that she, her husband and mother had been allocated a three-bedroom house in Doveton. Amber, who'd been hoping for a house close to the Camberwell tramline, kept the news to herself, and in the early morning of Wednesday, she caught a tram to the city, a train to Dandenong, a bus to Doveton, then walked past two and a half blocks of third-rate houses, each one much the same as its neighbour, many attached to its neighbour, and she wanted no part of them.

Dodged a bike rider who failed to give way to her, walked by snarling dogs, but found the house she'd been allocated. Number 12, not attached to its neighbour. She wasn't fond of the number twelve, and was less fond of the house. Stood for minutes eyeing the lopsided mailbox with its upside down two. She'd visualised a tall front fence of bricks and steel and received a low timber fence overgrown by a creeping weed. She'd been expecting bricks and mortar, long wide windows, a tall roof. She'd received small windows and the flat roof of a prefabricated structure an estate agent might have described as compact and she described as basic shelter. But it had only two steps up to a porch and it had three bedrooms. With a sigh, she opened the low gate and entered the yard.

A very small porch sheltered the front door and a small window, one of those wretched metal-framed things. She cupped her hands to its glass so she might see inside. Nothing inside to see other than a garish linoleum floor covering. Floors could be recovered, windows could be draped. She sighed again, then left the porch and followed a rutted driveway to the rear of the house. A rotary clothes line. She missed Lorna's line. A large expanse of newly mown lawn, no tree, no flower, grass growing halfway up the surrounding paling fences. Amber had not considered grass. At sixteen she'd made a pact with the earth to never disturb it if it kept its distance from her.

On the train back to the city, she composed Cecelia L. Duckworth's rejection of the offered house, editing it while crossing chaotic streets with the hordes, while fighting her way onto a tram, then off it, weary as she hadn't been in a while, weary with disappointment, and annoyance at what her years of scheming had delivered.

She entered the unit block behind a woman and her three daughters. They continued on towards the lift. She'd seen them before on the fourth floor, and the fifty-three steps being too many that afternoon, she hurried weary feet towards the lift.

On Sunday evening Cecelia L. Duckworth retrieved the good news, sealed in a new envelope, carefully readdressed, stamped with a used stamp and posted in her mailbox, and she read Duckworth interference into its every line. Reginald read it. He knew that Doveton was somewhere out beyond Dandenong. He'd spent most of his life in the city and knew its roads well.

'The inconvenience of . . . of position may well be . . . be balanced by the . . .'

'They're not moving me again,' Sissy said.

'. . . by the space,' Reginald finished as Sissy picked up the phone.

For two hours she dialled a variety of Duckworths, explaining to each in her own inimitable way how they were not moving her again, that they'd spent their whole rotten lives moving her around.

One-sided conversations are difficult to decipher, but it became obvious that no Duckworth was admitting his guilt. One had the audacity to ask for Reginald to be put on the line. His conversation was disjointed at its best. It was cryptic that day. 'Melway coordinates? Yes . . . Map 90. K 10 . . . Yes . . . that is so . . . The distance . . . Yes . . . Transport would certainly . . . certainly be a consideration . . . Yes. I would deem it impossible . . .'

It became clearer to Amber when the discussion turned to a vehicle. Reginald wanted a car. In Doveton, he'd require a car, and during the following days, when the phone rang, Reginald rose eagerly to take the call. A Ford Falcon could become available. Sissy, who had missed the car, began to see the fringe benefits of Doveton. And thus, while two states burned, the trio moved into the hot box of Number 12. A sweat box for Sissy. Amber shuddered as she passed – the floors shuddered. Reginald and a Duckworth fiddled with the television, unable to pick up a clear picture until a younger Duckworth climbed onto the flat roof to adjust the antenna.

Two days after the move, on the sixteenth day of February, fires swept through South Australia and Victoria, taking seventy lives and incinerating two thousand homes. It was a day most would remember as Ash Wednesday, the day dust storms, combined with smoke from the fires, blanketed Melbourne and blocked out the afternoon sun. Amber would remember that day for the gritty red dust that infiltrated every window and door. She'd remember it for the east-side neighbour's dog, barking nonstop from early morning to mid-afternoon – until the world darkened and the sun became an alien red glow in the western sky, when the dog's bark became a wolf's elongated howl. Sissy's howl continued longer. Reginald failed to hear her. His hearing was not good, a result of malaria caught during his years in the tropics. He stood to turn the television volume higher.

His head had been sized for a larger man, as had his limbs. His appearance when silhouetted against the undraped window was like one of the hairless, large-eyed, stick-limbed aliens portrayed in comic strips and on television. Sissy silhouetted against the same sun was *The Blob* – and it oozed vicious moisture from every pore –

and the floor plan of that basic shelter forced the trio into closer, not more distant, proximity. It was a common enough layout – three small bedrooms, small kitchen, front door opening into the sitting room, with the kitchen, bedrooms, bathroom and laundry feeding off a narrow passage. It reminded Amber of Norman's house, though his rooms had been larger, cooler, his ceilings higher. The kitchen with its west-facing window could have been Norman's – apart from the gas stove that stood where his wood stove had burnt – and had she possessed energy enough that Wednesday, she might have got down on her knees and stuck her head into the gas oven.

During that first week at Number 12, misery became a fourth presence. It sat at the kitchen table and sprawled in the sitting room while a motorbike roared in a tin shed behind the rear fence and Number 10's dog barked from seven thirty in the morning until six o'clock at night five days a week. It was silent on Saturday when the Duckworths came – two males, Ron and Charles. They delivered a six year old blue Falcon, now registered to Reginald and comprehensively insured for twelve months. Reginald patted its panels. He smiled. He sat in the driver's seat and roared the motor until a Duckworth claimed the keys so he could open the boot and remove an elderly lawnmower.

It roared on command and the dog, no longer silent, attacked the paling fence, determined to break through so he might kill that disturbing machine. The working neighbours, celebrating the cool change with barbecued sausages and beer, came to the dog's side to abuse the mower for disturbing the dog, so Sissy emerged to abuse the owner of the dog. Charles and Ron left the mower roaring to approach the fence where they attempted to offer a little Duckworth rationality to the discussion. Have mower, will mow. Reginald cut a swath through yellowing grass.

An elderly mower is a dangerous beast when driven by an inept fool wearing bedroom slippers. Reginald brought peace to that street in Doveton. Perhaps his big toe flew over the fence. Something silenced the dog. Charles Duckworth silenced the mower.

Many faint at the sight of blood. Reginald was a fainter. The men carried his minimal weight into the sitting room so he might bleed on the floor and couch. The dog owner, who also owned a telephone, called an ambulance. Amber fetched a towel to wrap the foot, and a mop and bucket to wipe up the blood. Two toes were missing, a third hung by a thread. Reg regained consciousness long enough to look at the stumps, then passed out again. They took him away. Amber and a street full of viewers watched the ambulance until it was out of sight. The Duckworths followed it.

So many of Amber's hopes had been centred on the possession of a house, and what had she received? Dead lawns, dogs, neighbours with motorbikes. The day was done before Sissy remembered what day it was. She'd forgotten to vote. Amber Morrison hadn't cast her vote in years. Elizabeth Duckworth had been on no electoral role.

Lorna, born the year Victorian women were given the vote, would have queued early at her polling booth but would not have been pleased with the outcome of the '83 election. Malcolm Fraser and his Liberal Party were given the boot by Australian voters. Bob Hawke, Labor man, ex-union man, would be sworn in as Australia's new prime minister. *That raucous larrikin*, Lorna had once named him.

On Monday Reginald was returned to Number 12 by a Duckworth husband and wife. His foot well bandaged, a mild heart condition had been diagnosed along with anxiety. The Duckworths lined up a variety of pills on the kitchen bench – vitamins, painkillers, pills to increase the strength of his heart, pills to relieve his anxiety, antibiotics – the dosage to be taken printed on each label.

Reginald sat, his foot propped on a pillow on the coffee table. Sissy slumped beside her new telephone, waiting for it to ring. The television belted out its advertisements, the dog barked and Amber tested an anxiety pill, which worked so well she caught the bus into Dandenong where she bought a pair of workmen's earmuffs, as red as Sissy's new telephone. That night she wore them while sitting at her embroidery.

Two days later her washing machine was delivered along with a new bedroom suite.

'Where do you think the money is coming from to pay for that?' Sissy asked.

Earmuff clad, Amber failed to hear the question. She failed to dose Reginald when he could no longer rise to get his pills. Dosed herself each morning with one of his anxiety pills. They and the earmuffs altered her perspective. She ordered two outdoor blinds, one for the kitchen, one for her bedroom window. She ordered blackout drapes, peacock blue for the sitting room, dusty pink for her own. She bought two cans of spray deodorant and with it sprayed Sissy's frocks, sprayed her bed linen. With multiple spray packs of weedkiller she sprayed along all the fencelines and around her clothes line. Sprayed the dog when he pushed aside a lose paling to poke his nose through, the better to bark. He was a big dog who would require more than one loose paling to squeeze through. For an hour, there was a war of wills at that narrow gap. The dog moved before Amber's spray pack was empty.

Sissy's well-shaped eyebrows became one. The roots of her hair grew through steel grey. She turned the deodorant spray on Amber one afternoon. She snatched her earmuffs and smashed them beneath her shoe. Amber took an extra pill, caught a bus and bought another two pairs, both red.

It came to a head, as an abscess will always come to a head if given time. Reginald's stumps became infected and an abscess developed in his groin. Again an ambulance carried him away. Alma and Valda came to pack his case and collect the pills his women had not been supervising. They stared at Amber's earmuffs but understood why she wore them. Alma turned the television off. Sissy screamed at her to get her interfering nose out of her house. She did. She walked out to the backyard to turn the hose on the barking dog. Accustomed to weedkiller, the pure hose water incited him to riot. He was halfway over the fence before Alma ran.

'Something needs to be done about that animal,' she warned.

Something needed to be done about the indoor animal, who barked and howled just as loud and long. She accused the Duckworths of cutting Reginald's toes off by expecting him to mow a lawn. She blamed them for her bedraggled state, for her mono eyebrow, accused Alma and Valda of applying for that house in the middle of nowhere where there was no tram, no bingo, no nothing and now no car and only doing it because they wanted a murderer to have her own bedroom.

'It wasn't of our doing, Cecelia,' Alma said. She and Valda, along with a dozen others, had been subjected to Sissy's phone attacks. 'You wrote multiple letters to the department demanding to be moved.'

'You liar! I didn't write to anybody!'

'Your cousin Steven's son has seen your letters, Cecelia.'

There'd always been a Duckworth capable of gaining required information. Amber backed off to the kitchen to cut steak into neat cubes for a stew.

'Steven's son said that you harassed the department, that your file is an inch thick,' Valda said.

Sissy wasn't dumb. She'd never been dumb. She rose from her couch, knowing who had harassed the Housing Commission for that cursed three-bedroom house.

The steak landed on the floor. Amber vacated the kitchen then the yard. The dog barked. Alma and Valda packed a second case for Sissy and they took her away – and forgot Reginald's pills.

Amber glanced at the lined-up bottles while picking up cubes of steak. She didn't cook her stew that night, but found occupation in making neat slits in each cube and carefully inserting into each cube one of Reginald's pills, in the main his heart pills, minute things. She added a few painkillers, but not those for his anxiety. They found a new home in her handbag.

At midnight, Number 10's house in darkness, Amber took a bowl of steak outside to the paling fence where she eased the swinging paling to the side. The dog rose to investigate, so she tossed him a bloody treat. Perhaps he recalled similar flying manna the day Reg cut off his toes. His snuffling told her he'd found the steak so she tossed another cube, and continued tossing. He was eating out of the bowl before it was empty. She may well have made a friend for life.

Slept well that night. It was after nine before she rose from her bed.

The dog didn't.

*

It took seven weeks for the doctors and the Duckworths to heal Reginald's stumps. They returned him and his new pills, his feet shod in toeless sandals. They returned him to a changed house. The floors were carpeted; the worn couch, stained by Reginald's blood, had been replaced by one of black vinyl, but the bathroom – it didn't really belong in a Commission house. The elderly green bath with its overhead shower had made way for a boxed-in shower recess with a folding glass door. The gruesome pedestal basin and wall cabinet with its stained mirrored door had given way to a small white vanity unit and a wall to wall mirror, which added both light and size to that tiny room. Its installation had so sorely depleted Amber's elasticised pocket accounts, Margaret Hooper had applied for her birth certificate. Amber knew Margaret's date of birth – somewhat later than Amber's. She'd died in '69.

Sissy, clad in diabolical floral, returned to Number 12. She believed the Housing Commission had renovated the bathroom in order to tempt her home to their taxpayer-subsidised house. The Duckworths, more worldly folk, didn't, but, delighted to be rid of Sissy, asked no questions. Nor did the city branch of the Commonwealth Bank when well-dressed, well-spoken Miss Margaret Hooper opened a bank account, only to simplify the cashing of her first pension cheque.

Life improved at Number 12 thereafter. No dog barked, Reginald was back behind the wheel of a reliable car and Sissy was again at his side on pension days, and off to church and lunch on Sundays, her hair again nut brown, her mono eyebrow two.

*My dear Lorna,*
*It is some time since I've written. I hope my letter finds you well as it leaves me. You will be delighted to learn that my family and I have moved into a lovely new home in the outer suburbs. Do note, however, that my postal address has not altered . . .*

# Potato Friendship

Sissy tested the menus in cafés and restaurants on pension days. She tested swollen plates of sweet and sour chicken on beds of fried rice, tested ham, pineapple and cheese pizzas. November was young when she discovered baked potatoes with cheese and bacon bits, buried beneath an avalanche of coleslaw and sour cream. She didn't like the owners of that small café; they hardly spoke a word of English, but if you held on to your receipt, you could get a slice of cake or a chocolate-iced, cream-filled doughnut and a cappuccino for two dollars.

She ate her fortnightly potatoes alone until January '84 when the streets and shops were overrun by mothers and their kids, as were the half-dozen tables in that baked potato café. She'd had her eye on a table when she'd ordered, but before the plate was in her hand, a woman with three kids claimed it. There was a table for two against the wall, and only one sitting at it. Her overloaded plate in hand, she had to eat somewhere, so she approached the lone eater.

'Anyone sitting here?' The woman had her mouth full, but she shook her head, so Sissy sat down.

'Very crowded today,' the woman said when her mouth was empty.

'I hate school holidays,' Sissy said.

She ate her potato down to the skin, then ate the skin, wiped her mouth and chin with the supplied paper serviette while watching the stranger use her serviette to wipe coleslaw from her ample breast.

'Will you look after my chair for me while I get my cappuccino?' the stranger said.

'Get mine while you're about it,' Sissy said, offering her receipt and two dollars. 'I'll have a cream doughnut.'

They discussed doughnuts while cream squelched as it ever had onto Sissy's top lip. They discussed the size of the cappuccino cups, then the stranger mentioned bingo.

'Me and Mum used to have lunch here every Wednesday then go to bingo,' she said.

'I used to play where I used to live,' Sissy said.

'Mum's dementia has got too bad to take her anywhere now.'

'My mother has had dementia since I was born,' Sissy said.

Women with a common problem will speak of it. They paid the full price for a second doughnut and cappuccino, and as cream squelched once more they compared mothers and spoke of long dead fathers, and Doveton. The stranger lived in a two-bedroom unit just around the corner from the bus stop. Sissy spoke of her three-bedroom house and her husband, who drove a car, who was probably waiting to drive her home.

*

Reginald had given up waiting at the car. He was seated in a locked cubicle in the public toilets, carefully pouring half of a litre bottle of cheap gin into a litre bottle of lemon cordial, half of which had been emptied into the toilet bowl. He had two small bottles of soda water at his feet, and when done with his decanting, he tilted the cordial to mix the brew, opened a bottle of soda water, poured a little on the floor, then carefully poured enough cordial to fill the space. Another tilt to mix the brew, then the taste test.

Oh, sweet, sweet memories of Port Moresby and black breasts.

*

The stranger's name was Lacy Hopkins and she was a talker. 'It was supposed to be Lucy. Mum always blamed Dad's handwriting, and he always blamed the bloke who typed up my birth certificate. Mum used to call me Lucy. Some days she doesn't know who I am now.'

A woman with a screaming kid and a baby came into the café, and all eyes turned to her.

'Have you got any kids?' Sissy asked.

'I was married for seven years but I couldn't get pregnant, then my hubby got a girl from work pregnant and he moved in with her. Have you got any?'

'Humph,' Sissy said.

Lacy was smaller than Sissy, though not a lot smaller. She was shorter, a few years younger.

'I get a carer's pension for looking after Mum, but my brother put her name down at a nursing home. He said his wife is sick of looking after her. And who is she to talk, I'd like to know. They only take her one day a week, or most weeks it's only one day. I've got her for the rest. Have you got help with yours?'

'Humph,' Sissy said.

'He said I can move in with him if we put Mum into a home, but I know how long that would last. I'd have to get a job. I used to be a nursing aide before I got married. I went back to it after he deserted me. There's always plenty of work for nursing aides at the homes.'

'How do you put people's names down at them?'

'Just go there and fill in a form, or I think that's what my brother did. He said Mum's doctor told him to. Doctor Kemp has been looking after her for years. He makes house calls now and he bulk bills us. How long have you been living down here?'

'Since February.'

'We've been living in our unit coming up three years, and I'd rather live there with Mum the way she is than with my brother – not that I don't get on good with him. It's his wife. I mean, I know she doesn't want me. She just got rid of her last son. They had three and two daughters. I've got three great nieces, and one on the way.'

The screaming kid drove them out to the street. They walked together down to the supermarket where they separated, but met up again at the magazine stand where each had picked up a copy of *New Idea*.

'I was thinking a minute ago that I should have asked you if you'd like to come to bingo with me on Wednesday. My brother can sit with Mum,' Lacy said. 'That's if you . . . if you're not doing something better.'

'I'm never doing anything,' Sissy said.

They found Reginald waiting in a hot car. Sissy dumped her bags in with his six pack of soda water and his bottles of lemon cordial. Lacy dumped her bags in the boot and when Sissy failed to introduce her, Lacy introduced herself.

'Reg,' he said.

Raised in the era of manners, when men lifted their hat to a lady, when they opened car doors, he opened the rear door for Lacy, and when he dropped her off at her unit, he opened the boot and lifted her shopping out.

'I'll give you a call if we're okay for Wednesday,' she said to Sissy. 'Nice meeting you, Reg. Thanks for the lift.'

That's how it began, with a baked potato and nursing homes and Wednesday bingo, where, on her first Wednesday, Sissy won a pair of green towels.

Lacy had lived. She'd done things. She'd flown to Queensland, been to stage shows and, until twelve months ago, she'd gone out to dinner at hotels when they'd had an entertainer who was worth listening to. She'd seen Kamahl. She drank wine and spoke about the night she'd drunk three gin squashes and could barely remember being driven home. Sissy had never stepped inside a hotel. The Duckworths didn't approve of drinking.

Lacy knew about cheap weekend bus trips to New South Wales to play the pokies. She'd been on a few trips with the girls she'd worked with and had taken her mother on one trip before she'd got too bad to take anywhere.

'It only costs ten dollars for the bus, the motel room and a cooked breakfast and all you have to do is put a few bob into the pokies. I put in twenty cents one night and won thirty dollars. It paid for my trip and then some,' Lacy said.

Sissy, having no experiences to offer, listened.

'We ought to book a trip, Sissy. My brother or one of my nieces would stay with Mum for the night.'

The Duckworths disapproved strongly of poker machines and of any form of gambling but Sissy wanted to do something and, never having gambled, she didn't know whether she disapproved of it or not. So she rode a bus to Moama with Lacy and rode it home full of approval for poker machines. Her purse was heavy with five-cent coins which had come pouring out of the throat of a machine two minutes after she'd started pulling on its handle.

'You're lucky for me,' Sissy said.

'You've been a godsend to me,' Lacy said.

Poor Sissy had never been a godsend to anyone. Poor, poor Sissy hadn't known friendship since Margaret Hooper. Nineteen eighty-four was turning into the best year of her life.

*

Not for Jim. *Molly Squire* was rejected for the second time that year. He was in one of his silent moods the day Trudy breezed in with Sophie and two males. Jim might have shaken himself out of the doldrums for Trudy, but his house full of youths, he sat alone for the two hours they were there. He walked them out to their car when they left, saw Joe Flanagan's maroon Toyota pull into the kerb on the far side of Hooper Street and back-pedalled to the house.

'Off you go, love,' Jenny said to Trudy. 'Drive carefully.' She didn't want her and her friends to witness a Flanagan brawl.

Jenny had witnessed a few this past year. They weren't pretty. The most recent of them had been caused by a final payment to Lila for permission to use the leftover photographs in a third witch book. She'd demanded five hundred, then taken off with it and Joe's car, which he'd reported stolen. Some women don't know how to handle men, Lila had once said. Some men refuse to be handled, and Lila had struck one.

Jenny watched him drag that well-travelled case from his boot. He didn't carry it across the road. He pitched it. Too heavy to fly far, it landed hard on the concrete guttering. He pitched a handful of banknotes after it and when Lila stopped cursing him to chase his notes, he took off around the corner, his passenger side door hanging open. Lila chased one flying twenty halfway to Blunt Street before she caught it. Jenny picked up another from the gutter. She picked up a five.

'Mean old bastard,' Lila panted. 'I'll go him for every penny he's got.' She claimed the twenty and the five, retrieved a ten blown into the rose hedge, rolled her loot, tucked it beneath her bra strap, then asked: 'Who were those blokes with Trudy?'

Jenny had forgotten the blokes and Trudy. 'What?'

'Trudy's blokes?'

They'd broken the mould when they'd made Lila Jones/Roberts/Freeman/Macdonald/Flanagan. Her case lay, half on, half off the road, spilling its load. She had two twenty-dollar notes, a ten and two fives to her name but could probably give a better description of Trudy's male friends than Jenny, who had fed them. What can you do with a woman like that, a woman who laughs when she attempts to pick up her case and everything she owns lands on the road? One hinge had ripped free from the cheap cardboard. There's nothing you can do with such a woman, other than make her a coffee, donate an old case as a replacement, give her a bed for the night, then buy her a one-way bus ticket to Melbourne.

'See ya when I see you, eh?' Lila said.

Jenny waved the bus on its way, praying that Lila Jones/Roberts/Freeman/Macdonald/Flanagan wouldn't come back, that she'd find herself a new bloke, or a job, or the Salvos.

Hope budded in Jenny's breast that Christmas. No tree that year, no cooking. They ate barbecued chicken in Nobby and Rosemary's backyard, with their sons and their grandkids and Trudy and Georgie, and on Boxing Day, in Myers, when Jenny saw the back view of a woman who might have been Lila, she grabbed Jim's arm and walked him fast to the exit.

In January Trudy moved from the Box Hill hospital to Frankston, and Jen and Jim were afraid she'd come across old hospital files which might give up the details of her birth, but she wasn't there long. In June she flew to India – and why, in God's name, would anyone choose to go to India?

She was due to fly home the night the doorbell rang at ten, and Jenny feared her plane had crashed when she opened the front door and saw the constable. Then she saw Lila. Didn't unlock the security door.

'Look what he did to me!' Lila wailed.

Jenny could see little through the security mesh. She unlocked it and looked at what he'd done. Old Joe was a dairyman. He'd been raised on a dairy farm. He'd never shorn a sheep in his life and he hadn't done much of a job of shearing his wife. Lila still had her ears, she still had a few hanks of two foot long hair behind her ears, but the rest was gone.

'He sat on me and cut it off then he pitched your case into the incinerator and poured petrol all over it. Everything I owned was in it, and he burned it.'

Jenny thought of the black leather hot pants and platform-soled boots, immortalised in the second *Witch* book.

'Come in,' she said.

'I'll leave her to you then, Mrs Hooper,' the constable said.

'No. I'll do what I can with her hair then you can have her back.'

She led her visitors through to the only warm room in the house and, in better lighting, saw why the constable was eager to be rid of Lila. She was naked, or nearly so, beneath Joe Flanagan's gabardine overcoat. Jenny took her arm.

'Bedroom,' she said.

'He ripped my dress off me and burned it too. It set me back fifty-five dollars—'

Jenny tossed underwear at her, slacks, a sweater, and while Joe's coat came off and the clothing went on, she fetched her scissors. There isn't a lot you can do to level up the wool of a badly shorn sheep other than to cut the rest of it off. The finished cut was shorter than Georgie's crew-cut, and there was nothing to be done about the gaps where Joe had cut a mite too close to the scalp. It would grow. Jenny offered the Collingwood beanie. Lila pulled it on before the constable drove her home. Old Joe was in hospital.

'That got rid of a night,' Jim said, then relayed what the constable had told him. Lila had split Joe's head open with the back end of a broom.

The Wednesday edition of the *Willama Gazette* featured Lila on page two. She'd removed her beanie for the cameraman: LOCAL DAIRY FARMER ARRESTED.

Maybe he'd been arrested, but by Wednesday he was back in his milking shed, limping, one eye closed, one side of his head as naked as Lila's, apart from the black stitches crawling across his scalp. He wasn't sighted in town for three weeks. Had he been himself, he might have noticed sooner that two bank cards, which accessed accounts he'd opened in joint names, for taxation purposes, which he'd believed to be safely hidden, hadn't been safe, a fact he remained unaware of until his bank statements arrived in the mail.

He closed both accounts but, as most know, it's of little use locking the stable door after the mare has bolted. This time she'd bolted with a haystack.

# Part Two

# Greensborough

Trudy had a trade she worked at so she might travel. Georgie had travelled, then acquired a trade.

In 1980, she'd become aware that universities had opened their doors to mature-age students and had applied to do law, driven by a burning desire to equip herself with the necessary tools to hang Dino Collins – and she hadn't heard a word about him since. He may have been dead, but had he passed on, that would have made headline news: JAMES COLLINS FINALLY AT REST WITH HIS BELOVED PARENTS.

During her last year at university, she'd become convinced she'd wasted five more years of her life, that she'd have little chance of beating any one of the bright young sparks in her lectures to a job. Spent a fortune on a black suit for the interviews – with pantihose. Wore that same suit and pantihose to five interviews, made up her face five times, pinned up her hair.

She bought a black frock when called back for a second interview at Marino and Associates – and she'd walked away with a job.

The money was unbelievable. She had her own cubbyhole office. The one drawback was its location. Marino and Associates' office was in the city, in Queen Street. She lived at Greensborough, miles away – and she couldn't move. Her tomato plants were loaded. She'd been picking tomatoes since mid-January. Tonight she'd picked a dozen and tomorrow she'd pick more.

Every year since arriving in Melbourne she'd grown a couple of tomato plants with varying degrees of success. On two occasions moving house had meant she'd had to leave plants loaded with green marbles for someone else to either let die or maybe enjoy. The day she'd moved to Greensborough she'd taken her six immature plants in pots.

On a Friday night in early August, she'd picked up those seedlings at a Doncaster supermarket and when she'd returned to her ute with her loaded trolley, there was Paul propped against its bonnet – the Paul disciple she'd met on her travels who she hadn't sighted since. He'd looked so clean she'd barely recognised him.

'I thought you might have traded the old girl in, and some big bruiser would walk out and claim it,' he'd said.

She'd bought the ute in '67, given it a bashing around Australia. Five years more of waiting all day in a university car park hadn't done its paintwork or tarp canopy a lot of good – and marked her as a country hick to a few of the brighter young sparks. That night it had marked her as a long lost mate.

'What happened to your hair?' He'd known her when she'd worn her crew-cut, when her daily uniform had been khaki shorts and boots.

'What happened to your face?' she said. She'd known him during the year he'd stopped shaving, when his uniform had been a navy singlet and matching boxer shorts. Shared a tent with him and John and Simon for a week in Karratha, and again when they'd gone grape picking in South Australia. She'd sat at night in the dust around campfires, smoking, drinking beer out of bottles while insults and laughter had flown with the sparks. That night in the Doncaster car park, she couldn't have kept the smile from her face had she tried – couldn't have shaken him off had she wanted to, and she hadn't.

He asked where she was living while they unloaded her trolley, then he followed her back to the trolley bay, attempting to catch up on six years of news in ten minutes. She told him she shared a rented house, just around the corner. He told her he shared a rented house with the other two disciples.

'John refused to let us get away until his credit card bill was paid,' Paul said, then he looked at his watch and told her he had to go, that he taught computer studies at one of the colleges and ran night classes in Doncaster for office workers.

The reunion could have ended in the car park, but his class only went for two hours, so she followed him to it, sat through it, then led the way to a hotel she knew where they talked nonstop until the lounge emptied while her frozen beans thawed and her tomato seedlings wilted in the ute.

She signed up late for Paul's computer class, and when she spoke of buying her own, he took her to a chap he knew, got her a good deal then set the machine up for her in her crowded bedroom. Leaned on her shoulder that night, instructing, kissed her cheek when he said goodnight.

In September on the last night of the course, John and Simon met them at the hotel where Simon kissed her within an inch of her life, then John and his fiancée, who lived with them, shook her hand. They told her that night that Simon was transferring to Sydney and asked if she'd be interested in renting his room. It was larger than her current room and the house had fewer inmates and no cats, no tray of kitty litter in the bathroom. She wasted ten seconds in making her decision and moved that weekend, her computer riding in the passenger seat, her tomato seedlings riding beneath the tarp.

There was plenty of dirt in their backyard and not a lot bar weeds growing in it. Her seedlings had got their roots into the earth and grown like weeds, like they knew they'd come home. For Georgie it had been a coming home. Since the night of the fire she'd lived in places, not in homes.

Then came Christmas and John's marriage to his long-term, long-suffering fiancée. It was a big wedding, heavy with relatives, sisters, brothers, mother, father, aunt, uncle and cousin of both bride or groom. Maybe it was the wedding that drew Georgie home to Woody Creek. She spent Christmas Day in Vern Hooper's house with Trudy and two of her girlfriends, with Jim who, after twenty years, was still a stranger, and Jenny, who was ever Jenny, and all Georgie had of family.

The day she returned to Greensborough, Paul had given her a Christmas paper wrapped gift he'd taken from the fridge . . . two slabs of Scotch fillet steak. She'd laughed, and fried it in Granny's pan.

Paul had always sat beside her on the couch when they watched television. She'd grown accustomed to him leaning on her, had grown accustomed to his hands on her shoulders when he demonstrated a new computer program. He started pushing the boundaries after New Year.

She shoved him off a few times. She gave him an elbow in the ribs once or twice but the day she landed that job with Marino and Associates, needing to tell someone, she'd phoned Paul at work. He came home that night with a bottle of champagne, and two more slabs of Scotch fillet. Roses wouldn't have got her into his bed. The steak, champagne and laughter did.

When she'd met those boys in Darwin in '78, Paul had worn a wedding ring. Of the three, she'd considered him the least threat to her footloose state. She'd found out since that he'd been their reason for travelling. According to Simon, Paul's wife had caught the seven-year itch and absconded with a workmate. They'd set off from Melbourne to hunt them down, but got Paul blind drunk in Townsville and kidnapped him.

The night they'd met up in the Doncaster car park Paul had told her that his wife and her solicitor had taken him to the cleaner's. She'd since heard his repertoire of solicitor jokes, none of which were complimentary to her hard fought for trade, but she got him back, a few days after they'd started sharing a bed. When he told her they ought to get married, she told him she'd spent too much of her life dodging chook dung to change her name to Dunn.

'The perfect name for a solicitor,' he said. 'You're all dung beetles, sifting through the piled-up bullshit of life.'

Loved his humour. Probably loved him. Didn't love battling her way through traffic into the city five days a week. Through January she attempted to convince herself that, if not for her tomatoes, she'd look into renting a flat in the city. Each morning while driving to work in peak-hour traffic she decided that she – or they – had to move, but on the drive home, she knew she was driving home and had no desire to change it.

Only two men had pursued her long enough to start talking marriage. She'd told Jack Thompson she was too young. Last week she'd told Paul she was too old. She'd turned forty-six in March. He never argued, but he cut an article from a newspaper about a fifty-three year old South American woman who'd given birth to her twenty-eighth baby. It was stuck on the fridge when she came home.

'Lay off,' she said.

'I only want one,' he said.

She stuck a photocopied page from a magazine beside his cutting, hers stating the percentage of retarded kids born to women over the age of forty was three times as high as it was for a twenty year old.

He'd had no kids with his absconding wife. He had two brothers. They had six kids between them. Paul had known his father for twelve years, he'd known both sets of grandparents. Georgie's blood line began and ended with Jenny. As a kid she'd believed Granny to be her great-grandmother by blood. She'd been Jimmy's blood, via the Hoopers' line – Granny and Vern Hooper were half-cousins. Margot had been connected by blood to Maisy, via her rapist fathers. Georgie's father was a framed newspaper mug shot of a redheaded water-pistol bandit.

She'd borrowed Itchy-foot's diaries at Christmas time, and since had keyed his pages of minute script onto a computer disc. She'd never met him, but he'd been her great-grandfather and Granny's husband. She'd married him at nineteen, left him eight years later and never referred to him by name. To Granny, Archibald Gerald Foote had been *that philandering, conscienceless sod.* He'd lived off women. It was in his diaries, as was his shipboard romance with Juliana Conti, the supposedly barren wife of a wealthy old banker. By the end of the cruise, she'd been pregnant with Jenny. Itchy-foot's diaries mentioned her *sow belly* – his only reference to the infant Jenny, though he had mentioned her as a ten year old, and later. There wasn't a lot of pleasant reading in those diaries, and they'd done little to fill in the jigsaw puzzle of Georgie's life.

*

Paul wanted to buy the house. The owners were moving back to England and had given him first option and a month in which to raise the money before they put it on the market.

Georgie had the money. During the last years of high interest her balances had ballooned. She'd invested what she'd got from the sale of Charlie's shop, and she still had much of her mouse money. She could sell the old Woody Creek house Charlie had willed to her. It needed money spent on it. She had shares bought for her by Charlie for Christmas bonuses or whenever she'd mentioned being overdue for a holiday.

*Hang on to them, Rusty. They'll be worth something one day.*

They were worth something. A canny old chap, Charlie White – he'd warn her not to put her money into a joint investment, but the De-Facto Relationships Act had come into being last year, giving unmarried couples similar rights and responsibilities to those who were married. She'd spent today sifting through pages of a joint property settlement. The unmarried couple, who had produced two kids and built a house during their nine-year relationship, were now at each other's throats over who had paid for what, and who would get the kids, and if they didn't stop arguing soon, Boss God Marino would get the lot.

She could see Paul moving around the kitchen. A long, long time ago she'd told Jenny that one of her prerequisites in a husband would be an ability to cook. He was cooking spaghetti bolognaise. She could smell it wafting out the back door.

His family believed her to be a fixture in his life. His mother, Irene, in her early sixties, was still working. The Dunns were a working family, a house-buying, mortgage-paying family. Paul had been paying off a house when his wife absconded. He'd spoken to the bank about getting a loan.

And he caught her staring at him. 'Are you going to stand out there all night?' he called.

'I'm considering my options,' she replied and went inside.

She'd liked his face. She'd liked his eyes when his face had been covered by a bush of beard. He was taller than her, though not by much, a few years younger, though not many.

The television news was on, showing Arabs at war. They'd been at war with someone for a thousand years and would still be killing someone – or each other – a thousand years from now. War was a genetic thing with them.

'Who was it who said that all religion should be strongly discouraged?' Georgie asked.

'The pope,' Paul said.

*

By April of '86, Georgie knew she was Marino and Associates' token female, that her age and lack of encumbrances might have swayed the Boss God's judgement. She'd replaced the former token female who'd retired pregnant. By April, Georgie knew she'd spend the rest of her days chained to her desk while the top dogs played God in courtrooms a bare block and a half from her fourth-floor cubbyhole. Chris Marino was a big name barrister – and currently playing God in Sydney – and while the boss was away, the atmosphere in the office relaxed.

He didn't approve of smoking. His office was smoke free. Georgie stole a smoke at lunch, lit up when she walked back to her car at night, had a couple with Paul at home but was considering calling it quits. She'd only started it because she'd liked watching Ronnie Hall blow smoke rings.

An elderly woman who'd been in this morning to make a will had been a heavy smoker. The smell of tobacco had exuded from her pores. A dear old bird, desperate to see that each of her seven kids received an equal share of next to nothing. Last week she'd made a will for a quarrelsome old bugger who had been determined to teach neglectful grandchildren a damn good lesson once he was dead. She'd made a study of humankind during her years behind Charlie's counter. Nothing had changed. Loved watching people, reading about people and attempting to work out what made them tick.

She'd spent the afternoon sifting through a stack of files for one of the top dogs who was currently attempting to get a big payout for a bloke with a bad back injured in a work-related accident, and at four twenty, she looked at her watch and decided she'd sifted sufficient dung for the day. She was packing up when the office girl knocked, then opened the door, with two customers in tow – clients. Bugger, Georgina Morgan Morrison, BA, LLB thought. She wanted to let down her hair and scratch, wanted to go home and fry the steak she'd removed from the freezer this morning.

'Michael Morgan and his wife Alison,' the office girl said, handing over a file.

A pretty, very pregnant Alison looked about fifteen, and Georgie glanced at the male accusingly. He was removing his baseball cap and beneath it, his hair was as red as her own. And his face – she was looking at the flesh and blood face of the redheaded water-pistol bandit who'd got another kid pregnant at fifteen.

Looked down fast at his file, at the *Morgan*, her heart slamming into her ribcage like a sledgehammer into concrete. She barely heard the office assistant explaining that Rowan, one of the senior associates, was Alison's mother's neighbour and that she'd made the appointment with him. Sadly, Rowan was in conference. Conveniently so. Georgie was the token female, the office dogsbody.

She got her clients seated then excused herself to escape to the passage where she poured a glass of water and told herself she'd gone stir crazy. It worked to a degree – as long as she didn't look at that male Morgan's face. She looked at Alison, looked at her notepad as they told the story of the house they wanted, and how Alison's mother was going to give them the deposit but she wanted all of the checks done before she allowed them to sign anything. Georgie took notes and wondered how two kids – kids compared to her – could consider tying themselves into a twenty-five year mortgage they'd still be paying when she turned seventy, but she was no longer watching the clock.

She shook their hands as they were leaving, told them to call her any time, then dared a close-up look at his face, at his eyes – as green as her own – and she wasn't fooling herself. He was the living, breathing personification of the mug shot she'd been carrying around for forty years. He had the height too. He had the same shape to his face, the forehead, the eyebrows. Less hair, but give him an inch or two more and an old-fashioned brush-back style and he could have been Laurie Morgan – and she had to ask him.

'You wouldn't be related to a Laurence George Morgan, would you?' She didn't mention the water-pistol bandit. 'I believe he worked in the menswear department at Myers during the fifties.'

'Dad,' he said. 'He worked at Myers when I was a kid. Did you know him?'

'Not personally,' Georgie said.

'Some long lost uncle has left him a fortune, I hope?' he said. 'Ali and I could use a bit of it right now.'

'Is your father still living?'

'He was last Sunday. They're down at Geelong – if you happen to come across the family's missing millions.'

She got them out the door, got it closed then sat down hard. Her legs were shaking. She had a smoke out of her packet before she realised where she was. Put it away fast, picked up her handbag and rode with her clients to the ground floor. Beat them out the door to the street where she had a smoke burning before her feet hit the pavement. It was unbelievable. She'd found him. Things like that don't happen in real life.

But they did. If Paul hadn't found a park two car spaces down from her ute that night, he wouldn't have recognised it, and she wouldn't have been living in Greensborough. If a tourist hadn't fallen to his death from Ayers Rock, Lindy Chamberlain would still be in jail.

Ayers Rock was an easy enough climb. Georgie had climbed it. How had he fallen? Why had he landed near a dingo's lair? The retrieval of his body had led to the finding of the jacket worn by the Chamberlain baby the night she'd been taken from the tent and Lindy had been released – and there'd been talk in the office for days, of how many millions she might sue for, for false imprisonment.

*Is your father still living?*

Your father. My father.

*He was last Sunday. They're down at Geelong.*

If she'd read that in a book, she would have tossed it. If she'd read about the tumbling tourist, she would have tossed it. And the manila envelope Jack's father had placed in his desk drawer in '59, still there twenty years later. Was it fate? Was it God? Until she'd opened that envelope, Georgie had seen Laurie Morgan as an old lag in Long Bay jail. Thereafter she'd seen him in Essendon with his wife and three kids.

Her mind wandering, Georgie damn near ran up the backside of a truck. Braked in time, then barely saw the road or the traffic until she turned into her own street.

Paul worked closer to home so was usually there before her. She parked behind his Holden then gave her tomatoes a drink. She still had a few ripening, smaller but as sweet. She picked two then let herself in via the back door.

The shower was running. The two pieces of Scotch fillet removed from the freezer this morning were bleeding onto the plate on the sink. All day she'd been craving it – or at least until the last hour of her day. Her stomach feeling jumpy, she placed the steak back in the fridge then went in search of the envelope and the mug shot Jenny had presented to her forty years ago, with her porridge.

Many times through the years it had disappeared, and for those years she'd forgotten Laurie Morgan. Like a bad penny, he'd always turned up again, in a carton, in a drawer, and each time she'd found him and dusted him off, his face had grown younger. She'd found him covered in dust on the floor behind her dressing table the day she'd moved out of the Surrey Hills granny flat. Hadn't bothered to dust him that day. Tossed him into the garbage. But removed him later and washed his face with a damp cloth. He'd lived in the manila envelope since, with the rest of his history. Wherever he was, he'd be dust free.

'What did you do with the steak?' Paul yelled from the kitchen.

'Tossed it out to a passing crow,' Georgie yelled back.

He opened a bottle of wine, so she fried the steak and served it with tomatoes and eggs, not as fresh as Granny's, but eggs. They ate while the news played. There was old footage of the exploding Challenger space shuttle, or of its smoke trail, and a Yank discussing why it had failed. Another elderly walker had been run over. Another level crossing crash. One dead. A woman at Doveton had her two minutes of fame. Someone had baited another of her dogs. She'd only had him for three weeks.

Paul packed the dishwasher then returned to his computer. Georgie went to a spare room, the room she'd called her own when she moved in. She continued her search for the manila envelope and found it, secreted away beneath the lining paper of the top dressing table drawer, as she'd secreted the framed mug shot away beneath the lining paper of Granny's top dressing table drawer.

A survivor, Laurence George Morgan, accidently saved from the fire while she'd been saving Jack Thompson's nautilus shell.

Back in the kitchen, she emptied the envelope onto the table, imagining Paul's mother's response should she walk in. She was Jenny's age, had been born and raised in Collingwood, and might have remembered the redheaded water-pistol bandit who for months had terrorised businesses around Melbourne.

Paul came out at ten to boil the jug for coffee. 'What are you working on?'

'A lost parent,' she said, sliding the papers back into the envelope. 'A young couple came in late today. They're borrowing a fortune to buy a house. He's a car salesman, and his wife looks about twelve months pregnant.'

'When we're young we believe we're indestructible,' Paul said.

'How much did you borrow when you bought your first house?'

'Too much,' he said.

'You still want to buy this place?'

'The repayments will be no more than what we pay in rent.'

'I've got an investment maturing in May.'

'Much?'

'The money I got for my shop.'

'What shop?'

'I told you I owned a shop.'

'You told me you managed a shop.'

'I did, then I inherited it.'

'From your father?'

'From my adopted grandfather.'

'You haven't got a husband and six kids out there somewhere, have you?'

She emptied the contents of the manila envelope again to the table, then riffled through the papers for the copy of a newsprint page headlined REDHEADED WATER-PISTOL BANDIT CAPTURED, then offered it to Paul.

'I've got a father,' she said. 'Or I had one last Sunday. I was born while he was serving a three-year jail sentence. He's got three kids – or he had three in '57. His son is the one buying the house.'

He looked at her, not comprehending. She lit a cigarette then told him a much condensed story of Jenny's brief Melbourne love affair. 'The police locked him up before he could marry her. I've never met him.'

She picked up the battered old frame. Silverfish had managed to get into it and have a nibble at the brushed-back hair, but she handed it to Paul. 'Jenny framed him for me when I was four and demanding my father. My brother and sister had fathers.'

'You've never mentioned a brother.'

'His grandfather claimed him. I haven't seen him since he was six years old.' She shrugged. 'My sister had two fathers.'

'Two?' he asked.

'Two – and to a four year old kid it seemed damned unfair.'

'Two?' he questioned again.

'Do you believe there's a higher power than man, Paul?'

'I don't believe in two fathers.'

'Identical twins.'

'Your mother couldn't choose between them?' he said.

'She wasn't given a choice,' Georgie said. 'She was fourteen; they were eighteen and drunk.' She drew on her cigarette. 'Do you believe in a higher power?'

'Something sent me into the Doncaster car park that day.'

'Why?' she asked. 'Why should Laurie Morgan's son walk into my cubbyhole today? Why pick Marino and Associates, and if he had to, then why me?' She looked at her cigarette and, knowing she didn't want it, mashed it into the ashtray.

'Jenny used to swear that there was a malevolent old God sitting up there, flipping through his account book, and when it fell open at her dog-eared page, he dished out whatever was written on it. Was *solicitor* written on my page at birth? Was I predestined to do law late in life so that I'd still be the junior dogsbody when Laurie's son was old enough to buy a house?'

'Lucky you didn't do psychology or the mean old coot might have had him develop a psychosis.'

'He'll develop one anyway. He's taken on the package deal, mortgage, missus, midget and in debt to his mother-in-law.'

'I'll take that deal,' he said.

'Quit while you're ahead, mate,' she said and started packing away the papers.

# The Meltdown

It was a Wednesday, bingo day, when news of an explosion at the Chernobyl nuclear plant in Russia leaked out along with the radiation. A secretive race, the Russians, they'd covered up the catastrophe until that deadly cloud spread across Scandinavia. MELTDOWN the headlines screamed. THOUSANDS EVACUATED. A city was evacuated, and while the world awaited the repercussions of yet another nuclear accident, Lacy Hopkins, who should have been celebrating her birthday, was dealing with her mother's little accident.

'You're so kind to me,' the old lady said.

'I'm your daughter, and I love you,' Lacy said.

The old lady chuckled. 'Lucy is my daughter, dear.'

'I'm Lucy, Mum.'

'You're too old. Where's my Lucy?'

Sissy had bought a box of chocolates. They shared them while watching television, Lacy unloading during the commercials.

'My brother and his wife came around at the weekend and both of them got stuck into me about putting Mum away.'

'I'd put mine away if I could,' Sissy said.

'How has she been?'

'She burns my underwear. I can't put a magazine down or she burns it, and the neighbour reckons she poisoned her new dog with weedkiller, and she probably did.'

'Talk to Dr Kemp about her,' Lacy said.

'It won't do any good.'

'If I was your age, I'd do it,' Lacy said, then quickly added, 'Don't take that the wrong way, Sissy. I didn't mean that you're too old to look after her, just that once Mum goes into the nursing home I'll not only lose her pension, but my carer's pension and probably this flat. With my nursing experience, if I try to sign up for the dole, they'll make me look for a job.'

'The Duckworths used to make me get jobs,' Sissy said.

*

Georgie couldn't get Laurie Morgan or his son out of her head, and on a Saturday in May she decided to stop thinking about looking him up and just do it. Not even as a kid had she imagined him being in her life; she'd wanted to know he existed, and to Georgie, adult or child, seeing had been believing.

Paul had left early to meet up with both brothers at the MCG. Their football team was doing well and win, lose or draw, they wouldn't leave until the last ball was kicked. She had all day, and at nine o'clock it promised to be a nice day.

She'd called the telephone exchange a week ago and been given numbers for two Geelong L. Morgans, addresses unknown. One was an L.G. That's the one she dialled, and somewhere a phone rang, Georgie's heart rate increasing the longer it rang. Visualised an old bloke with arthritis, cursing the phone, standing, knocking over his walking stick, finding it, limping to the phone.

A woman's voice came on the line: 'Hello.' She sounded as breathless as Georgie felt, and there were kids' voices in the background.

Georgie swallowed, convinced she'd dialled the wrong number. 'I'm attempting to locate a Laurence George Morgan. He was employed—'

'He's not here at the moment,' the woman said. 'Can I take a message for him? I'm his wife.'

'I'll call back later,' Georgie said.

'He should be home by six, or you could get him at the shop,' the woman said.

Georgie's quarry was seventy-two. A minute ago, he'd been crippled with arthritis. What was he doing at a shop?

'Could you give me the number?'

People are too trusting. For all that woman knew, Georgie could have been an axe murderer, or one of the jewellers her redheaded water-pistol bandit had robbed, but before the phone was placed down, she had the phone number and the shop's address scribbled on her phone pad. She ripped out the page and for a moment stood watching the paper shake in her hand. Jenny had once accused her of not having a nerve in her body. In recent years, she'd found a few nerves – or maybe it was old age tremors.

She changed her top twice before settling for Cara's old green top. Hadn't worn it since Darwin. Wore it today to remind her of how Cara had found the guts to track down her missing links.

What she'd say to him, she didn't know. Nor had Cara the day she'd caught a bus to Woody Creek – and been sorry ten minutes after she'd arrived. Georgie might well be as sorry, but one way or another, today she'd write the end to something she'd begun as a four year old.

By eleven thirty she was approaching Geelong for the third time in her life. In '79, she'd spent two months there, working as a checkout chick, and was relatively familiar with the city though had never learnt more than a couple of street names. She parked then walked, looking at street names until a woman waiting at the traffic lights gave her directions. Walked on then, not recognising a lot until she saw the side street that had housed a fish and chip shop and the secondhand bookshop in '79. She'd paid top dollar for faulty merchandise at that bookshop and, smiling at the memory, she turned left and walked on. The *PRE LOVED BOOKS* sign was still there, if a little faded. The fish and chip shop, now a motor mower repair shop, was still greasy but its odour not as inviting.

Her feet slowed at the bookshop window. Two of Stephen King's were on display. Paul liked his books. She'd read *The Shining*, but she wasn't in Geelong to buy books, so continued down the street, searching for a street number and eventually finding one over a take-away cum café's doorway. Found another over an accountant's closed door and, realising she'd gone too far, she turned and walked back. This time he was standing out the front of his shop, that same white-headed flirty-eyed bloke who'd sold her faulty merchandise and hadn't wanted to give her a refund. And the number over his head was the number she'd scribbled on her notepad.

'Morning,' she said.

'Still warm enough,' he said.

Georgie eyed him as he made way for her to enter. He looked sixty, was weighty but well dressed. She was looking for a seventy-two year old bloke. He'd be tall, stooped maybe, bald maybe, may still resemble Clark Gable, an old Clark Gable.

'Looking for anything in particular?' the white-headed bloke asked.

'*Leticia's Wardrobe*,' she said. She'd picked up a copy of that book a couple of weeks ago and if there'd been a sales assistant available to take her money fast she would have bought it.

'It's a new release,' he said. 'I won't be seeing a copy for a while.'

Secondhand bookshops have a smell of their own, a dusty scent of much-handled treasures, fused together with the defeated odour of the unloved. She sucked in a lungful, her eyes roving, seeking that tall seventy-two year old bloke. Jenny had always said that Georgie had inherited her height from Laurie Morgan along with his copper hair and green eyes. At seventy-two, if he had any hair, it wouldn't be red. Harry Hall's was no longer red. His eyes were still the same watery blue they'd always been, as Laurie Morgan's eyes would still be pea green.

The white-headed bloke was back behind his counter.

'Have you got anything by the author of *Leticia's Wardrobe*?' Georgie asked.

'Langhall,' he said. 'Should do.'

He knew his shop and led the way to the K to O fiction shelves. His hand reached up and he withdrew a beige and brown paperback. *Angel at My Door.* Georgie had heard of it. Hadn't read it. The title didn't sound like something she might be interested in reading, but she'd asked for it so took it from a hand which didn't appear to have done a day's physical work in its life. He had long fingernails for a man.

'Thanks,' she said, and he returned to his door to relight his butt.

She looked at the cover, an anaemic sepia photograph of a girl standing against the backdrop of a blurred city street, and it did no more for her than the title. Georgie turned to the rear cover, to the blurb.

*Australia is at war. Eighteen year old Jessica, pregnant and without family support, is befriended by her childless landlady . . .* It sounded familiar – like Jenny's life story. She opened it and flipped through to page one. *Dean James, a purebred cur, ran with a pack of mixed breeds. Smarter than the average cur, he was more vicious . . .* She read the page to its end and wanted to turn to the next. She could smell the leather jacket worn by Dino Collins the day he'd given Raelene a lift home from Moe on the back of his motorbike. Dean James was a similar bastard. Georgie wanted to find out if he'd get his comeuppance, which sometimes happened in fiction, if not in life.

The white-headed bloke had his back half-turned, and out of the corner of her eye, she studied him. Maybe he was tall enough. She was wearing heels. He didn't look like Clark Gable, was heavier than he'd been when he'd sold her his faulty merchandise in '79. Weight altered the structure of a jaw, as did the years, though it would take a better imagination than her own to superimpose that mug shot over his drooping jowls. She'd ask him – or ask him if he knew of a Laurence Morgan. And what would she say if—

He turned and caught her staring, so she flicked her hair from her face and approached the counter where he was now occupied in taping up a tattered paperback.

'This one's her debut novel,' he said. '*Rusty.* Have you read it?'

She looked at the open book as he applied tape to the flyleaf. 'I prefer them intact,' she said.

'No missing pages in this one, sweetheart,' he said, and the way he said it, she knew he remembered the redhead who'd returned *Papillon*.

'How much?'

'I never charge for faulty merchandise,' he said, adding more tape.

No one else in his shop, neither assistant nor customer; the woman on the phone had said her husband would be at work all day. It was the right shop, and if he was repairing books, then he didn't have an elderly assistant in a back room repairing them. He added tape to the cover, a colourful cover. No doubt the heroine was a redhead.

Charlie had never spoken Georgie's name. From infancy, she'd been Rusty – as he'd been Charlie – until Granny had told her she should call him Mr White when she spoke to him in town. She had for a time.

'How many has she written?'

'*Leticia's Wardrobe* is her eighth. It's set in England. She lives there. Her early books are set in Australia. I'd say she's spent a good few years over here. She knows the country well.'

He removed his glasses to polish them, and with only the counter between them, she saw the green of his eyes, and a choking lump of sadness rose up from her stomach to suck the air from her lungs, not because he was less than she'd hoped to find, not because he no longer looked like a movie star, but because she'd stood at this same counter eight years ago and she hadn't known her own father. That's how much blood meant. Nothing. The human race was no higher up the evolutionary chain than the chimp. She'd believed her friendship with Cara had been based on blood. They'd been friends, that's all, friends who had gone their separate ways – like Simon had moved to Sydney, like John who had bought a house way out east. They'd seen him only once since his wedding.

Wanting out of that shop, out of Geelong, Georgie placed a ten-dollar note on his counter, praying for a cloudburst over the MCG and for Paul to be at home when she got there.

'You live down this way?' Laurie Morgan asked.

'No,' she said, willing him to take her money and give her the change, but he'd found a few more pages threatening to leave home and was painstakingly applying sticky tape. Wasted a lot of time, a lot of tape, before placing both books into a plastic bag.

'Thanks,' she said.

'I'll hang on to *Leticia's Wardrobe* for you if it comes in.'

'I won't be back,' she said, and she got away from the man she'd been wanting to find for forty years, walked out to the street, the four year old kid inside her striving not to bawl her eyes out.

He followed her out. 'You wouldn't happen to be the redheaded Morrison solicitor young Mike told us about, would you?'

With six or eight paces between them, she turned. 'Gina Dunn,' she said, borrowing Paul's name, and right then it sounded a damn sight better than Morrison.

'I was hoping you might have come across Uncle Bert's lost millions.'

'Sorry,' she said. 'Just a checkout chick looking for a good read.'

'For the record, you're a dead ringer for Uncle Bert's sister – my mother,' he said. 'She was a redhead.'

'We all look much the same,' she said and, her stomach trembling like Elsie's white ant riddled house in a windstorm, she forced a smile, lifted her hand in a wave, then walked on.

'Not many of them look like you, sweetheart,' he said. 'Enjoy your read.'

# A Dog's Life

Joh Bjelke-Petersen, Queensland's benevolent dictator premier, decided to make a push for a seat in federal parliament, believing that he alone could save the Liberal Party from internal combustion. They'd been kicked out of office because of infighting and had not yet learnt their lesson. They were still playing musical chairs for the job of leader of the opposition. Joh's ambition may have encouraged the Hawke government to obtain a double dissolution of parliament. Anyone who'd driven on Queensland goat track roads could see how much Joh had done for Queensland.

In July when Australia returned to the polling booths – where they'd queued too often these past few years – what did it matter which boxes they ticked? It made little difference to the general population which parrot-mouthed, self-serving coot occupied the lodge. As it happened, Bob Hawke retained the keys, even increasing his majority. He'd aged in the job, hadn't matured into the role of statesman but become more shifty eyed, and who could blame him? Paul Keating, his treasurer, who fitted the general image of a mafia hit man, had his eye on the keys to the lodge. Australia's politicians had gone to the dogs and the country was going with them.

Lacy's brother and his wife were self-funded retirees, and with interest rates higher than they'd ever been, they were living off the fat of the land. They bought a brand new car, then bought plane tickets to Brisbane to spend the last of winter with their middle son. They had five offspring, and an obese, spoilt-rotten, ginger-haired, squashed-faced, evil-tempered little mutt of a dog they dropped off at Lacy's unit before flying away. He spent the last of July and half of August snuffling, peeing and attempting to mate with Lacy's mother's immobile legs – or her fluffy pink boots. And he refused to eat dog food. He'd eat chocolates and fine slices of fillet steak if they were hand fed to him. He'd eat sliced chicken livers.

He tried to mate with one of Sissy's tree stump legs in August, and it responded to his advances. He climaxed mid-flight, hit the crystal cabinet and didn't get up. With his owners due home in a week, Lacy panicked and rang for a taxi to take him to the vet. Sissy had to sit with Lacy's mother.

'Who are you?'

'Cecelia Duckworth.'

'I don't know you.'

'Lacy's coming soon.'

Not soon enough, and when she came, she didn't have enough money to pay the taxi driver. Sissy had to lend her five dollars. No bingo to spend it on. No overnight trips to the country to play the pokies. No pleasure for Sissy in visiting Lacy just to watch her mop up dog pee or change her mother's bed sheets. She stopped visiting.

Two days after her brother and his wife picked up their limping mutt, Lacy capitulated and the shell of what had been Mrs Ellen Hopkins was moved onto a four-bed ward where the un-dead lay in various stages of decomposition.

Not a good winter for Sissy, the winter of '87.

*

Nor was it for old Joe Flanagan. He'd been hospitalised with pneumonia in late June, and when his sons drove him home, his cows were missing and his bitch of a wife wasn't. He called her the winter boomerang. She spent most of her winters with him. He liked a warm house, as did she. He accused her of selling his cows. Then his sons came clean. They'd sold them. They told him that the money they'd got for them was in the bank, then left him with his winter boomerang, who would release them from their obligations until the weather warmed up.

There were days when Joe didn't recognise his wife, which had nothing to do with pneumonia or dementia. Many Woody Creek residents failed to recognise Lila Jones/Roberts/Freeman/Macdonald/Flanagan. If it wasn't for her outfit, Jenny might not have recognised her when she turned up at her door twelve months after absconding with Joe's bank cards. Before he'd come to his senses and cancelled them, they'd paid for a facelift and breast implants. She'd been a short-haired blonde for a time. Joe had been greeted by a fire engine redhead this winter.

By October '87, Lila was piebald. Her red had faded to pink and her silver roots were an inch long. The couple spent their days snarling. They snarled at the breakfast table. She snarled when he drove her into town to shop, then followed her around, putting back on the shelves what she'd tossed into the trolley. She wanted spring. She wanted a dye job. She wanted Melbourne. She snarled at him while he attempted to watch the six o'clock news, which in October '87 wasn't good.

*Following the collapse of Wall Street, the Melbourne All Ordinaries index crashed by 20.3 per cent, wiping $37 billion off the value of share prices today . . .*

'Shut your flapping mouth and turn that bloody thing up,' he ordered. Lila turned the volume up until the television howled its bad news at him.

*With the markets in free fall, the crisis threatens the stability of the international economy.*

'Thousands wiped off,' Joe bawled over the news broadcaster.

'Serves you right, you mean old bastard,' Lila snarled.

'Turn the bloody thing down.'

'Who was your bloody slave last week? Turn it down yourself or buy a decent television you don't have to get up to turn down.'

'Get off your wrinkled backside and turn that bloody thing down, I said.'

She got off her wrinkled backside and turned it up.

*The collapse eclipsed the crash of 1929, which triggered the Great Depression.*

The volume blew the speakers. Lila, or the stock market crash, blew an artery feeding blood to old Joe's brain. His heart was still beating when the ambulance carried him out on a stretcher, though not before Lila had emptied his pockets of car keys and wallet. For eight hours more old Joe's determined heart beat on, time enough for his sons to say their final goodbyes had Lila bothered to give them a call. The hospital contacted them the following day, when their phone calls failed to raise his widow.

His sons organised the funeral. They, their wives and children arrived at the house to tidy up before they went to church. Lila opened the front door to them, her hair red from the crown back, and black to the fore, a perfect match for her skin-tight floral frock, bought to display all bar the nipples of her marble breasts.

'You will not make a laughing stock of that old man in church,' a daughter-in-law said.

Lila had no intention of making a laughing stock of him in church. She'd loaded the car boot with his first wife's wedding presents and anything else transportable and of value. Left them to lock up the house, and before the full mass was celebrated, before old Joe was lowered into the earth on top of his missus, Lila was halfway to Melbourne.

*

Lacy's mother had been buried before the stock market crash. Had she waited a day or two more to die, her son would have chosen a less expensive coffin. He might have chosen cremation instead of interment. The crash hit him hard.

Her mother's death hit Lacy hard. Since she'd allowed her brother to talk her into letting her go into the home, Lacy had taken one hit after the other. The Housing Department's letter arrived first, then a letter telling her she was no longer eligible to receive a carer's pension. She'd made an appointment with Dr Kemp, had gone to him in tears, but he'd refused to fill in the forms to transfer her onto the invalid pension.

'With your trade, you could walk into a well-paid job this morning,' he'd said.

'I'm in no fit state to work, doctor.'

'I'm in no fit state to pay your dole, but I pay it,' he said.

Over a cup of tea she told Sissy about her morning. 'He took no notice that I was bawling. He just stood up and held his door open, like telling me to go.'

Sissy didn't want her to get a job. She had a best friend for the first time in forty years. She didn't want her to move in with her brother at Glen Waverley either. She wanted Amber in Lacy's mother's vacated bed at the nursing home and Lacy in Amber's room.

Two overweight witches, stirring a cauldron while packing up a two-bedroom unit, will eventually raise a broth of trouble, and on a Wednesday morning in late October, at ten minutes past eight, Amber opened the door to the aging Dr Kemp, there to assess the ninety year old mother of Mrs Duckworth.

He was expecting bedridden and demented, not the diminutive, apron-clad old soul who told him her daughter was still sleeping, then invited him to breakfast. He observed her over a cup of tea and raisin toast in an immaculate kitchen. He asked her date of birth, asked the prime minister's name, the names of Queen Lizzie's children. She replied to each question without thought. He asked if she had other children to care for her. She told him she'd given birth to five babies but only Cecelia had survived.

His hostess was refilling his teacup when the surviving daughter came to stand in the kitchen doorway, her hair uncombed, her dressing gown gaping across the bulge of her stomach.

'Ask her about her earmuffs,' Sissy said. 'Ask her about poisoning the lawns, and two of the neighbour's dogs with weedkiller, and throwing my clothes and everything else in the rubbish bin.'

As the odour of the unbathed infiltrated the immaculate kitchen, Amber rose to show Dr Kemp to the door. He patted her shoulder before he left.

*

Harry, who still kept an eye on Gertrude's land, asked Jenny what had happened to Joe's kelpies.

'His sons probably got rid of them when they sold his cows.'

'They were there last Saturday. I heard them,' Harry said. 'There's not a sound out of them this morning.'

That evening he drove down to the deserted property to take a closer look. The dogs didn't bark. He found out why, found the two lying at full stretch of their chains, eyes glazed and close to death. He filled their empty water containers then called in to tell Jim that the dogs were dying, and that old Joe's place looked deserted. Jim had little interest in dogs. John and Amy were there. They were dog people from way back.

Come morning, John went shopping for dog food but, uncertain of Lila's whereabouts, he called by Hooper's corner and asked Jenny to drive with him to Flanagan's. A shy man, he was afraid of the woman he'd named the Wild Witch of the East. There was no sign of Lila, but Harry's water had revived the kelpies. John changed his mind about scraping dog food into their upturned bowls and sprang out of reach of the two crazed mongrels.

'They're ravenous,' he said.

'They're rabid,' Jenny said, watching him spoon out and toss the contents of the tins. The kelpies didn't refuse the meal. They swallowed it along with the dust.

'He bred the best dogs in the district until a few years back,' John said.

'Their forebears found little Tracy,' Jenny said.

They had no idea how long those dogs had been tied there, but going by the stink, they'd been chained since Joe died.

'We'll need to have them put down,' John said. 'It's a hell of a pity. They're a breeding pair.'

Jenny might have been able to pick the male from the female had she been able to get close enough to look at their undercarriages. Before returning to the car, she'd named them Vern and Lorna.

John didn't phone the vet, not that day. He bought more dog food. Again, Jenny drove with him down to Flanagan's. Still no sign of the maroon Toyota or Joe's sons.

They used the hose to refill the water containers, then John started tossing dog food, and the pair, preferring their meals not covered in dust, started catching the lumps of congealed meat midair, so John started ordering 'Catch' before tossing the dog food.

A dog's trust, its love, is stomach related. The next time Jenny drove in through the front gate, the duo recognised her car and started yipping. They sat, tails almost wagging as their meal approached, and remained sitting until John ordered 'Catch.'

After five days of regular meals, when John yelled 'Sit' they sat, tongues lolling, then ate their meals out of bowls. On the sixth day, John offered the back of his hand to the male. Jenny stood back waiting for him to lose it, but Vern sniffed it, smelled kindness and dog food on it, then licked the hand that fed him.

Jenny's dog experience limited to John and Amy's variety of well-groomed breeds, she started regretting her early choice of names. Vern sat when she told him to sit. He lifted a paw to pat her when she'd had enough of patting his stinking flea-riddled coat. She bought flea powder and two of Trudy's old hairbrushes, Vern wriggling in ecstasy when she brushed the flea powder into his coat. Lorna, perhaps worn niggly by too frequent motherhood, was less effusive but tolerated John's powdering, his brush.

The stink they lived in was intolerable. At ten paces their wolf-pack odour was overpowering, and for his own comfort, John decided to move the dogs to the shelter of Joe's veranda.

He tied ropes to their collars, then while he attempted to release the rusting chains from bolts secured to the shed's doorway, Jenny held the two ropes. So occupied was she in watching John's progress, she was unaware the maroon Toyota had joined the white Holden in the drive until the dogs sat without command and started wagging their tails and yipping for old Joe.

No more Joe. Lila got out of the driver's seat and Joe's dogs again became rabid killers, wanting fresh meat. In their desire to eat Lila, they almost pulled Jenny from her feet.

'Sit!' John bellowed. His voice was commanding. They sat. Didn't want to – Lorna's fine set of teeth showing exactly how much she didn't want to.

'What do you think you're doing with them?' Lila yelled from behind the car door.

'We're taking them home,' Jenny yelled back.

She'd had no intention of taking them home until witnessing their response to Lila, which was much like her own response to that woman who had allowed a surgeon with a knife to deduct ten years from her face and to give her the breasts of a marble statue, and who shoved Jenny's extra two years up her nose at their every meeting and bruised Jim with her breasts if he didn't dodge fast enough. With Vern at her heels and Lorna looking back at the bitch she wanted to fight, Jenny headed through the long grass of the top paddock, John close behind.

'What's going on?' Jim asked, half-in, half-out of the front door.

'Lila's back,' Jenny said.

'Then what are they doing here?'

'They don't like her facelift and neither do I,' Jenny explained as John took both ropes, freeing her to go indoors to fetch old bowls she could live without, and four eggs and the remainder of a bottle of milk. She served up two meals on either side of a veranda post, and while the dogs lapped eggs and milk, one eye on Jim and one on their feeder, John tied their ropes to the post and Jim placed more than his artificial leg out of doors.

The men drove together to Flanagan's to pick up the Holden. Jenny went shopping at Fulton's for dog bowls, worm pills, dog collars, chains and flea collars, guaranteed to keep a dog flea free for three months. She called into the butcher's on her way home to buy bones and, on John's instructions, and for the first time in her life, to pay for a liver she would have buried in Armadale.

The Toyota was parked in her drive when she returned, Lila terrorising Jim on the veranda. John stood between two rabid dogs, safe from her attack.

'You have to bring those mongrels back,' Lila said.

'They're staying where they are,' Jenny said, silencing the dogs with the matching leg bones of a cow. They would have preferred to sink their teeth into Lila's more meaty legs, but accepted the bribe and lay down to gnaw.

'I just got off the phone from Joe's solicitor and he said you have to bring them back.'

'Go away and spend your money. You worked hard enough to get it,' Jenny said.

'I won't get a red cent unless I've got those mongrels.'

'Which didn't worry you when you left them on their chains to die. If Harry hadn't found them, they would have been dead a week ago.'

'I didn't know what was in the mean old bugger's will then, did I? Anyway, I'm here now and you have to bring them back.'

'You're two weeks too late. They're mine.'

'Well I'm telling you that you can't have them. He signed most of his money over to his sons before he married me and he tied up the rest in a trust fund for his dogs. Unless I stay in the house and feed his mongrels I don't get a red penny.'

'Get a job like everyone else. You look young enough.'

'You finally admit it?' Lila said. 'Anyway, his solicitor said I could sue you for pinching them. They've got pedigrees a mile long.'

'They've got fleas too, and worms, and I've got witnesses to prove you left them for two weeks to starve on their chains, so charge me.'

'You wouldn't care if I starved.'

'I'll guarantee that when the last cow on earth is slaughtered, you'll end up with one of its hind legs,' Jenny said. 'Go, Lila, or I'll let my dogs off and you'll need plastic surgery on your sagging backside.'

'You're blind jealous, that's what's wrong with you, and you never got over me marrying Macka.'

'I pity him,' Jenny said. 'Want to know something else? I couldn't stand old Joe Flanagan when he was alive, but by God, he's gone up in my estimation since they buried him.'

'Yeah? Well you should have heard what he used to say about you,' Lila said.

'He called you the winter boomerang,' Jenny said. 'It didn't matter how far he pitched the thing, it kept on coming back – and I know exactly how he felt.'

*

Jim didn't want the dogs. Had Amy not been so frail, had John owned dog-proof fences, he would have taken then. He'd recently lost his well-behaved dog who'd understood unfenced boundaries.

Maisy's sheep farmer son-in-law said he'd take them, until he came around to get them and they told him in no uncertain terms that they weren't going anywhere. They liked Jenny. They loved John. Gave Jim dirty looks when he ventured out to the veranda but no longer snarled at him. They used one of his old sweaters as bedding – John's idea.

There had once been a gate to that driveway. They'd closed it when Trudy was small. Stopped closing it once she'd learnt not to wander from the yard. The years had buried it beneath a creeper, but it was still there. Two days of Jenny and John's labour with saw and secateurs released a galvanised gate, still intact. They didn't expect it to swing, but with a little oil applied to rusting hinges, it swung and latched.

'Vern Hooper only ever bought the best,' John said.

They were smart dogs and, of the two, Vern the more obedient to Jenny. She released him first from his chain. He had a sniff around, watered a couple of trees then returned to his chained mate where he remained until Amy approached Lorna and ended up scratching behind her ears. Jim, embarrassed by Amy's lack of fear, came out to watch her release Lorna. She approached Amy, wanting more scratching. She sniffed Jim's artificial leg. He froze, his hands raised, but she lost interest and sniffed her way to the closed gate where she barked her warning.

'Bad dog,' John said, and led her by the collar to the veranda. Three times she barked at that gate, and three times John led her back. She'd learn town manners or she'd know no freedom. She lay then to watch that gate but kept her distance from it.

Lila didn't return for her meal tickets, but a letter arrived from her solicitor. It led to two nights of searching for old receipts. Jenny's handbag was a gold mine, as were the pockets of John's tweed jacket. A typed, itemised account for dog food, flea powder, chains, collars, worm pills, butcher's bills, plus kennelling fees and petrol used while feeding the dogs twice a day at Joe's property was posted to old Joe's solicitor. A cheque for the total amount arrived by return mail.

# Lacy Hopkins

In early November, a taxi arrived at Number 12, and Lacy Hopkins emerged from it, as did her many cases. She was followed soon after by a small removalist's van. Powerless to prevent that homeless stray's invasion of her house, Amber removed her earmuffs and left via the rear door. She walked. She rode a bus, a train, a tram. She stood for minutes at Lorna's gates, remembering the clean calm comfort, the silence and serenity of that red-brick house.

Lost that day in wandering through a red haze of impotent anger. Couldn't recall eating lunch. Weak and weary when she returned to Flinders Street Station, she sat a while to rest, and slept where she sat. Lost the hours between seven and ten, dreamed of Norman and awoke in fright, confused, alone and too far from home, and too hard to get home. Walked out to the taxi rank.

A young driver, a gentle boy, opened the door for her and helped her out. She tipped him well, and for that he walked with her to the door, found the right key and the keyhole. Then, his car lights gone, she stepped inside and into the dark, closed the door and, as she had many times before, made her way through the dark towards her bedroom with a hand on the wall.

And fell. Fell hard over boxes, bags. The noise of her fall might have woken a sleeper, but no one came. For minutes Amber lay as she'd fallen, shaken. Not until the shock eased did she feel the pain of her fall. Her left breast, her shoulder, hip, ear, and . . . moisture. Her first movement came from her right hand. It rose to wipe the left side of her face. Tears are salt water and she had no more to shed. Blood has a stickiness to it. She identified the moisture as blood, and got a knee beneath her.

She knew where she was. She could feel carpet beneath her knee. Her left hand held to her breast, her right hand felt for the familiar and found . . .

Wrong. Found Norman's mother's crystal cabinet. Knew its doors. Knew its curved central drawers. She'd polished them a thousand times. She knelt there, running both hands over carved timber. And she didn't know where she was.

Using the crystal cabinet, she got her feet beneath her, then felt for the wall, then the light switch. Couldn't find it – not where it should have been. She found one. And in that blinding white light everything was wrong. Her mother-in-law's peacock feathers were there, in a brass urn, a long narrow urn with handles. The vase they belonged in was blue, blue/green, a china vase, and it should have been on Norman's wireless.

The wireless was in the corner where it belonged, a walnut cabinet model chosen by him to match the crystal cabinet's timber. She walked to it, her hand feeling for her glasses. Lost them in the fall, cut her nose with them. Looked for them on the floor beside the boxes. Ran her hand again over the crystal cabinet.

She'd married him for that cabinet, and for the dainty tea set with its gold-rimmed cups and delicate sugar basin. The cabinet was empty.

She turned in a half-circle towards the cardboard cartons where she'd fallen. The tea set would be in one of them. She'd forgotten something, that's all. There was no need to panic. It would come to her. She turned to the feathers and the brass urn, certain she'd never seen that urn before. Walked to it, touched the feathers. Beautiful things, though dust gatherers, and they belonged on Norman's wireless, which wasn't his wireless but a television.

Gave up attempting to work out where she was, whether she was old or young, dreaming or awake, but whoever had emptied that crystal cabinet was not getting away with it.

She opened the smaller carton. Didn't find the gold-rimmed tea set, but as we do in dreams, she found previously unseen treasures. A crystal sweet set with a gold leaf pattern, a perfect cut glass vase. She found six crystal wine glasses. Found a lacquered bowl where Japanese ladies danced and, too weary to do more, she rested a moment on the couch to admire that bowl, to turn it in circles, watching the Japanese ladies dancing in an endless circle, and she thought of the six china sisters she'd found in the dark of Lorna's cabinet, soiled sisters she'd bathed back to beautiful . . .

Amber slept where she sat, on the couch, the bowl on her lap, and woke to the voice from hell.

'You had no right to touch Lacy's things,' Sissy yelled and Amber reached for the earmuffs she kept beside her bed. No earmuffs. No bed – then remembered why she had no bed.

'She's got blood everywhere,' Lacy said. 'She's hurt herself, Sissy.'

And thus the two women in Sissy's life met.

*

Twenty-two years Lacy had spent at her trade, before her marriage, after her marriage. She'd handled all types, the old and the young, the sweet natured and the foul. For years she'd cared for her mother, who'd progressed from fastidious to foul. Had she known Amber's history, Lacy might have kept her distance. Sissy had mentioned that her father had died young, but withheld how he'd died. Lacy went to the bathroom to fetch a damp cloth. Amber went to her bedroom and closed her door.

Sissy had spoken for hours about her mother's dementia. On that first day at Number 12, Lacy saw evidence of her dementia.

Amber, earmuff clad, went about the house oblivious to its other occupants.

As she ever had with the elderly, Lacy smiled too much, she called Amber dear. She told her that she was a nurse and asked if she might have a look at Amber's injured ear, her swollen nose. Amber left the house and returned in a taxi – late but in daylight – and she handed the driver a fifty-dollar note then walked away without her change.

'That was a fifty-dollar note, dear, not a five. How far did he drive you?' Lacy asked. Amber ignored her and walked to her room to fetch her earmuffs.

Lacy liked a tidy house. She was vacuuming the bedroom she shared with Sissy when Amber entered with a can of deodorant spray which she used liberally on Sissy's frocks, her sheets, and in Lacy's face when she dared to reach for the spray can. She dropped the vacuum cleaner and ran to the bathroom, and when she returned Amber had control of the vacuum.

Lacy bought two kilos of minced steak on pension day. She portioned it into four plastic bags which she flattened with a palm, sealed, then stored in the freezer. Amber opened the freezer, removed the minced steak and tossed it into the kitchen tidy. Lacy rescued it and returned it to the freezer. It went missing again that night.

She'd been patient but was becoming annoyed, and alone she took the bus to town where she bought two kilos more, then took over the kitchen for a day while turning that meat into a minced-steak stew, a meatloaf, bolognaise and a curry. She served the curry that evening. Amber scraped her meal into the kitchen tidy.

Reg in the front seat, the two women in the rear, the trio went to church on Sunday. Amber put a leg of lamb in the oven to roast. It was sizzling when the churchgoers returned, when Sissy's stray peeled four onions, impaled them two by two on skewers, opened the oven and tossed them into the pan fat, her eyes daring Amber to remove them.

She didn't. She stole Lacy's skewers when she washed the dishes.

A cold war, it continued until one pension day in mid-December. The house was still Amber's on pension days, but that day when the two returned, Sissy's neglected hair had been cut short and bleached to the same shade as her homeless stray's.

Amber stood, her back to the sink, until the shopping bags were heaved onto the table, a lump of minced steak removed from one and dumped determinedly on Amber's sink where bacteria bred while they made tea, while they opened a packet of Tim Tams.

Then Lacy removed a large picture book from a plastic bag.

'They wrote it,' Sissy said to Amber.

Amber could see a family of sparrows stepping down to . . . to Norman's railway station. She stepped closer to the table.

'It's them and the McPhersons,' Sissy said.

Amber was staring at the station, at the family of sparrows, the Daddy Sparrow toting the family's luggage, and beneath the sparrows the words *J. and A. McPherson, J. and J. Hooper.*

It was Norman's stray, the motherless brat he'd decided to raise and the swine who'd ruined Sissy's life. For a time Jim Hooper had been engaged to Sissy. Amber turned back to the sink and the mound of disease-riddled minced steak. It angered her. Sissy's stray angered her. A world in which others were in control angered her.

There is a dark place where the damned dwell, where red mists rise to engulf and the fine threads of self-control unravel. Blame that meat, its blood seeping. Blame the television blaring in the parlour, and the barking dog, and Sissy's stray blathering on about little Cathy, and little Sean and little Thomas. Get rid of her meat and she'd buy more. Get rid of her and there'd be another. Always another homeless stray to infiltrate the clean, the calm Amber required to survive, as there'd always be another stray dog to bark at that fence.

Amber picked up her handbag and walked out. She stood on the footpath for a moment, staring at the house she'd schemed to possess, the house she'd spent Amber's and Elizabeth's savings on making more than it had been. She'd chosen the carpet – and stained it with her blood. She'd chosen the drapes, the lounge suite, the washing machine, and that homeless stray had walked in and taken the lot – and Sissy.

Five babies Amber had carried. She walked away from the last of them that day to become Maryanne Brown. Rode the bus, the train, then rode a tram to Richmond where she used her private mailbox key to retrieve six envelopes and two bankbooks, Maryanne's and Margaret's. It was a long trip from Doveton. Once a month she emptied that box. She cashed Elizabeth's cheques at the post office. They knew her there. They thought they knew her. A middle-aged woman asked after her health.

No chatter in Elizabeth Duckworth today. Amber zipped her notes into her handbag's inner pocket and she went on her way. Such a grand game she'd played, but too old to play any more. Such a grand life she'd led as Elizabeth. Lost her. Lost her Royal Doulton vases. Lost her Waterford crystal bowl. Lost Number 12.

She had her pocket accounts, but in a world that had long outpaced her, how could she start again? Caught a tram into the city. Margaret Hooper's bank was in Swanston Street. She made her way there, joined the queue. She was reaching for the correct envelopes when she stabbed her finger on one of the stray bitch's skewers, in her handbag since the day of the roasted onions. She'd had plans for those skewers. Another plan that wouldn't come to fruition. Dripping blood onto one of Margaret's envelopes, she stood staring at it, and at her middle finger where blood oozed up rich and red. Aged skin rips like paper. A woman queuing behind her offered her a tissue. Amber took it, wrapped her finger and moved forward to pay in Margaret's cheques then to withdraw what she'd paid in last month. She didn't need the money, her pocket accounts were bulging, but Maryanne and Margaret had never allowed their balances to grow large.

Walked on then towards Maryanne's bank, a red flower blooming on white tissue. Red for Christmas. She crossed over Bourke Street, wondering if Myers were ready to display their Christmas windows. How many days left until Christmas? Didn't know. Didn't care. Sissy's stray would cook the Christmas chicken. Amber Morrison was redundant. And those magical windows had been unveiled for Amber to see one final time, and there was space to see them today. She pressed in between a woman with a fat brat of a child and an elderly male and his woman.

Alone between them. Always alone, though never alone in Kew. She'd lived a companionable life there, had walked with Lorna, read with her, sat with her in theatres and restaurants, sat at her side in church each Sunday. Led a good and useful life until mud-eyed Sissy had ruined it. Born to ruin. Her birth had ruined Amber's dreams of beautiful Ruby Rose. For years she'd tried to make her be Ruby Rose. She'd bought her pretty frocks, spent hours on her hair, Sissy's one saving grace, that mass of heavy hair.

*There was a little girl and she had a little curl,*
*right in the middle of her forehead.*
*When she was good she was very, very good*
*and when she was bad she was horrid.*

Amber was unaware she'd mouthed that old rhyme aloud until the brat pulled on her mother's arm.

'That lady said I was horrid, Mummy.'

The woman looked at the well-dressed lady, then took her daughter's hand and they walked on, Amber watching fat little thighs rub together.

She sniffed. Smelled whining brat on the city air, smelled age on the old man at her side; his wife's perfume brought back memories of Maisy.

The smells of life, she thought. She'd never forget the scent of her father's hair. How many years had she waited for him to come back and take her away to his fine house with his maids to iron her pretty gowns and polish her fancy shoes?

*A bud near ripe for the plucking.*

Loved the scent of his hair. Loved him. Hated him when he hadn't returned. Always confusing, the love, the hate. Confusing, too, how the eye recognised beauty while the heart rejected it.

Amber swayed but steadied herself against the plate glass while shaking the past from her mind. Old age too often sent the mind reeling back to yesterday.

Every year since '61, she'd stood here. Next year's display would be different and the year after that, and the year after that and soon she wouldn't be here to see them. She placed her bleeding hand flat on the glass to bid those clockwork creatures goodbye, then walked on, her tissue lost, her injured finger leaving blood on her frock as she felt her breast, still bruised from her fall, painful, swollen and leaking red milk, fit only for the devil's child. Felt the other breast, sucked flat and dry by Sissy.

The traffic lights green, she crossed over and walked on towards Maryanne's bank, glancing in windows at beautiful things, stopping to admire a tray of diamond rings. She'd once owned a diamond ring. Looked at her left hand, old, the knuckles swollen. As a girl she'd had beautiful hands. Maisy had said so. Buy Maryanne Brown an engagement ring.

Far better she buy gloves to hide her hands than a diamond to laugh at them.

Gloves no longer in vogue, the shop doors were closing before an assistant found her a pair of lacy things, white. Amber paid, and while waiting for her change she pulled them on. Blood still seeping. Nothing she could do to stop its seeping.

Norman's blood had seeped into the pillow, into the mattress—

But she'd saved him from old age. He would have thanked her for that. She'd never wanted it, never expected to grow old. Age crept up while the back was turned.

She was close to Maryanne's bank when her feet came to a halt before a restaurant where only the finest meals, the best wines were served. She'd sat in that restaurant with Lorna, had eaten lobster there and craved a glass of wine. Lorna had ordered water. Tonight she'd drink her wine.

A black-clad waiter eyed her as she entered, but it was still early and he had empty tables. He led her to a table for two in a corner where she got her back to a wall, and when he asked if she'd be dining alone, she told him her companion would be joining her.

'A glass of water?' he asked.

'Champagne – and a bandaid, if you please,' she said.

*

An unforgettable two hours for that black-clad waiter. He'd speak of it and of Maryanne Brown many times in the coming year, how she'd been the size of a sparrow, but over a two-hour period had managed to put away two-thirds of a bottle of champagne and two serves of lobster when her companion hadn't arrived. He'd speak of how, when he'd presented her with the bill, she'd placed the uncorked bottle into her shopping bag and asked to borrow his biro. He'd given it to her, believing she meant to check his addition, but she'd taken an envelope from her handbag, removed a pension cheque, signed it and offered it to him with the bill. He'd gone to get his manager, who'd explained to the old dear that they couldn't accept her cheque as payment.

'When we can't trust our own government's cheques we're in a bad way, aren't we?' she said, and reached again into her handbag – not for cash, but for a second envelope.

They watched her sign a second cheque, watched her stand, watched her walk away, the uncorked bottle in her shopping bag.

# Funerals

In January '88, Australia celebrated two hundred years of European settlement. Prince Charlie and Lady Di arrived in Sydney to add their royal presence to the occasion. The six o'clock news that night was full of them and the re-enactment of the First Fleet's landing. There was barely time to slot in half a dozen words about an elderly woman found dead in her bed.

At ten thirty they broadcast more Charlie and Di, and again mentioned the elderly woman believed to have been dead for some weeks. They interviewed the neighbour who'd raised the alarm after junk mail from her neighbour's overflowing letterbox had been blowing across the road onto her front lawn for days.

*When I saw one of the junk mail deliverers piling in more, I went over to tell him that the owner was on holiday. Then the woman who lived next door came out and said that maybe we ought to call the police, that she hadn't seen the old lady since about a week before Christmas, and that when her son had climbed over the fence to get his ball yesterday, he'd said there was a bad smell coming from the bathroom window. That's when we contacted the authorities.*

'What a world,' Jim said. 'Someone must have missed her.'

'People don't know their neighbours down there,' Jenny said.

It was getting to be that way in Woody Creek, or so it seemed to her. Maisy knew everyone. She still called in for a cuppa on her way home from Willama on Tuesdays, still kept Jenny abreast of the town news. She came the following day. The dogs were tied up on Tuesdays and the gate left open so Maisy could drive in.

'Guess who I just ran into in Willama?' Maisy greeted her.

'Who?'

'The unmentionable. She came straight at me in that big new roundabout they've put in down the bottom end of Main Street.'

'Lila?'

'Who else? She got out of her car and started snarling at my window, so I backed up and drove around her,' Maisy said.

Most agreed that Maisy shouldn't have been driving. She'd hit one or two of the town cars. Bernie had stopped having her dents straightened. Most also agreed that if Maisy's wheels and freedom were taken away from her, she'd curl up and die.

'You should have heard what she called me, and it wasn't my fault anyway. They've got no signs telling you that you have to take the long way around it to make a right-hand turn so I took the short way, and she slammed straight into me. Is Jim home?'

'He's in Willama with John.' Everyone knew that Amy was dying.

'How is she?'

'She's been in a coma since Sunday night.'

Jenny had sat with her on Sunday. John sat with her every day. Her kidneys had shut down. It was only a matter of time.

'John won't handle it. Remember Nancy Bryant, how she was dead a month or two after she lost Lonny? Maureen O'Brien was the same. She was dead in six weeks. How old would John be?'

'Gone eighty,' Jenny said.

'He was just a kid when Amy started teaching up here. He didn't have a word to say for himself, but he set his sights on her and never looked at another girl. She must be close to my age.'

'Eighty-eight. She goes with the century,' Jenny said. 'What did you want with Jim?'

'I was just wondering where his car was,' Maisy said. 'They say Melbourne will get forty degrees tomorrow. It's lucky they found that dead woman when they did.'

'She must have had relatives somewhere who'd missed her,' Jenny said.

'She was a spinster,' Maisy said. 'Sammy told Maureen that they had to cut a padlock off her gate and break into the house.'

'Heart attack?'

'Murdered, Sammy said, but you can't breathe a word of what I'm telling you. He wasn't even supposed to tell his mother. They reckon that it was someone she knew, someone she let in. No windows were broken.'

'How was she killed?'

'Bludgeoned,' Maisy said.

The beeping of a car horn ended their conversation. Jim was home and Maisy's aging Chrysler was blocking the drive. He never beeped at Maisy. He'd park in the street for Maisy and walk in. Jenny knew why he hadn't today.

'I think Amy's gone,' she said, standing, picking up Maisy's handbag and car keys. If Jim had John with him, the last person he'd need to see would be Maisy.

*

An appalling night. They'd been four for so many years. Now they were three – or two and one broken man. John didn't want to return to his empty house and he wouldn't go to bed, so they sat half the night with him, pouring wine and speaking of better nights. He hadn't slept for weeks and at two fell asleep on the couch. Jenny was asleep when the phone rang at eight the following morning. She rose to silence it, wanting John and Jim to sleep, but the caller, a male, asked to speak to Jim.

He came on one leg and his crutch and Jenny watched the blood drain from his face.

'It's Lorna,' he said. 'The woman on the news. It's Lorna.'

Jenny moved the chair she kept in the hall so he might sit, then stood, her hand on his shoulder, her own ear close to the phone, listening secondhand to the distant voice. As Lorna's next of kin, Jim was expected to make the official identification.

'My sister and I were estranged,' Jim said. 'I haven't seen her for many years. Our cousin, Ian Hooper, will have seen her more recently than I.'

He spoke for five minutes more, but Jenny walked away to dress for a day like no other.

'Murdered,' Jim said when he put down the phone. 'Blunt force trauma to her head and face, then they . . . mutilated her eyes . . . with kitchen skewers.'

'Stay where you are,' Jenny said as he tried to rise. 'I'll get your leg.'

She had two silent men, two dogs and a telephone to deal with, had gone to bed too late and been woken too early. She had no time to mourn Amy – didn't give Lorna a second of thought.

She drove with John to the undertaker where she learned that Amy would be forced to queue up for burial, that they'd have to wait through a weekend before they could put her death away. It was too long.

John surprised her. He had a strength she hadn't expected. He didn't want to be alone in his empty house so they gave him the big bedroom on the north-eastern corner; it had twin glass doors opening onto the veranda where the dogs spent their nights. They had a telepathic understanding of his loss, and each time he opened those doors, they were at his side, to offer their silent sympathy, to walk the garden with him.

Ian Hooper phoned, eager to rehash the details of Lorna's death. Mrs Watson called to offer her condolences, Jenny believing her condolence was for John and realising late it was for Jim. Lorna's notorious death was more newsworthy than the slow fading away of gentle Amy. Missed her. Sat alone at night turning the pages of the books they'd created together, free to mourn her in the dead of night. Not by day. She was strong by day, and she'd said her goodbyes on Sunday.

'Finish *Molly*,' Amy had said. 'Finish it in your own inimitable way, Jennifer.'

It was Jim's book. He'd spent years writing and rewriting it. Four publishers had rejected it and the last time it came back he had tossed it into the wood box.

'Light the fire with it,' he'd said.

The manuscript spent one night with the chips and kindling. She'd attempted to crumple a page to use as a firelighter. Couldn't crumple that anonymous poem, or any one of his pages. She knew the work, the hope that had gone into it, some of it her own, so she'd bundled it into a supermarket bag and taken it and the dogs for a walk down to the McPhersons'.

Her first teacher, Amy, her singing teacher and accompanist, her best friend and a hard editor. They'd gone through those pages together, had burnt many and added many more. Their secret this last twelve months, their private game.

Missed her, and on that gut-wrenching, soul-destroying morning when they carried her from the church, Jenny couldn't follow the coffin out. She sang 'The Last Rose of Summer' while the church cleared, and when it cleared, she escaped out the side door and went home to her dogs, who comforted her while she cried her heart out.

She fetched their leads when the men returned. John removed his suit jacket and tie and walked with her, the dogs wriggling with the pleasure of his company, and craving Amy's they turned towards the bridge. Too many times Jenny had walked them that way to Amy. Not today. She turned them towards the school.

'He's such a shy boy,' Amy used to say of John, but he spoke that day, to the dogs and to Jenny, he spoke of the retirement units being built down the bottom end of the school road, six single-bedroom brick units, built wall to wall on a block where Mrs Owen had lived and died. Two units were nearing completion. He spoke of buying into one, or into the Willama retirement units.

To Jenny the units looked like prison cells. 'Give yourself time,' she said.

A bad week followed before Lorna's body was released for burial. Jim brought her home to the vacant plot beside Vern's grave. It was the right thing to do. Had Lorna been born a male, she would have been the son Vern Hooper had wanted at his side.

It was a better attended funeral than Amy's. Many of the old brigade were there, not for Lorna, who in her lifetime had endeared herself to no one, but for the memory of Vern and the notoriety of her death. Jenny was there only for Jim, and for that wisp of hope that Jimmy would come home to bury his aunt. He didn't.

Jim's hand was well shaken that day. Jenny's remained firmly on her handbag. A few women who couldn't get to Jim offered her their condolences. She could have used them in '47. She was there only to make certain that the hole had been dug deep enough, and when Bill O'Brien told Jim that Vern would never be dead while Jim was alive, it was time to go. Jenny had spent the past thirty years denying that there was a skerrick of Hooper in Jim.

There was. Age has a habit of bringing to the fore family resemblances. Jim's steel-grey wire hair was his father's, as was his long jaw, and he'd always had his father's hands, though Vern's had been broadened by the heavy labour of his youth and Jim's refined by his years of typing. He walked with a limp, as had Vern, though only after he'd had his stroke.

Two couples had driven up from Melbourne to pay their last respects to Lorna, Jim's cousin Ian and his wife Lorris, and an elderly couple who introduced themselves as Martin and Mary Leeds; Martin was the former minister of the church Lorna had attended.

'Your sister's absence would have been noticed in our time there,' he said. 'She and her companion never missed a Sunday in their pew.' He looked to be ninety and his wife looked as old. Jenny asked them back to the house for lunch. She'd already invited Jim's cousin and his wife.

They were leaving the cemetery. They were outside the gate when Lorna got in her last hit from the grave. Dust, flicked up by a breeze, landed in Jenny's eye. A finger or handkerchief raised to remove it might suggest she'd shed a tear for Lorna and, a terrible death or not, let no one believe that Jenny had shed a tear for the woman. She drove home with dust in her eye.

Trudy removed it. She'd come home because of Lorna's will. *To my niece, Gertrude Juliana Hooper, I leave my all.*

'Why me, Mum?' Trudy asked again. 'She didn't even know me.'

That will had set Jenny back on her heels. Lorna had seen Trudy once in her life. They'd collided in the entrance hall, back in the mid-sixties. Trudy, a three year old at the time, couldn't remember the collision but had retained an image of a black-clad witch sitting on their floor, showing her knee-length bloomers. It was the first time she'd seen such bloomers. She remembered the haunted house where she'd been taken that night, and that's all she remembered.

'Why me, and not Dad?'

'She didn't approve of his choice of wife,' Jenny said.

'I'm not even her blood.'

'As far as she knew, you were her father's granddaughter.'

'Why not Jimmy? You said they'd adopted him.'

'Lorna's sister adopted him and gained control of the Hooper estate. That time you collided with Lorna, she'd come up here wanting your dad to go to court to stop the sale of the Monk portion of the land the haunted house was built on.'

'Dad's family owned Monk's?'

'They did for a lot of years.'

'What's Lorna's house like?'

'Brick, tiled roof, high fence and a tramline half a dozen houses away.'

'Kew is a good area. It could be worth a lot of money. Georgie and Paul paid over a hundred thousand for a house way out at Greensborough,' Trudy said. 'When did you see her house?'

'Back in the fifties.'

Jenny sliced lettuce and tomatoes, Trudy worked at her side, efficient in the kitchen. She'd spent much of her early life at Jenny's elbow.

'I'd feel like such a fraud if I took her money, Mum.'

'It's yours, darlin', to do with what you will.'

They served their guests in the dining room, served a ham salad followed by trifle, Trudy's specialty. Ian Hooper spoke of Lorna, whom he hadn't seen in three years though he'd heard from her more recently. Martin Leeds, Lorna's executor, who had last seen Lorna three months ago, told them that both he and his wife had suggested Miss Hooper sell her home and move into a church-run retirement home.

'It was obvious to us that she wasn't managing alone,' he said.

'Your sister was a very determined woman,' his wife said.

'However, one had to respect her desire for independence,' Martin said.

The visitors left in convoy. John closed the gate and released the dogs, who chased the scent of strangers to the gate where they warned them not to return. John raised his voice and they came to his side, heads and tails down. They were more than half human, and if it was possible to fall in love with middle-aged dogs, Jenny had fallen hard. Vern Hooper's garden belonged to them and for Jenny, they'd altered its character – and its scent.

They spoke of Lorna's house that night, Trudy wavering between signing it over to the church and selling it as it stood and donating the money to charity. It was not in a saleable condition, according to Sammy, Maisy's grandson. He'd suggested Jim hire professional cleaners – with shovels and a truck. He'd offered the name and phone number of such a company. Jenny wanted to call them. Jim wanted the old Hooper documents he'd handled in his youth.

'If any of them have survived, they'll be in Lorna's house,' he said.

'I'm not going anywhere near that place, Jim.'

Trudy went near it. She phoned on Friday. 'Tell Dad I've got Monday and Tuesday off next week and that I'll give him a hand to find what he wants before I get in the cleaners. It's chaos, Mum. Sophie and I had a quick look through it, and you've never seen such a mess in your life.'

Then Georgie rang. 'Trude said that you don't want to leave John on his own up there.'

He'd moved home before Lorna's funeral, his means of evading any obligation to attend, though he spent little time in that empty house. He ate at Jenny's table, walked the dogs with her, and there was no way Jenny would leave him or her dogs to search Lorna's house for Hooper history.

'We're a long way from Kew,' Georgie said, 'but we've got two spare rooms and a spare bathroom between them. Tell John he's more than welcome to one.'

'I can't leave the dogs, love,' Jenny said.

'Harry will feed them.'

'His leg might. They don't like him. I'll try the Willama kennels and get back to you, Georgie.'

She wanted to stay at Greensborough. She'd heard about Georgie's house but had never seen it. In recent years she'd seen too little of Georgie, and as for Paul Dunn, he'd been up here twice, briefly. She might have spoken ten words to him and heard ten back.

On the phone half an hour later, she was discussing immunisations, unaware dogs had immunisations, and she didn't have a clue whether old Joe's dogs had been immunised or not. Knowing him, probably not, and the kennel wouldn't take her dogs until they'd had their shots, and how was she supposed to get them down to Willama to have their shots—

John tapped her on the shoulder. 'I'll look after the dogs,' he said.

# HATE

They left John, installed again in the rear room, the refrigerator full of easy meals for him and the dogs. He'd done most of the food preparation this past year and, unlike Jim, wasn't useless in a kitchen. Left him on the Sunday morning, a dog at each heel. Hoped he'd be okay.

'We'll phone you tonight,' Jenny called.

With the aid of a Melway's directory, they found Georgie's street, and eventually her house, a brown brick with a terracotta tiled roof, triple fronted, relatively modern but with a narrow drive, where by seven that evening, five vehicles were parked nose to tail. Trudy was spending the night in Georgie's second spare bedroom, and before the morning traffic was too heavy, she'd guide Jim via an easy route across town to Kew.

The house woke at six and by seven thirty four of the five vehicles had cleared the drive, leaving Georgie's old ute to stand alone, and Jenny to wait alone in a strange house in a strange land. That Monday morning may have been the longest of her life. She weeded the garden, made a pot of soup out of what she could find – and she couldn't find much. She baked a lemon cake to use up a few of the stockpiled eggs. Could find no icing sugar, and had used most of Georgie's butter in the cake.

The keys to the ute hung on a hook beside the fridge. Georgie now drove a cream Datsun and went to work in a business suit. She didn't look like Jenny's Georgie. She looked like half of a business couple, and Jenny felt out of place in that couple's house. Wanting out of it, she took the ute keys from their hook, locked the back doors, deadlocked the front door behind her and walked down to the ute. She'd seen shops on a corner when they'd driven in yesterday. She'd find them.

The ute coughed. It coughed, caught, shuddered then died. She persevered until the battery died. Locked it and looked at her watch. She still had almost five hours to fill before the workers came home. Reversing her actions, she unlocked the front door and phoned a taxi. Waited twenty minutes for it to arrive, then told the driver that she needed to go to a big supermarket somewhere. Should have been more specific. He took her touring for miles, then pulled into a rank out front of a huge enclosed centre where she spent the next half-hour searching for a supermarket.

Dangerous things, supermarkets. They offer you a massive trolley and somehow you manage to fill it. And she got lost on the way back to the taxi rank.

Taxi drivers used to open their door for passengers. There were three lined up waiting for a fare. She opened the rear door of the first in line, tossed in three bags, propped the trolley against a no parking sign and crawled into the taxi with the last two bags.

'Greensborough,' she said, and she gave him Georgie's address.

Smell of stranger in the taxi – of stale stranger sweat. She opened a window, just a little, considered lighting a cigarette, glanced at him, hoping the driver would light one and give her leave to. He didn't. Dark greying hair, something familiar about the back of his head, or the way it was attached to his shoulders. She shrugged her own shoulders down and told herself that she was in Melbourne where one in ten people looked familiar. She'd seen a younger Maisy at the supermarket.

He knew the roads, or she hoped he did. She sat back, found the end of the seat belt beneath her shopping, buckled herself in then settled back to watch the traffic, pleased she was being driven and not driving in it.

It wasn't only his hairline and neck that was familiar. She could see his left ear and she knew it.

Idiot, she thought. Ears all look the same.

But they don't. Ears could be as different as eyes. Jim's ears were big. John's ears were small and the driver's ear looked like . . .

She was being ridiculous. She'd last seen those ears in a courtroom, their wearer strapped into a wheelchair, oxygen bottles strapped to that chair. The driver wasn't sucking on bottled oxygen.

She checked the money in her purse. Taxis were expensive these days. Back in the forties she'd caught one once from Spencer Street Station to Armadale and paid the driver a few coins – her last few coins, which back in those days would have fed her and her kids for a week. She'd empty her purse today. Supermarkets swallowed money.

Again her eyes were drawn to the driver's ear. There was not much else she could see of him – his ear, his neck and his hairline. Wished he'd say something. Most taxi drivers wouldn't shut up. This one hadn't said a word. His concentration was on the road, as it should be, she told herself – and no longer believed herself. He'd recognised her when she'd walked out with her trolley. That's why he hadn't spoken.

His ear had no lobe. The first day Raelene brought him to the house, Jenny had spent a lot of time looking at that ear. Hadn't liked it, or his eyes. If she could see his eyes, she'd know him. Determined to get a look at his eyes, his face, she moved her shopping bags, eased more of the seat belt free and slid a little towards the centre of the seat.

He was wearing the taxi driver's cap, its visor pulled low to meet wraparound dark glasses. She could see the side of his jaw. Dino Collins had been left with scars, very few teeth and a section of his jaw caved in. Which side of his jaw? The jaw she could see wasn't scarred or caved in.

Closing her eyes, she attempted to see the face in the courtroom. Saw the oxygen bottle. Saw the nurse seated beside her patient, saw his bandaged hand—

Knew how she'd recognise him! H A T E had been tattooed across the knuckles – of his left hand. She sat higher in her seat, sat forward. His left hand wasn't on the wheel, or not until he made a right-hand turn – and he was wearing a leather half-glove, skin toned, fingers free. Why, on a day like today? Because it covered up his H A T E as he'd covered it up in the courtroom, as he'd covered it with bandaids the first day Raelene had brought him home . . .

It *was* him, and she'd given him Georgie's address and, her heart-beat quickening, she cursed herself for a fool. Then cursed herself for being a fool with an overactive imagination and for giving herself the jim-jams over nothing. Even if it was him, he had no way of knowing that it was Georgie's address – and taxi drivers' hands on the wheel all day in heavy traffic probably sweated – as were her own.

She'd know his voice anywhere.

'A lot of traffic on the road,' she said.

His reply was barely intelligible, a comment on school holidays, his accent marking him as some breed of European, newly arrived on Australian shores, and every nerve in Jenny's body screamed with relief as she sat back to watch the meter.

He found the street and the address. She handed him a ten-dollar note, didn't wait for her change, then, her hands loaded with five heavy shopping bags, she closed his door with her hip and walked towards the house next door, hoping to get a look at his face when he turned the car around. He continued forward. There must have been an alternative route back to the highway.

Everyone has a double, she thought, the shopping at her feet, her fingers fumbling to unlock the front door. She'd seen John McPherson's double once in Willama and had almost spoken to him, and everywhere she went she saw Maisy's double.

She stocked Georgie's pantry and fridge, placed the pot of soup back onto a hotplate, added a pinch of ground ginger, a dash of Worcestershire sauce, a shake of black pepper and four chicken drumsticks. Stood watching it until it settled down to a simmer, then had a shower, needing to wash the thought of Collins from her skin, her hair. By five thirty when Paul walked in, she was seated in the kitchen, doing a crossword.

'I didn't hear your car,' she said.

'It's out the front,' he said. 'I've got a class tonight.' He lifted the lid of the soup pot. 'Smells good.'

'I had a long day to fill,' she said.

'They are all long,' he said.

That was the extent of their conversation. He disappeared into his study and fifteen minutes later, Jim arrived, or came as far as the back door where he took his shoes and shirt off, asked if Georgie was home and, when Jenny shook her head, removed his wallet and car keys from his pocket then dropped his trousers and removed his socks and singlet.

'That bad?' she said.

'You don't want to know,' he said. And she did want to know, but he'd walked inside, clad in his boxer shorts.

With finger and thumb Jenny transferred his clothing to Georgie's washing machine, fifteen years junior to her own. She was still attempting to work out which buttons to push when Georgie came in via the rear door.

Solicitor Georgie started the machine, in her white shirt and grey skirt, grey stockings and smart shoes, her hair pinned up in a roll. She'd never been a stocking person, or a shirt and skirt person.

'I smell home cooking,' she said. 'I'll have a fast shower then we'll eat if it's ready. Paul's got a class at seven thirty.'

Fast had always meant fast with Georgie. She was back in the kitchen five minutes later clad in t-shirt and shorts, barefoot and her hair hanging – Georgie again. With still no sign of Jim, Jenny went to their borrowed room and found him seated on their borrowed bed, considering his leg.

'Get it on. We're ready to eat,' she said.

'Start without me,' he said.

'How bad?'

'Uninhabitable,' he said.

She picked up his boxer shorts. 'Did you find what you were looking for?'

'She's got two filing cabinets full of every piece of paper she's received in her life. The old stuff will be there. We need to clear some space before I start going through the cabinet.'

'Your trousers were filthy.'

'We should have thought to pack my gardening clothes,' he said, and his leg on, he hitched his trouser leg down then followed her out to the kitchen. The laundry was next door. Jenny lifted the lid to toss the boxer shorts in with the rest, then the machine worked on, unsupervised.

Fifteen years ago, her twin tub machine had been modern. Thirty years ago, the old Pope washing machine with its built-in mangle had been a miracle of modern man. Forty-odd years ago, she'd almost bowed down and worshipped running hot water and a scrubbing board. Georgie's machine had inbuilt intelligence. Where would it end? Would it end?

The house was eight years old, but to Jenny it was another miracle of modern man's ingenuity. The kitchen was down one end of a large family room which opened out to a paved barbecue area. Where the paving ended, the garden began. A door in the kitchen opened into the laundry. Jenny had to walk through sun, wind and rain to get to her own laundry. Georgie's kitchen had a built-in dishwasher with its own intelligence. At home, Jenny was the dishwasher.

Space for a couch and comfortable chairs in the family room, and for a good-sized television, positioned so the eaters could keep up with the news while they ate. Jenny had to screw her neck around to see it. Jim's back was to it, but his mind was elsewhere tonight.

*A mother and her three small children died in an overnight house fire.*

*Thirty-five year old male arrested for the rape and murder of a nineteen year old girl.*

*New leads in the investigation into the murder of Lorna Hooper, found dead in her Kew home . . .*

Jim flinched.

'Have you heard anything in recent years about Dino Collins, Georgie?' Jenny asked.

'Not in years,' Georgie said.

'Do you ever hear from Jack Thompson?'

'I saw him on the box a month ago. He looks like his father.'

Paul left before seven, with a slice of lemon cake to eat on the way. Georgie stacked the dishwasher and Jim went into the sitting room to watch the ABC news – or to sit alone and process his day.

'Is he okay?'

'He's been quiet since he heard about her murder. He said the other night that she'd been more mother than sister to him when he was a kid. A dominating bitch of a mother, but there, I suppose,' Jenny said.

'He looks shell shocked,' Georgie said. 'Are you going with him tomorrow?'

'I told him at home that I was having nothing to do with that house – and I'm not – and I'm not going to feel guilty about it either.'

And she had more on her mind than Jim's shell shock. She couldn't get that taxi driver out of her head. Kept seeing his gloved hand. Kept seeing that covered-up H A T E. And though his accent had made her feel mistaken about recognising him, anyone could put on a convincing accent for half a dozen words. Get a few glasses of wine into John and he could do a perfect Scottish accent. She could do a half-reasonable Italian. If it was him, he would have recognised her before she'd recognised him. He'd hated her. He'd hated Georgie more. She'd been closer to his age than Raelene and she'd spurned his advances.

And I've led him to her.

Of course it hadn't been him. Driving a taxi would be the least likely occupation Dino Collins would choose. He wasn't the type to spend his days at the beck and call of passengers.

Jim went to bed early. Had they been at home she would have gone with him. She wasn't at home so she phoned John, just a quick call. He said that all was well with him and the dogs, so she phoned Nobby and spoke at length to him, or he spoke at length. He told her of a house full of newspapers, of clothing piled in corners, of empty tins and packets, plastic rubbish bags spilling their loads of rotting food. He told her of unwashed dishes, and a car rusting in the drive.

'Trudy was worth her weight in gold. She got Jim interested in the furniture. He said he'd grown up with it. There are a few nice old pieces, neglected but intact.'

Jim was still tossing when she slid into bed at eleven. She told herself that she had to go with him tomorrow, but by one she'd changed her mind. Tossed until two, when she dreamed of Collins. He was inside Georgie's house and she was alone. Woke gasping for air, and decided to track Jack Thompson down in the morning, or ring Maisy and get Maureen's number. Sammy would know if Collins was alive or dead. She'd talked herself out of that come daylight and decided to go into the city with Georgie. She could fill a day there. She and Jimmy had filled many days riding city trams when Ray had been on the nightshift. No way was she staying here alone tomorrow, not after that dream.

*

They were in the city before eight thirty, as was everyone else. She caught a tram to Armadale, got off at the old tram stop then walked the streets that were no longer familiar. Tall brick houses now stood on blocks of land where small weatherboard homes had once stood. Ray's house was unchanged apart from its concrete driveway and its altered garden. The woman watering the garden might have been Flora Parker. Jenny's footsteps slowed to stare at her back, but forty years ago she'd had nothing in common with Flora, so she walked on to the corner, where Wilma Fogarty had hosted her Friday night card games. No sign of her ramshackle old house. A block of double-storey units now stood on Wilma's land, and God help Doreen's little house next door, which would see no sunlight.

No one to visit now in this sprawling city, only Nobby and Rosemary, who'd be at Kew again with Jim and Trudy – where she should have been but wasn't.

Walked back to the tram stop and returned to the city. Trams hadn't altered. Still rattled down the same lines, stopped at the same stops, squealed around the same corners and shed their load in the middle of Swanston Street. She went shopping for workman's overalls for Jim, and two t-shirts, a pair of drill trousers, then she walked down to Fletcher Jones to order a replacement pair of grey slacks. The company had Jim's measurements on file. The last pair they'd made for him she'd left swinging dolefully on the clothes line this morning.

She found a theatre where *The Man from Snowy River* was playing and, her shopping on the seat beside her, she watched a movie she'd been wanting to see for months. There was no scent in the world like the scent of Melbourne theatres. She loved it, or the memories it raised of sitting in old theatres with Jimmy at her side. He'd sit as quiet as a little mouse, watching anything that flashed on that screen. He'd liked going to Coles cafeteria for an ice-cream sundae, so that's what she ate for lunch there, a raspberry sundae, Jimmy's favourite, three big scoops of ice-cream and a wafer cut into triangles. The sails, Jimmy had named those pieces of wafer. In the forties, Coles had served their sundaes in metal, boat-shaped bowls. Their metal bowls had given way to glass, but she scraped it clean.

A dragging day and, weighed down by her load, she envied a woman hurrying by with a small shopping buggy so decided she was old enough and went in search of one of those shopping bags on wheels. Found one in the doorway of a cluttered little shop, and it was her colour, a deep peacock blue. She went on her way then, just another elderly shopper walking free and filling up its emptiness on the way back to where Georgie had parked her car. She bought a ton of fruit and, just for fun, a kilo of sausages.

'Sausages? How rare,' Georgie would say.

She'd started it as a twelve year old, the day Jenny had come home from Willama with sausages for dinner, halfway between cheeky brat and woman then. Her 'How rare,' had continued through thirty years. She'd be forty-eight in March, two years away from fifty, and to Jenny the idea of Georgie being fifty was ridiculous. Only yesterday Jenny had been fifty, only the day before yesterday she'd been fifteen.

*How did I get to sixty-four?* How did little Jenny Morrison grow a solicitor, a schoolteacher, and Margot, who in turn had grown a nursing sister – one with a charitable heart. Trudy was determined to sell Lorna's house and give away half of what she received for it.

No sign of Georgie. She'd said she could become tied up and not get away on time. She wasn't smoking, or only smoking at parties. Keeping her eye on the corner, Jenny lit a cigarette, intending to smoke it before Georgie turned that corner. Her mind was far away when solicitor Georgie tapped her on the shoulder.

'I was expecting you to come from the other direction.'

'You're twisted,' Georgie said.

'I was born that way,' Jenny said, crushing the butt beneath her shoe.

'You don't need to waste it. I smoke if I feel like smoking.'

'I know what I was like when I stopped,' Jenny said.

'You look as if you've been buying out Melbourne.'

'Most of it's working clothes for Jim.'

They lifted the loaded buggy into the boot, then they were in and away, and nothing more was said until a traffic light stopped them.

'Do you like your job?'

'I didn't have to pay to get the legal work done on the house.'

'That's it?'

'I've got the wrong attitude for it, Jen. I can't yet see as innocent those who are guilty as sin. I want to hang the mongrel Boss God Marino is defending at the moment but he'll probably get him off.'

'Then why do it?'

'Your fault.' Georgie braked, ten or so cars back from another red light. 'You spent half your life telling me I had brains enough to do anything. I decided to prove you right – or wrong.'

'Why law?'

'I had a dream,' Georgie said with feeling.

'What?'

'Me standing in a courtroom convicting Dino Collins.'

'I could have sworn he was driving my taxi yesterday,' Jenny said.

'I used to see him on every motorbike that roared by.'

The traffic crawling at a snail's pace, they made it through the next lights as they changed to red. Two other cars made it through behind them.

'I don't know how you stand this day every day.'

'I can't,' Georgie said. 'If you want to smoke, smoke.'

'I'll smoke when we get home. When I lived down here before the war, no one could have conceived of this many cars in the entire world,' Jenny said.

'Your water-pistol bandit managed to get his hands on a few.' They'd done most of one block before she spoke again. 'I found him a while back.'

'You found Laurie Morgan?'

'The one and only,' Georgie said.

'Where?'

'Where you lost him.'

'In Geelong?'

'He owns a secondhand bookshop.'

'My God. How did you track him down?' Jenny asked and she lit a cigarette and wound her window down.

'I didn't.' Georgie braked. 'His son walked into my office one night and he was the spitting image of him. Red hair, green eyes, same face, tall. Light me one, Jen.'

She drew on her cigarette and, as the traffic moved, slipped into the central lane, which appeared to be moving. 'I asked him if he was a relative of Laurence George Morgan, and he was his dear old dad.'

'And?'

'I drove down to Geelong and bought two books from him.'

'What did he say when you told him?'

'I didn't.'

'Why not?'

'Because he would have thought it was a bloody good joke – and at the time, I didn't feel like laughing.'

They drove on in silence until a solid block of traffic in front and behind slowed them to a first gear crawl.

'There must have been an accident,' Jenny said.

'It's normal here for this time of day. We'll be right once we get off this road.'

'Why buy so far out of town?'

'House, trees, price, and dirt that will grow anything.' She ashed her cigarette. 'Your bandit told me I looked like his mother. I've got a feeling that he had his suspicions.'

'He was worldly wise when I knew him, world weary too,' Jenny said.

'Hardly a fifteen year old's type.'

'I wasn't old enough to know what type he was. He was better than the alternative.'

'Namely?'

'Margot. Her fathers.'

'How do you have a kid you don't care about, Jen?'

'I don't know, love. I'm sorry now that I couldn't care about her. Before she was born, Granny used to tell me that I was making her from my flesh and blood. I never believed her – and still don't.

She was their flesh. I used to . . . used to hope she'd grow more like Maisy, that one day we'd find a common meeting ground. It wasn't fated.' They got through the next traffic lights. 'Are you going to see Laurie again?'

'I considered it for a time – considered taking you down there with me to see if he recognised you.'

'When did you find him?'

'April of '86.'

'And you left it until now to tell me?'

'He was something I had to come to terms with. I saw his son again, as a client, in my office. He's not my type.'

'Why?'

'I dunno,' Georgie said. 'And he's not much older than Trudy.'

They were stuck again in solid traffic before she spoke once more. 'I never wanted to know your water-pistol bandit, just to know that he was real. He was a bit like Santa Claus and Jesus to me when I was a kid, unseen, unknown but supposedly there.' She shrugged. 'I've seen him. He exists, and I don't need him in my life.'

'His kids are your blood.'

Georgie pointed to a couple in the lane beside them. 'Do you want to know them?'

'They're not my blood.'

'How do you know? From what I've read of Itchy-foot's diaries, he could have seeded the earth with relatives.'

And probably had, Jenny thought as she looked at the couple. The woman had curly blonde hair.

'I used to envy Jimmy's Grandpa and Margot's Nana, and all of their aunties when I was a kid,' Georgie admitted. 'I remember the night Granny got us out of bed to meet our grandfather, Norman, and I remember thinking, oh boy, I'm catching up with them. I had an aunty too, who needed two chairs to sit on, then the next thing I knew, Grandpa Norman was dead and Aunty Sissy had disappeared. My tongue was probably hanging out for a blood relative when Cara turned up. I welcomed her into my pack like a thirsting man sinking his head into a water trough.' She drew on the cigarette. 'She didn't hang around long.'

They were creeping towards a green light, but the red beat them. 'Blood is overrated,' Georgie said.

'I'm no expert on it.'

'Want to know the weirdest bit about the whole water-pistol bandit deal? Back when I was working in Geelong, I bought half a dozen books from the flirty-eyed old coot, and I didn't have a clue who he was. So much for the old genetic fireworks display.'

'What does he look like?'

'Like every other old coot who still thinks that women from fifteen to fifty are after his body. He's nothing like his mug shot. I wasn't certain he was who he was until he took his glasses off and I saw my own eyes looking back at me.'

'He probably saw his looking back at him.'

'Probably.'

'He'd be in his seventies now,' Jenny said.

'He doesn't look it. He's carrying too much weight, still got a good head of hair. Did you ever see a photograph of his mother?'

'He never mentioned her. He spoke about his sister once or twice. At the time I didn't know she was dead. He's still married?'

'I spoke to his wife on the phone. She sounded normal. There were kids in the background. The papers Jack's father dug up on him in '59 said he had two sons and an infant daughter. He could be breeding up a second family with a second or third wife. He looks capable of it.'

'They'd be his grandkids,' Jenny said and they drove on. 'I'm pleased you found him. I'm more pleased that you found him in a bookshop and not a jail. I've thought of him from time to time through the years.'

'He took advantage of a fifteen year old kid. You're supposed to hate him.'

'He thought I was nineteen, and he gave me you,' Jenny said.

'I know he cared about me, and if not for me, he probably would have been long gone from Melbourne.'

'He cared enough about me to find an abortionist.'

'It's what I wanted. Don't think of him as the bad guy. He was kind, and he did what he could to protect me at the end. "When it's over, it's over, sweetheart," he said. "Walk away from me. We're out of options."'

'Did he know where you were from?'

'Granny reported me missing in the papers.'

'He never bothered to look you up when they let him out,' Georgie said.

'Granny would have greeted him with her rifle.' Jenny drew on the cigarette. 'For three weeks he didn't touch me, other than to bandage my sprained ankle, and as soon as I could walk on it, he gave me a five-pound note and told me to buy a ticket home. I told him I wanted to stay. Had I been old enough to see outside of my own problems, I might have realised that he was as mixed up as me. Fifteen year old kids don't see far.'

'How come you didn't have an abortion?'

'Granny – and maybe him. The last day I saw him, when I asked him for the abortionist's address, he gave it to me and said, "Poor little Georgie." He would have been a kind father to you.'

'But wasn't, isn't, and such is life,' Georgie said. 'It makes you wonder, though, doesn't it?'

'About what?'

'Why his son chose Marino and Associates. Why he was brought into my cubbyhole. Paul reckons there's a big computer out there, a fat old controller sitting behind it, playing computer games and shaking with laughter as he looks down on the blood and guts and chaos he manages to create.'

'Do you love him, Georgie?'

'None of your business, Jen.'

'Do you like your job?'

'I'm making good money.'

'Is it what you want to do for the rest of your life?'

'Ask a plague of fleas if sucking on your smelly dogs' backsides is what they want to do for the rest of their lives. That's all we are, a plague of humanity, sucking the blood from some greater life form, each one climbing over the others to get to the juiciest spot.'

'Are you a happy flea?'

'I looked up *happy* in a dictionary once. *Glad*, it said. *Content, fortunate, prosperous, successful.* I fit the criteria. What about you?'

'Jim is prosperous enough. We've had success with our kids' books.'

'What about you, I said?'

'I miss Amy like I miss Granny. We worked on *Molly Squire* together until six weeks before she died. I miss that too.'

'I thought it was Jim's magnum opus.'

'No one wanted to publish it. He spent years on the thing, changing bits of it, but not the bits that needed changing. I told him to self-publish. He told me to burn it, so I took it down to Amy. We'd tried for years to convince him to add in my Wadimulla bits. He wouldn't so we did. Amy's fingers were twisted with arthritis at the end, but she could still type faster than me. She owns – owned – a little portable typewriter, more modern than Jim's – not as noisy.'

Jenny looked at her hands, at her fingernails. Cook and laundry maid, chief gardener and seamstress, her hands were work worn and old. Were they happy hands? They had been. They were nicotine stained since Amy had died – then Lorna. Strong hands. They'd been afraid to hold Amy's hand too tightly during her last days, scared they'd hurt her, but on that Sunday, Amy had gripped Jenny's hand.

'"Promise me that you'll finish *Molly*," she said to me the last time I saw her. "Write it in your own inimitable way, and dedicate it to me, Jennifer."'

'So do it,' Georgie said.

'She was the driver. I used to nick off down to her place with the dogs and stay for hours. We'd kill ourselves laughing over some of the things I made poor Molly do. I don't think I can stand to look at it without her. I don't think I can stand that town without her either.'

'Get out of it.'

'I'd move tomorrow. Jim won't budge.'

'What does he think of Trudy giving his sister's money to charity?'

'I doubt he's even heard her. He's wrapped himself up in guilt because everyone in town knows that Lorna lay dead for weeks and that her only brother didn't miss her. Before we knew it was Lorna, he'd said that she must have had family – and she did – and I can't raise a smidgen of sympathy for her. I can't. I try to imagine her afraid of some young bloke with his bludgeon but keep seeing her carrying Jimmy out to the car, hearing her clashing the gears as she drove him away. I hated that woman and dead or alive, I can't change what I feel about her. I'm lacking in human kindness.'

'What do you think about Trudy giving the money away?'

'It's her money,' Jenny said.

'This is me, Jen.'

'Okay, then I think that charity begins at home, and that one day Trudy will appreciate the money – and that she must have got her charitable inclinations from Teddy's side of the family because she didn't get them from me or Margot.'

'She doesn't seem interested in getting married,' Georgie said.

'She's got itchy feet and a trade like Itchy-foot's that will get her a job anywhere – and I'm scared she'll go somewhere one day and won't come back, and I wish to God that Lorna had left her money to the church – and speaking of marriage, am I likely to be making a wedding dress for you?'

'Marriage is out of vogue, Jen,' Georgie said.

'How did you get together with him?'

'What's wrong with him?'

'Nothing – as far as I can tell. I meant, how did he run you down?'

They drove through a set of lights before Georgie replied. 'I convinced myself the night of the fire that I'd been saved for a reason, and I drove all over Australia looking for that reason. When I put the rock through my sump, I started thinking I'd been saved to die alone beside a dusty road, fifty miles from Wittenoom, and along came Paul and his mates. We were Victorians and way over there any Victorian was home. I came back to stand in the witness box, convinced that I'd been saved to convict the swine, and the mongrel wriggled out of a second trial. I started the uni course so I could get him when they let him out of the psych ward, but he dropped off the face of the planet. I was planning to hit the road again when I finished the course, then I went to the Doncaster shopping centre one Friday night and when I came out to my ute, Paul was leaning against it.'

'So you decided he was the reason you'd been saved?'

'Something like that.'

'I think,' Jenny said, 'I've just decided to stop nagging Jim to move down to Melbourne. I wouldn't drive in this traffic if you paid me a million dollars to do it.'

# The Commission House

While Georgie duelled with peak-hour traffic, Sissy and Lacy stood out the front of Number 12 waiting for a taxi. They ate out on Wednesday evenings then went to bingo. A car turned into their street. Lacy identified it as a police car and the two women watched it cruise by then stop opposite the house with the dogs.

'Someone died,' Lacy said.

They watched a middle-aged male and the young female driver step from the car as a taxi made the turn. Sissy and Lacy were in it and away before the uniformed pair left their vehicle and crossed over to Number 12's side of the street.

Jack Thompson had read what there was on file about Amber Morrison. He'd seen old photographs of her. Uncertain what to expect, he rapped on the front door, rapped several times before it was opened by the white-headed, apron-clad little woman.

'Mrs Amber Morrison?' he asked.

'So they tell me,' the old one replied.

'We'd like a few words with you, if we may,' he said.

'It's dinner time,' she said.

Old records stated that Amber Morrison was five foot four and a half, had greying/blonde hair, blue eyes, and weighed eight stone three ounces. The woman blocking his entrance might have weighed thirty-five kilograms, she'd shrunk in height, but her eyes were blue. She wasn't what Jack had been hoping to find in that house, but he showed her his badge and, when it didn't move her, he told her he had a warrant to search the house. Amber Morrison stepped to the side and removed her apron, and Jack and his colleague entered the kind of sitting room they hadn't expected to find behind that door.

Through the years they'd had reason to enter a few similarly constructed Commission homes. Some were well cared for, as many were not. Money had been spent in this room. Jack glanced at an old cabinet on his right, then he turned to the mantelpiece – and there they were, set on either side of an old marble clock, Miss Hooper's missing vases. Her minister and his wife had mentioned that pair of vases.

'You are alone, Mrs Morrison?'

'My son-in-law is about,' she said, then placing her folded apron down she stepped forward to reclaim a vase from his careless hand. He'd upended it to glance at the maker's name, but returned it to Amber, who placed it back where it belonged.

'An attractive pair,' Jack said.

'There was a grace to the old days,' Amber said.

'A few would agree with you there,' he said. His colleague was interested in a pair of twelve-inch statuettes on the polished cabinet – also missing, according to the minister and his wife.

'Has there been . . . an accident?' asked a shrivelled male who'd materialised in the doorway.

'We believe Mrs Morrison may be able to assist us with our investigations,' Jack replied.

Amber knew why they were here. There had been an accident of sorts. Things happened at times, happened so fast she failed to consider the possible consequences. She watched the female place the statuette back where it belonged, a beautiful thing, one of six. She'd only taken two. The blue sisters. They matched this room.

Out of nothing she'd created it. She'd always done her best with what she'd been given. Had never been given enough, that was the trouble.

She looked up at the ceiling, prefabricated like the rest of the house, looked at the door they'd left open for the street filth to blow into her parlour. Norman's front door had opened from a veranda into a passage, and when they'd taken her away from that house, there hadn't been a speck of dust in his parlour.

She turned to the crystal cabinet and the statuettes, turned one slightly to the left, just a fraction, so she might face her blue sister. A week after moving in with Lorna, she'd found those statuettes hidden away in the dark of a sideboard, their perfection buried beneath years of grime. She'd washed them clean. Had planned to take all six before the accident. Wrapped them well in layers of newspaper, intending to call a taxi when she was done – but when she was done and the mist of anger had washed away, she'd changed her mind about a taxi and caught the last tram back to the city. Had to leave the other four behind. Her Waterford crystal bowl was heavy.

And how dare that filthy old bitch allow that house to get into such a state. How dare she!

'We'd like you to come to the station with us, Mrs Morrison,' the sergeant said.

'I'll fetch my jacket,' Amber said.

Reginald blocked the doorway. He looked green, and she thought of a bug-eyed grasshopper, useless without its hoppers, a big-headed crawling thing.

'There's stew on the stove,' she said, and walked by him to her bedroom, the female at her heels. She needed time, not a jacket. She needed space in which to think. She'd got rid of Lorna's keys. They'd gone down a grating in the city.

A blunt instrument, the newspapers had said. Amber had read every report. There'd been no mention of the champagne bottle. She'd washed it, washed it in the bathroom because she couldn't get near that filthy old bitch's sink. That's what had angered her. The kitchen. On that final morning when they'd walked off to church they'd locked an immaculate house, a chicken left roasting in the oven with potatoes, carrots, pumpkin. They'd sat side by side in the front pew, she turning the pages of both hymn books. Lorna had taken her arm as they'd walked from the church – then she'd been flung away like a piece of filth. And after all those years of *Fetch this, fetch that, Duckworth. Time for my eye-drops, Duckworth. Read this, read that, Duckworth . . .*

Amber closed her bedroom door, attempted to close it. The female in blue was standing so the door wouldn't close. Wouldn't give her that time, that space in which to think.

It was Sissy's fault too, and her stray bitch's with her skewered onions. Never had Amber roasted onions in the meat pan. They fell apart, and their overpowering flavour ruined the gravy's.

It was her wretched finger's fault too, the blood on white lace. Bloodstained.

'Are we ready, Mrs Morrison?' the female said.

'You, perhaps, are ready. We are not,' Amber replied.

*Are we ready, Miss Hooper?*

*You, perhaps, are ready, Duckworth. We are not.*

Old bitch. She'd deserved what she'd got.

Amber slid her dusty pink frock from its hanger. On her final day in Kew, Elizabeth had worn her dusty pink and matching hat. Hadn't worn that frock and hat since, and where had she put that hat?

She found it on the upper shelf of her wardrobe. She removed her house frock and pulled on the pink. She brushed the hat then set it on her silky white curls, and Elizabeth smiled at her again from the mirror.

She slid her maroon jacket from its hanger. She'd paid a small fortune for it, and that old bitch had seen fit to toss it into a pile of dog shit on the nature strip. Amber slid her arms into it then opened her top drawer. Elizabeth had always worn white gloves to church. They'd covered her hands' sins from God's sight. Old gloves and older gloves in her top drawer, gloves that no longer fitted her hands, but she chose a pair of white kid, and smiled at the memory of white lace. They'd gone down the grating with Lorna's keys.

Left the house she'd schemed to acquire, an escort on either side. A ludicrous assignment for a burly sergeant. Jack Thompson had arrested drunks and addicts, wife killers, thieves and rapists, and felt a fool walking that white-headed old granny to the police car. He took her arm to assist her into the rear seat and when she couldn't find the end of the seat belt, he found it and buckled her in before sliding in beside her.

Four kids delayed their game of cricket to lean against fences, against a telephone pole, to stare. Their mothers peered through windows. A few came outside to get a better look. Amber waved a queenly gloved hand as the car drove towards the setting sun.

At the police station they offered her tea and a biscuit and they asked her many questions. They asked about Kew.

'My memory isn't what it used to be,' she said.

They asked about her husband.

'I have been told that he was a station master in a small timber town. I have no memory of him.'

'In '47, you were arrested for his murder, Mrs Morrison.'

'That may well be so. I suffered life-threatening head injuries in a car accident twenty years ago and recall nothing at all of my former life.'

They asked about the Royal Doulton vases.

'Now that I can help you with. I came across them at an opportunity shop in Richmond, and what a buy they were. I enjoy having a poke around in those shops, and that day, there they were, in a cardboard carton with a pile of other goods. The woman who sold them to me had no idea of their value. She offered me change from a two-dollar note.'

They led the subject back to Kew, to Lorna Hooper. 'When did you last speak to her, Mrs Morrison?'

'The years go by so quickly. I'm sorry, but I can't help you there.'

Lorna Hooper's murder had made the front page for a day; it had gained a mention for a few days more, but old news is like a pair of pantihose, worn once or twice then relegated to the bin. Police sift through bins. They flip through old files, speak to neighbours, to relatives, to taxi and tram drivers. They take photographs, measure with their tapes and make copious notes.

They'd found the champagne bottle, the only wine bottle in the house, and its clean new state was an alien presence there. They'd found no fingerprints that matched those on Amber Morrison's file, but they'd found the prints of lace gloves, finger and hand-prints, and who in this day and age wore lace gloves?

An elderly woman might. They knew an elderly woman had been seen standing at the Kew gates when a neighbour had driven in at around ten o'clock on 17 December, the neighbour certain of that date. She'd been at the Royal Women's hospital visiting her daughter and her brand new grandson, born that morning.

They knew an elderly woman had caught the last tram in from Kew on that same night. Had the tram driver not recently buried his own mother, he might not have noticed Amber, but he had, and had been concerned for the poor old dear struggling home with two heavy shopping bags. He'd been able to give the police a description, and the time he'd seen her. He'd clocked off for the night soon after.

Police speak to taxi companies. It had taken many phone calls and much footwork, but they'd found a driver who recalled picking up an elderly woman and her shopping bags at the Flinders Street taxi rank. He remembered dropping her off at an address in Doveton. Drivers don't forget the big tippers. He was dead certain of the address. His sister and her five kids lived two streets away from the old dear.

Martin Leeds and his wife had been helpful. They'd known Miss Hooper and Miss Duckworth well, had taken tea with them regularly during the sixties and early seventies. Martin Leeds, the dead woman's minister for years, and her executor, had been given charge of Lorna's house keys. Both he and his wife had been to the house. They'd seen the state of the rooms. It was the wife, Mary, who noticed Miss Hooper's Royal Doulton vases were missing from the parlour mantelpiece.

'My wife had always admired those vases,' Martin said. 'Eight or ten years ago she came across an auction house catalogue containing a colour photograph of a pair of near identical vases.'

Two weeks ago, the minister's wife had found that catalogue in the drawer of her writing desk. It was now in Jack's possession, and on page four the vases, Lot 57, had been circled. He'd handled one of those vases today.

The dust Amber had chased for the greater part of her life led to her undoing, and the vases she had found in a carton at an opportunity shop in Richmond. Dust settles not only on a folderol but around it and when, after several years, that item is removed, the dust-free circles leave mute evidence of that which has been removed. As with the six figurines of fine ladies. Four had been found in the house, found wrapped in layers of three month old newspaper. They'd found evidence of six on a begrimed blackwood sideboard, on a small table, on the television.

Jack had the probable murder weapon, a champagne bottle with not a fingerprint on it. He had the vases, the figurines, Amber Morrison's prior record, but no confession. It would have taken strength to do what had been done to Miss Hooper. Amber Morrison looked as if she'd be hard-pressed to swat a fly.

Twice Jack asked her if she'd like him to call her a solicitor. On the second occasion, she told him that all she required was a bed.

'Please,' she said.

The tram driver came in at eight. He identified her as the old dear who'd ridden his tram into the city on the night in question. So Jack charged her with the murder and mutilation of Lorna Hooper, and Amber yawned.

He asked her if she understood the seriousness of her situation. She asked him to make sure that she was given a private cell.

'My hearing is acute,' she said.

And how could he lock a ninety year old woman in a cell? He made alternative arrangements. It took time, and by the time he led her out, the vultures had gathered.

Most want to hide their faces from the media. They'll cower beneath jackets, beneath blankets when they're led away. Amber smiled for the gathered hoards, smiled as she was assisted into the rear of the police car, and once seated and buckled in she waved her queenly white kid gloved hand.

Her handbag gave up little, a handkerchief, a gold mesh purse containing twenty-five dollars, the keys to Number 12 and a small key, pinned into the lining of a zipped pocket.

Her undergarments gave up more.

She'd been admitted to a private ward at St Vincent's hospital where a doctor noticed the pockets, stitched neatly to the hip and buttock region of Amber's girdle – button-down pockets.

They were packed with bank notes totalling eight thousand, six hundred and fifty dollars, and come morning, Jack learned how Amber Morrison had come by that money.

That small key unlocked a private mailbox at the Richmond post office where a mess of mail awaited collection. The box, registered to Elizabeth Duckworth, contained six pension cheques, two addressed to Elizabeth Duckworth, two addressed to Maryanne Brown, and the last two to Margaret Hooper. Two manila envelopes, addressed to Elizabeth, contained the bankbooks of Margaret Hooper and Maryanne Brown.

*

*Ninety year old pensioner Amber Morrison was charged tonight with the murder of Lorna Hooper, her lifelong companion . . .*

It was on the ten o'clock news. Television news writers don't always get it right.

'My God,' Jenny said, springing to her feet. 'Oh my God.'

Jim turned to her and for an instant, when their eyes met, Jenny saw his father's eyes, his father's expression in those eyes.

'It's almost incestuous,' Georgie said, putting Jenny's thoughts into words.

Jim rose and left the room, and Jenny sat down to watch, to listen.

'Did they say ninety, or nineteen?' Paul asked.

'Ninety. She's your adoptive grandmother-in-law,' Georgie said.

'Jesus,' he said.

They sat late, but learned no more. They saw her, fleetingly, saw her gloved hand, her smile for the cameras.

'My God,' Jenny said, recognising little other than the grimace of a smile, then she too went to bed. Jim was asleep. Perhaps he was asleep. She didn't disturb him.

Cecelia Duckworth, daughter of Amber Morrison, was on the six o'clock news the following evening, or the rear end of an overweight woman was on the screen as she struggled into a large and modern car, her rear end protected by a stocky male. The news broadcaster identified the two as Cecelia Duckworth and her husband.

'That's not Sissy,' Jenny said. 'And that male is no Duckworth either.'

'How long since you've seen her?' Georgie asked.

'Years, but those legs aren't Sissy's.'

The reporters got it right on Thursday when their cameras caught Sissy opening her front door to pitch a saucepan of water at a cameraman. Jenny recognised her through a dripping lens.

Given time, the Duckworths rallied as Duckworths ever had. They removed the useless duo from Doveton to a farm fifteen miles from Bendigo, and with nothing more to aim at, the cameramen moved on to greener pastures. The neighbour's dog stopped barking and the kids got on with their cricket match.

# FAME

Nobby owned a large trailer. He, Rosemary and Jim emptied Lorna's house while Jenny remained at Greensborough, locked in, the television playing from morning to night. On the Friday following Amber's arrest, Jim arrived home, the car boot loaded with old files, moth-eaten albums, his great-grandfather's Bible and four statuettes.

'They were Mum's,' he said. 'There were six of them when I was a kid.'

Jenny didn't want them, or the files that had transferred their odour to her car boot. She changed her mind about the ornaments when Jim unwrapped the first twelve inch tall lady, clad in a maroon and green gown and carrying a basket of delicate china flowers. Beneath its layers of grime it was beautiful. She helped remove the newspaper from the others.

'They're old,' she said.

'Older than me. I was allowed to look at them but not touch,' Jim said, and they carried them into the laundry where Jenny ran them a bath in the sink then bathed them with dishwashing detergent and a toothbrush.

They were air drying on the family room table when Georgie came in. Like Granny, like Jenny, she saved used tissue paper. They wrapped each lady well before placing it into the case, well protected on all sides by clothing. Jim wanted to go home in the morning, as did Jenny – until they watched that evening's current affairs program.

Reporters had tracked the woman they'd named the Grinning Granny to Woody Creek where, in 1946, she'd been arrested in connection with the murder of her husband. They'd found Maisy, neighbour and childhood friend of the Grinning Granny, and there she was, on the box in full living colour – and knowing Maisy, the tape editor must have worked overtime to patch together three minutes of usable interview. For Jenny, even those three minutes were too much.

'I'm not going back there, Jim.'

'We're packed,' he said.

'I went through it when she killed Dad, and again when Raelene and Margot died. I can't do it a third time. I can't. And I won't.'

Jim phoned John, who suggested they stay where they were. 'The dogs have been worth their weight in gold,' he said.

'We'll move over to Nobby's in the morning,' Jenny said.

'Stay where you are,' Georgie said. 'I was hoping to get a look inside Lorna's house.'

'Paul is sick of the sight of us,' Jenny argued.

'I've been thinking about offering you a job as cook,' Paul said.

'Live in, ute supplied? I'll take it.'

He'd bought a new battery for the ute. Twice Jenny had driven to the local shops. The roads around Greensborough were viable in the late morning or early afternoon.

Georgie, who battled peak-hour traffic daily, should have been content to stay home on Saturday, but she drove Jim to Kew in the ute. There was an old oil painting he hadn't been able to fit into his boot, and with room for only two in the ute's cabin, Paul stayed home, Jenny barely aware that he was there. Like Jim, he typed, but his computer keyboard was near silent.

At one, she heated a can of tomato soup and made two toasted cheese sandwiches. She called him, and when he didn't come out to eat, she took a mug of soup and a sandwich to his study.

'It's getting cold,' she said.

'Thanks,' he said. 'I'm inclined to become involved when I get in here.'

He cleared a space between his computer and half a dozen flat squares of what appeared to be cardboard. One fell to the floor at Jenny's feet. She placed the mug and plate down then picked up the cardboard square.

'What is it?'

'A floppy disc,' he replied.

Discs were round flat things, not square. She placed it with the others, turned to go, then changed her mind.

'They're the things Georgie said she'd put her grandfather's diaries on?'

'Her Itchy-foot? He's here somewhere,' he said. 'Would you like to see what she did?'

'You're working,' she said, but he opened a drawer to riffle through a dozen more of the same-sized squares of cardboard until finding the one he sought. He slid a square disc out of a slot in the computer, slid the other one in, hit a few keys and, half a minute later, up popped THE DIARIES OF ARCHIBALD FOOTE FILE ONE.

Jenny moved closer as the screen filled with words then, elbow to elbow with this quiet man who had somehow managed to run Georgie down, she watched as page after page slid by, until she glimpsed what appeared to be a poem.

'Can you make it go back to the italics bit?'

He could, and did, and she read words she recognised, astonished that a skinny piece of cardboard could contain so many words.

'How?' she asked. 'How can so much fit onto that thing?'

He attempted to explain between sips of soup. He spoke of bits and bytes – meaningless jargon to Jenny. She was mesmerised by the screen.

Then he vacated his chair and gestured to her to sit.

'No,' she said.

'I need to shower,' he said. 'Hit the *page down* key when you're ready to move on.' And he left her with the humming beast that would probably explode if she touched anything.

It didn't.

There were passages of Archie Foote's diary he'd recorded in mirror writing, which, like the poems, Georgie had typed in italics. She was reading one when Paul returned to stand behind her. Hit the *page down* key twice before springing up from his chair.

'Playing games is the best way to lose your fear of the beast,' he said, reaching to turn on the second computer. He set it up to play a game of solitaire.

'I'll wreck something,' she said.

'It's a mindless tool, Jen. You're the controller. How did you learn to control a car?' he asked.

'When you're young you have no fear.'

'I bet you didn't take off at a hundred k's an hour?'

'I remember kangaroo-hopping down a country lane while my teacher killed himself laughing,' Jenny said.

'Playing solitaire is kangaroo-hopping. If you run into trouble, you hit the brake – the *quit* key.'

She'd been playing solitaire since she'd discovered the game. He showed her how to move the cards and she sat down to play. That's how she got to know Paul Dunn, after almost a week of sleeping beneath his roof, a week of well-mannered monosyllables.

She'd liked the way he hadn't turned a hair when the news broke of Amber Morrison's arrest, or when Georgie had explained Jenny's connection to the Grinning Granny. She liked watching him and Georgie seated side by side on the couch. They looked right together. He was almost four years her junior, but Georgie had never looked her age. What a pity they hadn't found each other years ago – or recognised what they'd found years ago.

The computer beat her. It beat her three times before she gave up.

Stood a while in the passage, listening to his keyboard's chuckle, and thought of Jim's rattling, zipping, bell ringing, clanking relic. Before Amy went to hospital, Jim had taken on a typing job for the Forestry Commission. He was a whiz at typing facts and figures.

The ute returned at three thirty. Jenny went outside to tell Jim she'd used a computer and that he had to buy one. He was more interested in removing a life-sized portrait from the rear of the ute – no wonder he hadn't been able to fit it into the boot.

'I thought you were talking about a landscape,' she said.

'It's Pop's grandfather,' he said, propping a mean-faced old coot against the wheel of the ute, then stepping back to admire him.

'His frame might be worth keeping. He isn't,' Jenny said.

'He'll clean up,' he said. 'What would you use on oil paint?'

'A splash of petrol and my cigarette lighter on that one,' Jenny said. 'And just for the record, I'm not giving him house room, Jim.'

In all, they stayed for twelve nights in Greensborough, and when they left for home on Wednesday, James Richard Hooper rode on the floor behind them, and he blocked the view, and he stank of Lorna, so Jenny lit a cigarette.

'Not in the car,' he said.

'It's a sweeter smell than his, and I'm not having him in the house, Jim.'

'Trudy wanted to keep him.'

'There are places down here she could pay to store him,' Jenny said.

'We've got the space,' Jim said.

'He's going in the shed.'

They were halfway home before he told her there were a few pieces of furniture Trudy also wanted to keep. 'The removalist will deliver them on Thursday.'

'What?'

'Only the best of it,' he said.

'Not "what" as in "what's coming?", but "what" as in how dare you agree to store it, and how dare you leave it until now to tell me.'

'I knew what your reaction would be.'

'If you knew my reaction, then why agree to store it?'

'I grew up with it, and most of it was Mum's before it was Pop's.'

'That thing wasn't your mother's,' she said, gesturing to the rear seat. 'And I'll bet she didn't give it house room.'

'It was in the farmhouse until I was six or seven. We found out that one of Monk's English relatives had painted it—'

'The one who shot himself,' Jenny said.

'Did he?'

'He would have if he'd had a conscience,' she said.

'It's old, Jen. It's got historical value.'

'Hysterical value,' she corrected. 'His moustache looks like a white rat perched on his top lip – and your mother's furniture or not, you had no right to agree to storing it without talking to me about it, and then not telling me until we're on the road and there's not a thing I can do about it.'

'The dining room setting could be over a hundred years old—'

'I've got my own dining room suite.'

'Trudy brought an antique dealer in to give us a valuation on it and the sideboard. He offered twelve hundred, and if he was prepared to pay twelve, it's worth twice that or maybe more.'

'Every stick of furniture, every floor covering and drape, we've chosen together—'

'All things pass,' he sighed and said no more.

*All things pass?* She smoked in silence for a kilometre or two, each revolution of the wheels drawing her back to that town, to no Amy, to hours of Maisy and her rehashing of the Amber, the poor Sissy, the Granny rolling over in her grave story. And she didn't want any of it.

'Nothing passes,' she said. 'Our arguments don't pass. They congeal and grow scabs until you go and do something like this that rubs my scabs off and I bleed again – and I'm sick of bleeding, Jim. Stop the car and let me out. I'm going back to Greensborough.'

'We'll talk about it at home,' he said.

'Woody Creek isn't home. Your father's house has never been home—'

'You're being unreasonable.'

'Being reasonable hasn't got me far, has it? How did you lose your leg, Jim?'

'I'm driving, Jen.'

'Then stop the bloody car and let me out.'

He didn't stop. He didn't make the usual halfway stop for toilets and petrol, and when he turned into the drive, the motor was running on empty and Jenny's bladder wasn't.

The dogs were pleased to see her. John looked well and he had news.

'Lorna is in pup,' he said.

An unfortunate choice of name that Jenny had considered changing. Not today. Today it sounded fine as she ran for the bathroom.

# Good Dog

John went home. Jim wanted the dogs to go with him and, if not for the portrait leaning against the entrance hall wall, Jenny might have let them go. But it was there, eyeing her as she walked by, and the removalist was coming with more junk, so the dogs stayed.

She threatened to leave them free to hunt the removalists. Jim wouldn't go near them. He threatened to phone John, or the Willama dog catcher. There was a stand-off until Maisy beeped her horn at the gate. Jenny chained the dogs for Maisy, and two minutes after she drove in she had to give up her space to a huge van.

Two burly males carried Vern Hooper back into his house – or carried in his tapestry-upholstered dining room chairs, ten of them. Jenny had sat on those chairs way back when her feet couldn't reach the floor. She'd traced their carved backs with a tiny finger. As each chair was carried inside, she promised it that it would never feel her weight again.

Jenny's dining room suite made way for a heavy oval table and matching sideboard. That suite may well have been worth twelve hundred dollars – or thirty-six hundred. Jenny could see its value, which didn't alter its stink of Lorna.

Her convenient phone table and chair made way for a grand hallstand. As a kid she'd admired it. She hadn't previously sighted the large camphorwood chest with five deep drawers. Plenty of space for it in Trudy's bedroom, and who can ever have too much drawer space? Its drawers were magnificent but, camphorwood or not, it smelled of Lorna, and Jenny escaped with her dogs, went for a walk down to John's and found him, sitting alone in the garden, looking into space.

'Will I leave the dogs with you?'

'I've paid a deposit on a room at the retirement home in Willama, Jen. The house is on the market.'

'A deposit on a room?'

'It has its own bathroom,' he said. 'All meals are provided by the hospital.'

She went home late – went home, and when she flicked on the entrance hall light she saw him glaring down at her with his cockroach eyes and his white rat moustache. They'd hung him high where Simon Jenner's landscape had hung that morning. Jim couldn't climb ladders. The removalists must have hung him.

All things pass, or weeks pass. The Grinning Granny didn't. The newspapers loved her. Ninety year old women didn't wander around at night bludgeoning other old women to death with champagne bottles. She had a young solicitor, who might not win the case but his face would become as well known as Grinning Granny's before the trial began, if it ever got to court.

Jenny's face was well known in Woody Creek. She couldn't walk into the butcher's shop to buy her dogs a bone, or into the newsagent's to pick up her paper, without the stares, the whispers. Stopped shopping in Woody Creek. Stopped walking her dogs. Stopped.

She nagged John into a trip to Willama to have his hair cut, and that half-hour on the road with him was a relief. She drove him up to the hospital to look at a room similar to the one he'd be moving into.

'You won't survive in that,' she said.

'It's enough,' he said.

'It's not enough. And the dogs will miss you. You're their alpha male, and we've got rooms rotting for lack of use, and you're part of our pack.'

'It's done, Jen.'

'It's not done until it's done. What am I supposed to do with a pregnant dog, and pups?'

'Lorna has done it before. She'll handle it,' he said.

'She won't, and I won't. I can't handle what I've got now. Cancel your room and get your deposit back.'

He didn't agree, not that day.

By February's end Vern Hooper's antique dining room table was buried beneath piles of antique Hooper documents, moth-eaten photograph albums, the typewriter and the familiar pile of Jim's notes. He'd started compiling a book on the history of the Hoopers, and who did he think would be interested in reading about them?

Jenny read a letter written by the first James Hooper, a shepherd, or a letter he'd paid the town scribe to write to James Richard. It told him that his mother had died and that her final words had been of her son – interesting – but Jim wasn't writing about the old shepherd. He had details of the boat James Richard had sailed on, and the date he'd set out for Australia, and the date he'd arrived, and his date of birth, and the date that he and Maximilian Monk were named as joint owners of the thousand-acre property they'd named Three Pines.

March, eight days of unrelenting heat. It broiled the musty scent of old documents and aged furniture, and the distilled essence of Lorna seeped from the dining room and hall into every room, and into Jim, who spent his days and nights sitting on Lorna's chairs, his knees beneath her table, became steeped in that musty scent of dusty old age. John's house was Jenny's escape, and morning, noon or evening she walked her dogs to his door.

Found him packing up one morning. Found Amy's typewriter on his kitchen table with *Molly Squire*, a bulk of pages, tied into a bundle with a blue ribbon. She undid the bow tied by Amy's hands then sat down to read. They'd done a lot of work on poor Molly; they'd got rid of much of Jim's work, his umpteen excess names had gone, his dates too. She found a pencil in Amy's desk drawer and ran a cross through two pages of Mr Kennedy, who would later become Molly's son-in-law. Then, after a late lunch, she erased her erasing and wound a sheet of typing paper into Amy's typewriter and while the dogs roamed free in John's garden, Jenny created a battleaxe mother for Mr Kennedy then, fifty pages deeper in the manuscript, after Molly's daughters had wed – or bred – she allowed the one with the illegitimate son to bump off her sister's mother-in-law with a spear.

Jim hadn't appreciated Jenny's suggestion that Molly had managed to raise her infant daughters because the blacks had taken her in. In Jenny and Amy's version of Molly, she'd taken a black husband, Wadimulla, and her daughters had grown wild.

Jim missed out on lunch that day. She made him a sandwich at half past two. He ate it in the dining room while she set about cooking something for dinner. She'd left the dogs with John, had told him he could walk them home at around six and stay for dinner. Hoped he'd come. She cooked enough for three.

He was at Jenny's side the day Lorna produced six pups, blind, rat-like and as red as their parents, and they looked underdone to Jenny. It was the pups who moved John back into the rear bedroom, and while he split his days between the pups and their parents, Jenny escaped alone to Amy's house where she lived a happier life with Molly – and Amy's chuckling ghost, who urged her labouring fingers on.

*She needs a reason to have gone back to the whites, Jennifer.*

She did. The whites had hanged her husband. They'd left her and her babies to their fate, then along came Wadimulla and his tribe to save her. She'd had a life of freedom with the blacks and Jenny had never found a good reason for her to leave Wadimulla.

When in doubt kill them off had been Shakespeare's method

of problem solving, so she killed her noble savage, or allowed one of the new settlers to shoot him, then during the night the rest of the tribe had taken off, leaving Molly with no alternative but to return to the whites, which meant that Jenny had to lose half a dozen pages in order to slot the new pages in, but they strengthened the chapter where Molly's daughter speared her sister's mother-in-law. Jim would have a fit if he ever saw what she'd done to his manuscript.

Trudy came home in April. She took precedence over all else. Lorna's house had sold.

'Sophie and I have booked our tickets to Greece,' Trudy said.

'When?'

'We fly out on the eighth.'

'Where will you stay?' Jim asked.

'Sophie's got scads of relatives. We'll relative-hop until we wear out our welcome then backpack across country to England and see if we can get work there for a while.'

'Two girls hitchhiking? You're putting yourself in danger, Tru,' Jim said.

'Backpacking isn't hitchhiking, and there'll be three of us, Dad.'

'To go over there without a plan is dangerous.'

'I've been an adult for a while now, and India was more dangerous than Greece is likely to be.'

'You travelled there with a group,' Jenny said.

'Three is a group, Mum.'

'Who is the third?'

'Sophie's cousin, Nicky,' Trudy said.

'Are you shouting the trip?'

'I'm paying Sophie's fare – if the solicitor pays the money in when he said he would, otherwise our credit cards will be shouting.'

She was an adult. She had a profession, she spoke serviceable Greek and Sophie spoke the language like a native. They'd be safe together, with Nicky, who Jenny couldn't place. Trudy had a lot of friends.

Jenny had Maisy, and if today was Tuesday then she'd lost a day somewhere. She waved to her, couldn't open the gate until the pups had been rounded up and placed into their pen, a chicken wire construction John had built behind the shed. He tied up Lorna and Vern, Jenny opened the gate and Maisy drove in – and got out of the car with a parcel, and its floppiness suggested fabric.

'What have you been spending your money on?' Jenny asked.

'I know you said that you've retired, love, but young Glenda bought me a dress-length. She's having an evening wedding and she wants me in an evening gown. It's not until August,' Maisy said.

Since Amy's death, Jenny had refused half a dozen orders. She had enough to fill her days without her sewing machines, but how could she refuse Maisy? She led her down to the kitchen, hurriedly vacated by Trudy, who preferred the pups' and John's company to Maisy's.

'I wouldn't ask you if she hadn't gone and bought the material, and just look at it. It must have cost her a fortune.'

Jenny looked at it. Chiffon, but beautiful, a deep blue with metallic silver and blue/green thread woven through it, a fabric she might have chosen for her own gown had she been the mother of a bride. Not to be. Maybe never to be. She'd done something wrong with the raising of her girls.

Cara had married; Jenny had played no part in her raising. Jimmy had married. She hadn't played a long role in his raising either. She'd raised Georgie and Trudy, one determined to rise to the top of her profession, the other destined to die a charitable pauper – and both of them childless. Maisy was grandmother to the multitudes and the multitudes were marrying and producing great-grandchildren.

'In August?'

'The second last Saturday, love. I just want something very simple.'

She stayed for two hours. Jenny learned that one of Patricia's sons was in hospital with a broken leg and head injuries, that Sissy had suffered a nervous breakdown, that one of Amber's breasts had been cut off.

'Sissy said she had a lump in it as big as a golf ball,' Maisy said.

'When are they trying her?' Jenny asked, feeling no sympathy for Amber's breast.

'Sissy said they'd found cancer in it.'

'I was hiding behind a door when forgiveness was handed out, Maisy,' Jenny said. Forgiveness, forgetfulness, motherliness, wifeliness.

She'd given up nagging about the stink of Lorna's furniture. She never looked up when she walked through the entrance hall – she'd stopped vacuuming it. Stopped vacuuming the dining room – her room once, and a beautiful room. Her dining room setting, now relegated to the small sitting room corner, looked like the modern junk it was. Its chairs were comfortable, though. She'd chosen it for its six comfortable chairs, and Jim had been at her side when she'd chosen it – on her side.

Didn't know what was going on in his head lately. He'd become obsessed by his family. She'd known him as a boy who had called his father 'sir'. Had known him as a young man dominated by Vern Hooper and Lorna. Knew as much as Nobby knew about his missing years in psychiatric clinics after the war – next to nothing. Since she'd got back together with him he'd had nothing to do with his family. Lorna hadn't let him know that Margaret was dead. His cousin had passed on that piece of news, after the funeral.

Maisy was still talking. Maisy never stopped talking, and Jenny drew her mind back to the kitchen.

'. . . terrible photograph in Saturday's paper?'

'I saw it,' Jenny said.

The Grinning Granny business settled down for weeks at a time. Her breast had returned her grin to the headlines. Jenny knew it well, Amber's snake-getting-ready-to-strike smile she'd named it as a kid. She wanted her convicted, not for Lorna's murder but for Norman's.

'She's been on pills for it,' Maisy continued.

'Pills for cancer?'

'Sissy. For her nerves. She's living with one of your cousins in Hamilton, and she said that the cousin puts an eggtimer on whenever Sissy picks up the telephone.'

'I was born without compassion for the great human horde, Maisy – and I don't count Amber and Sissy amongst them anyway.'

'You were raised as sisters,' Maisy said. 'She took Amber in when she had no place to go, and that friend of hers too when she had to get out of her unit, and because of what Amber did, Lacy won't even talk to Sissy on the phone.'

Jenny leaned, elbow on the table, face supported on her palm, her mind searching for a safe place to go. It found Molly Squire. Jim had written her death scene. His Molly had died alone in her bed, but Jenny liked her and didn't want her to die alone.

'She phoned Lacy before she phoned me last Sunday, to tell her that she'd been given a two-bedroom unit and to ask her to move into it with her. All Lacy did was bawl. Then her sister-in-law came on the phone and demanded that they be let into the Doveton house to pick up her mother-in-law's furniture before Sissy moved, like she was scared Sissy would take off with it.'

'Where was she going to put Cousin Reg?'

'He's with some other cousins. Sissy said that they can keep him if Lacy changes her mind. She's going to write to her.'

'Poor old Cousin Reg,' Jenny said.

'The new unit wouldn't be any good for him anyway. It's close to a big shopping centre with a hotel, and it's got a bus stop at the front door, Sissy said.'

'If I had to live with her, I'd drink too.'

'Don't let life make you hard, love.'

'You're too soft, Maisy.'

'It stops me getting wrinkles,' Maisy said.

*

By July Trudy had flown away, the pups had moved on to new homes and Ray's insurance money account had paid for a concrete drive. Pups dig. They'd dug up bulbs, dug holes beneath the side fence, excavated beneath the gate, tormented their parents when they wanted to sleep and scuttled around the veranda when Jenny had wanted to sleep.

She'd sat Vern down the day the last of the pups was driven away and told him in no uncertain terms what she'd do to him if he ever did it again. Hoped he understood *castration*. He understood everything else.

Most dogs will heel when told to, they'll sit, even stay. Old Joe's kelpies would stay until ordered to move. Ask 'Where's your bone?' and they'd run to retrieve it, ask 'Where's the cat?' and they'd scare that cat up a tree in the blink of an eye. 'Bad dog' meant 'Go to your chain'. 'Good dog' meant 'Have a good time', and the more Jenny and John laughed at their good time antics, the better time the dogs had. Mention 'Walk' in their hearing and they'd run to the gate. 'Where's your lead?' or 'Get your lead' and they'd run to the shed where their leads hung and return with both, or arguing over the one they'd managed to unhook.

At times they behaved like pups, but John, the dog expert, put their age at around six. All things being equal, Jenny could expect to be a dog owner for another five or six years – as could Jim, and he didn't want them defiling his lawn, and they knew it. They kept their distance from him, except when Jenny asked 'Where's Jim's gammy leg?' at which point they'd approach him warily, sniff his plastic leg, then move away, the fur on the back of their necks standing on end.

From time to time they barked at a passer-by, but only if the passer-by was too slow in passing. They barked at Amy's garden pixies, her leadlight winged butterflies which had found new homes in Jenny's garden.

Spring would come, it always did, but not to Amy's garden. Jenny knew its fate. She'd seen land developers at work before. They'd arrive with their bulldozers. They'd level that old house and garden, then cut those two and a half acres up into building blocks, fifty per cent of which would be bought by Melbourne retirees.

And who could blame them for getting out of a city where murders had become commonplace, where strikes crippled. Truckies throughout four states had blockaded major highways, protesting about fuel tax and the cost of registering their vehicles. And could you blame them? The cost of living kept skyrocketing, housing prices in Melbourne had gone mad. With what the owners might get for a grotty little weatherboard house in Richmond, they could build a mansion in Woody Creek – and did.

The town's businesses should have been thriving. They weren't. Too many of its six hundred residents did their major shopping in Willama. Robert Fulton now ran a one-man business. He could order a television, refrigerator or washing machine and within two days deliver it to your door. He could order any piece of household furniture required, if you were prepared to choose it from one of his catalogues. Catalogues might have been good enough in the old days but they weren't any more, not when there were two big furniture stores in Willama where a buyer could test the comfort of a chair or bed before handing over his credit card.

Woody Creek's butcher no longer employed an apprentice. Charlie's grocery store, now a supermarket, had changed hands twice since the day Jenny handed the keys to N. and B. Wallis. The café cum fish and chip shop did well enough, though the service station out on the highway sold take-away meals and coffee, and had a better range of ice-creams along with clean toilets for travellers. Stock Route Road had been extended through to connect up with Three Pines. It got rid of the heavy transports that had roared through town night and day, but also got rid of the travellers on the way to some place better. They used to break their journey in town, buy a meal, a beer or an ice-cream.

The Taylor couple who'd bought Blunt's drapery no longer stocked drapery. John Taylor baked fresh bread and rolls on Saturday and Sunday mornings, and every day during the holiday season. Pauline Taylor served tea and light midday snacks three days a week. Some days they did well enough. Some days they didn't.

The old post office had become a community centre. City retirees pine for their clubs and centres. The city chap who bought Freddy Bowen's hotel turned the rear section of his backyard into a beer garden with a shade cloth roof. Once a month he brought in city entertainers with their screaming guitars and pounding drums. Closed doors and windows couldn't lock their noise out. Hooper Street was narrow. Jen, Jim, John and their dogs were entertained free of charge once a month.

'They're driving me to drink!' Jenny moaned.

'That's the idea,' Jim said. 'Go to sleep.'

Then August, a deathly cold August, and the Grinning Granny was back in the news.

IT WAS A MERCY KILLING, GRANNY CLAIMS.

AMBER MORRISON TO SPEND REMAINING DAYS IN SECURE HOSPITAL WARD.

Staring, whispering people.

'They say that she's that woman's daughter.'

'Where does she get the nerve to walk around town the way she does?'

Wouldn't – if I had a face like yours, Jenny thought. Wouldn't if I had a choice.

GRINNING GRANNY ADMITS TO DEFRAUDING SOCIAL SECURITY DEPARTMENT

*A spokesman today told reporters that prior to her arrest, Amber Morrison was collecting pensions in her own name and in the names of Elizabeth Duckworth, Maryanne Brown and Margaret Hooper . . .*

Even the Grinning Granny's underwear was big news in August. There was a photograph of her girdle on page two. She'd been examined by a doctor shortly after being charged. He might not have found the lump in her breast but he'd found four rectangular bulges in the hip and buttock region of her girdle. In excess of eight thousand dollars was removed from those pockets.

The Royal Doulton vases and the two statuettes taken by the police from the Doveton house now belonged to Trudy. Jim knew where vases belonged. Pretty things, Jenny was admiring while standing close enough to the open fire to burn.

'Jen!' Jim said. 'She's on the news.'

She turned to face the flashing screen – and there she was, filling the screen, the rounded shoulders, the flat round face, the bulge of floral frock.

Sissy?

Knew that mouth, that heavy jaw. Knew that heavy brow. Remembered Sissy's parrot beak nose, her eyes. Didn't know her red-rimmed glasses.

*She wrote to Lorna almost every week for years and years even though Lorna kept posting those letters back*, Sissy said. *I still think there was something like . . . something romantic going on between them before she moved in with us. I think that's why she did it.*

The interviewer asked why, being aware of her mother's past, Sissy and her husband had taken Amber into their home.

*'The Bible tells us that we need to be . . . to be charitable to people who aren't as well off as us. I've always been a good Christian woman*, Sissy said, and Jenny escaped to the kitchen.

Sissy was on the front page of the morning newspaper. They'd printed her television interview. And there was a promise of more Grinning Granny on page two.

On page two, *Jennifer Hooper, Woody Creek* jumped out and hit Jenny in the eye.

Then the phone started ringing.

You can kill a phone by leaving it off the hook. She killed it.

Then the dogs started barking.

'Good dog,' Jenny said, and if that day it translated into *Climb that bloody gate and dine on bloody cameramen*, who was she to interfere with their game?

The newspapers didn't get a shot of the Grinning Granny's second daughter, so they recycled the Grinning Granny in the weekend supplement, with a photograph of her elasticised girdle, its pockets enhanced by an artist's hand. And below it:

*My dear Miss Hooper,*
*How can I ever repay you for your kindness to a stranger in her time of great need? I fully understand your response on Sunday. Your shock was no doubt as great as my own. Had the deception been a conscious ploy for your sympathy, I would not beg your forgiveness now, but until yesterday I was unaware of my cruel deception . . .*

*. . . As you are aware, my Royal Doulton vases have great sentimental value to me. I thank you for not placing them at risk with my other belongings. I can only assume that one of the young street louts vandalised my case's contents. As to my Waterford crystal bowl, I am sure it and my vases will be safe in your care until I can arrange to collect the last of my belongings . . .*

*In closing, I bless you for your kindness to me when we met as strangers and I hope that one day you can find it within your heart to forgive my accidental deception.*
*My very best regards to you always,*
*Elizabeth*

That was the day winter hit Jenny's soul, the day she removed Amber's vases from the sitting room mantelpiece, wrapped them well then packed them into a box and hid them in the storeroom, behind John's boxes of negatives – and that room colder than a tomb, as was the entrance hall where that cockroach-eyed old sod glared at her and told her to crawl back into the gutter she'd crawled out of.

She walked to the door of the sitting room, vacated by Jim for the winter. He was warm in her kitchen. Tappity-tappity-tap-tap-tap. Bang! Zing! Tappity-tappity-tap-tap-tap.

Cold. Cold. Cold. Cold enough to light the sitting room fire, then to enter the dining room and light a fire in there. The dining room chimney must have been blocked. Smoke billowed into the room. She didn't kill it. She closed the door, allowing that smoke to fumigate Lorna's furniture.

There were five open fireplaces in Vern Hooper's house. By mid-afternoon three were burning and she had a full-time job carrying wood to feed them.

Jim watched her enter with another armload. 'Give it up, Jen. You're wasting wood,' he said.

'I'm a fighter,' she said.

'Are we eating today?'

'The take-away place sells fish and chips.'

Before Christmas he might have followed her, put his arms around her, kissed her and told her that all things pass. Today he turned back to his tappity-tappity-tap-tap-tap.

John opened a can of baked beans. He made toast and tea while Jenny phoned the wood man, who told her that everyone wanted wood yesterday, that he couldn't deliver before next Wednesday. She put the phone down and, aware she was fighting a losing battle, went for bigger guns. Dialled Robert Fulton's number then, without need of a catalogue, she ordered a briquette heater, his biggest, his best.

'I need it installed yesterday, Robert.'

'I'll do my best,' he said.

# The Fire God

A Willama chap installed her metal deity. It ate a bag of briquettes in a day, but before the day ended the sitting room was an oven and heat was trickling through into her sewing room.

For years she'd spoken to Jim about installing a heater. He'd liked the old fireplace as it was. He wasn't happy. He was so unhappy, he refused to learn how to open its door to stoke it.

Black things, dusty, dirty things, briquettes; a briquette stoker's hands turn black, as do their fingernails. Robert delivered a dozen bags of briquettes on Saturday – and his bill. Jenny placed his bill on the hallstand and told him to dump the briquettes in the hall, which would save a good portion of her day walking out to the shed and walking back in. She'd made a start on Maisy's frock.

Jim came from the kitchen to take charge of the bill, and to countermand her order. Robert stacked the bags in the shed while Jim wrote a cheque. Jenny clad herself in an overcoat, beanie and gloves then spent two hours opening bags, and wrapping briquettes four at a time in newspaper. She wrapped four in the Grinning Granny's letter and took pleasure in it. She turned Bob Hawke's face black – apologised to Hazel, then changed her mind about apologising to her and told her that if she wanted to pose with him, then she deserved what she got. Loaded the briquette gifts into the gardening barrow, lost one parcel while manhandling it up the back step, but got it up and wheeled the barrow through the kitchen, through the house and into the sitting room, where she built a pyramid of newspaper wrapped gifts on the left-hand side of the god, the father of all fires, then went out to the shed for more building blocks.

Wind howled through Vern's pine tree, sobbed in the power wires, but for the first winter night in the years she'd lived in that mausoleum, she wasn't wearing a heavy cardigan over her sweater.

'The small dining room is as warm as toast. Take your typewriter and papers in there tomorrow, Jim,' she said.

'The light is no good,' he said.

'Then have a couple of fluorescent lights installed in there so it is good.'

'Every wire in the house needs replacing,' he said. 'And in a month's time we'll be complaining about the heat.'

'If you want to eat, I need my kitchen to cook in.'

'I thought it was our kitchen,' he said.

'I could work around one. I can't work around two.'

'You wanted John to stay.'

'I want him, and my kitchen.' Jim rolled out a completed page, rolled in another. 'What would it cost to have the house rewired?' she asked.

'You've spent our quota for this month,' he said.

She had her own money, her sewing money and Ray's insurance. There was plenty in Vern Hooper's blood money account, and why not spend his blood money on his house, and get rid of that account which had been haunting her for years?

She drove to Willama the following day and got a park out the front of the bank. The changes I've seen, she thought as she joined the tail end of a queue of six waiting for service at a solo teller's window. Until the mid-fifties most Willama businesses had closed their doors for an hour between twelve and one; there'd been a mass exodus of bike-riding staff heading home for a cooked midday meal. Lunch hours had shrunk to half-hours; staff had become thin on the ground, and what there was of them ate in shifts while the customers queued.

She glanced at the withdrawal slip, made out for eight thousand five hundred dollars. Prior to the crash of '87, banks had been paying incredible interest. She'd empty that blood money account today, then dig a deep hole in the back garden and bury that book.

The queue moved too slowly. She had too much time to think. She was only one away from the teller when she admitted to herself that the book meant more to her than the money in it – like the five-pound note she'd won at the talent quest. In Armadale, desperate for sixpence, she hadn't been able to spend the note that had somehow attached itself to Jim's life. He'd been a part of that talent quest night. He'd stood watching more proudly than Norman when the photographer's camera flashed. When he'd gone missing in the war, she'd placed that five-pound note safe in the frame of their family photograph. It was still in the frame, on their bedside table.

And she couldn't spend a penny of that blood money account. Knew that updating that account each June hadn't been to keep the account up to date, but to keep it alive – and to keep Jimmy alive. If she closed it, he'd be gone.

She had no problem spending her own and Ray's insurance money and as a young male moved away, she took his place at the head of queue, tucked her bankbook away and offered a plastic card to the teller.

'Five thousand, please,' she said.

*

John was in bed before Jenny placed the rubber-banded notes beside Jim's typewriter – still in the kitchen.

'I don't need your money,' he said.

'You will,' she said. 'An electrician is coming in next week to rewire the house and install fluorescent lights in the small sitting room.'

He looked at her, then rose from his chair. 'You go too far,' he said, and left the room, left his typewriter and her money on the table.

Five minutes later she followed him to bed. And he wasn't there. She found him in Trudy's unused room.

'Are you asleep?' No reply, and he didn't go to sleep that fast. 'Talk to me, Jim.'

Still no reply.

Maybe she'd gone too far. She went to her sewing room where Maisy's evening gown waited for its hem. Chiffon frocks in stores had machine-stitched hems. Miss Blunt had hand stitched them. She'd taught Jenny how to roll a chiffon hem. She'd rolled a few since, though none of her own. She'd never worn chiffon. She'd never owned a long ballgown.

Picked up Maisy's blue. Picked up a reel of blue thread and her pincushion and returned to the kitchen to stitch, and to think.

At fourteen, she'd worn a long gown and felt like Cinderella. It had ended its life in shreds. As a ten year old she'd worn a magical ankle-length froth of crepe paper frills, designed by Amy for a school concert. It ended its life in a lavatory pan. Sissy's daffodil-yellow dress, altered by Maisy for another of Amy's school concerts, had ended its life in Norman's kitchen stove. She'd almost owned a brand new blue dress to wear to the talent quest. She'd tried it on in Miss Blunt's fitting room. Amber hadn't approved. She'd brought home a gruesome brown.

Jenny's hands, requiring no direction, worked on while she smiled at the memory of her attempt to dye that gruesome brown blue – and created a dirty grey. That same dye-bath had turned Amber's moth-eaten creamy beige ballgown to the prettiest shade of blue – and it had ruined her life.

Shook that thought away, made three fast stitches then rolled another inch or two of hem.

Not often did she allow her mind to roam back to the night of that blue gown with its sheen of green when the light caught its folds. If she hadn't dyed it, if she hadn't worn it to the ball, if she hadn't argued with Norman, if she hadn't climbed out of her bedroom window, there would have been no Margot. Too many ifs, and if there'd been no Margot there would have been no Georgie. Couldn't have survived her life without her beautiful Georgie. And Jimmy. And if not for Margot there would have been no Trudy and no beautiful books with Jennifer Hooper's name on them.

Jennifer Hooper. Would I have been a Hooper if not for the ball and Margot? Would I have married Jim anyway? Probably not. If not for that blue gown, my entire life would have been different. I would have sung in other talent quests, and might have won the next one. I might have sung with the Willama band. I would have gone to that Bendigo boarding school, would have got an education and done something, been something.

What?

Something.

Might-have-beens don't count for much. She shrugged her shoulders, stretched her neck, adjusted her glasses, knew she should have stitched the hem by day but stitched on, determined not to think of Jim, who hadn't been her Jim since he'd heard about Lorna – and had been even less like him since Amber's arrest. Thought of him before the war. Thought of him in Sydney. Loved him. That week in Sydney had been the best week of her life. Loved watching him with Jimmy.

Bloody Sydney.

She'd hand stitched a blueish/green taffeta frock in the boarding house kitchen, the first frock she'd made without Granny watching her every cut, her every stitch. She'd worn it to Barbara's twenty-first birthday party and Lila wouldn't believe Jenny had sewn it. Wore it a second time, to the Sydney club on New Year's Eve, on her twentieth birthday, and those bastards had ripped it from her on a beach, five of them.

You can't fight five. She'd thought she was dead that night, had given in to death and been pleased to give in. Woke stark naked in the sand, an old dog licking her face. He'd guided her eyes to that frock, caught up on a tussock of beach grass, and she'd crawled to it, crawled through sand, every inch of her hurting. It had covered her nakedness – later she'd burnt it in Myrtle's incinerator.

Blue frocks had always been her downfall. Even the blue linen dress-length bought for her twenty-first birthday by Granny. She'd loved that dress. Wore it the night Ray King took her to a New Year's Eve dance. Wore it the day she married him. Had been buttoning it up the day Lorna had driven away with Jimmy.

Black was safer. The red dress Laurie Morgan had bought in Melbourne ended its life black. A frock of many personalities, that one. She'd dyed it in Sydney and stitched a strip of lace to its neckline to offer it respectability. In Armadale she'd removed the lace, respectability not required when she sang at the jazz club with Itchy-foot.

She'd stitched herself a smart black suit in Armadale and worn it for years. After the fire, when she'd been looking for clothing that might fit Georgie, she'd dug that suit out from the back of her wardrobe, and its light wool blend fabric had pressed up as good as new.

And the hem was done. Jenny frowned, checking her work, doubting that it was done. It was. She'd done too much sewing; her hands now worked on automatic pilot. She anchored the thread before snipping it. She checked the seams for dangling threads. Found a few she tied off well before snipping – as Granny had taught her to tie off all threads before snipping.

It was Granny who'd taught her to use the old treadle sewing machine, who'd taught her to measure three times and cut once. An urge to create was her only guide until Miss Blunt, a fabric artist, had taken her in hand and taught her how to draft a pattern, and to roll chiffon hems – and how to charge like a wounded bull. She never charged Maisy, but Maisy always found a way to pay.

Brides paid, or their fathers paid. She'd stitched a lot of fairytale wedding gowns. As a twelve year old, she'd dreamt of marrying Clark Gable. Gave up early on that dream and started dreaming for Georgie. Gave up on her and started dreaming for Trudy. And might as well give up on her too. If she ever married, she'd do it on holiday, in a t-shirt and jeans.

She gave the frock a shake. It needed pressing, but that was for tomorrow. She thought about crawling into Trudy's bed with him. Knew she should. Knew she'd gone too far today – or hadn't gone far enough before. He'd had the money. She'd allowed him to make the decisions on how to spend it.

Maisy's frock returned to the sewing room, she fed her new god another gift, adjusted his air supply for night burning, told him he was the one true god, then returned to the kitchen to stoke and close down the stove.

Didn't want to go to her lonely bed so stood reading Jim's half-completed page. He always left an incomplete page in his typewriter. He'd written two paragraphs beneath *LORNA 1908–1987* and before Jenny was done with her reading she wanted to rip that page from his typewriter and pitch it into the stove. No matter how bad a death might be, it doesn't wash away the deceased's past sins.

She turned to the pile of completed pages he'd placed face down on the table, and she picked up a bunch of eight or ten, hoping to see what he'd written about his father. He wrote well. He wrote too well. Molly Squire had been written well. He wrote in solid blocks of words, dialogue free, a documentation of bland facts. She stood, scanning more pages – and found old James Richard's four wives. They'd warranted a paragraph each; their birth dates, marriage dates, death dates, and the names of the infants who'd killed them.

She hadn't considered Jim to be super intelligent as a kid, though he'd always been a reader, or he had been until his obsession with *Molly Squire*. She sighed and placed his pages down as she'd found them, made a cup of tea, lit a cigarette and thought of Georgie, of Laurie Morgan, found in a secondhand bookshop – and of all of the occupations Jenny might have imagined for him, bookshop proprietor hadn't been one of them.

Georgie had been disappointed in who she'd found. She had a face Jenny could read like an open book. The night she'd driven in late with Jack Thompson's manila envelope, her eyes had been flashing green sparks. Father and daughter, meeting across a counter after forty-six years. That would make a book Jenny would want to read. As would the tale of Lila's many husbands. As would Granny's life story. As would my own, Jenny thought. The world was full of stories people would want to read – and Jim was wasting his time and talent again in documenting a cleaned-up history of a family of pig-headed, bigoted swine.

She glanced again at the half-filled page in the typewriter, *LORNA 1908–1987*. He'd mentioned her mother, Lorna Langdon. She'd died in childbirth. Granny had known her. She'd described her once as a slim-hipped Englishwoman, nine years Vern's senior, approved of by old James because of her connections to the English gentry and her five hundred pounds a year. She'd died with Lorna stuck inside her. A Willama doctor had cut her out of her mother's dead body. Did Jim know that? It was a detail Jenny would have been interested in reading.

She looked at the wall clock. Its small hand had crept past the two. Had to go to bed. Didn't want to, so lit another cigarette and sat down at the typewriter to write what she knew of Lorna Langdon who, according to Granny, Vern hadn't been able to get close enough to, to impregnate.

She completed the page, wound in another and wrote of the totem pole Lorna, of her childhood, and poor dithering Margaret too.

More pages rolled in and out. She wrote of the morning Jimmy had been taken.

Then her rhyming gremlins came out to play.

*RHYME FOR LORNA*
*Morning has broken, a fine day for hunting*
*Carrion bitch is eager to feast*
*Lives to extinguish while daylight comes creeping,*
*Blown out to appease the greed of a beast . . .*

# GOD IS KIND

It was after ten when she woke and she would have slept later had John's elderly Morris not complained for ten minutes before it roared into life.

'Where's he off to?' she asked.

'Willama,' Jim said. His typewriter had gone and his pages. He was stacking his notes.

'What for?'

'Film.'

His one-word replies told her he hadn't appreciated her addition to his Lorna chapter.

'To see one or to buy one?'

'Buy,' he said as he walked from the room, her money and her *Lorna* pages left on the table.

She picked up both and followed him to the dining room. 'The small sitting room is warm.'

'Go away, Jen.'

She tossed the rubber-banded wad down beside his typewriter. 'My sewing money has paid for half of the food on your table. What's the difference?'

'I'm attempting to work,' he said. 'Close the door on your way out.'

'You're into factual material. My chapter is all fact.' There was only his tappity-tap staccato in reply. 'Every word is fact. The bit about your father marrying Lorna's mother for her five hundred pounds a year is fact,' she said.

'If you are attempting to annoy me, you are succeeding,' he said.

'Excellent,' she said. 'You've been annoying me since she died.'

'Have you any idea of the amount of work involved in rewiring a house?'

'No more than five thousand's worth.'

'You didn't discuss it.'

'I didn't have another twenty years to waste discussing it, like I wasted on discussing a heater for the sitting room – and I didn't hear you discussing how you planned to turn what's supposed to be my home into a bloody Hooper museum.'

'I grew up with that furniture.'

'I grew up with Norman's. Can you see any of it about?'

'Go away, Jen.'

'I might take my photograph of Norman out to Simon Jenner and get him to paint me a life-sized portrait – and a matching one of the Grinning Granny.'

She'd got him to his feet.

'Did you ask me before you brought those dogs home to defile every lawn I walk on?'

'Do you prefer tripping over Lila? She hasn't been inside that gate since the dogs started defiling your lawns – and John picks up most of their leavings anyway. And how often have you been outside this winter? You sit all day writing pages of muck that a reader would need a bulldozer to work his way through. You're doing exactly what you did with Molly, mixing up an acre of wet, waist-high mud then pitching a few handfuls of diamonds into it. It's not worth the digging through mud, Jim, and you need to be told before you waste the rest of my life in your puddle.'

'You want to see me angry, Jen?'

'It would be a change from the well-mannered act you've been putting on lately.'

'Go.'

'I should have given you my "Rhyme for Lorna": *Morning has broken, a fine day for hunting, carrion bitch is eager to feast . . .*' she quoted. 'And there you sit conferring sainthood on an evil bitch who took what she wanted from life and didn't give a tuppenny ha'penny damn for the devastation she left behind.'

'Go!'

'If there was a goods train full of sheep passing through town right now I'd stow away in one of their trucks – and they'd be better company than you.' The phone was ringing. She walked into the hall. 'Incidentally,' she yelled, 'I'm bringing the ladder in here and pitching that rat-mouthed old coot. He's polluting the atmosphere.'

She silenced the phone with a sharp 'Hello!' And if it was someone wanting her to sew something, she'd hang up in their ear. But just when you think your world can't get a whole lot worse, it up and proves you wrong again.

'It's Paul, Jen. Georgie has been taken by ambulance to St Vincent's hospital. I'm leaving the college now. I'll call you when I know more.'

'Georgie! What?'

'She was attacked at home. She was able to phone the police and tell them where I worked,' he said. 'I have to go, Jen. I'll call you.'

'Tell her I'm on my way,' Jenny said.

Jim was behind her when she placed the phone down. 'Someone attacked Georgie. She's in St Vincent's hospital. I'm going down there.'

'I'll drive you,' he said.

'You'll need to be here for the electrician,' she said.

Ten minutes later, she was away, two hundred of her five thousand in her handbag. She filled the tank at Teddy's garage, then drove, drove too fast, not daring to pray for Georgie. Nothing she'd ever prayed for had been given. She'd got down on her knees and begged for Jimmy to be given back to her. She'd got down on her knees to plead to God for Jim to be found safe. She'd prayed for weeks for God to take the Macdonald twins' leavings out of her belly. She wouldn't dare a prayer for her Georgie, the only brightness in her world during the dark times. Beautiful Georgie, who'd howled with her when Granny died, who'd sat at her side through the hours of waiting to learn if Ray was alive or dead – her Georgie, who knew every mistake she'd ever made and who'd never blamed her.

It was a three and a half hour trip to the western outskirts of Melbourne; Jenny did it that day in three. Sydney Road, a solid block of traffic, stopped her flight. Frustrated, jammed between trucks, choking on exhaust fumes, she wasted twenty minutes in that jam, then gave up and turned down a side street, parked the car, locked it and ran to catch a city-bound tram. It was four forty before she found the hospital and was directed to the lifts.

She saw Paul first, then Georgie, flat on her back. The tubes dripping into her proved she was alive, and Jenny bawled with relief and throat-choking love for that girl, that woman, her red hair spread on a white pillow, her face near as white as the pillow. Kissed her. Kissed her face and bawled.

'Don't go mushy on me, mate,' Georgie said. 'I look awful when I blush.'

She looked awful already. They'd clad her in a hospital-issue gown, clad a part of her. One shoulder and her lower neck were gauze padded. Her left arm was immobilised, fluid dripping through a tube into it. Paul was holding her right hand, which he released so he might fetch a second chair. Jenny stole that hand awhile.

'I need a pillow,' Georgie said.

'You need to lie flat. You're held together by stitches,' Paul said.

'They didn't give me any blood with AIDS in it, did they?'

'You told them no blood transfusions before they knocked you out,' Paul said.

'A bloke is suing for . . .'

'We're only allowed to sit with you if you sleep,' Jenny said.

Georgie sighed, licked her lips and tried again. 'He crept up on me,' she said. 'I swung the shovel. Or I heard him and swung, or swung then heard him. I can't remember.'

'Did they get him?' Jenny asked.

'I did,' Georgie said, and she closed her eyes.

They thought she was asleep so spoke quietly across her bed. Paul knew little more than he'd known four hours ago, other than that the intruder had driven a taxi he'd parked in the drive, that the police had found the taxi licence of a Novak Wazinosky.

'A taxi driver?' Jenny asked.

'It may have been stolen,' Paul said.

'God is kind,' Georgie said.

'Why?' Jenny asked.

'That's what he said. *God is kind.* I think I heard him say it before I swung.' They looked at her. She sighed, again licked her lips then tried to explain the finer details. 'I wanted to hang him, not murder him,' she said. 'It replays when I close my eyes. It's like watching an action movie on fast forward.'

'You're supposed to be resting,' Paul said.

'Tell them he's not What's-his-namesky.'

'Go to sleep,' Paul said.

'I'll go,' Jenny said.

'Did you charter a plane or something?' Georgie asked.

'I'll probably go home to ten speeding tickets,' Jenny said.

'I'll represent you in court,' Georgie said.

She was drunk on painkillers or the anaesthetic, a different-sounding, sleepy Georgie, her eyes closing between utterances. This time she closed them for so long, Paul attempted to release her hand.

'Just remembered. I mightn't be able to represent you,' she said. 'Did Marino call?'

'I haven't been home,' Paul said.

'I was taking a sickie. You'd better tell him when he calls that I was digging a hole to vomit into.'

'Stop talking,' Jenny said.

'He'll probably sack me, not represent me,' Georgie said.

Jenny stood, brushed the hair back from Georgie's brow, kissed her scarred eyebrow and knew she'd have more scars after today. But she was alive, and now she needed rest.

'I'll see you in the morning, darlin'.'

Georgie reached out a hand to prevent her leaving. 'Didn't you tell me once that Amber tried to cut your father's head off with a shovel?'

'She broke his collarbone,' Jenny said.

'That would make it . . . make it premeditated,' she said.

'You've got forty-odd stitches in your arm and shoulder,' Paul said.

'They only put five in my eyebrow. He had one of those carpet layer's knives.' She swallowed. 'I need a beer.'

'You need to stop talking and we need to go,' Paul said.

'I was on the phone to the cops and I looked out the window to see if he was coming in and saw a trail of blood heading for the door. I thought he was coming in. It was me . . . my blood. Did they give me a blood transfusion?'

'You told them not to,' Paul repeated.

'There's probably some by-law . . . some council by-law . . . about how sharp a shovel is allowed to be before . . . before it's reclassified as a lethal weapon.'

'Go to sleep,' Jenny said.

'You're easier to look at than what I see when I close my eyes.'

Jenny sat again. There was nowhere else she wanted to be.

'I only meant to flatten him,' Georgie said. 'I hit a kangaroo in Queensland and killed it and felt like a murderer. I hit him and I don't. What's the time?'

'Ten past five,' Paul said.

'You'll get someone at the office. Have they got a phone in this place?'

'I'll call him tomorrow,' Paul said.

'He defended a bloke . . .' She swallowed, licked her lips then continued, '. . . who brained a druggie with a cricket bat and the cops charged him . . . not the druggie. You can't go around hitting druggie thieves with hard luck stories.'

At five thirty, a nursing sister hunted Jenny and Paul from the ward.

'Where did you park, Jen?'

'Off Sydney Road somewhere. In Brunswick – or close to it.'

'I'll see if I can get word to Georgie's boss, then we'll get going,' he said.

Chris Marino wasn't in the office, but the woman who took the call said she'd see that the message reached him tonight.

There are a lot of side streets off Sydney Road around Brunswick, a lot of tram stops, but they found the Holden, and Jenny followed Paul down back road and highway, aware that if she lost sight of his car, she herself would be lost. Tonight, drunk with relief, she stayed on his tail, barely aware of the traffic. He caught the end of a green light. She caught the beginning of the red, but didn't lose him.

He served leftover spaghetti bolognaise that night, and while he spoke to his mother, Jenny stood outside blowing smoke into the night and looking at the trail of Georgie's bloodstains on the paving.

Paul's brother called, Jim called. Then Chris Marino called and Jenny and Paul learned that that Novak Wazinosky had died at the scene.

*

They were back at the hospital at ten thirty the following morning and found Georgie in a different ward, a private ward, found her propped on pillows, two uniformed men on her left, a chubby, balding chap on her right. Paul introduced him to Jenny as Chris Marino.

'Have we met?' he asked, studying her face intently while shaking her hand.

'I've heard a lot about you,' Jenny said.

'All good, I hope,' he said, then turned back to the business at hand.

The room being too small for six and the uniforms and the notebooks speaking of repercussions for Georgie, Jenny left and walked downstairs. She ordered a cup of tea, picked up a newspaper, its headlines screaming: PREGNANT WOMAN ATTACKED IN HER HOME.

That's Melbourne for you, she thought. She'd known it as a safe city where the bad had been locked away, the mad hidden away in asylums, when governments had spent their money where it had needed spending. It went on renovating Bob Hawke's lodge now, on ex-prime ministers' overseas trips, on communal junkets, while the mad and the bad walked the streets.

She paid for her tea and newspaper then, in need of a place where she could smoke, found her way to an outdoor table, complete with ashtray. Sugared her tea, got her smoke burning then spread out the newspaper.

*Georgina Dunn, a solicitor with Marino and Associates, was attacked in her Greensborough home yesterday by a knife-wielding intruder . . .*

Dunn? Georgina?

Jenny looked back at the headlines. PREGNANT WOMAN ATTACKED IN HER HOME. She looked again at the name. Georgina Dunn?

Georgie? She was too old to be pregnant.

Dunn?

If she was pregnant, she would have married him – and, knowing Georgie, she wouldn't have bothered to tell anyone. And Jenny was on her feet, her cigarette mashed into the ashtray. She gulped a mouthful of tea, another, then left the remainder to grow cold as she returned to that private ward at a near run, her newspaper gripped as evidence.

The uniformed men had gone but Chris Marino was still there. Jenny waited until he'd left then closed the door and, her evidence held high, approached the defendant.

'Is it true?'

Georgie's one available hand reached for the paper. 'The buggers,' she said. 'How did they get onto that?'

'It would be Marino's doing,' Paul said. 'He makes every post a winner.'

'Is it true?' Jenny repeated.

'Yeah, but don't count your chickens before they hatch, mate. I've already lost two and I'll probably lose this one now – and not another word about it or I'll have you evicted.'

'How far along are you?'

'It's due in December,' Paul said.

'On Jimmy's birthday. Now, the subject is closed, Jen,' Georgie said, and she read aloud from the newspaper: *'The intruder, Novak Wazinosky, a Polish immigrant, had been with the taxi company since the mid-eighties, a spokesman told reporters yesterday. He said that Novak was a reliable driver.*

'I told the cops before they loaded me into the ambulance that it was Dino Collins. What's wrong with them?'

They got it right by nightfall. It was in the morning newspapers, and when Jenny and Paul arrived at the hospital at eleven, Georgie had her own copy of the Melbourne *Sun*.

> *Police yesterday officially identified the Greensborough intruder as James Robert Collins, who was involved in the Grenville kidnapping in 1977. Collins' de facto wife, Raelene King, the natural mother of the kidnapped infant, died when she was trapped in the Woody Creek house fire that killed her stepsister, Margot Morrison. Margot Morrison was the granddaughter of Amber Morrison.*

There was more, a lot more, but Georgie had read enough. 'They'll join their dots,' she said. 'They'll have me connected to the Grinning Granny by morning and have found me a motive for murder.'

'You defended yourself in your own backyard and if you hadn't, you'd be dead,' Jenny said.

'You're thinking with your head, Jen, as an individual. The new world is reverting back to a pack mentality. They don't think. They sniff each other's backsides then bay for blood. Cast your mind back to Lindy.'

'That sort of thing wouldn't happen these days,' Jenny said.

'No,' Georgie said. 'It would happen a damn sight faster. The human pack thrives on its daily dose of soap opera, celebrities and drama, and Dino Collins was the whole damn deal. Born of the Virgin Mary, beloved only son of Joseph, Dino was orphaned at the age of eleven in a horrendous accident, when the boy hero turned to drugs to mask his pain. He was tempted by forbidden fruit, and for love of his temptress, was crippled in a car accident. He descended into clinical depression, but after years in hell, he rose and ascended into heaven, or into the arms of his loving wife and nurse, who with her love and compassion cured him of depression and miraculously repaired his damaged spine. And they lived happily ever after. But no, enter the devil, in the guise of the evil redheaded solicitor, stepsister of the temptress, granddaughter of well-known killer, Amber Morrison, who with one blow from her razor-sharp shovel, stole poor long-suffering Dino Collins' life. Get me out of here, Paul. Shave my head and carry me if you have to,' Georgie said.

They took her home that evening.

# The Manuscript

Chris Marino came, and when Jenny opened the door to him, he stared a moment, forced a smile, then got down to business. It was a busy week in Greensborough. She opened the door to Irene Dunn, to her sons. She hung up the phone on newspaper reporters, who had not connected the dots yet between Georgie Morrison, grocery shop proprietor, and Georgina Dunn, solicitor.

Jim rang twice, each time asking when she'd be home.

'Georgie needs me down here,' Jenny said.

He needed his car, though he didn't say so, not straight out. He spoke of driving with John to Willama and leaving a trail of blue smoke behind. He spoke of the severe knock in the old Morris motor, and how that day he hadn't expected the car to get them home.

'Use Trudy's car. It needs a run,' Jenny said.

'It's a manual,' Jim said.

'John drives a manual.'

'John sits on thirty miles an hour,' Jim said.

Jenny had been a passenger in John's car once, and if he'd got his old heap up to thirty miles an hour, she'd have been surprised.

'I'll bring the car home at the weekend,' she said.

The worst of Georgie's injuries was to her upper arm. The knife had cut deep there. Muscle takes a long time to heal. There was little she could do. She read. She talked and Jenny talked. On the Thursday, Jenny was at the letterbox when Chris Marino drove in. She walked him around the house to the rear door, and once more he gave her his piercing stare, and this time didn't look away.

'I had a call yesterday from a girl I knew many years ago, a Cara Grenville, previously Norris. Your resemblance to her is quite striking,' he said.

'Where is she?' It was a reflex question and, aware that an explanation was necessary, Jenny added, 'She's a distant relative.'

'I noticed the similarity at our first meeting,' he said. 'She's in London. She married an Englishman and moved over there with her children in '78.'

Georgie was in the family room. 'Chris had a call from Cara,' Jenny said.

'She called to verify an Australian friend's information. The friend had mentioned that Collins had attacked one of my solicitors.'

'He kidnapped her foster daughter the Christmas of '77,' Jenny said.

'I was her solicitor at the time, Mrs Hooper,' Chris said.

'You don't know her phone number?' Georgie asked.

'No. She had little to say other than how she and her children could now sleep safe in their beds – and to enquire after your injuries and wish you a speedy recovery.'

Jenny had intended leaving at daybreak on Saturday morning but altered her plans when Irene Dunn arrived at ten on Friday morning. Jenny left at ten thirty, following Georgie and Paul's route out to the Hume Freeway, through Whittlesea. It was an easy drive. She was home before two and Jim pleased to see his car.

'A good trip?'

'Fast,' she said. He didn't kiss her hello, so she turned to the dogs, who didn't give a damn about the car; they loved her, and told her so.

She'd shopped in Willama. The men unloaded the car while she ran for the toilet – it smelled like a public loo, and the main bathroom looked as if it had been hit by a cyclone. Her bed hadn't been made for a week and the kitchen looked like a squat for the homeless. She cleaned while she cooked. She swept, turned a kilo of steak into a stew, then vacuumed while a lump of corned beef boiled. Cut up half a loaf of stale bread and turned it into a pudding, mopped floors, lit the briquette heater, served dinner, then Jim went into the sitting room to watch the news in comfort, and she washed the dishes. John dried them, then went to the bathroom.

It was eight o'clock when he said goodnight; Jenny was weary enough to go to bed. She'd showered, was clad for sleep, but instead began searching her wardrobe for garments Georgie might wear. Although she refused to discuss what she was growing, she'd grown out of her jeans. Jenny found a black pinafore dress she'd worn in the seventies. Plenty of room in it. It wasn't long enough but she could cut it shorter and turn it into a smock. She found a pair of elastic-waisted stretch slacks which, with an inch or two off, would make serviceable pedal pushers. She folded them and placed them into an open case.

'What are you doing, Jen?'

'They'll fit Georgie.' She stripped a seventies caftan from its hanger.

'You're going back?'

'On the Sunday bus.' She added a long shirt to the case. 'She needs someone with her.'

'You said she was well.'

'She is well, but her arm isn't, and you can't go around decapitating people with a shovel. She'll be charged with something.'

'It was self-defence,' he said.

'I know that, you know it, but he's dead and she's alive, and the last thing she needs right now is to be stuck in that house by herself all day, thinking about what might happen.'

He left her to her packing and she heard him at his typewriter in the dining room. The electrician had been and gone, the new fluorescents were hanging in the small sitting room, but he'd chosen not to move there.

She looked at a muted floral shift frock, a late sixties style, and what the hell was it still doing in her wardrobe? She'd never learnt to throw anything away – Granny's doing, her 'waste not, want not' having been drummed into Jenny's head for too many years. She added the shift to the case then walked across the hall to the dining room doorway.

'The little sitting room is warm. Amy's desk is in there. It would make a perfect study.'

'I'm comfortable,' he said.

'You've done a lot while I've been away.' His stack of completed pages had grown, and grew one page higher while she stood.

'I thought I was going to lose Georgie.'

'What do you do down there all day?'

'She's been teaching me how to work her computer. You need to get one, Jim. It would save you a ton of rewriting.'

'I'm too old to learn new tricks, Jen,' he said and, the conversation over, he wound a new page into his typewriter.

'I've been away for a week, John's in bed. Can't you stop that for a minute and talk to me?'

'I've been attempting to finish this chapter all day.'

'And tomorrow there'll be another chapter, then another one, then another one.'

'I'm trying to finish a book, Jen.'

'I'm trying to work out what's going on in your mind. You wanted your car, I brought it home for you. I cooked your dinner, washed your dishes. What else should I have done to be worthy of your attention?'

He typed another line, his ten fingers working as a team, flying across those keys.

'When we got back together you made me believe that I was the most important person in your life. I'm less important to you now than your car.'

'Stop,' he said.

'You stop. You couldn't even kiss me hello.'

Zing! Bang!

'You refused to have anything to do with your family before we got back together. Nobby told me how he'd found your cousin and you refused to speak to him. I had to plead with you to write to Margaret – and when you did you wrote her a business letter.'

Zing. Bang.

'She wasn't the black-hearted bitch Lorna was. If you'd begged her, if you'd pleaded with her, I might have got to watch Jimmy grow,' she said.

Zing. Bang.

'And now that they're all dead and safely buried, you surround yourself with them. This house is supposed to be my home too, and the whole bloody place stinks of Lorna.'

'It was my mother's furniture!'

'You're not writing about your mother. You're turning every Hooper who ever walked into a hero. They weren't heroes. They were a kidnapping, self-serving mob of pig-headed swine, and the reason why you didn't kiss me hello was because you're now seeing me through bloody old James Hooper's cockroach eyes.'

'You're talking arrant nonsense,' he said, his hands hovering over the keyboard like wounded birds who'd lost their way.

She'd said too much. She stepped back to the hall, but that old swine was looking at her, and tonight he knew he'd won. It was in his eyes, in the angle of his rat moustache, so she turned back.

'I told you when we were in Sydney that there'd come a day when you'd start seeing me through your family's eyes and that you wouldn't like what you saw.'

'For God's sake, drop it, Jen.'

'Admit it and I'll drop it. Admit that every time you look at me you see Amber bludgeoning your sister. She isn't my mother, Jim, and it's not my fault that your sister was such an old bitch that no one noticed she was missing. It's not my fault that you cut yourself off from them. I would have kowtowed to her, I would have licked the soles of Margaret's shoes if it would have bought me one hour with Jimmy.'

'Stop it now,' he moaned.

'They're haunting you,' she said. 'They're haunting this house and that rat-mouthed old coot out there is their medium.'

He rose and attempted to get by her. She caught his arm. 'Talk to me.'

'What do you want from me?!'

'Start with why you prefer to spend your night with dead Hoopers than with me, why you haven't touched me since they arrested Amber.'

'Put yourself in my place,' he said.

'I've been putting myself in your place for years. I've been pussy-footing around your place, your space, since that day in Ringwood when I found out that you'd let Margaret adopt Jimmy. Every time you get into one of your sitting, staring at walls moods, I pussy-foot around you. And I'm done with it, Jim, and I'm done with that evil-eyed old coot hanging up there too, and to tell you the unblemished truth, had it been anyone other than Amber who'd murdered Lorna, my sympathy would be with the murderer.'

He shook off her hand and went to the bathroom. It had a lock on its door.

*

Jenny didn't sleep, and when there was light enough to see, she rose and went out to the shed to fetch the stepladder. John, early to bed, early to rise, caught her manhandling the ladder in through the front door. He helped her position it and steadied it when she climbed to remove the portrait's chain from its hook. Not an easy task. The frame was heavy, but with him supporting it, the chain came off – and he had to dodge it as it crashed to the floor.

She climbed down, expecting the noise to have woken Jim, but Trudy's room was a good distance from the hall and he didn't come. She expected some damage to the frame, but the old ones had made their frames to last for a few lifetimes. She climbed again to hang Simon Jenner's landscape, then together she and John returned the ladder to the shed. She dragged and carried the portrait out to the front veranda then along it to the east side where she leaned it against the wall.

The dogs came to sniff, and if they did more than sniff, then the old coot deserved what he got. He'd married four young wives and at a time when he should have been too old to need a wife. All four had died in childbirth or soon after.

Jim retrieved the portrait before she carried her case from the house. 'If he's hanging when I come back, I'll cut him from the frame and burn him next time.'

The case was small but heavy. Get enough sheets of foolscap together and they become weighty. The *Molly Squire* manuscript consisted of four hundred and fifty-two pages, his and hers.

# Sent in Chains

Georgie read *Molly Squire* in two days, Jenny watching her face all the while, watching her smile, rub her eyes, watching too as she flipped fast through bunches of pages, then hearing her chuckle.

'Well?' she asked when Georgie was done.

'Well, well, well,' Georgie said. 'Do you want the scrupulous truth or the toned-down version, Jen?'

'Scrupulous?'

'The major problem, as I see it, is you can pick where your chapters begin and Jim's end. They need smoothing out, or you need to make it obvious that there are two separate viewpoints.'

'How?'

'How would I know? You need to get it onto a computer.'

'Amy would have been able to type it in. I'd die of old age before I'd typed fifty pages.'

'Use a scanner,' Georgie said, picking up and sifting through a few of the pages. 'Paul's college has got one. It should do most of it.'

'What's a scanner?'

'A machine that reads text then copies it to disc,' Georgie said.

'I wouldn't be game to let anyone see it.'

'Machines don't see – and why write it if you don't plan for anyone to see it?'

'That old rhyme got into my head.'

'Where did it come from?'

'We don't know.'

'Number two problem,' Georgie continued. 'Molly and Wadimulla are gripping. There are bits in those chapters that are so you, it's hilarious. Then you hit me with a slab of history and it's like moving from fast forward into slow.'

'It's Jim's book. Amy and I tried to leave as much of his work in it as we could.'

'Get rid of him and you'd have a damn good read.'

Paul took the manuscript to work on Friday and returned it that night along with three discs, more of modern man's magic to Jenny. She didn't understand it, and didn't try. Georgie flipped the first disc into her computer, hit a few keys and up came Molly's poem.

'My God.'

Thereafter the days flew by too fast, the red and the fading gold heads side by side at the computer, Georgie instructing, at times commanding, Jenny selecting paragraphs confidently, Georgie reaching across occasionally to hit the *delete* key Jenny couldn't make herself hit. But the text moved up to fill the gap and left no scar behind.

Within three days they'd deducted thirty-two pages from file one. Jim's pages. He hadn't phoned. Jenny had phoned once. He was well mannered. He asked after Georgie's health, and when she put the phone down, Jenny felt guilty. He'd spent years researching and writing *Molly* and she'd just wiped out fifty per cent of his research.

They were nearing the end of disc three when Georgie came up with the idea of an addition – Molly's half-white son.

'They were at it like rabbits on disc one. Molly probably had half a dozen kids to Wadimulla. What happened to them, Jen?'

'There was no Wadimulla. I cooked him up,' Jenny said.

'Then cook him up a son,' Georgie said. 'And while you're about it, cook up a few of Molly's starving siblings in Ireland. There's too much telling in your first chapter. Open the book with a death scene for one of them and the rest dying of starvation before Molly goes out and sells herself for a loaf of bread.'

'How could I cook that up?'

'Think back to Armadale, Jen, and making us pancake sandwiches for school lunches – and minced vegie pancakes and fried dough-balls for dinner. Send a few of her siblings out to the paddocks to pick nettles.'

Jenny wiped out five hours that night remembering her fight to feed three kids back in Armadale when Ray had taken her purse and bankbook. Before she shut down the computer she'd written Ray into the story. Molly had traded her virgin body for a loaf of the stuttering baker's bread, and Jenny knew exactly how young Molly had felt, like a beached starfish attached by a ravenous beak. She'd sold herself to Ray so she could give her trio his name.

That chapter became the opening chapter, hopeless, sad, but moving, and when Georgie read it on the screen, she shook Jenny's hand.

'That's what I'm talking about, mate,' she said. Amy had said much the same when she'd read a similar chapter. *That, Jennifer Morrison, is what I've always known you were capable of.*

*

Chris Marino phoned to let them know that the hearing into Dino Collins' death had been delayed again. Georgie wanted it done. She wanted to go back to work. Chris wanted her to look pregnant.

He stage-managed Georgie's day in court. He told her he'd need her to present herself in a feminine maternity frock, her hair worn in a soft style. By the end of September she was living in stretch slacks and oversized sweaters. She didn't own a maternity frock. Chris Marino's wife, who had spent most of her married life pregnant, owned plenty. He arrived the evening before the hearing with a choice of two – a pink, ultra feminine frilly thing and a spring green with box pleats but no frills – and a two-inch hem Jenny could let down.

The show went according to Chris Marino's plan. The magistrate, a white-headed grandfather, came back with the right decision, the only decision. Justifiable homicide. Georgina Dunn, who had already lost two infants, had defended herself and her unborn baby with the only weapon at hand. There had been no intent to kill the intruder. She'd raised the shovel only to parry her attacker's knife.

They drank champagne that night at a hotel, and Jenny ate a meal she hadn't cooked. Too relieved, too wound up to sleep, they sat talking until twelve, and when Paul and Georgie went to bed, Jenny started up the computer. She found Molly's half-black son standing at the tall gates to his mother's mansion. He'd walked for miles, led by some ancient awareness that the mother he'd known for six years was dying. Near dawn, he crept up to the house and in through a rear door. And Molly had known him, had reached out a hand to him, and with her final breath, spoke his name.

*'Joeyboy? My Joeyboy,' she whispered.*

And having found him old, Jenny wanted to find him young. She knew how Molly had lost him. He'd been stolen away by the tribe after the white settlers shot Wadimulla.

Had Georgie not returned to work, *Molly Squire* might have grown to a thousand pages, but Chris Marino wanted her at work. He told her she'd be joining him in Sydney in October.

'I get to stick my nose inside a courtroom, Jen.'

'For how long?'

'He said a week to ten days. He's not often wrong.'

'You'll be seven months pregnant,' Jenny said.

'Wrong choice of subject matter, mate.'

'Why, Georgie?'

'Donny,' Georgie said.

Donny, Ray's retarded son, Jenny had babied for seven years. She glanced at Georgie's growing bulge. Thought of her age, of the O'Briens' youngest girl, thirty-odd and still a child in her mind. It could happen – but wouldn't happen, not to Georgie's baby.

The printer churned out three hundred and ninety-eight numbered pages, including the title page, *MOLLY SQUIRE*, in large print, *J. AND J. HOOPER* beneath it, and on the final Sunday in September, those pages travelled home in Jenny's case, though not on the bus. Paul and Georgie drove her home.

Paul Jenner's landscape still hung in the hall. She glanced into the sitting room, expecting to find old rat mouth had taken up residence over the mantelpiece. He wasn't there. The bathroom was a pig pen, the kitchen a mess. She walked by the mess to the laundry to fetch bleach and mirror cleaner. Gave the main bathroom a wipe, splashed bleach into the toilet, dusted the floor with a soiled towel, hung clean towels and was sweeping the kitchen floor when she heard Georgie mention power points in the sewing room. Jenny stopped sweeping to see why she needed power points.

She knew Paul had ordered a new computer, a bigger, faster model. She hadn't been aware that his old model had made the trip up with them. Paul was setting it up on the cutting table, close to a power source.

'You can't just give it away,' Jenny said.

'Done,' Paul said.

Dust was thick on her sewing machines and cutting table. She gave the table a wipe with a scrap of fabric while Jim and John stood back watching the bits and pieces of that magical machine being connected, cables with weird fittings plugged into weird sockets. And Paul had brought his printer. Jenny watched him fit its plugs, her mind darting to what was in her case. She looked at John, who stepped in closer to watch, looked at Jim, and their eyes met. She'd told him a dozen times that he ought to buy a computer.

'It's Paul's,' Jenny said.

'I need its space for my new model,' Paul explained and plugged in his own power board.

And the magical beast awakened and Georgie slid the first *Molly* disc into it. Up came the title page.

'What have you been up to down there?' Jim asked.

'I'll show you later,' Jenny said, demonstrating how to close that file fast, flip it out and flip in another, the safer, solitaire game.

She played it, on her feet before the computer, and for the first time the cards fell in exactly the right way. She won.

Georgie and Paul didn't stay for lunch. Jenny fed the men an omelette, and two hours later, when the kitchen looked and smelled like her kitchen again, she fetched the manuscript and dumped it on the dining room table beside Jim's typewriter.

'That's what we've been up to,' she said.

He was interested and, feeling sick with the knowledge of what they'd done to it, she left him to read and took the dogs for a walk down to Granny's land.

The manuscript was on her cutting table beside her computer when she returned, a red line through one of the *I*'s and the *and.* He was in the dining room. She placed the title page down near him. 'I take it that you don't want your name on it.'

'It's all yours, Jen.'

'How much of it did you read?'

'Enough,' he said. 'Can we leave it at that?'

'Fine,' she said, her stomach aflutter. Amy had liked what she'd done. Georgie had been impressed. She trusted their opinions.

Had trusted his once.

Walked away from him. Walked around the veranda, then returned to her sewing room and closed the twin doors. For half an hour she sat turning the pages of the manuscript, attempting to see, to feel how much of it he'd read. Shrugged her shoulders and turned on the computer, then riffled through the discs Georgie had copied for her until she found Itchy-foot's diary. Barely thirty pages into it, she found the young Gertrude . . . *a feisty young beauty who resides in a pig pen and has opinions above her station.* He hadn't mentioned her name, but there was no doubt in Jenny's mind that his feisty young beauty was Granny. She read on, absorbing every word, read of a grand garden party at Monk's, and less than four months later, according to Itchy-foot's dates, she found Gertrude again, this time in verse.

> *The feisty new missus, though she has tasty kisses,*
> *Of late begins dodging her lover.*
> *Much prefers yarning out in the garden,*
> *than sliding beneath the bed cover.*

Two days later, on the disc containing the diary, she found Juliana Conti. There were mentions of Itchy-foot's many love affairs scattered throughout, so many that Jenny hadn't recognised his early description of her mother, the barren banker's wife, until . . . *a scratching, biting, fighting lioness, protecting its lone cub. Why am I attracted to fighting bitches?* Until that moment, Juliana Conti had been John's black and white photograph of a dead foreign woman; she'd been *J.C. LEFT THIS LIFE 31.12.23* cut into a small grey tombstone in the cemetery. That disc gave her life.

By November, Jim's old rattler was silent. He'd completed his history and posted it up to Sydney. *Molly Squire* was gathering dust on Jenny's cutting table where she might never cut again. She'd found a more absorbing occupation. With the help of Itchy-foot's diaries and her Tuesday afternoon sessions with Maisy, she was creating the young Gertrude Hooper and her world of horse-drawn ploughs and long gowns and garden parties and lamplit balls, and to hell with *Molly Squire.*

Deep into organising a grand wedding for young Gertrude, Granny's own brocade wedding gown hung over a chair at her side, the phone rang. She sat, her hands hovering over the keyboard, hopeful that Jim would think it was the publisher and pick it up. He usually did. Not today. She hit *save* and caught the phone before it rang out.

'We have a six and a half pound daughter, Jen,' Paul said.

'It's too early!' Jenny said.

'Three weeks and three days, but that's Georgie, always in a hurry.' Silence then, and emotion in his voice when he continued. 'They're both well. She's perfect, Jen, and as red and beautiful as her mother. Katie Morgan Dunn, Georgie said.'

'Tell her we're on our way,' Jenny said.

'We're in Sydney. I flew up last night.'

*

Thanks to Chris Marino, Georgie had barely felt a ripple from the Dino Collins affair. He hadn't billed her for his time, but she'd always known he'd claim his pound of flesh one day. She called him the Boss God. A few called him the Godfather, and some, the Little Dictator. He resembled Marlon Brando – not the aging Brando of *The Godfather*, more the balding, pot-bellied Brando of *Napoleon.* The courtroom was his theatre, and just as he'd stage-managed the James Dino Collins affair, he staged each production.

When he'd told her that she'd be with him in Sydney in October, she'd known why. The Collins affair had been newsworthy and he'd be defending a young mother of four charged with the murder of her brutal husband. The trial was delayed, then delayed again, and when you're seven and a half months pregnant, a three and a half week delay takes you into your eighth month. She could have got out of it, but had wanted to watch him at work.

She'd watched him for four days. Watched him in fancy restaurants, too, where he'd taken her each night to eat. They'd been in court when the pains started.

Their client was acquitted five days later. Chris flew home, but the company paid for a hire car and, when Katie was a week old, they drove her home via Woody Creek.

Week-old babies don't win beautiful baby contests and Katie was no exception. She looked like a tiny orang-utan, as had her mother forty-eight years ago, and as had that earlier orang-utan, she stole a large handful of Jenny's heart.

'What have you done with *Molly*?' Georgie asked.

'Nothing,' Jenny said, the tiny orang-utan grunting in her arms.

'Why not?'

'Jim.' Jenny shrugged.

'What about Jim?'

'It was his factual history of a town. To use his words, I've turned it into a penny dreadful.' She shrugged again. 'I can't go sullying the Hooper name, can I – not even for money.'

'Where is it?'

'In my sewing room, on the table.'

'I'll get rid of it for him,' Georgie said.

*

She was on maternity leave for six months. Katie slept in four-hour shifts – sometimes. Georgie had the original discs. It took one four-hour shift to cut the last of Jim's long-winded chapters down to two vital paragraphs, then to dump those paragraphs into the following chapter.

There was little of the original left, so Georgie spent another four-hour shift altering names. *Squire* became *Flanagan*, so *Molliston* had to go. *Flanagan Hill* grew in its place. The giant gum tree turned into an elm; Molly's daughters became *Myrna* and *Laura*. The hotel moved into the middle of town and the police station slid halfway down the hill. She came up with a new title during Katie's six to ten o'clock sleeping shift, and typed a new title page: *SENT IN CHAINS by Jennifer Hooper.*

Still sullying the Hooper name. She deleted it and typed in *Morrison*.

'Add *daughter of the notorious Grinning Granny* and it will make the bestseller list,' Paul said.

'Yeah,' Georgie said. She deleted *Jennifer Morrison* and tried *Juliana Conti.*

'That looks good,' Paul said. 'Who was she?'

'Jenny's mother. She had Jenny beside a railway line and died a few hours later.'

During another morning shift Georgie wrote a thumbnail synopsis and a brief letter, which included the titles of the McPherson/Hooper children's books, published by their company. She put her own address on it, her own phone number. Didn't want them contacting Jenny, who she had no intention of telling what she'd done, but it was a damn good read and, as Granny had always said, waste not, want not.

She enclosed a cheque for its return postage, sent it on its way to Sydney and forgot about it.

# A Wrong Year

Nobby's son phoned on the evening of the twenty-ninth of December. 'Mrs Hooper,' he said. 'It's Steve, Nobby's son. It's bad news,' he said. 'Dad had a heart attack this afternoon. He was gone before the ambulance got here.'

It was the wrong time. It was so wrong. Georgie and Katie and Paul had spent two days in Woody Creek over Christmas. Trudy had called from Venice. Jim was still on a high from that call, as was she. With old James Richard's cockroach eyes gone from the entrance hall, all had been well with their world. Jim was back in his own bed, and certain his Hooper tome would be accepted for publication.

He was watching a television comedy. Jenny turned it off. 'It's Nobby,' she said, and it was the wrong thing to say. He stood, believing Nobby was on the phone. 'His son, Jim,' she added quickly. Maybe her face said what she couldn't say. Jim stood waiting. So she said it. 'He had a heart attack this afternoon.'

Then she bawled.

*

They drove to Ringwood via Lilydale. They sat through the funeral, saw Rosemary collapse, saw her son carry her from the church.

A dozen of Nobby's RSL mates were there. Two remembered Jim. Hoop, they called him, and they wanted him to go to the pub and have a final drink for Nobby. He looked to Jenny to get him out of it, but she didn't know how.

Four wives went with their men and Jenny didn't know the RSL wives. She did her best. She counted the glasses of beer Jim emptied, listened to too many conversations that included 'Rosemary won't survive this.'

Most do, Jenny thought, and lit a cigarette, but one of the wives was allergic to smoke, so she stood and walked out to the pavement to smoke with the lepers.

Jim was no drinker. Three beers were too many. She stopped counting after three. When he was done her shoulder supplied a crutch out to the car park. He had the keys. She refused to get into the passenger seat. He argued that he was fine to drive. She argued that he wasn't, but he wanted to go home so gave up the keys. Somehow she got the car back to Greensborough, through peak-hour traffic, Jim asleep beside her. To her dying day she'd never know which roads she'd driven. Jim was in bed before Paul served dinner.

Jenny wanted to stay a few days in Greensborough, to allow the new life of her Katie to wash away Nobby's death. Jim wanted to go home. They left early, Jenny behind the wheel. She drove out via Whittlesea, Jim sorry and sober beside her. Home to a dusty, dirty new year, to forty-degree temperatures, blistering north winds that dried the first sheet before the last was pegged, sheets which smelled of burning forest when she brought them in. Back in the old days when five mills had screamed their victory over logs, when the loggers had kept old timber truck tracks open, when farmers had cleared wide firebreaks around their properties, bushfires and grass fires hadn't been as common.

Then two days later, Harry came to their door on a day when the smell of smoke was on the air and the heat so intense the dogs could barely raise a bark of protest. Jenny knew when she saw his freckles, like blotches of mud on grey clay that day.

'Else,' he said. That's all he said. He didn't need to say more.

Jenny didn't speak. Was there one word worth saying, one question worth asking? She stepped out into the heat to hold him on Vern Hooper's veranda, to hold him tight, then tighter, and to howl. A howling month that January. The calendar hanging on the hook behind the kitchen door was too gay with its beachgoers and its boats on cool water, and its 1989. All wrong. This was the year Jenny would turn sixty-six, and if she looked at 1989 upside down, there were those two sixes taunting her: 6861. She was old. Her friends were dying.

Harry asked her to sing at the funeral. She tried. She opened her mouth to sing for Elsie. The organist played the introduction a second time, then Jenny ran out into the burning heat, hot enough, dry enough, to turn her tears to salt. Walked home through the railway yard, walked fast to the shade of the veranda and elm tree where she sat and howled with her arms around her dogs. They kissed her. They calmed her before Jim and John came home with the key.

A blank of days. A black pit where Elsie had always been. She'd been there before Margot, before Georgie. She'd been there the day they'd carried Jenny out to Maisy's car, Jimmy stuck inside her. Always there. And she'd been so well at Christmas time when she'd held Katie. *All good things come to those who wait, lovey.* Dead of a brain haemorrhage. She'd had a bit of a headache. Dead in minutes, Harry said. Gone.

And lanky, raw-boned Harry, smoking faster than he could roll them, his freckled hands never still, and looking so wrong without little Elsie at his side.

Trickling eyes eventually run dry. Harry came with his watery blue eyes that never cried. Jenny and the dogs knew he was full up with tears. They greeted him at the gate and tried to make him better. He ate at Jenny's table. He pottered around the garden with John, in the shed with John, who owned every tool known to modern man. He made toys for the hospital auxiliary. Harry could paint. They worked together while Jim sat on the veranda watching for the postman.

John and Harry were fitting new hinges to the small gate when the postie delivered Jim's manuscript. Jenny watched him open it, praying for him, pleading to God – or to the publishers – to give him what he needed. They had enclosed a brief letter. 'Rejected,' he said. Jenny put her arm around him but he didn't want to be held. He took his pages into the dining room. She took the dogs for a walk. The gate repairers downed tools to walk with her.

They walked to where Hooper Street dead-ended on Blunt's Road, then turned left and headed to Joe Flanagan's land – no longer old Joe's, though whoever had bought it hadn't yet moved in, so they took the short cut through to Granny's land. The fig tree, always loaded, had been stripped by the birds. They'd beat Jenny to the apricots this year – or someone had. Harry picked a pocket full of plums.

'Else always wanted to move back here,' he said. 'Three days before she died we spoke about buying a caravan.' He ate a plum and pitched the stone, and the dogs, freed from their leads, chased it, thinking food.

'We look on the old days as utopian,' John said. 'We forget the disease, the death.'

'And no water on tap,' Jenny said. 'I must have spent half of my life carrying water before we put the big tank in.'

Harry took another plum from his pocket and Jenny held her hand out for one. John shook his head, and he'd made the better decision. Those plums had always been sour. She took one bite then pitched it. The dogs gave chase.

'The chap who bought Flanagan's made me an offer before Christmas. I was thinking about selling,' Jenny said.

'They say he beat Joe's sons down in price,' Harry said.

'He offered me a fair price. It's just the land. Every fence needs replacing,' Jenny said.

'Maybe it's time for it to live another life,' Harry said. 'Young Ronnie says it's time I did. He reckons he could use my help over there.'

Ronnie lived in Mildura, miles away. Jenny didn't comment. John whistled the dogs to his side and they crossed back over old Joe's land, perhaps for the last time.

Jim was typing when they returned. He told her Georgie had phoned. 'She said she'd call back tonight,' he said.

She called at nine. She said she had some good news and a confession. 'Which one do you want first, Jen?'

'I need a dose of good news,' Jenny said.

'The publisher likes *Molly*.'

'How?'

'That's the confession bit, Jen. I posted it to them.'

'No, Georgie. They sent Jim's book back today,' Jenny said.

'They sent *Molly* back too, but they want to see it again,' Georgie said, then read aloud: '*We feel that the novel could stand an extra ten thousand words . . . a chapter on the birth of Joeyboy . . . a scene where the six year old boy witnesses his father's death and perhaps scenes showing the relationship between father and son.* They like Wadimulla. I changed most of the other names – oh, and Juliana Conti now wrote it.'

'It's the last thing Jim needs to hear right now. He's been down since Nobby's funeral.'

'What do you need, mate?'

'For people to stop dying and life to get back to normal.'

'There's no such thing, Jen, so live what you've got while you've got it because it's all that you've got – unless you believe in reincarnation – and stop attempting to live it through Jim.'

She read out the letter in its entirety, then the two-page reader's report, and it was like . . . like hearing someone else's mail read, not Jenny's.

'I'll come down and we'll talk about it. I was thinking of coming down—'

'I made copies of the letters. *Molly* is in the mail.'

'No! It will kill him!'

'You've done something, Jen. Pull your head out of the kitchen and your flea-riddled mutts and finish what you started.'

They spoke for half an hour. Jim had gone to bed. John had been in bed for two hours. Jenny, a night owl, went to bed when they'd hung up.

'Are you awake, Jim?'

'I am now.'

And she told him what Georgie had done. His breathing altered but he didn't comment.

'How much of it did you read?'

'Go to sleep, Jen,' he said and he turned his back.

She rolled onto her side and placed her arm over him but, feeling his tension, removed it and rolled to the other side. Didn't sleep well.

The parcel came the following afternoon. Jenny was cutting her way into the envelope with her dressmaking scissors when the dogs started their killer bark. John was out there.

He came in as she removed the stacked pages. 'It's the Wild Witch of the East,' he said, his name for Lila since their last couple of kids' books. Jenny went out to deal with her.

'You look well heeled,' she greeted her.

'They paid me out,' Lila said.

'That's what you wanted, wasn't it?'

'I didn't want the bloody solicitor to take half of it,' Lila said.

'They usually do. Where have you been?'

'Wherever. I'm going up to Sydney. Barbara is still up there.'

'Have a good time,' Jenny said, taking a better grip of the dogs' collars.

'After all these years, that's all you've got to say to me? Ask me how much I got.'

'How much did you get?'

'Twenty-two lousy thousand. He was worth millions.'

'Put it in the bank and spend it wisely,' Jenny said.

'Like hell I will. I've been living on a pittance these last years, but you wouldn't know what that's like.'

'I spent a lot of years living on a pittance, Lila.'

'Bullshit you did. You caught yourself a rich bloke and have been on easy street since.'

'If you say so,' Jenny said.

'Are you going to tie those mongrels up and give me a cup of tea?'

'Not today.'

'I used to be your best friend.'

Jenny sighed. She'd lost her two best friends. She sighed again. 'I just gave you a best friend's advice, Lila. Put your money in the bank and make it last.'

'Stuff your friendship and your advice,' Lila said and walked back to her car.

*

Planes crashed that year. An oil tanker spilled thirty-eight million litres of oil off the coast of Alaska, wiping out seals and birds by the thousands. Ninety-odd sports fans were crushed to death in a people stampede at a football match in England. In June, the Chinese government sent in troops to open fire on students in Tiananmen Square, in Beijing, China's capital city. Thousands, there only to protest for democracy, were mown down by rifle fire, crushed beneath the army's tanks.

And Jim had the nightmare to end all nightmares. Jenny, deeply asleep, wore the bruises of his battle with the Japs.

'What were you dreaming?'

'Nothing.'

'It wasn't nothing. Talk to me.'

'Go to sleep,' he said.

'I can't. You punched me. I'll have a bruise in the morning. What were you dreaming?'

He took his pillow and his crutch and he went to Trudy's room, which Jenny would need to stop thinking of as Trudy's room. She was currently sleeping in Ireland and working in one of their hospitals, as was Nicky. Sophie had come home.

Jim's nightmares didn't stop in Trudy's room. Two nights out of seven she ran through the house, turning on the lights. She always heard him. He was vocal in his dreaming state and his voice was not the controlled Jim's of daylight hours. He never swore by day, and when she did, he told her that her use of expletives displayed a lack of vocabulary.

He was certainly lacking in vocabulary when he fought the Japs. He screamed at crazy bastards to get their heads down, and too often when she turned on Trudy's light, she expected to find him on the floor. The light woke him and, on his back, sitting, or halfway out of bed, well-mannered Jim said, 'Sorry I woke you, Jen.'

His dreams had been rare during the years of the kids' books. The loss of Amy, then Lorna, Trudy flying away, then Nobby's death – then the rejection of his Hooper tome.

She brought home brochures for a bus tour to Alice Springs. He wasn't interested. In July she talked him into a trip to Greensborough. A bad month to visit Melbourne. Unionists who refused to work prevented those who wanted to work from getting there. Bob Hawke didn't call out his troops to mow the protesters down. These days, if a constable spoke harshly to a drunk he was accused of police brutality.

They spent the weekend in Greensborough, and even Katie's antics couldn't make Jim laugh. With Georgie now back at work, Katie spent her weekdays at a crèche, and Jenny wanted to stay longer, to give Katie a week's holiday. Jim wanted to go home.

They left at seven thirty on Monday morning, Jim behind the wheel, and he missed the right-hand turn that led down to the Hume Freeway.

'You'll have to find somewhere to turn around,' she said.

'I'll take the next turn,' he said, and he did, but the road was unfamiliar and, judging by the amount of traffic on it, was heading into the city.

'You need to turn back, Jim.'

He didn't reply, or turn. There was no sun to tell her which way they were going, no landmark presenting itself, and he too was so occupied in looking for one, he damn near ran up the back of a truck at the traffic lights. Unfamiliar traffic lights.

'Put your left blinker on and get over to the left. We need to get off this road and find out where we are.' The map book now open on her lap, she was searching its pages for the names of the streets they crossed over, but with no idea which road they were on or which suburb they were passing through, she gave up on the book to watch the road – and finally recognised an intersection she'd driven through with Paul, back when Georgie had been in hospital.

'We're heading into the city,' she said. 'Get off this road and stop.'

There was nothing wrong with his hearing. His problem was deeper. She reached across and turned on the left blinker. He turned it off and drove a curving road too fast. A red light stopped him and when it did, she opened the door and got out, dodging between trucks and cars to the nature strip. That got through to him. She saw it on the face she'd known since childhood, a face she could once read like an open book.

The lights changed to green. He continued forward with the traffic, but she saw his blinker signalling a left-hand turn, so crossed over and walked on. Found him down the next side street, a residential street where, frightened by his behaviour for the first time in her life, she attacked him with her tongue.

'You pig-headed fool of a man. You're not your bloody father so stop acting like him.'

'Get in,' he said.

'Get out and let me drive, or I'll hitchhike back to Greensborough and stay there.'

She polluted the residential gutter with two butts before he gave up the wheel.

# The Silencing of Screams

She drove back to Georgie's house, then drove out through Whittlesea, and with Jim trapped in the passenger seat, she continued her attack.

'It's killing you what I did with *Molly Squire*, admit it.'

'You wanted to drive, so drive.'

'Amy and I told you what was wrong with it. You wouldn't listen to us, and you need to listen to what the publishers said about your Hooper tome.'

'What did they say, Jen?'

'That as it is, they don't want it!'

'Concentrate on the road,' he said.

'I know where I'm going.' She wanted a smoke. He didn't like her smoke, didn't allow it in his car. A smoke might have shut her mouth.

'It could be the perfect family saga. You've got the dominant James Richard, then his two sons, one determined to live his own life, the other remaining with the old man so he might one day inherit the property, then dying before he did.'

He sat, his eyes closed, and whether he was listening or not, she said more.

'Then Granny and Vern, the next generation. Gertrude and Vern, cousins? They were much more than cousins, and you know it. If you were prepared to write the truth about their relationship, you'd have the longest love story ever written.'

'You're the love story expert,' he said.

'There are a lot of readers who enjoy a love interest and I'm not ashamed to admit I'm one of them.'

'I write historical fact, as Molly *was* historical fact.'

'She was too much fact and not enough humanity – like your Hoopers are all fact and no humanity.'

'No doubt it too needs a Wadimulla,' he said.

'No. It needs your old shepherd. His one-page letter told me who he was and he'd be a brilliant character – as would each of the four wives of old James Richard. That's a story in itself, how the old coot kept marrying these young women, dragging them out to the middle of nowhere then letting them scream themselves to death in childbirth.'

'I don't recall mentioning the screaming.'

'You didn't. You silenced their screams, Jim, and that's your main problem.'

'Melodrama is your field,' he said.

'Every birth is a drama. Dying with a baby stuck inside you is very dramatic. Old James' wives screamed for days. They exhausted themselves with their pushing and their screaming. Then they died – like I would have died if Jimmy had been my first baby, if Granny hadn't got me down to the hospital.'

He'd put Jimmy away. He hadn't mentioned his name in years. He usually walked away when she mentioned his name. He couldn't walk away that day – and Jenny couldn't put Jimmy away. Still saw that little six year old boy, still felt his sweaty little hand in her own, and she'd never put him away – and today she wouldn't let go of the Hooper tome because it did have the makings of a brilliant family saga. She'd read every solid page of the thing and the story was in there, just lost in a mass of names and dates.

'Who buys books, Jim?'

'Those who read, Jen.'

'Why are publishers in business?'

'To print books?'

'To print books, Jim, but *business* is the operative word. A business is in business in order to make money. Writers produce the raw product the publishing business turns into money. They're not patrons of the arts.'

'As the writer says to the novice.'

'As the reader says to the pig-headed writer who has got himself so wrapped up in his power over words, he's forgotten about me, the reader. You used to be a reader. Get your book scanned onto a computer disc then read it, as a reader. Your words coming off the screen might alter your perspective.'

'My perspective is fine, Jen.'

'Your perspective stinks. Your tome is a wallow of facts and dates that mean nothing to anyone other than you.'

'I write history and history is full of facts and dates.'

'Old rat mouth wasn't Captain Cook or Australia's first prime minister. He was a no one, and who gives a damn when he was born, when he sailed away from old England. If you'd shown him saying goodbye before he sailed, I might have given a damn. Your book needs truth.'

'Look up *truth* in your computer's dictionary. Unless your screen alters its perspective, it will define the word as a conformity to fact: reality: veracity.'

'The truth of man and woman goes a damn sight deeper than their birth, marriage and death certificates.'

'Watch the road.'

'Unlike some, I always watch the road when I drive.'

She watched it while she wound down the window, while she found her cigarettes in her jacket pocket, found a lighter and, one handed, got it lit. It silenced her for a kilometre or two. It silenced her until she drove into rain and had to pitch her butt to close the window. Locked in then by heavy rain, the wipers doing what they could to clear her windscreen, she dropped her speed down to sixty, slowing other drivers on the two-lane road.

'Your father's chapter tells the reader that he was a successful farmer, a mill owner, town councillor and a respected man who in midlife married a forty year old widow who gave him a son, ten months after the wedding. I knew Vern Hooper. He might be in there somewhere, but if he is, he's as flat and lifeless as a cardboard cut-out. Whatever your father was, no one could call him a cardboard man.'

'Stop the car until the rain eases.'

'There's nowhere to stop.'

'Stop the car. I can't see the road.'

'There are a lot of things you can't see lately. Did you see Katie?'

'She's very visible.'

'You used to know how to talk to babies. You dodged Katie.'

'Enough!'

'It's not enough, and you're not either lately. Tell me what's going on in your head.'

He turned his face to the window and a kilometre or two on, she drove out of the rain, and one by one the tail of vehicles following her whizzed by, and when the road had cleared behind her, she wound her window down again and reached for another cigarette. Got one out, then dropped the packet. He picked it up, crumpled it and aimed it towards the open window. It hit her, landed on her lap.

'That, at least, was an uncensored response,' she said. 'Remember the censors' blackout during the war? One of your letters was more blackout than words.' No reply. 'You've become your own censor. Every word you say is censored, as is every sentence you put on paper.' No reply. 'Your head is so involved in blocking out whatever it is that you don't want to remember, you're turning into a cardboard man. The Jim Hooper who made Jimmy censored nothing.'

'Goddamn you,' he said.

'He did, at birth – and you too. Your father married your mother for her sawmill and her first husband's house and his money – and to nark Granny, who wouldn't marry him because she had brains enough to know what she'd be getting herself into if she did. That's what you need to tell your reader, how he was a dominating, cold-hearted bastard of a man who for three years allowed me and Jimmy to believe that you were dead.'

He slapped both palms on the dashboard. 'Stop.'

'I'll stop when you talk to me.'

He didn't talk so she didn't shut up.

'Tell them too how that mean-hearted old bastard believed it was his God given right to take my son away from me and raise him to think his mother was the town trollop – which is how you've been treating me lately – like some worn-out old bugger you keep around because she can cook. Well, she can write too.'

'It's shit!' he said.

'Excellent uncensored response. Your tome isn't shit, Jim. It's too dry to be shit. Any highlights in it are so buried in your four-syllable intellect, your reader becomes breathless attempting to get to the end of each line.'

'What do you want from me?' he yelled.

'A book I can read, not an obese attack of words, written by a hung-up English professor with a guilty conscience. You've taken a pair of cowyard boots and plastered them with boot polish in the hope it will hide where they've been.'

'Tell me where they've been, Jen.'

'Wallowing in wet cow dung and my blood and guts, that's where. Telling it as it was won't make me like those boots, but I might respect their bloody honesty – and yours too.'

*

In November of that year, his Hooper tome was rejected again. In February of 1990, Jenny drove to Willama to post *Sent in Chains* up to Sydney. She'd taken too long to return it. The publisher had probably forgotten it. They'd suggested the novel could stand ten thousand words more. She'd given them an extra twenty thousand. She was on her way home, her mind still with the manuscript, when she heard a siren on her tail. It was a first. Woody Creek's brand new constable wrote her a speeding ticket before she knew his name was Quick.

Constable Quick wrote more speeding tickets that week. The road to Willama was straight, flat and newly bitumined. Then he confiscated Maisy's driving licence. Few blamed him for that. She'd developed a bad habit of backing out first and looking over her shoulder later. A cop car is the wrong car to back into, and it's never a good idea to accuse a man in blue of coming too fast around the corner.

Bernie bought her a four-wheeled, top of the range electric runabout, known locally as a *gopher* – they'd go far enough for most on a charged battery. Maisy drove it into Jenny's yard on a Tuesday in early March. A more silent beast than her Chrysler, she crept up on the chained dogs and frightened six months of sex out of them – hopefully.

Jenny and John admired her new set of wheels. They test-drove her gopher around the garden.

'The salesman said they'll do twenty-five kilometres on a fully charged battery,' Maisy said. 'I've ordered a spare.'

Jenny should have asked why she needed a spare battery. She found out why on Friday. Val, Lenny Hall's wife, sighted her seven kilometres short of Mission Bridge. Maisy had managed to disconnect the flattened battery and connect up the new, but her gopher refused to go. Val Hall waited with her until two of the Watson boys came along in their farm truck. They transported her gopher home. Val drove Maisy. Then, the following Tuesday, Bernie Macdonald's ute drove into the yard.

Jenny stood inside her screen door and watched him get out from behind the wheel, watched him walk around the ute and take his mother's arm while she stepped out, and the dogs, so attuned to Jenny's emotions, strained to get off their chains and eat meat. Through the security mesh she watched him approach the steps, then climb up the steps to the veranda. She was closer to him than she'd been in thirty years, close enough to see the age of him. Too close. She stepped back.

'I'll give you a beep at half past three,' he said, and returned to his ute. Jenny opened her security door.

'He hid my battery charger. I can't find it anywhere,' Maisy said.

'I would have tossed it in the bin. I heard what you got up to,' Jenny said.

'I was all right, and I paid enough for that spare battery. You'd think that they could have charged it up for me.'

'How did you plan on getting home?'

'Bernie would have picked me up.'

'I would have driven you down there too if you'd asked me.'

'I hate being dependent on people,' Maisy said, settling herself in her usual chair so she could look out both the window and the door. 'Are we doing your taping thing today?'

'If you feel like it.'

'I thought of something this morning that you might be interested in. I was talking to Hilda O'Brien about poor old Dottie Martin. She's fading away to a shadow. Anyway, we got onto how Dottie damn near died in a diphtheria epidemic when we were kids and how your gran saved her life and half a dozen more with a spoon handle.'

Jenny set up Jim's tape recorder with her *Maisy* tape, turned it on and went about making a pot of tea. Maisy didn't like teabags. They were the lazy way of making tea, she claimed. Jenny had become one of the lazy – except on Tuesdays.

'Hilda remembers watching your gran wrap a bit of flannel around a spoon handle, dip it in kerosene, or a mixture of kerosene and something else, then poke it down Dottie's throat to break the membrane that used to grow over the windpipe or something.

She'd be interesting to get on your tapes. I'll bring her around with me sometime if you like.'

Jenny didn't like. 'No thanks, Maisy.'

'What are you going to do with what we talk about?'

'Lock it away in a time capsule,' Jenny said. Since Paul had given her his old computer she'd been filling a file she'd named *Granny* – with Elsie gone, it somehow seemed more important to trap Gertrude Foote in something more substantial than her memory.

'Bernie told me that you sold your gran's land,' Maisy said.

'It seemed like the right thing to do at the time,' Jenny said.

'Because of Elsie?'

'Because of a lot of things, Maisy.' Because Ray's insurance account was empty. Because Jim had lost interest in chasing high interest, because inflation was eating into his capital, because she wanted that land to have another life.

'That new owner has got twice as many cows as old Joe had,' Maisy said.

'That's the way of the new world. Get bigger or get out of the game.'

'Bernie is thinking about getting out of the sawmill game. Those new people who built on John's land spend their lives complaining to the council about the noise.'

Never a silence in that kitchen when Maisy came. She knew everyone, knew the ins and outs of the local news the *Willama Gazette* didn't mention. She was still talking when the ute horn beeped at three thirty on the dot, and by the time Jenny walked her visitor to the front door, he was waiting on the veranda to take charge.

Georgie phoned that night. The publisher had made an offer for *Sent in Chains.*

And God save her – not that he'd ever listened.

# Part Three

# Communication

*May, 1991*
*Dear Juliana,*
*My great, great-grandmother's name was Molly Flanagan and she was sent in chains to Australia in the early eighteen hundreds. My sisters and I are wondering if your Molly Flanagan was a real person . . .*

*July, 1991*
*Dear Juliana,*
*It's two o'clock in the morning and I just finished your book. I bought it this morning to take with me on holiday, then made the mistake of opening it. I couldn't put it down . . .*

*December, 1991*
*Dear Juliana,*
*My name is Angela Luccetto. I bought your book because of your name but read it with great enjoyment. The sister of my grandmother, also a Juliana Conti, disappeared in mysterious circumstances in 1923. According to family legend, her husband, a*

*banker and a very rich man, took her on a world cruise and didn't bring her home. He told the family she'd decided to stay on with friends in Australia. That was the last my grandmother heard of her sister.*

*I have enclosed a photograph . . .*

*January, 1992*
*Dear Juliana,*
*I was given your book as a slightly used Christmas present by my mother. She said she bought it because of Wadimulla on the cover. Her grandmother was an Aboriginal woman. My mother ended up reading it before she gave it to me and she said to tell you she loved every word, as I did. I found Molly's relationship with Wadimulla and his family group, and the loss of Joeyboy, very moving . . .*

*February, 1992*
*Dear Juliana,*
*I was given your book by an Australian friend for Christmas. Your name is very familiar to me. It was my maternal grandmother's name. I was adopted at birth and know little of my natural family's history, other than, like you, my Juliana was of Italian origin, and that she separated from her husband, had a love affair with her doctor, and in 1923, died in giving birth to my biological mother. She was buried nameless in a country cemetery where for twenty years her identity remained a mystery.*

*I congratulate you on your novel. I too am a writer, and well recall the delight of holding that first copy of my novel to my heart. May you write many more.*
*My regards,*
*Cara*

Juliana's mail came via the publisher to Georgie, who filed each item. She replied to the fan mail with a half-page letter she had on file, only changing the name before it was printed and posted. When she deleted *Joan* and typed in *Cara*, she knew who would read that copy. During the weekend she'd spent with her in that tiny Armadale unit, Cara had picked Georgie's brains for family information. She'd taken pages of notes on the Juliana Conti/ Itchy-foot story.

*I too am a writer . . .*

What did she write? An avid reader, Georgie hadn't come across a book by Cara Norris or Grenville.

Again she read the letter. Chris Marino had said she'd called from London. The return address on the letter was London, *c/o Hillary Rowe*. Did she write under a pseudonym, and why *Hillary Rowe*?

For ten seconds Georgie considered enclosing a personal note. For ten more she considered putting Cara in touch with Angela Luccetto. Knew what that would lead to. Cara would mention Jennifer Hooper and the Luccetto woman would turn up in Woody Creek. Cara's letter had been written to Juliana Conti, the writer who, according to her biog, was the second daughter of Italian immigrants, born on 11 April 1939, midway between Australia and Italy. She was the mother of two daughters and resided with her husband on a property in Gippsland where they bred dogs – Georgie's fiction.

She reached for the printed letter, signed it, the J dominant, the smaller C trailing into a squiggle, a circular dot over the tail of the squiggle.

'Done?' Paul asked. 'It's going on eleven.'

'If not for him, she'd be doing this herself, and enjoying it too.'

'Has he seen a doctor?'

'She can't get him near one.'

The filing cabinet was to the left of her computer. She filed Cara's letter in the *Juliana* file, closed the drawer and thought of Christmas, pleased Katie wouldn't remember it. She'd known Jim for twenty years but never known him, as in known who lived inside him. He was an intelligent, pleasant bloke, very well mannered.

He hadn't been at Christmas time. He'd eaten with them, then gone to the bathroom where he'd remained locked in for an hour. Paul diagnosed prostate problems. Georgie's diagnosis placed the problem higher up, somewhere between his ears.

She knew he'd come home from the war screwed up in the head. She knew third or fourth hand that he'd spent six or so years in private clinics. Nobby had found that out from Ian Hooper, Jim's cousin, who'd kept in touch with Margaret Hooper until she died. According to Ian Hooper, Jim had been given electric shock therapy at one of the clinics, which had apparently sorted out his head but wiped out his memory. According to Jenny, he had nightmares, he tried to sleepwalk – not easy to do on one leg and a stump. According to Jenny, he was back to what he'd been when she'd visited him in a Melbourne hospital, after they'd first brought him home from the Jap prison camp.

The last time he'd spoken to Georgie, he'd claimed that he suffered constant pain in his missing leg. Maybe he did. Jenny blamed *Sent in Chains*, which hadn't made it to the top of the best-seller list but had been on it for weeks and had got up to number three. He should have been celebrating with her, not hiding his pain in a locked bathroom.

Paul hadn't known him during the kids' books era. He'd had little to do with him until the Lorna business. On the second night Jen and Jim had stayed with them during the clearing out of Lorna's house, he'd asked how Jenny had become involved with a bloke like Jim.

She'd got pregnant to him too young, but should have been old enough to know what she was doing by '59 when she'd married him.

Georgie filed the royalty statement, slid the attached cheque, made out to J.C. Hooper, into an envelope and addressed it. Jenny wanted no part of that book, or the fame that might have gone with it, but she didn't refuse the money it made.

She missed John. He'd been her rock until a few months before Christmas when he'd gone to bed one night and hadn't woken up the next morning. Harry was her leaning post now, when he wasn't with Ronnie and his wife and grandkids in Mildura.

Wished Trudy would come home. She knew her father wasn't well, though knowing Jen, she probably didn't know how unwell he was. She was currently in Norway. She'd spent last Christmas in Spain with Nicky, who wasn't a Nicole or a Nicola as Jenny had believed when they'd flown away. He was a Nicholas.

*Dear Jen,*

*More money for the coffers. Your publisher also wants to know if you're working on a follow-up book. They're still nagging about photographs too, and a literary lunch somewhere. You could be out there having fun with this. How many times did you nag me about wasting my life? You've done something big, and if you were prepared to do it, you could turn your Granny file into something publishable instead of sitting up there playing nursemaid and dog lady.*

*Enough nagging, now for the interesting bit. Cara wrote, not to me, or to you, but to Juliana, a sort of one writer congratulating another letter. She mentioned her link to a former Juliana Conti and how some Aussie friend had sent her your book for Christmas. You haven't happened across anything written by a Cara Grenville, or a C.J. Grenville, have you? . . .*

'Come to bed. It's almost midnight,' Paul called.

'Five minutes,' Georgie said.

# The Sewing Room

In July of '92, Harry brought his chainsaw around to prune the rose hedge. Its noise roused Jim, who came to stand in the doorway, on one leg and a crutch, wanting to protest at the desecration of those rosesbushes but unable to find the words.

'You can't kill a rosebush,' Jenny told him. 'They'll bloom better than ever come spring – if it ever comes.'

Unpruned last year, the roses had grown tall and rangy – like the thorny brambles imprisoning *Briar Rose*. Harry, Elsie's Prince Charming, freed Jenny not with a kiss but his chainsaw. Before the day was done two trailer loads of brambles had been offloaded at the tip.

In August, he suggested he prune a bit off Vern. The dogs were at it again, and both Lorna and Jenny were too old to cope with another batch of pups.

'At what age does a female dog become menopausal, Harry?'

'I think they die of old age first, Jen,' Harry said.

*

Georgie and Paul spent Christmas Day setting up Paul's second retired computer in Jenny's sewing room and copying her large floppy discs onto the smaller plastic ones the new computer read. Jim sat nodding off in the sitting room while Katie, a beautiful being with hair as red as her mother's and as curly as Nanny's, assisted Nanny in the kitchen. She dropped an egg Jenny had given her to hold, poked a finger into the spilled yolk to taste it and considered it a grand joke when Jenny invited Vern inside to clean up the mess.

Dinner was late that day. Jim ate at six, and at six he came out to the kitchen to sit and wait. He wasn't fed until seven.

Vern lost his male privileges to a Willama vet in January, a mild case of locking the door after the horse had bolted. In late February, Lorna popped another batch of the blind-eyed little coots while Jenny stood by counting and willing her to stop. They kept coming and coming, ten of the little blighters, and one of them dead. She buried it. By March, they were trying to trip her over each time she stepped out the door, or get in before she could close it. The other litters had run to John to learn good doggie manners. No John to train this lot. Lorna taught them bad manners while Vern slept his life away in the shade of the elm tree and Jim slept his life away in the sitting room.

Jenny was reading in the kitchen when she heard Lorna's killer bark at the gate. Hadn't heard it for a long time. Didn't want to hear it. 'Please God, let it be one of your salesman,' she moaned and, placing her book face down on the table, she went to the front door to peer out through the security mesh.

The pups were yipping at the small gate Lorna was attempting to climb over in order to de-sex Lila. All greying red hide, dangling teats, sinew and bone, Lorna – and Lila – who was wearing most of a red sweater that clung to sagging marble breasts, which looked lopsided. She had an inch of grey roots showing beneath her fading red dye job, and she looked hungry enough to eat Lorna.

Jenny walked down to get a grip on Lorna's collar and haul her back from the gate.

'Sit!' Lorna didn't want to sit.

'I need a bed. I'm stony motherless broke,' Lila said.

'What happened to your payout?'

'Try paying board and living on a few measly thousand and see how far you get. I've been on a single pension since my last one croaked, and the pittance they expect a single person to live on wouldn't be half enough to live decent on even if they gave you twice as much,' Lila said.

'Your idea of living decent has never corresponded with most,' Jenny said, surrounded by six week old pups whose mother was now teaching them how to show their teeth. Then Vern, roused by the ruckus, came to add his sexless 'woof' to the chorus.

'Sit,' Jenny ordered, and eleven dogs disobeyed her command.

'I'll only be here for a day or two.'

'Jim's sick.'

'You've got your photographer living with you.'

'He died before Christmas.'

Lila shrugged. 'He was always an up-himself old bugger anyway.'

'Far better to be up oneself than to have half of Australia up you,' Jenny said.

'Bitch. Have you got a spare fag on you?'

'No.'

'I can see a packet in your pocket.'

Jenny retrieved her smokes, offered one, not the packet. Lila didn't have a light, and again Jenny patted her pockets. She found a lighter.

'I haven't slept in a decent bed for two weeks.'

'No,' Jenny said.

'I'll be out on the Friday morning bus. My pension gets paid in on Thursday.'

'Try the hotel,' Jenny said, then, releasing Lorna's collar, she turned to walk back to the house and her book. Hearing the gate squeal open, she turned to see Lorna riding it while the pups fell like ninepins before it.

'Eat me, you mongrels, and see if I care,' Lila said, and she came through, dragging a case with only three of its four wheels intact.

An embarrassed Lorna, her four feet again beneath her, snarled her challenge, as did her pups, but the unwanted visitor and her case continued up the bricked path towards the house. It's one thing to snarl and bark when there is a barrier between antagonist and defender. Actually ripping out a wrinkled throat is another matter entirely. Lorna retreated with her troops to make a second stand at the veranda where Jenny stood, watching her nemesis coming to get her.

Some are haunted for life by their yesterdays. Jim was, and there was not a thing Jenny could do or say to change that. Some wake each morning to a brand new day, their every yesterday washed clean. Lila had only ever believed in tomorrow. Jenny sighed and opened the wire door. At Christmas time, Georgie had suggested a dose of shock therapy might jolt some sense into Jim. Maybe a few days of Lila might do the trick, or at least get his leg on. He'd spent a lot of years dodging Lila's scarlet kisses.

'Let those pups inside and you'll be rounding them up,' Jenny warned, and returned to her book.

Georgie, on the hunt for Cara since she'd written to congratulate Juliana, had posted up *Balancing Act*, by C.J. Langhall, because of the photograph of the author inside the rear cover. The initials were right. The photograph could have been Cara. Georgie swore it was, but if it was, she was wearing a shoulder-length wig and glasses. Her biography was of no help. *Ms Langhall lives on a rural property outside of London with her partner and their three children.*

The last time they'd seen Cara she'd had a seven year old boy, and she'd been fostering Tracy. They'd be adults now. She could have had another baby. They knew from Chris Marino that Cara had married her Englishman, so why write partner and not husband? *Partner* could mean anything from husband to lesbian lover.

Jenny did no more reading that day. She led her visitor to the room beside Trudy's, threw sheets and pillow slips at her, an extra blanket, then returned to the kitchen to round up something for dinner. If Jim's meal wasn't on the table at six he became agitated. He'd be agitated anyway when he woke up and saw Lila.

*

Her pension was paid into an account she accessed with a plastic card, and on Thursday morning Lila disappeared early. Had she taken her case, Jenny might have believed she'd left town. She hadn't. She returned before six, her demeanour suggesting she hadn't had a good day.

'Where have you been?'

'Nice to know you missed me,' Lila said.

Never an early riser, Jenny woke her in time to catch the Friday bus.

'I'll go tomorrow,' Lila said, rolling over. She slept until midday when she showered, put on her makeup and disappeared again. She returned at five.

'When are you leaving, Lila?'

'That bloody bowling club took every penny I had.'

Anyone with a brain in their head knew that poker machines were the government's recycling agency for pensions.

'You mindless halfwit.'

'It wouldn't have kept me for a day in Melbourne. If I'd doubled it I would have gone.'

'You're going.'

Jenny packed her case, stripped her bed and, when Lila refused to leave, she carried her case down to the gate and dumped it on the footpath. Lila dragged it back. She retrieved her sheets from the laundry and made up her bed.

'I won six hundred dollars up in Sydney one night. Sooner or later I'll win again.'

'And until you do you expect to bludge on me.'

'I don't eat much.'

'You're not staying here, Lila. Jim isn't well.'

'Put him away and come up to Sydney with me. We'd have a ball.'

Couldn't take another day of her – or Jim. Wanted . . . wanted life, wanted Georgie, wanted Katie, wanted to howl with frustration, and what good had howling ever done? She lit a cigarette instead, and made the mistake of leaving her cigarettes on the refrigerator while she hid in her sewing room, the twin doors closed, a chair jammed beneath its doorknobs. It remained in place until five to six, and when she went out to the kitchen to find something for dinner, her empty cigarette packet was on the table, Lila smoking the last one.

Couldn't get the car out, not unless she rounded up and penned nine pups. She opened a tin of tomato soup, slotted bread in the toaster, and with the hands of the clock now pointing to six, Jim came to the kitchen on one leg and his crutch. Couldn't stand the sight of his crutch. Ran from it, from him, from Lila to the take-away shop. They sold cigarettes – at a premium price – and disposable lighters for twice the price she'd pay for one at the supermarket. She bought one, then ordered two dollars' worth of chips and three slabs of flake and went outside to smoke while she waited for the fish to fry.

Didn't set the table. Dumped the parcel onto it along with a bottle of vinegar, salt and pepper, then sat down to eat off the paper, with her fingers. Hoopers didn't eat off paper. Jim looked at it, then actually looked at her, expecting her to fetch him a plate, knife and fork, to serve him his fish and chips. She ate scalding chips, and he reached for his crutch and got his own plate, his own knife and fork, served himself the last piece of fish and a dozen chips. There was nothing wrong with his appetite.

There was nothing wrong with his stump either, or his artificial leg. Six months ago he'd stopped wearing it. Every night since, his crutch had been a third presence at the table – now a fourth. He leaned it on the chair to his right, beside Jenny's chair, and every time she saw it, heard it, she wanted to take to it with an axe. For months and months and more months, she'd pleaded with him to put his leg on. He suffered terrible pain, he claimed. She no longer believed in his terrible pain. He refused her aspros, her Panadol, refused to see a doctor, refused to set foot or crutch outside the door. He sat, staring at windows, at walls or sleeping – sat and rotted and she rotted at his side.

Lila ate her meal from paper, with her fingers. She'd never been skin and bone before. Wouldn't be for long. She cleaned up the last of the chips then ate both pieces of toast. She dropped three teabags into three mugs, poured the boiling water over them, then left Jim to fish for his teabag – and look at it as if he'd retrieved a dead mouse from his cup when he finally got it out.

Jenny escaped, with her smokes, to her sewing room, where she no longer sewed but gave her problems to her gods, the computers, preloved, though never loved more than she loved them. Tonight she emptied her anger into the original god, already stained yellow by her smoke. It didn't accuse when she lit another.

She created a new file she named *Boomerang*, and closed it down fast when the chair jamming the twin doors gave way to Lila. She wanted a smoke. Jenny went to bed and took her cigarettes with her.

On Tuesday, Maisy's visiting day, Lila hunted Jim from the sitting room. He holed up in the bathroom. On Friday, Lila begging for a loan, Jenny offered her ten dollars to cook dinner, clean the bathroom and wash the kitchen floor.

'That's bloody slave rates.'

'It's bludger's rates, Lila, and more than you deserve.'

She cooked, she cleaned, she got her ten dollars. Spent it on hair dye, but the supermarket didn't have a good range of colours in stock. The faded red and silver turned dark brown. She looked semi normal.

# SANCTUARY

Lila's battered handbag was hanging over the back doorknob as usual. Jenny removed it each night when she locked that door. Tonight she dropped it, scattering its general chaos of makeup and used tissues, purse and perfume. She picked up each item, tossed it back in, then tried to close it. Its zip no longer zipped.

Her plastic card would be amongst that mess. She'd collect her pension in the morning and recycle it at the pokies – or maybe not. Last night she'd diagnosed Jim's illness as 'mad as a rabbit'. She might catch the bus on Friday.

Georgie's diagnosis was kinder than Lila's though much the same. She'd suggested a psychiatrist. Maisy had suggested the doctor who set up shop in the old bank building every Wednesday. She'd made an appointment for Jim. Jenny had kept it. She'd spoken to a young doctor about Jim's breakdown after the war, about his years in psychiatric clinics. He'd told her he couldn't fix her husband by remote control and to bring him in. As if.

She emptied her cup and went to the bathroom. Clean. She hadn't cleaned it. Maybe the Muslims had got something right with their many wives. Every wife needs a junior wife. Jenny hadn't asked Lila to stay but no longer told her to leave. The *Boomerang* file was growing. Lila shed gems daily, gems Jenny swept up and fed to her computer. She'd made a superb Molly.

*The publisher wants to know if you're working on a follow-up novel* . . . She was now.

She brushed her teeth, creamed her face, then crept back to the kitchen to open Lila's purse. Her bank card was in it, and not much else. She stole it. She hid it in her sewing machine drawer, then went to bed.

Lila missed it when she went to the post office to pick up her government pay and was back in ten minutes. 'I have to phone the bank. I've lost my money card.'

'You'll get it back when you're on the bus out of town, Lila.'

'You'll give it back to me now or I'll bloody report you to the copper.'

'Go for your life. When he comes around to arrest me, I'll ask him to evict you.'

'I can't live without money!'

'Bernie Macdonald has got plenty. Try your luck with him on Tuesday.'

Their exchange became louder when Jenny suggested Shaky Lewis, who still had a room at the hotel. 'Two pensioners can live more cheaply than one,' she said. They became loud enough to raise Jim. He stopped the argument – or his clunk-clunk across the hall stopped it. Jenny left via the back door.

He was in the kitchen, close to the open back door, when she returned. His crutch was leaning beside his chair. Lila was vacuuming.

On Tuesday, Lila claimed his sitting room where she terrorised him with afternoon television. He clunk-clunked to the bathroom to take refuge, and that night he spoke to Jenny – or moaned.

'When is she going?'

'I don't know,' Jenny said, looking at his eyes, which, for the first time in months, appeared to be seeing her.

There were days when she felt like lining both of them up

against a wall and borrowing Granny's rifle back from Harry. He still had it. There were days when she missed John so much she sat on his bed, in his room, and invited the pups in for company. Missed his clever hands every time Lila opened her sewing room door. He would have worked out how to fit a lock that would keep her out.

'Why do you need two of those things for?'

'I run a retirement home for Paul's old computers.'

'What do you do on them?'

'Play games.'

'Show me.'

Not bloody likely. Jenny saved, shut the computer down and went for a walk that ended at Fulton's hardware store.

Robert Fulton sold her two solid slide bolts and, as always, asked after Jim. He'd stopped visiting him around the same time Jim had stopped wearing his leg.

'As usual,' she said. 'Would you know if old Shaky Lewis is still capable of screwing in a screw?'

'They took him down to the old-folks' home, but there's a chap living out Cemetery Road who does a bit of handyman work.' He gave her the phone number.

Jenny looked at the phone when she walked in. Jim would take to his bed to hide from him. She studied the fittings. All they needed was a couple of screws and a few holes drilled. She'd once been capable of using tools. In Armadale, she'd drilled holes to repair an old cabinet, to hang curtains, to attach a form of lock to Ray's back door. When she'd lived with Granny, she'd sawed and hammered and worked like a labourer. Only since she'd been with Jim had she become useless. John's toolbox was still in the shed. He'd owned two electric drills and a huge set of multi-sized drill bits.

And maybe Jim wasn't quite as usual. She roused him from his chair when she started drilling a hole through the carpeted floor, which took a few attempts and a larger drill bit before the hole was big enough for one of the slide bolts to fit into. He watched while she positioned the bolt plate on the bottom of the left hand side door and marked its four holes with a pencil.

'Hold the door still for me,' she said.

He held it still. He held it when she got down on her knees to drill. She'd used Norman's hand drill in Armadale and wished for it now. John's electric model was too powerful, but fast.

'What are you doing?'

'Building myself a barricade,' she said, and selected a screwdriver. She got the screws in and, when the slide bolt was driven down through the floor, she had the left hand side door locked.

'In or out?' she said. 'I need to close the other one.'

He came in, no doubt wanting to protest against the ruination of another of his possessions. His mouth slapped open and shut a few times but she closed the door, then, closer to him than she'd been in months, she started measuring up for her second slide bolt, which, if attached in the right place then anchored into the locked door, should give her privacy.

He held the bolt plate above the doorknob while she marked its holes, and again while she got the screws started. He watched her mark the keeper's holes, and when the screws held it firm, when the second slide bolt was in its keeper, they were barricaded in. It wasn't a pretty job. A couple of the screws had gone in on an angle and their corners were sharp, but she hadn't been looking for pretty, only effective. And he wanted out.

'Thanks for your help,' she said, then locked him out and turned on Paul's second retired computer. He'd bought a faster model with a larger built-in brain, or hard drive, as he called it. Jenny's second computer had a small hard drive which she didn't quite trust yet.

It took one night for her to trust her handyman skills, because shove as she might, Lila couldn't get in. She knocked, she yelled, but not until Jenny took pity and slid that bolt did Lila get her cigarette.

Jim knocked on Monday afternoon, his knock a foot higher than Lila's. Jenny slid her bolt for him.

'Seeking me or my sanctuary?' she said.

'She took Trudy's car,' he said.

'I told her to take it for a run.' Jenny had given her ten dollars to wash the sheets and hang them on the clothes line. Lila had gone to Willama to spend it.

'She won't bring it back,' he said.

'If she doesn't, it's celebration time,' Jenny said. 'In or out?'

He came in, leaned his crutch against the table. It fell. She picked it up, took it to his bedroom and returned with his leg. Didn't say a word, just placed it down beside her older computer.

Only two chairs in that room, her discarded dining suite chairs. He sat to stare at the bulbous screen, so she turned it on to give him something to stare at. It took time in doing its warm-up exercises, and when it finished, she inserted the solitaire disc, and up it came, ready to play. He didn't like it but, trapped there without his crutch, he sat while, from a standing position, she played the game, hearing herself echoing the words Paul had spoken to her the day she'd first sat in front of a computer.

'Playing games is the easiest way to lose your fear of computers. Learning to control them is like learning to drive a car.'

He looked at her, helpless without his crutch. 'Get it, Jen.'

'Ah, he knows my name. I got your leg for you. Put it on – all the better to dodge her, my dear.'

She played a second game. The machine won, but her concentration hadn't been in it, nor was his. He was looking at his leg.

There were new age antidepressant pills that might help him, if he'd take pills. He'd never taken pills. If he had the flu he wouldn't swallow an aspro unless she disguised it in Granny's flu brew, which she had many times. She did what she could for him. Lived the best way she could around him. He wasn't interested in the computer, so she shut it down and returned to the faster model, still clean. Watched him. Watched his hands. One was hovering over the keyboard. She stopped typing to watch that hand. He didn't touch the keys. How many years had he spent on *Molly Squire*? How many had he spent on his Hoopers? Then he'd stopped, stopped dead, like a battery toy out of power.

He stayed with her until he heard Trudy's car at the gate. There was no mistaking its motor. Its exhaust pipe and muffler had rusted for lack of use.

'If she opens that gate and lets those pups out, I'll murder her,' Jenny said, and ran out to stop her opening it. When she returned, Jim and his leg had gone.

He came back the next morning, on his crutch.

'Bring that crutch in here and you know what I'll do, Jim.'

'The pain,' he said.

'Take an aspro.'

He went away and didn't return to her door for two days. Came early the next morning on two legs. She locked him in her sewing room, ruffled his hair when he sat and turned on the computer, inserted the word processing program and created a file she named *Jim*. Then turned off the monitor.

'Now it's a typewriter without paper. You can pour your every thought into it then, with a few strokes of the keys, delete the lot,' she said and sat again at her own computer.

He touched a key, and when the machine didn't explode, his fingers started searching the keyboard.

Jenny married Lila off to Billy Roberts and moved her to Woody Creek, and so engrossed in what she was doing, she was unaware he was typing. He wasn't as fast as he'd been on the old rattletrap typewriter, but his ten fingers had found a rhythm she'd never found with two fingers and a thumb.

He remained with her until lunchtime and when she turned his monitor on to read what he'd written, she'd expected more. *The quick brown fox jumped over the lazy dog*, repeated. Repeated umpteen times. He'd filled two-thirds of a page with that one sentence, then progressed to *The crow flew over the river with a lump of red raw liver in his mouth*. In all he'd filled three pages, but better he fill a hundred pages with his fox and his crow than sit staring out the window. She deleted his morning's work, closed down both machines and went out to make him a sandwich for lunch.

He beat her to the sewing room the next morning, on two legs. She turned on the two computers, turned his monitor off and, without comment, sat down to work.

And he spoke. 'What are you doing?'

'Getting Lila out of my head and onto disc. It's therapeutic,' she replied.

He typed a few more lines. Amy had timed him once on his typewriter. He'd done seventy words in a minute. Paul's newer computer had come with a touch-type teaching program already installed. She'd wasted a day attempting to give her ten fingers eyes. The computer told her she could do twelve words a minute. Her two fingers and thumbs could do around forty.

'Where did you first learn to touch-type, Jim?'

'Somewhere,' he said.

'At one of the hospitals?' There would be no more topics which were out of bounds, not for her. He didn't reply. She turned back to her computer and for half an hour their keyboards chattered companionably.

Nobby believed Jim had lost his leg before he'd been captured, that he'd received the wound in battle. From what Jenny had read of the Japs, if he'd been injured in battle, they wouldn't have wasted medical supplies on him. Through the years she'd asked him a hundred times how he'd lost his leg. He claimed to have no memory of it, or of the war. Only once had he mentioned the prison camp, to John. *I saw the worst of mankind and the best of it*, he'd said. Jenny knew when he'd gone missing. She knew when he'd been returned to a Melbourne hospital, but that's all she knew.

'Did they have doctors in the Jap camp?'

He looked at the blank screen, his hands still.

'Talk to me,' she said.

'It's the past,' he said. Like a parrot. For thirty years he'd been parroting those words. Thirty years? It was too long, and today his words failed to silence her.

'The past isn't ever gone, Jim. Scars from the past don't heal. I've got one on my calf from a pair of scissors Amber threw at me one day. I'll wear it to my grave. You'll wear that stump of a leg to your grave. How did you lose your leg?'

He'd stood then, and let himself out; she returned to her *Boomerang* file. She had a hundred and twenty-two pages now, and was having a no holds barred ball with Lila. She'd celebrate her absence when she was gone, but while she was here, she looked on her presence as less of an irritant and more a subject to be studied, and recorded.

And he was back. She unlocked the door.

Until the moment his batteries had run down, he'd filled his every day at his typewriter. At times she'd wanted to drag him away from the thing, to dig a pit in the garden and bury it. Today she wanted to watch his hands fly. Knew those hands so well. Knew the scar on his middle left finger, the scar on his wrist.

'You're getting your old speed back,' she said.

'It's flat,' he said. 'The keyboard.'

'It doesn't demand paper,' she said.

'Where does it go?'

'It stays inside until you save it to a disc,' she said. 'If you don't save it before you turn the computer off, it's lost.' She watched him type another line. 'You can tell a computer your worst secrets. Its blank expression never alters, and when you've finished baring your soul to it, you can hit the delete key and erase the lot. Do you want me to erase it?'

He nodded, so she turned on the monitor and up came the *The quick brown fox* and *the crow.* She held down the *shift* key, selected the pages on the screen, hit *delete* and the screen's blank face looked back at them.

'Look, no white-out,' she said. 'Rubbed out as if it never was.'

She'd done a lot of her own deleting when she'd filled her *Jenny* file. Had almost wiped out the night of the five American sailors and the beach and the taxi driver and the factory and her belly growing with Cara and the ripped taffeta dress. Hadn't. Hadn't deleted Laurie Morgan, or the Macdonald twins either. Knew deleting it would do no good. It had happened, all of it.

Every Tuesday, rain, hail or shine, at one o'clock Bernie Macdonald drove into her yard. Every Tuesday at three thirty, he returned to collect Maisy. Jenny never spoke to him, but constant subjection to the sight of him may have been a form of therapy. And she loved his mother.

She loved that fool of a man sitting, typing his fox and crow epic. Should have tried harder to make him talk about his war when he'd been well, and he had been, for years and more years. They'd created eight kids' books. Then they'd lost Amy. If he hadn't insulted her version of *Molly Squire*, if he'd put his name on it beside her own, if he'd taken one scrap of notice of her when she'd told him to turn the car around that day, she wouldn't have attacked his Hooper tome.

He'd burned half of it. He'd stood feeding a few pages at a time into the stove and when that had proved too slow, he'd opened the briquette heater's door and pitched in half of his tome before the smoke choked him. She'd retrieved some of it, and burnt her hand in doing it, and before she'd done it, he'd driven off to the tip with his typewriter. Should have kept her mouth shut. Should have burnt *Sent in Chains*—

And if she had, the house would have been falling down around them by now. Her advance had paid to restump Vern Hooper's house – and her floors felt better for it.

Shook her head and her fingers returned to her keyboard where she sat Lila down at a Sydney poker machine and had her feed it her last ten cents. She was working her way towards allowing her to win the jackpot, when he spoke.

'Tell me again how I erase it, Jen?'

'You have to . . .' She stood and turned on his monitor. Saw no crows and foxes. Saw . . . *prisoners dying like flies from disease and dysentery and starvation . . . little bastards were starving . . . waste no food on us . . .*

He sat watching her select the eight pages he'd typed. She didn't *delete* the pages but removed them and, her heart racing, she lied, 'All gone.'

The screen was blank. He stood and let himself out. She locked the door behind him, opened a new file, dumped what she'd removed from the *Jim* file into it, saved it as *Memory* then shut down the computer. Opened it late that night and read of Jim's war, or his final years of it. She learned how he'd lost his leg. A Jap did it – and he'd been lucky not to lose his head. He was a blocked conduit, finally releasing his load of debris, and with the minimum of punctuation and words of four syllables.

*A man can't survive on a cup of water and a handful of filthy rice. I watched them give up and their eyes looked relieved to give up.*

*My leg wouldn't heal. I knew I was dying and I found out why their eyes looked relieved. Something happens inside your head. One of the blokes there called it the God centre of the brain. If there's a God he lives somewhere in man. He wasn't in that bloody camp.*

She couldn't read for howling, but she read, swiping her tears away with wet fingers, sobbing in breaths before she reached the end of his pages, when she wiped her eyes on her dressing gown and closed his *Memory* file. Knew now why he'd erected his neon-lit *Don't Look Back* signs. Wanted to go to Trudy's room and climb into his bed and hold him, howl in his arms. Knew it wasn't the right time, not yet.

Each day thereafter she dumped more of his pages into his *Memory* file. Each night she read what he'd poured into that old computer. She forgot to put the ad in the paper to get rid of the pups – or she didn't forget, just knew what would happen when that ad went in. The phone would start ringing, the buyers would start coming and, right now, Jim didn't need the disturbance.

She knew she couldn't get rid of Lila when her next pension payment was paid in. Lila therapy had driven him to the sanctuary of her locked sewing room. Lila was due for another payment the night Jenny read about Jim's final days in the camp.

*'It's over, Hoop,' one of the chaps said. 'They dropped a bloody big bomb on the bastards and blew them all to hell.'*

*He had a sheet of paper they'd dropped from a plane that circled the camp that day. I remember one of the chaps was spoon-feeding me something sweet. Those little yellow bastards had cleared out, and our boys had cleaned out what they'd left behind. Jap jam maybe, or what had come from the sky in crates.*

*They dropped down warning leaflets, telling us not to eat too much, to allow our stomachs to get used to dealing with food slowly. We were skeletal men clad in loincloths. I was too weak to feed myself, a dead man breathing. Someone, maybe the chap feeding me, must have found the ribbons of Jen's poem. Someone copied it onto the back of one of the warning leaflets. It was days before our blokes got in to get us out. We were in a jungle camp. They carried me out on a stretcher. I was in the first hospital when I found the poem.*

*I wanted to live then, but damn near died. It was months before they brought me home. I still had it with me. Then I lost it. I lost everything . . .*

# The Unforgiven

Tuesday afternoon, Jenny was swinging the big gate open when the postie came. He handed her three envelopes, two addressed to Jim, the third addressed in Georgie's handwriting to *Jennifer Hooper*.

The dogs, defeated by Lila's ongoing presence, had lost their killer instinct and might not have bothered getting to their feet to eat Bernie Macdonald, but Jenny had chained them, just in case. She'd given up penning the pups. Too well grown now, they climbed on the backs of their siblings and scrambled over the sagging fence as fast as she could lift them into their pen. They'd learnt that the gate was out of bounds and that's about all they'd learnt, and not from Jenny, but from Lorna.

She opened Jim's mail. He had no interest yet in opening a bill or in paying it. She was opening Georgie's envelope when she heard Bernie's ute drive in. She removed two pages, a handwritten page from Georgie and one typewritten and addressed to Juliana Conti. Juliana Conti was dead. Folded the two together fast and slid them beneath her bra strap as Lila came from the kitchen.

'He's out there,' Jenny said. 'Skitch him, Lila.'

'One of them was enough,' Lila said. She went into the sitting room and closed the door.

Jenny stood behind the screen door, watching Bernie help his mother down from the ute then walk her to the veranda, one arm around her. Watched him support her up the steps. Maisy would celebrate her century in '96, and her legs were beginning to let her down. Jenny pushed the door wide for her, held it wide. Half a dozen pups accepted the invitation to enter – and they hadn't learnt that from Lorna.

'Sorry,' Bernie said.

Jenny ignored him and his apology, and once Maisy was in the hall, she closed the front door.

Pups skittered everywhere, sliding on the polished kitchen floor while she got Maisy seated on her favourite chair. She called to Lila to help round up the pups.

'Boo,' Lila said as she entered, a pup beneath her arm.

'Your face is enough to scare the tripe out of me without your boo,' Maisy said. And when she was gone: 'What's she still doing here?'

'She's incapable of surviving on a single pension,' Jenny said.

'Sissy's been struggling since Reg died, and now the Housing Commission want to move her out of her two-bedroom flat. They've given her a choice of Richmond and some place way to blazes out past Lilydale.'

Jenny moved Maisy's handbag and a small brown paper wrapped box she'd brought with her, then went about the making of afternoon tea, her Tuesday ritual, her mind with Georgie's letter, not Maisy's news of the week. Maisy didn't require lengthy replies, a nod and an 'Mmmm' usually sufficing.

'She'd be better off dead,' Maisy said, and Jenny dragged her mind away from the folded pages pricking her collarbone.

'Three years now she's been in that home. I was warned not to visit her, but Bernie took me down to see Patricia's new grandson, so I popped in to see poor old Dottie. I didn't recognise her. She's like a shrivelled-up little parcel of bones . . .'

Maisy's monologue of the dead and the dying continuing, Jenny placed two mugs down, then sat.

'He was two weeks early and weighed eight pound nine ounces. If he'd gone full term he could have been a ten pounder. That blonde-headed Duffy girl had a nine and a half pound son. How old would she be?'

'I don't keep track of them,' Jenny said.

'You know her. She rents the old Roberts' place in King Street with her sister,' Maisy said.

'Her!' Jenny said. 'She's already got umpteen – and a new two-door refrigerator. I saw it being wheeled in while I was walking the dogs.'

'We paid for it – and her kids,' Maisy said. 'God help them.'

'Granny used to say that Duffy babies did well in the womb but God help them when they hit the ground.'

'Nothing much has changed,' Maisy said. 'God help this town too. They're running wild.'

She spoke then of the bloke who owned the bush mill, spoke of log quotas and culls. Jenny was relieved when her monologue moved on to the new house going up on the last portion of John's land.

'That house is going to leave nothing over for a garden. It's huge, Bernie was telling me.'

Ten long minutes of Bernie followed, Jenny silently smoking and sipping tea, hoping Maisy would move on from Bernie this and Bernie that. Like his father before him, Bernie had become a fixture on the town council. He kept Maisy up to date with council permits, council decisions. He was a good son to her. Even Jenny had to admit that. If not for him, she would have been shuttled around between her daughters, half of whom weren't capable of looking after her. Maureen, her eldest, was eighty, and the rest weren't far behind.

'. . . he was saying last Sunday night when I phoned Sissy that I ought to tell her that Macka's widow needs a place to live and, you know, it wouldn't be a bad idea. The Housing Commission isn't going to put two widows out of their unit.'

'I wouldn't know which one to feel sorrier for, Maisy,' Jenny said. 'Did I tell you that Trudy got married?'

'She didn't! When?'

'On Saturday, in Greece. She phoned us on Sunday morning.'

'Who did she marry?'

'That Nick she's been travelling with.' Nick, an Australian-born Greek with a name Jenny couldn't spell. 'They're in Africa by now.'

'I can think of better places to go for a honeymoon.'

'They're volunteering for twelve months with some medical group.'

'She's already done that,' Maisy said. 'For most of my life we've been pouring food and medicine into that country. Has it done any good?'

'About as much as our handouts have done for our blacks – and the Duffys.'

'How does Jim feel about her going back there?'

'Startled.' 'Startled' was good. It was a response from a man who for too long hadn't been responding. Jim wasn't greatly improved, but was improving.

The two pages tucked beneath her bra strap prickling, Jenny stood and opened the firebox. The stove needing wood, she excused herself and went out to the wood box to scan Georgie's page.

*Dear Jen,*

*Don't come out firing. Make yourself a cup of tea and at least think about it . . .*

*. . . there's stuff on those discs that deserves to be read and with a few changes, could be . . .*

*. . . here comes the emotional blackmail bit. If you decide to go along with it, we'll come up for a week in June and I'll work on it with you . . .*

*Love G. X X X Kisses from Katie.*

Work on what? She hadn't seen the *Boomerang* file. Jenny glanced at the final paragraph. She wanted that week. She needed it. Jim didn't, not right now, but June was still three weeks away. She glanced at the typewritten page, the *Dear Juliana* page – and it was an offer of a contract for three books.

Three? Where the hell did they think she was going to get three from?

She stoked the stove, Georgie's and the publishers letters beneath her bra strap again, where they irritated her even more now.

At three she added more tea to the pot, more water, and was placing the full mugs down when Maisy, back on the topic of Sissy's unit, knocked her mug flying. Tea went everywhere. Jenny snatched up the parcel as she tossed a tea towel over the spill, hoping to catch the tea before it ran down to Lila's polished floor. She gave the box into Maisy's hands and grabbed a second tea towel, then went out to the laundry for a mop and bucket.

'I can never wait to open parcels,' Jenny said when the table was dry and the floor almost dry. 'They bring back memories of Sissy's catalogue orders from Melbourne. I used to love watching her rip her way into them.'

'I know what's in it,' Maisy said.

'What?'

'Your mother,' she said, and Jenny dropped the mop. 'She wanted to be buried with her babies, and Sissy went and had her cremated.'

She'd died three months ago. Maisy had been down to say goodbye. A forgiving soul, Maisy Macdonald. She had sat in this kitchen one Tuesday and attempted to talk Jenny into going with her. The shell of who she'd been or not, Amber would have risen up from her hospital bed to kill the stray.

*Your mother*? Maisy always referred to Amber as 'your mother'. She'd never been Jenny's mother. Her only infant memory of Amber was of a white-clad monster, then for six years she'd gone away. Good years, the best of Jenny's childhood, just her and

Daddy and Sissy and Maisy always in that house full of light across the road. Sissy must have remembered those good years. Since Norman's death, she'd kept in touch with Maisy.

'Sissy refused to say goodbye to her. I think she was pleased to see the last of her.'

As was I, Jenny thought, and I don't want her ashes in my kitchen.

'Every week, I'd ask Sissy to pick up the ashes, and every week she'd tell me that one of the Duckworths was going to pick them up. Sammy got them for me last weekend,' Maisy said and she placed the box back on the table. The child in Jenny still wanting to run, she returned the mop and bucket to the laundry and lit a smoke.

'As I said to Bernie when he picked them up at the post office, if you can't get what you want at your own funeral then it wasn't much use living, was it? I've told all of my kids not to put me in with their father when I go or I'll spend my life pregnant in paradise.'

Jenny sat until three thirty, and when no ute beeped in the drive, her ears strained to hear it. If nothing else, Bernie was punctual. At three forty-five she walked to the front door, willing him to come.

'He said he could be a bit late picking me up today,' Maisy said. 'I told him I'd ask you if you'd like to come out to the cemetery with me.'

'No,' Jenny said, then tempered her statement. 'No thanks.'

'I could be stuck here for another hour or more, love. He had some council thing in Willama today, and when those blokes get talking they're worse than old women.'

Jenny wanted to phone Georgie, and she didn't want that box of Amber in her house, and the weather was deteriorating.

'Lila,' she called. 'I need you to keep an eye on the pups while I get the car out.'

The easiest way to keep an eye on nine pups was to get them together in the laundry with food in their bowls. Lila came. The rattle of food bowls brought pups running from every direction.

She left Lila tormenting them with a bag of Puppy Chow, then went inside to get Maisy. The easiest way to get her out was via the back door. There was only one step down from the back veranda. It was a longer walk to the car, but once on her feet, Maisy walked well enough on flat ground. There was only flat ground in Woody Creek.

Jenny got her out of the car and onto her feet at the cemetery gates, but as she walked off alone, Jenny changed her mind about waiting in the car. She locked it and in a few strides caught up to Maisy. They walked together then.

So close to town, that cemetery had been an extension of little Jenny Morrison's playground. She, Dora and Nelly had spent hours playing there, reading the stories told by old tombstones. Both childhood friends were out here, Nelly only ten when she died, Dora barely into her forties. Too many of those she'd known had moved out to this place to print their own stories in stone, a few she'd loved – Norman, Granny, Amy, and John now, back with his Amy.

Maisy was familiar with each gravelled path, each stone. 'That's old Nelly Watson,' she said, pointing to a fancy stone.

Raelene had no stone. Jenny hadn't been at her early morning graveside service and was uncertain of where she lay. She knew where Margot was buried, had heard much about her tombstone but hadn't seen it, had made a point of looking the other way when forced to come out to this place. Bernie Macdonald had chosen it, paid for it.

Maisy continued on slowly until they reached the aged stone guarding Amber's lost babies. *CLARENCE. SIMON. LEONORA APRIL. REGINALD.*

'Was the last one Cousin Reg's?' Jenny asked.

'It wasn't your father's, I can tell you that much,' Maisy said.

'When I was a kid I used to believe they were my lost brothers and sister. Who might they have been had they lived, Maisy?'

'Who might Amber have been had they lived, love?' Maisy said, ripping her way into the box.

'You'll forgive the devil when he throws another log on the fire,' Jenny said.

'I like a warm house,' Maisy said, and she laughed and dumped Amber Morrison back onto the earth from whence she'd come. Jenny stepped back, one pace, two, then four more, not wanting one speck of Amber to stick to her. The wind was blowing stronger now, but blowing the wrong way. She was safe.

The letter prickling, she adjusted it.

Heard the box tapped, heard: 'Rest in peace, Amb.'

'All set?' Jenny asked.

'I might visit George and the kids while I'm out here, love. Bernie hates following me around this place.'

And well he might, Jenny thought. This was the place where he and his twin had sacrificed a fourteen year old kid to their drunken pleasure, where they'd held her down while, one after the other, they'd ripped and gouged every dream out of her – on old Cecelia Morrison's tombstone, three chubby angels smiling down on the scene.

Macka was out here, lying beside his father. Dawn was out here, the only one of Maisy's daughters who hadn't married. Cancer stole her life. A scary word, cancer, a death sentence. Doctors could transplant the heart of the dead into a living person and that heart would beat on, but they couldn't kill cancer. They couldn't cure AIDS either. Back when it first hit the headlines, it was believed to be a disease of homosexual habits, then it started turning up in those who'd had blood transfusions. It was rife in Africa. Nurses spent their lives up to their elbows in blood and body fluids. And what if Trudy's Nick was like Itchy-foot?

Granny had been a nineteen year old kid when she'd tied herself to trouble. Trudy was well into her thirties, and she'd been travelling with Nick since a few months after Lorna's house was sold. Wondered why they'd decided to get married in such a hurry. Initially Jenny had thought 'baby'. Then Trudy said 'Africa' and 'volunteering', and Jenny had cancelled her second grandchild.

'Be careful,' she called after Maisy.

'Everyone keeps telling me to be careful and I keep telling everyone that I don't intend moving out here until after my century party.'

Jenny wandered back to the area where they'd buried Margot, knowing today she'd run out of excuses as to why she'd never seen her tombstone. Didn't know how she hadn't seen it. It wasn't easy to miss. He'd bought her a near life-sized angel with spread wings to stand guard over a large white slab of stone.

*MARGOT MACDONALD MORRISON 11.4.39 – 20.12.77*
*LOVED DAUGHTER OF JENNIFER AND BERNARD*
*GRANDDAUGHTER OF MAISY. R.I.P.*

She stood staring at the words linking her name to that of her rapist. How dare he?

But what did it really matter? Since Jim's decline over the last few years, nothing much mattered, or not as much as it had. A hundred years from now, when Woody Creek had forgotten Margot, forgotten Jenny Morrison and Bernie Macdonald, that stone would suggest that Margot Macdonald Morrison, a woman of prominence, had been the beloved child of a happy couple.

'You'll stump future historians,' Jenny told the angel, then walked on and down to Granny's grave.

And what would future generations think of her unconventional stone? The day of Ray's accident, Jenny had been in Willama, describing the stone she wanted, a large and wise old owl perched on a fencepost, *GERTRUDE MARIA FOOTE* cut deep down the front of that post and the date of her birth and death hidden at the rear, as Granny had hidden her age until the day she died. She reached out a hand to rest it awhile on the owl's head. Aged now, green/grey moss covered, the owl looked timeless and very wise.

'Miss you still, me old darlin',' she whispered, then turned to look for Maisy. She was on her feet, no doubt passing on the latest gossip to her dead cronies, so Jenny took a seat on Granny's cement blanket, removed the prickle from her bra strap and, free to read, she read every word.

*You could sing, and you wasted it in that town, Jen. You can write, and now you're wasting that too . . . and if you do, I swear I'll put 'Jennifer Morrison Hooper, who could have been . . .' on your tombstone.*

'You bugger of a kid, Georgie. You prize bugger.' *Who could have been . . .* Jenny thought, and took her cigarettes from her cardigan pocket, a small disposable lighter squeezed into the packet. She sighed out smoke, looked for Maisy, then sucked hard on nicotine. Since Jim had fallen into his hole she'd been smoking like a chimney, and even more so since Lila. Had to get rid of her. Had to get rid of the pups. Had to remember to pay the rates too.

Or just keep everything stable, just for a week or two more, just until . . .

Until she'd lost a couple more years? 'Who could have been,' she said aloud, then drew in more smoke then flicked ash to the earth.

*You may as well light up a ten-shilling note*, Granny, or the owl or the wind, whispered.

'A ten-shilling note wouldn't buy much these days, Granny. The dollar note that replaced it has been replaced by a coin and it takes six of them to buy one packet – if you buy them in cartons,' Jenny said, looking again at the publisher's letter.

*Most of it would be banned reading*, all-knowing Granny, or the wise old owl, or the wind, whispered.

'You were reading over my shoulder!' Jenny accused. 'You taught me that that was bad manners, Granny – and you're wrong anyway. Nothing is banned these days. They show naked women on the television screen, in full living colour. They advertise condoms and safe sex. Brothels are legal and homosexuals have become gay.'

*That's not the sort of thing to talk about to your grandmother.*

'No,' Jenny said, 'but it gives a whole new meaning to the words of that old song I used to sing. *When I pretend I'm gay, I never feel that way, I'm only painting the clouds with sunshine.* All of the old boundaries have fallen. Itchy-foot could have bought his drugs on a street corner in the middle of Melbourne – or up here. Per capita, Woody Creek has got as many addicts as Melbourne – and if anyone ever wonders why, they only need to look at their televisions. They run a permanent fear campaign. Everything kills us. We've been brainwashed into spreading birdseed paste on our toast. And remember that little olive oil bottle you used to keep with your medicines? We buy it by the litre now and fry our fish and chips in it. They don't taste as good as the chips we fried in lard but we might live a few years longer.

'Doctors have become so clever, they can give you a new heart when you wear out your own. They can keep the dead breathing. Remember Dottie Martin, who once called my kids a trio of little bastards? She's a shrivelled-up Egyptian mummy with a brain the size of a walnut, but she's still breathing, thanks be to the grace of God – and modern medicine.'

Jenny sucked on the cigarette, her eyes searching again for a splash of maroon amid the grey, the white, the black tombstones.

'Cigarettes kill too. Smokers are quitting by the thousand. We've got a pandemic of depression and diabetes—'

She glanced again at Georgie's letter. *I stole your Granny file* . . .

She'd seen it ages ago. She'd spoken of that file half a dozen times. Must have made herself a copy at Christmas time when they'd brought up the second computer and were showing her how to copy the big discs onto the smaller discs.

The publisher's offer was for three novels! What else had that bugger of a kid sent them? The *Granny* file might have been printable. It was Jenny's recreation of the young Gertrude, built from Maisy's taped monologues, from Itchy-foot's diaries, from Granny's own stories about the old days, and from the ever young Granny she'd known. She had a *Jenny* file too, and if Georgie had sent bits of that up to Sydney, she'd murder her. She changed the names in *Sent in Chains.* If she'd changed the names—

Maisy was working her way back. Jenny stood, passed a kiss to the owl with her fingers and was walking away when the wind or the owl or Granny whispered, *I always wanted to change my name to Gloria.*

'I knew where I'd find you,' Maisy called, and with *Gloria* ringing in her ears, Jenny walked up to where Maisy waited.

'Does the name Gloria mean anything to you, Maisy?' Jenny asked.

'Gloria Swanson, the old movie star. We saw her on television the other night, or I saw it and Bernie slept through it.' Maisy talked as she walked, and Jenny's mind wandered back to the week of *Sent in Chains*' release. She'd lost that week. She'd lost the next month, had lost that year attempting to drag Jim out of the pit he'd fallen into.

'Did you see the name on a tombstone?' Maisy asked.

'What name?' Jenny's mind had travelled far from Granny's '*Gloria*' to possible titles. There was only one, *Before Her Time.*

'Gloria,' Maisy said.

'No,' Jenny said, then changed the subject. 'They need garbage bins out here. There's nowhere to toss anything.'

'There's one outside the gate,' Maisy said. She was still hanging on to Amber's box. 'It's sad when you think about it. Me and your mother were such good friends as kids and for a long time after. If things hadn't gone like they did for her, we would have grown old together.'

'If pigs had wings we'd call them birds,' Jenny said.

'She's at rest now,' Maisy said.

'I hope Norman is lacing on his running shoes.'

Maisy laughed. Her laugh hadn't aged. 'I can almost hear your dad. *You keep your distance, Mrs Morrison, or Saint Peter will hear about it.*'

They laughed together then and walked on arm in arm, the wind lifting Maisy's skirt and cutting through Jenny's lightweight slacks and cardigan. This morning had been pleasant with barely a breeze.

'Bernie told me to take a coat,' Maisy said. 'He's a good judge of what the weather's going to do. His father used to be too. He'd go out to the veranda, look at the sky for a few minutes, and come in and say: "There's rain on the way. Don't forget your brolly." Bernie does the same thing now.'

He'd been a swine of a kid, a drunken bastard of a youth. If not for him, Jenny might have done something grand with her life. Whether he was good to his mother or not, she'd never forgive him for altering the pathway of her life. Nor would a few in town; he'd been a councillor for years, but had never been offered the mayoral robes.

'Did you see Margot's stone?' Maisy asked.

'It's big.'

'It cost him a fortune. I think it was his way of . . . you know, of confessing what he and Macka did that night,' Maisy said.

'His monumental apology?'

'Pretty much,' Maisy said. 'He was deadset on having both of your names put on it. I told him a dozen times not to do it, but he did it anyway.'

He'd been apologising for years, in deed if not in word. Offering her and her kids a double-header ice-cream that day at Crone's café, back after the war, might have been his idea of an apology. She'd ground the ice-cream and cone into his earhole – or into Macka's. It was Bernie who'd helped her with Donny the day of Ray's funeral, maybe another form of apology, as might have been the abomination he'd helped to construct around Granny's hut. She'd never lived in it. Would have lived on the street with the homeless rather than in something he'd had a hand in building.

But she loved his mother – as did he – and since she'd lost her licence they'd become her private taxi drivers. If Jenny said they'd be leaving for Willama at ten and be back by three, he'd deliver his mother at ten on the dot and be waiting to take her home at three, and until Maisy's final visit, he'd walk her to Jenny's door on Tuesday afternoons.

'Sorry,' he'd said today when the pups had run inside. Every time anyone opened a door, half of them got in. Had to get that ad in the paper this afternoon and get rid of them, though maybe not all of them. Vern was on his last legs and Lorna, who John had believed to be the older of the two, wouldn't live forever, and the thought of that yard without a red dog wandering in it was untenable. Keep Tiny perhaps, and one of the males – or Olejoe and Lila, named for Olejoe's white goatee beard and because Lila had been tumbling him since she'd found her legs.

'They were both good kids when I could separate them,' Maisy said, still on about her twins. 'It was the two together, the one egging on the other one, that got them into all of their trouble. And it was George's doing too. After having eight girls, he thought those boys were the reincarnations of Jesus Christ himself and could do no wrong.'

No comment from Jenny. They were passing Norman and his mother's tombstone, and the wind was making the three angels howl. From infancy, she'd loved them. As a three and four year old she'd walked out here each Sunday morning with Norman and Sissy to give Grandmother Cecelia a bunch of flowers and to visit with her angels. There'd been no question in Jenny's mind as to where Norman should spend his eternity. In life he'd needed protection; in death, who better to protect him than his mother? She patted an angel's head, which moss and grime had done nothing to wizen up.

'They could use a scrubbing brush and a damn good clean,' Jenny said.

'Did I tell you that that young bikie granddaughter of Irene Palmer's cleans my house once a week?'

'Lila cleans mine,' Jenny said.

'You don't pay her, do you?'

'She gets ten dollars pocket money a week.'

They were walking by Juliana Conti's small grey stone. It looked much as it ever had. *A tenacious woman*, Itchy-foot had written of her. *A fiery-tempered Latina.* She was in the *Granny* file, towards the end of it. Call her Maria. Alter Gertrude to Gloria, Vern Hooper to . . . to Raymond Cooper. Itchy-foot could become Oswald. Dr Oswald Hand. It sounded good. Amber could be a Ruby.

'Sissy didn't like Reg much, but she misses him – or his car. She's having a hard time getting around lately, she said.'

'When have I been interested in Sissy's problems, Maisy?'

'She's your sister, or she was for a lot of years.'

'Dad might have turned us into sisters if Amber hadn't come back.'

'She's dead, love. Give her a wave and let your anger at her go.'

'I never learned the art of forgiveness,' Jenny said.

'It's easier on the heart than holding a grudge,' Maisy said. 'Grudges rust your organs – not that I'll ever forgive that pug-faced cop who took my licence – or the woman you live with. Every time I set eyes on her I want to brain her with a blunt weapon.'

'She'll be gone as soon as I've saved enough of her pension money.'

'How about I put it to Sissy to take her in?' Maisy said.

'Are you holding a grudge against Sissy?'

'I am not. I'm thinking of her stuck in a poky little single unit some place where she doesn't know anyone. She's got to know the neighbours where she is.'

'I'd prefer a prison cell to living with Lila,' Jenny said.

She got Maisy settled in the car, closed the door and walked around to the driver's seat, imagining a unit containing both Sissy and Lila, who would jump at the chance. She liked cities. Sissy wouldn't have a bar of her – though she might if Macka's widow drove a car.

Kill two birds with the one stone, Jenny thought. Jenny had paid Trudy's registration and third party insurance so John could drive her car occasionally. Had intended not to waste money on reregistering it this year. It was twenty years old, and worth nothing.

She turned to Maisy. 'Ask her if you like.'

'Ask who what?'

'Sissy. If she'd like a lodger. Tell her Lila owns a car.'

'Since when?'

'Trudy's. We need to get rid of it.'

Jenny drove Maisy home – and Bernie's ute was parked in the driveway. Cursing silently as she pulled in behind it, then prayed silently that he'd stay inside until she got Maisy out.

Not bloody likely. The front door opened as she braked, and he came out, suit-clad. He'd always looked ridiculous in a suit. No neck, ape arms, too much shoulder, his bald bullet head somehow attached directly to his shoulders. He nodded in Jenny's general direction, didn't attempt to meet her eyes. She didn't return his nod. Didn't bother turning off her motor; he was big and ugly enough to get his mother out of the car. But too close while he was doing it. She held her breath, determined not to inhale the air he expelled – and her brain, momentarily starved of oxygen, brought forth an image of his monumental apology.

She sucked in a breath of Old Spice shaving cream, and breathed it out fast. So what if he had spent a small fortune on that stone? He had plenty of money and nothing to spend it on. No wife. No kids. Nothing at all. And he deserved nothing. He'd stolen her childhood—

Maybe she'd stolen more from him. His granddaughter was now a Mrs Pappadimpoppa-doppalous – something unspellable – and Bernie would never know it.

She glanced at him. An ugly, clumsy hulk of a male – but as gentle as a woman with Maisy, supporting her with a long ape arm until she was steady on her feet. He'd spend his night with her. He'd sit watching old movies with her until it was time to go to his lonely bed, where maybe he dreamed of one day wearing the town's mayoral robes – and far better he wear Woody Creek's chains of office than another blow-in retiree.

Jenny shook the thought away and wound the window down, sucking in untainted oxygen enough to kill that mindless ripple of sympathy in her brain stem. Why should she feel sorry for him? Because he wouldn't even have his mother to sit with a year or two from now and nor would she.

'See you next week, love,' Maisy said.

'See you, Maisy.'

He was closing the car door when Jenny's lips, already open, allowed that ripple free. Didn't know why she did it. Maybe because grudges rust the organs and she didn't want her organs to rust, not yet. Maybe the ripple in her brain stem got together with the vibration from the car's motor and forced her vocal cords to vibrate.

'Margot would have been pleased with that stone,' her lips said.

He stopped closing the door and looked at his mother, believing Jenny's words had been for her. Maisy was making her slow way up the ramp he'd built for her, clinging to the handrail he'd built.

His eyes were focused on Jenny's, needing verification that her words had been for him, and for the first time in fifty-odd years she looked at eyes like fading twin violets near buried beneath overgrown clumps of the bone-dry grass of eyebrows. And fifty-odd years was long enough.

'She liked white,' Jenny said.

His bullet head nodded. 'Mum said she always liked white.'

Embarrassed by what she'd done, Jenny slid the selector into reverse, wanting that door closed now. He didn't close it.

'Thanks for taking her out there, Jenny. I hate going near that bloody place.'

Once she'd been Jenny, a fool of a girl. Now she was Jen, and it was well past time to let that fool of a girl go. And to let that drunken youth go.

'She knows she's always welcome,' she said.

He closed the door, and she backed out of the drive, feeling light-headed. Too much oxygen, or too little. And relief, a weird sense of . . . of freedom, like . . . like she'd turned the key in the door of little Jenny Morrison's cage and set her free.

Maybe she wasn't too old to learn how to fly.

# The Final Year

There is a calm before a major storm, a stillness to the air. Animals recognise the signs. Birds fly home; a dog's tail will curl between his back legs, and he'll stay close to his people, or to the door he last saw them enter.

Jenny had felt the calm of this last year of the old millennium. She'd put it down to old age, and to Johnny Howard in the Lodge and hope of stability for Australia. Trust is an odd thing. It hadn't been built into Jenny's psyche. She trusted Johnny Howard and his Liberal Party.

*Before Her Time* had been released in '96. She'd trusted Georgie to stand between her and the publisher. Juliana Conti, its writer, was a recluse, resided on her property in Gippsland with her husband and dogs, but it was Jenny Hooper who had drunk too much champagne at Maisy's century party the week it was released. What a crazy, crowded, rowdy night that had been. The council had donated the hire of the town hall and the whole town was there, and umpteen dozen from out of town. Georgie and Paul and Katie had been there, to celebrate Maisy's century, or Johnny Howard's win, or the release of *Before Her Time*.

It was Granny's story, her childhood, girlhood, marriage and womanhood, though Gloria, Ray and Oswald now cavorted between its covers. No Amber in it. Her history was too well known to camouflage so Georgie had suggested they delete her, apart from the pregnancy, which had given Gloria the impetus to escape Oswald. A miscarriage on the boat home had done for Amber.

Juliana Conti was in that book, with a name and nationality change. Maria Georgio, a Greek woman, died giving birth to the baby of Oswald, who was still a ship's doctor. Gloria, still the town midwife, was left holding the motherless baby, which supplied a possible happily ever after ending for childless Gloria and Ray Cooper – who Jenny had left studying Juliana's ruby and diamond encrusted brooch. Given the benefit of hindsight, Jenny wouldn't have suggested using Juliana's brooch on the cover.

Maisy came for her final visit in September '97, a few days after the death of Princess Di. She'd died as she should have, in the middle of a sentence, wound up that day about that beautiful, innocent little Cinderella girl who had married her Prince Charming and hadn't lived happily ever after.

'It's those little boys that will . . .'

For an instant, Jenny had waited for more. There'd been no more. No more that day, or ever. The chair that had known Maisy's shape so well had supported her until Jenny could hold her. Jim called the ambulance, the constable and Bernie, in that order. Bernie had come fast, had come into Jenny's kitchen, then the constable arrived. They'd waited half an hour for the ambulance, Maisy seated on her chair, Jenny on one side, her arm around her, Bernie on the other side, his ape arm brushing Jenny's. It hadn't mattered, not a bit, not that day.

In '98, *The Stray* was released. It was the *Jenny* file – Jenny's life – with alterations. As Amber had dominated Jenny's early life, she'd dominated the early pages of *The Stray*. Unable to delete her, Georgie suggested they alter her name to Vera, the ex-prostitute, wed to John, a widowed country parson with three children. Thereafter, the story stuck close to the original, other than the character of Sissy, who they'd turned into twins. There'd always been too much of Sissy for one person. Jenny had left out the Sydney rape and Cara. Jim didn't know about that and he was now her editor, and a damn good editor.

He knew she had his *Memory* file. She'd told him he ought to do something with it. He wouldn't. Maybe she would one day.

Lila hadn't returned. She'd moved in with Sissy and was still with her, and Jenny was still unable to decide which one to feel sorry for. She felt sorry for herself when Lila phoned, which she did once a month when the Duckworths removed Sissy from the unit for an hour or two. Sissy placed an eggtimer beside the phone every time Lila picked it up.

Jenny lit a cigarette and turned to glance at a women's magazine, the July issue. September now, and that magazine had lain open on the cutting table at pages twenty-two and twenty-three long enough to wear a film of dust. Shouldn't have used Juliana's brooch on the cover of *Before Her Time.* It had raised Angela Luccetto out of Sydney. Way back in '91 when *Sent in Chains* was released Georgie had received a letter from her. She claimed to be the granddaughter of Juliana Conti's sister. They'd heard nothing more from her until that magazine, which had printed a two-page spread about a beautiful Italian woman who had gone missing in Australia in 1923. Now that magazine wanted to interview Juliana, the writer – as did a newspaper.

Jenny drew the magazine to her side, wiping and blowing it free of dust. Vern Hooper's ceilings leaked dust. She'd given up chasing it. They'd printed a photograph of Angela Luccetto, a woman who might have been forty, a blood relative – distant blood relative but, as Georgie always said, blood is overrated. They'd printed an old sepia-toned photograph of Angela's grandmother standing with her two sisters. The one on the left was Juliana, and if there'd been any doubt in Jenny's mind, the brooch pinned to the shoulder of her frock killed it. They'd printed a blow-up of that brooch and the brooch on the cover of *Before Her Time*. They were identical. Maybe the jeweller had mass produced them. He'd been dead for a hundred years or more so who was to prove he hadn't? It would go away. As Jim was still prone to saying, all things pass.

He was eighty and he had a gammy hip now to go with his gammy leg. She couldn't think of him as eighty, but couldn't deny it. Woody Creek had begun its preparations for her seventy-sixth birthday party – or for the birth of the new millennium – and the year 2000 sounded like science fiction. According to the media, every computer in the world was going to crash when computer clocks attempted to turn over to 2000.

Paul said it was more media hype, their latest fear campaign. 'Got to keep the viewers' adrenalin pumping or they'll stop tuning in for their daily hit,' he said. Hype or not, Jenny was making copies of her files – that's why she'd come in here tonight, to copy, not to worry about Angela Luccetto.

Then the phone rang. It would be Georgie. No one else rang her at ten o'clock at night. Busy Georgie, getting to where she wanted to go – and playing literary agent in her spare time, of which she had none.

'What do they want now?' Jenny greeted her.

'Do you want the good news or the bad first, Jen?'

'Angela Luccetto's been at it again?'

'Worse. The release of *The Winter Boomerang* will be delayed until November. They're doing a reprint of your earlier books to release at the same time.'

'Is that the good or the bad news?'

'Good. I'm working my way down. There was a ton of stuff on the computer when I came home tonight, a ton of stuff from your publicist too.'

'Juliana Conti does not do publicity.'

'Get off your soapbox, mate,' Georgie said. 'The bad news is some literary coot has got hold of a copy of *The Stray* and he's accusing Juliana of plagiarising C.J. Langhall's *Angel at My Door* . . .'

'*Angel at My Door*?'

'By C.J. Langhall,' Georgie repeated. 'I told you she was Cara.'

'I've never read it. How did I plagiarise it?'

'I read it, years ago, and I think it could drag you out of the closet, Jen.'

'I've had enough whispering behind hands and fingers pointing at me to last me until 2099. What's her book about?'

'From what I remember, it's about an unmarried girl who has four kids and gives the last of them away to her landlady.'

'We cut the Sydney baby out of *The Stray*. What are they on about?'

'Lots of things, Jen. When I read that book I saw a few similarities to your life.'

'Can you post it up to me?'

'I need to read it again. Give the Willama library a call and see if they've got a copy – it will look good to have it on record when I have to defend your plagiarism charges in court.'

'That's not funny, and my library card is in Jennifer Hooper's name. They're accusing Juliana.'

'At the moment.'

'Has Langhall responded?' Jenny asked.

'Not yet,' Georgie said. 'But I'll guarantee if she does, she'll name Jennifer Hooper as her inspiration for *Jessica*.'

'The photograph in her latest book looks nothing like Cara.'

'I hate to tell you, mate, but you don't look a lot like you used to look thirty years ago either,' Georgie said. 'It's her, and I know it now. She knew the ins and outs of your life story. She used to pick my brains for details back in the sixties – and I know she spent half her life writing and posting off bits of her book to publishers.'

'That Angela Luccetto brought me out into the open with her magazine story.'

'She's the reason they're reprinting your early books.'

'Not *Sent in Chains*?'

'All three, Jen, and you need to get on the internet. I've got a pile of stuff down here I need to send you.'

'They have viruses on the internet that eat your computer's brains.'

'They have virus killers too. I got an email from Trudy tonight.'

'Where is she?'

'Back in England.'

'Can you read it to me?'

'I'll post it up with the rest. She said in it that if Mum and Dad would come out of the dark ages and connect up, it would make life a whole lot easier – and it would.'

'If I did it, it would have to be connected to one of the old computers. I'm not putting anything odd on my new one.'

'They're too old for the internet. Get yourself a little laptop and we'll connect you up when we bring Katie for the holidays. She'll teach you how to use it.'

'What else did Trudy say?'

'That a while back she found out her mother's name was Margaret Morrison and that she lived in Vroni's street in Frankston, and was she some distant relative?'

'My God.'

'Are you going to come clean, Jen?'

'It's too late.' Jenny lit a cigarette. 'It would be Vroni's old address. They changed the street numbers when they continued her street through.'

'She also wants to know the names of the people who adopted Jimmy. She said she'd see if she can find him while she's there. How come she doesn't know?'

'She would have heard the Langdon name – or was she at school that time Lorna came up? Maybe she was. Tell her, Georgie. Tell her that the last we heard Jimmy was in Thames Ditton.'

*

Ask most of the Thames Ditton locals if they knew the Langdon family and they'd admit to knowing the name. Get some of the old chaps talking, and they'd tell how there'd been Langdons living at The Hall for five hundred years. Trudy and Nick had a well lubricated octogenarian bailed up in the local pub; he was a gold mine of information.

'They owned half the county at one time. Henry Langdon was the one who started the breaking up of the estate when he come into his inheritance.'

'Is he still living?'

'Old Henry? No. He passed on in '52, the same year as King George. Leticia, his good lady, made old bones, then the young Langdon come into it. He sold off all bar twenty acres then spent the lot on putting the old place into good repair. He had workmen out there for twelve month. They did a grand job on it.'

Trudy paid for a shampoo in Thames Ditton. Her hair was long; it took the hairdresser some time to dry it. She learned that Mrs Langdon didn't frequent the salon, though the youngest girl came in when she needed a trim.

'She's a cripple,' she said.

'She'd be the daughter of James Langdon?' Trudy asked.

'Morris Langdon,' the hairdresser said. 'My mother knew him, or she knew the girl he was engaged to at one time. Mum worked in the girl's father's office. They had a big wedding planned, the dress bought and all, then less than a month before the wedding, this Australian girl turned up, and the next thing everyone knew, the wedding was off and Morris was squiring the Australian around.'

'Is her name Karen or Carlene?'

'I wouldn't know. She's Mrs Langdon to me. She's been living out at The Hall since the late seventies. They say she writes books. One of the girls who served her apprenticeship here told us she was in London one day with her mother and they saw this crowd in one of the big stores' book departments. They went over to see what was going on and there was Mrs Langdon, sitting signing books. They bought one, thinking it would be about our area, but it was about Australia. Full of violence and murder and what-not, she said. To look at her, you wouldn't think she'd know about such things.'

'You don't know of a Jim or a James Langdon?' Trudy asked.

'I've never heard of Jim or James,' the hairdresser said.

Nick had more luck. He learned that the Langdon family had no living offspring to carry on the name, and that Morris was an offshoot of Henry Langdon's sister.

'His mother's maiden name could be on her tombstone. He said she's buried in the local graveyard.'

They walked the graveyard that afternoon, searching for Margaret Langdon, *née* Hooper. They didn't find her. They found umpteen Langdons. They found a Margaret Grenville-Langdon, beloved wife of Bernard and mother of Morris, but no mention of Hooper.

It was a perfect autumn day in a land where perfect days were few and far between. Their sweaters were off.

'Mum used to call a day like this an ice-cream day,' Trudy said, so they drove away from the graveyard and bought ice-cream, then drove on to find Langdon Hall. With no gates closed against them, they drove in and up to the house.

'Wow!' Trudy said.

'Ye olde family estate, yer 'ighness,' Nick said.

'It could be Jimmy's. Georgie's email said that Jimmy was adopted by Margaret Hooper and her husband.'

'You never met him?'

'He was gone long before I was born, and they never spoke about him. I've seen baby photographs of him. From what I've been able to glean, his grandfather claimed him when he was a tiny kid.'

'How come?'

'Mum and Dad weren't married when he was born. It was during wartime and Dad was away in the army, then a prisoner for years. They never talk about that either.'

'The house of secrets.'

'It seems like it at times,' Trudy said.

Nick knocked on a massive front door. No bustling maid came

to open it. They looked for a bell they might ring. No bell. Only the power wires feeding into that old building gave away the fact that they hadn't stepped through a hole in time and back into the seventeenth century.

They knocked again, then walked to the corner and down the eastern side to knock on a smaller, more utilitarian door. No bell. No maid.

'The hairdresser said they have an open day in spring. I wish I'd started searching earlier.'

'Wish in one hand and spit in the other, Tru,' Nick said.

They walked back to the car then, and turned its nose towards London.

*

A rare day, and not many more such days to look forward to, Morrie and Cara were walking their dogs. He too was craving an ice-cream. He too had removed his sweater.

Cara didn't share his craving, or his idea of warmth. Her conditioning to England's chill having commenced later than his, her cardigan was buttoned to the neck today.

'Will you go?' he asked.

'I'm considering it,' she said. 'They've been at me for years to do a book tour over there.'

They hadn't been back to Australia since Robert's funeral and had no desire to sit on a plane for twenty-four hours, but publicity sold books and the tour would coincide with the release of her latest novel.

She picked up and tossed a stick towards a tiny streamlet and the two dogs, still arguing over an earlier stick, bounded after the new. They followed the dogs and caught a view of the distant house, at its best from this angle. He'd spent a fortune on removing the rot of generations, along with generations of renovations. He'd brought in an architect and a building supervisor, but had personally supervised the removal of every stone, had watched every ancient wall reinforced, every rafter in the old section replaced.

There was no garden when Cara had arrived with the children, and neither she nor Morrie gardeners they'd hired professionals. The present grounds might not have been as the old Langdons had known them, but who was alive to say if they were or not? They were pleasing to the eye.

They rarely opened the front door, rarely opened the front rooms, other than on open day. They lived at the rear of the house, spent most of their days in the long flagstone-floored eastern room, their living area – sitting room cum study cum kitchen – modern enough to work in, but not obviously so. They'd replaced ancient windows with new, paying a fortune to make the new look exactly like the old. At seventeen, Morrie had fallen in love with the age, the immovability of Leticia's house. He loved it still. Cara had fallen in love with its sanctuary.

They'd fallen in love with each other before learning that their love was forbidden, though not in Leticia's house. In Thames Ditton no one had heard of Woody Creek.

On two occasions letters posted in Woody Creek had found Morrie, and shaken him to his core. For a time he'd considered replying, but a man is who life makes him, not who he'd been born to be. These days, if he looked back too far, if he remembered Jenny's frizzy lemon-scented hair beside him in a dark theatre, remembered the photograph of the man with big teeth who'd painted the rainbows in the sky, he shook himself and turned to Tracy, conceived during a business transaction, born in jail to a drug addict, but now Tracy Langdon, a ballet dancer in London. He looked at pretty Elise, born with a crippled leg and dumped at birth at a Romanian orphanage. She'd never dance like her sister, nor sing like her brother, but she'd teach like her mother.

Robin could have, perhaps should have, been taking his bows on stage. His voice was a musical instrument. Place any instrument in his hands and he'd make music on it, but he preferred a surgeon's instruments. He'd married two years ago and now had a three month old son – and for the nine months their grandson had been growing in the dark, Cara had feared he'd be born imperfect, that Robin would be punished for his parents' sin against God. Their grandson was perfect – but Cara would continue to suffer that same torment if there were more grandchildren.

'When are they suggesting we go?' Morrie asked.

'November, Hillary said.'

'For how long?'

Cara shook her head. 'A book tour. That's all she said. I told her I'd think about it and get back to her.'

They walked on then, admiring the land, the trees clad in their autumn garb. It was a day when Morrie wished himself an artist so he might capture the trees and the sky and the laughing dogs, rolling in fallen leaves.

'My father must be around eighty now, if he's still living,' Morrie said.

'Jenny will be seventy-six on New Year's Eve,' Cara said. 'If you ever plan to see him or her, the time to do it is now. It won't be much good wishing you had when they've gone.'

'No,' he said.

'If we go, I'd want free time in Sydney with Pete and Kay, and a few days with Cathy – and I'm going back to the house, Morrie. I'm cold.'

'You've got ice in your blood,' he said.

'I've got Australia in it. Summer will be coming over there. I'd like to feel its heat, just once more. I'll give Hillary a call and see if she can find out exactly what they've got in mind, then we'll decide whether we're going or not.'

Still a good-looking pair, both tall, both slim. Cara's hair, once cut like Jenny's short spring-coil gold, was shoulder length, bleached a few shades lighter, tamed by a brush and blow dryer. Wasted effort when the wind blew and fine English rain fell, when that hard worked for smooth style reverted to spring coils, when she still looked a little like Jenny around the brow, around the eyes. No wind, no rain today, a long fringe covered her brow, sunglasses hid her eyes, and her mouth and chin had never been Jenny's.

His brow was. His nose was Jenny's in male form, and his ears. He had the Hooper hair, steel grey like his father's, his grandfather's. Jenny's lack of height had saved him from the excessive height of his forebears. He'd made the six foot two inch mark, then no more. He had his forebears' double-jointed thumbs and hands, which he clapped now. The dogs stopped rolling to lead the way down the track that would take them home.

# The Lady in Pink

*The Winter Boomerang*, released the first week of November, made the bestseller list and Jenny's publicist was tearing out her hair, according to Georgie, who came to Woody Creek with Katie two weeks after the book's release. They'd brought a bundle of emails from the publisher. Jenny gave them only a cursory glance before placing them down.

'Juliana doesn't do publicity!' she said.

'The days have passed when writers sat in their cold garrets and wrote with a quill, Jen, and hiding from this plagiarism thing isn't making it go away. She suggested that you write something for one of the women's magazines stating that you hadn't read *Angel at My Door*, and include a bit about your personal knowledge of Sydney during the war.'

'Let them talk. It's selling books,' Jenny said.

'They're talking about it on the ABC now. It's growing, not dying down,' George said.

Jenny's pile of free books was also growing. Georgie had a boot full of things. Every time the publisher did a reprint Jenny had to find space for another carton of their free copies. She used to want to move to a smaller house but had stopped nagging about that. The bedroom they used as a storeroom was full. They loaded the new cartons in a corner of the small sitting room.

'If you keep this up, I'll end up a kept man,' Jim said.

'If you'd see a doctor about your hip, you might be worth keeping,' Jenny said. He'd been having trouble with his hip for months – and refused to see a doctor about it.

'Your publicist wants you to go on television, Nanny,' Katie said. Now a leggy eleven year old she'd had her spring-coil curls cut short like her nanny's and looked older with her mop of hair gone – a beautiful kid with a beautiful nature.

'That will be the day, my Katie,' Jenny said.

'Mum said in the car that you could wear a wig and that no one would even know it was you.'

'How old are you, Jen?' Georgie asked.

'You know how old I am, and don't bother waking it up.'

'You'll turn seventy-six on New Year's Eve. That's four years away from eighty, Jen. What have you got to lose?'

'Twenty-four years. I'm going to live to a hundred, aren't I, Katie?'

'A hundred and ten,' Katie said.

'You've got nothing to lose and everything to gain, mate,' Georgie said.

'It's bad enough now. Maisy's Patricia read *The Stray* and she sent it to Rebecca and I had both of them up here the other day telling me that someone in town wrote my life story.'

'I'll make you up so Jim won't recognise you,' Georgie said.

'Do it, Nanny.'

'Enough,' Jenny said, her hand raised as Norman's hand had been raised when he'd commanded 'enough'.

'It's a morning show, not some literary thing. You could handle the host.'

'I said no, Georgie.'

'You've got no outstanding features.'

'Thanks.'

'That's to the good. Cover up your hair, dress in some way-out writer's gear, plaster on the makeup and no one would have a hope of recognising you. It would shut your publicist up, and Patricia and Rebecca.'

'You put the wig on and do it. Or Jim can,' Jenny said, and Katie giggled. 'He'd look good with a long ponytail and a fake beard, wouldn't he, darlin'?'

'It would be half an hour out of your life, Jen,' Georgie said.

'Half an hour would be more than enough to make a fool of myself. I was listening to a writer on the ABC a few weeks back and he sounded like a university professor.'

'Anyone who has read your books knows that you're not a university professor, Jen,' Jim said.

'Thank you, Jim.'

'You've been standing on stage singing since you were knee high to a grasshopper,' he said.

'Truly?' Katie asked.

'Once upon a time,' Jenny said.

'When I was a kid she played Snow White in a pantomime,' Georgie said.

'Were you famous, Nanny?'

'No I wasn't, and I don't want to be.'

'It would be like going on stage again,' Georgie said. 'You'd be playing the role of Juliana. You looked nothing like yourself as Snow White. Jimmy kept pulling on my arm and asking, "Where's Jenny?" and you had a ball doing it too.'

'I made money doing it,' Jenny said.

And she'd had a ball. She'd become Snow White once her wig had been pinned down and her costume laced up. She'd done three two-hour performances at the Hawthorn town hall and when the last show ended, she'd been Jenny King again and four months pregnant, and she'd wanted to howl. Maybe she could play Juliana for half an hour.

Then Georgie said the magic words. 'We're proud of you, Jen. Katie drags me into every bookshop to count your books.'

No one had ever said that they were proud of her, or not since little Jenny Morrison had sung about the lonely petunia in the onion patch. *You make me proud*, Norman had said that night.

And goddamn it all, what did a woman four years away from eighty have to lose?

'Could you make me look like a Juliana?'

'We can, Nanny. Papa will be pulling at Mum's elbow asking, "Where's Jen?"' Katie said.

*

Papa didn't go to Greensborough. The night before they were to leave, his hip crippling him, he couldn't lie still, couldn't sit in his chair, let alone sit in the car for three hours.

'I'll go by myself,' she said.

He couldn't walk as far as the letterbox and she couldn't leave him without his car, which he was able to drive if he took a couple of painkillers half an hour before setting off.

She walked to the bus stop. Georgie picked her up at the Melbourne depot at one.

'We found the perfect wig at an opportunity shop, and a choice of outfits. Katie has laid them out on your bed for a dress rehearsal after school.'

Their purchases hit Jenny in the eye when she carried her case into the spare room. A pink suit and matching platform-soled sandals and an emerald-green mother of the bride floating chiffon thing.

'I wouldn't be seen dead in either of them,' Jenny said.

'That's the idea, Jen. If you're going to pull it off, you need to think outside the square of you.'

They picked Katie up at three thirty. At ten days old, she'd asked for Jenny's heart and it had been given. She gave her her dress rehearsal.

The pink sandals were too big. Had they not been, Jenny would have claimed that they were too small. She tried both outfits – and had no intention of wearing either. She'd packed her black slacksuit and a blue top, and who could tell one black suit from the next?

She'd never been overly busty and didn't have a lot left of what she'd had in her youth. Georgie tossed a padded bra onto the bed. 'Try it, Jen.'

She tried it, and it gave her a bustline equal to Lila's marble breasts – before they'd gone lopsided. She played busty Lila for Katie; she did her voice, then did Juliana's accent, and Katie laughed and Jenny laughed, then Georgie offered the wig, a dark brown neck-length bob with a long and heavy fringe.

It covered most of her face and felt like one of those head-hugging hats from the thirties. 'It itches, Georgie.'

'I checked it for lice.'

'We sprayed its inside with Mortein fly spray, then shampooed it,' Katie said, and Jenny looked at her image in the mirror. She didn't look like herself. She felt the textured fabric of the pink suit which might have been expensive in its day.

'No one wears pink suits now,' she said.

'Except Juliana. It looks good,' Georgie said.

'I haven't worn pink since Sissy's hand-me-down sixty years ago. It ripped while I was on stage and put me off pink for life.'

'That suit was tailored for you.'

The jacket might have been. The skirt barely covered her knees and it had no hem to let down.

'It's too short.'

'You've still got good legs. Flaunt them,' Georgie said.

She slid the pink sandals off and put her black high heels on. She'd need to wear stockings if she was flashing her legs, but Georgie had thought of everything. She'd bought pantihose. It was just a game she was playing to amuse Katie, so Jenny played it. Played mother of the bride later in green chiffon, and at dinner she drank two glasses of wine so she might continue the charade. Made silly jokes for her beautiful girl, made up silly poems.

'There was an old lady in pink, who had far too much to drink. When she rose from the table, she was quite unable, and down to the floor she did sink.'

'There was an old lady in green, the funniest that ever was seen. When she went on the telly, she got a pain in the belly, and how that old lady did scream,' Katie countered.

'There once was a lady of law, who stood barricading the door . . .'

But eleven year olds have to go to school. At nine Katie went to bed and Jenny took her cigarettes from her case and walked out to the street to light up and blow smoke into the dark. She never smoked when Katie was around. Kids learned in school that smoking kills. As did living, but they didn't learn that at school. She walked to the corner, hoping to trip over in the dark and break a minor bone, and when she returned to the darker dark of Georgie's backyard she damn near got her wish. Stubbed her toe on a rock and almost went for a sixer.

It was eleven when she went to bed the first time. Rose at midnight and made a cup of tea she took outside. Lit a smoke. Lit two. She was out of bed again at three o'clock, and eventually fell asleep propped on the family room couch, the television silent but flashing its mind-numbing commercials. Paul woke her at seven when he turned her sleeping pill off. He didn't ask why she'd slept on the couch.

'It will be a breeze, Jen,' he said.

'I feel stretched to breaking point,' she said.

'You don't break, mate,' Georgie called from the bathroom. 'You've got the recoil of a rubber band.'

Last night had been warm, but while they'd slept a cool change had blown through turning midsummer to winter. Jenny took her coffee to the glass door where she stood looking out at the yard, seeing nothing, her mind going over and over the hours ahead. She watched the morning show from time to time. The host had been on television for years. She knew his interview style. Jim had made a list of questions she might be asked. They'd rehearsed Jenny's replies. She couldn't remember the questions this morning.

Georgie's foot now well in the door of Marino and Associates, she'd arranged her appointments so she might play literary agent cum taxi driver, and when Katie was at school, she slid into her literary agent role.

There was a poem about a wolf and a vain little pig, a kids' poem Jenny had long ago memorised. She recalled it now as she dressed for her date with the big bad wolves . . . and when Georgie saw her blue top and black slack suit, she told her to get them off. Then she dropped her bombshell.

'Your publicist arranged for a photographer to come to the house. Everyone and their dog will recognise you in that. Put the green on first – and that bra too.'

Other than a swipe of face cream and a dash of lipstick, Jenny rarely bothered with makeup. Georgie plastered it on her that morning, a sheet protecting the flyaway green. She added eye shadow, eyebrow pencil, mascara and layers of pale pink lipstick, guaranteed not to kiss off. Then they pulled that crawling wig into place and when every fading tendril of gold had been tucked beneath it, they pinned the wig down with a multitude of bobby pins and slid long dangly green earrings through her lobes.

'Where are your black-rimmed glasses, Jen?'

'They're my reading glasses.'

'They'll do for the photographs. Those frameless things look like you,' she said.

They had trouble sliding the arms of the glasses beneath the too well pinned wig, but they covered much of her face and matched the wig. If she'd been wearing her black slacksuit, she might have looked like a writer.

'Let me wear my slacksuit.'

'Jennifer Hooper doesn't wear green and pink, now behave yourself.'

She couldn't run from this, couldn't hide from it. Couldn't sit down on the floor and kick her heels. Couldn't think of her list of questions but remembered every word of that poem and recited it in her mind while the photographer carried in half a ton of paraphernalia.

*She preened in the mirror. She made herself neat . . .*

He took umpteen dozen shots of her, first in her green with her green dangling earrings, then in her pink, with pink and gold ear studs. He shot her full length, head and shoulders, pink suit walking, pink suit sitting. Hair hanging forward, hair held back to show one earring. He took shots of her wearing Georgie's maroon jacket, a few with one of Georgie's scarves. Then he wanted her to remove her glasses. She clung to them and raised her hand at Georgie.

'We're out of time,' Georgie said.

*And she opened the door – to be swept off her feet . . .*

Greensborough was a long way from the city but that morning the trip was too short. She saw no traffic on the road.

'Where were you born?' Georgie asked.

'Halfway between Australia and Italy.'

'What year was that, Juliana?'

'I can't give them Margot's date of birth. She would have turned sixty this year.'

'They'll know you haven't had a facelift – and they won't ask anyway.'

'They'll bring up that plagiarism thing again.'

'What will you say if they do?'

'Rape is all too common, as were Sydney boarding houses during the forties. And until that coot started—'

'Don't call him a coot, Jen.'

'Until that literary gentleman started his plagiarism thing, I had not read *Angel at My Door.*'

'And?'

'And I thought I was here to discuss *The Winter Boomerang*, much of which is also set in Sydney during wartime.'

'Good enough. What are you currently working on, Juliana?'

'Thanks to you, I'll probably die of a heart attack before I finish it.'

'Relax and be yourself – as much as you can,' Georgie advised.

'In pink, with a thirty-eight inch foam rubber bust and my knocking knees on show – and as blind as the proverbial bat in those reading glasses. With a bit of luck I'll fall over and break my neck before I get in there.'

'Try my glasses,' Georgie said, offering them. They were black-rimmed but sunglasses.

'You said I couldn't wear sunglasses.'

'They're only tinted once you're inside,' Georgie said.

'You've got a weak muscle. They'll send me cross-eyed.'

'Which could be a good thing this morning.'

*

Jenny had never ridden a roller-coaster. She rode one that Wednesday morning and all she could do was hang on until it stopped or she was flung off flat on her face. You can imagine an experience over and over, you can practise your replies until you're word perfect, but all of that didn't matter a damn. Once out of the car, her mind turned to baby mush and any second now she was going to spit up. She almost vomited when they ushered her away from Georgie – just as she and Sissy had been ushered away from Amber on the night of the talent quest, and just as Amber had attempted to follow Sissy, Georgie attempted to follow Jenny with the glasses she'd required for driving. Someone brought them in to the makeup room. Jenny slid her sunglasses from beneath her wig and put the other pair on, then the makeup woman asked her to take them off so she could powder her face.

'I've already powdered it.'

The woman not satisfied, Georgie's glasses came off and, Georgie's eye makeup or not, the eyes looking back from the mirror were Jenny's and they were petrified. She clung to her wig, refusing to allow the makeup woman to touch it then, when the glasses were poked and prodded back beneath it, she dared another look in the mirror. Maybe Juliana Conti looked back at her – a somewhat blurred Juliana.

They led her out, pointed her in the right direction, gave her a nod when it was time for her to make her entrance. Then she was on her own. She'd made a few entrances in a past life so, grasping at straws, she reached for the past and for Miss Rose's final instructions before kid Jenny had made her entrance on stage: *Head high. Give the audience a big smile, Jennifer.*

Head high, stomach threatening to lose its two bites of breakfast toast, she fixed on her fake smile and walked across to the host – to applause. Maybe the applause helped. If the worst came to the worst she could stand up and sing 'I'll Walk With God'.

Georgie hadn't told her there'd be a second guest. With too much else to see in the studio, Jenny didn't notice the already seated stranger until the host introduced her to Ms Langhall.

# A Match Made in Heaven

Sissy and Lila usually watched the morning show. It came on before *Days of Our Lives.* They knew the host well.

'He wasn't a bad-looking sort when he was young,' Lila said.

'All you ever talk about is men. If you're going to watch it, shut up and let me listen.'

'They're writers. Who's interested in what they say?'

Sissy was. She'd read about Juliana Conti in a magazine. 'She had a grandmother who went missing in the war or something. She's Italian.'

'When I was young, blokes used to ask me if I was a dago,' Lila said. 'My hair was as dark as hers and long enough to sit on.'

'So was mine,' Sissy said.

'You ought to dye it. Grey hair is aging.'

'So is going bald. You're so thin on top I can see your scalp shining through. A friend told me once that too much dying kills all the hair roots.'

Sissy had plenty of hair, the Hoopers' steel grey. At eighty, she took up less of the couch than she had at seventy. Lila would wear the weight off anyone. Watching her incessant movement burned calories, as did sucking in her secondhand smoke.

She rose to get the remote, then to flip through the channels looking for something worth watching, and while her back was turned, Sissy helped herself to another Tim Tam. She'd almost got rid of it before Lila gave up flicking and settled for the writers. She caught her crunching.

'We paid half each for those,' Lila said, claiming the packet and placing it out of Sissy's reach while the Conti woman spoke about her small country property.

'She looks like a cat on hot bricks,' Lila said.

'Can you keep your mouth shut for five minutes?'

The camera swung to the other writer, clad in a silky beige shirt and brown slacks. *I wrote the first drafts of* Angel at My Door *in longhand during my first year at college*, she was saying. *It began as a search for my own identity.*

The Conti woman said she'd never considered writing a book until her son-in-law introduced her to a floppy disc that knew how to play cards.

'She sounds familiar,' Lila said.

'She doesn't sound Italian. That other one reminds me of someone.'

They sat forward as the camera moved in on Conti, who was speaking about being born on a boat halfway between Italy and Australia. *It must have been traumatic. I haven't been on a boat since*, she said, and the audience laughed.

'She sounds like Jenny!' Lila said. 'Her and Jim and those up-themselves McPhersons used to make kids' books years ago. I was in three of them.'

'If you think I believe that, you've got rocks in your bald head.'

'It's true. I had a copy of one of them until the old mongrel I was married to burned it. Jenny's still got copies of them. Ring her up and ask her.'

'If I've told you once I've told you a thousand times not to mention her name in my house.'

'She's my best friend and I'll talk about her if I want to, and I pay half the rent and half the bills.'

'The bills come to me so it's my house.'

*You write directly to your computer, Miss Conti?*

*Why do it twice?*

'Close your eyes and listen to her. She sounds exactly like Jenny.'

'As if I'd know what she sounds like. I haven't seen her since . . . years.' Conti had said something. The audience was laughing. 'What did she say?'

'Who cares? It probably wasn't funny. They have a bloke on stage who holds up signs telling the audience when to laugh,' Lila said. 'I went to one of Tommy Hanlon's shows once. I didn't get picked to be on it, but one woman who did, she got a new washing machine and dryer.'

The camera was on the second writer, who had a lot more to say than the one in pink. She'd flown over from England yesterday and was flying up to Sydney tomorrow, then on Monday she was off to Perth.

'They have a good life, jetsetting around all over the country. I wish I had the money to fly somewhere,' Lila said.

'I went on a boat to Tasmania once,' Sissy said.

'Tasmania's not somewhere.'

*I like your title,* A Hand of Cards, the writer in pink said. *I've always thought that we're dealt a hand of cards at birth and good, bad or indifferent, we play the best game we can with what we've been dealt.*

'That's Jenny, or I'll eat my hat! Her legs look like Jenny's.'

'I haven't seen her legs in fifty years and if I don't see them in another fifty I won't care, now shut up!'

'You'll be dead in ten – if you're lucky.'

'You'll be dead in fifty seconds if you don't stop talking – as if it's her! She looks ten years younger than you.'

*You deal a few of your characters a difficult hand, Miss Conti,* the host said as the camera swung back to the woman in pink and caught her trying to break off a dangling thread.

*Life wasn't meant to be easy.*

*What was your inspiration for* The Stray?

*I'm here to discuss* The Winter Boomerang.

'What did she say?' Lila yelled.

'Who cares?'

*I'd be remiss if I didn't take this opportunity to discuss the plagiarism accusation,* the host said. *Your protagonist in* The Stray *is raped at fourteen, and by the age of eighteen is a single mother of three, and in an era when few unwed mothers raised their children, when those who did were frowned upon. Ms Langhall's Jessica, in* Angel at My Door, *is also raped at fourteen and an unwed mother of four by the age of twenty.*

The writer in pink shrugged. *When I was a kid I knew a woman who wandered around town with a pillow stuffed under her pinny so she could pass her unmarried daughter's baby off as her own – which is where I got my idea for the landlady's cushion in* The Stray.

*Where did the idea for your book come from?*

*Life*, the writer in pink said as she glanced at her watch.

*Are we keeping you from an appointment?*

*My dau . . . agent is waiting for me.*

'Did they say how old she was?'

'You haven't shut up long enough for me to hear anything,' Sissy said. 'Did she just say *The Stray*?'

'I dunno.'

Sissy reached for the Tim Tams, but Lila snatched them away. 'You pinched one before,' Lila said.

'If not for me you'd be living on the street.'

'If not for me, you'd be catching a bus to bingo.'

Lila was agile. Sissy had height, weight and determination. They squabbled over Tim Tams while a commercial played, and when it was done the Tim Tam packet was in the kitchen.

'What's plagiarism?' Lila asked.

'If you listened you might find out.'

*There are many similarities between the two protagonists*, the host said, then the camera swung to the one in pink, who was more interested in the hem of her skirt, so it swung to the other one.

*My research for* Angel *was done in Traralgon, where the fifteen year old daughter of family friends was brutally raped. I set it in Sydney because I knew the city well.*

*You are familiar with the city, Miss Conti?*

*My grandmother lived there. She used to talk about the Yanks pouring into Sydney during the war.*

*You appear to know the city.*

*I bought a street directory.*

'I lived in Sydney during the war,' Lila said. 'It was the best time I ever had in my life, then my first husband got out of the army and got me pregnant that same night. I didn't hang around after it was born to give him another chance at me.'

The one in beige was on the screen still yapping about plagiarism. The watchers were silent, attempting to work out what the word meant.

*Did Daphne du Maurier plagiarise Charlotte Brontë? I've always seen a similarity between* Rebecca *and* Jane Eyre. *Juliana's Sally has three children. My Jessica has four. Sally marries an abusive American. Jessica ends up with the love of her life. Where is the similarity?*

The host turned to the one in pink, who shrugged, and when the camera didn't move away, she sighed and spoke her longest sentence.

*There are only X number of words in a dictionary and X number of stories to tell. There might be one book in a hundred I read these days that doesn't remind me a bit of one I've read before. And to kill this subject, which I've had enough of, a fool of a girl I once knew was my inspiration for Sally. She grew up and moved on with her life, which is what I'd like to do right now.*

The host wanted more. He didn't get it, not from the one in pink, so turned his attention to the other one.

*The fictitious country towns may well be the same town, Ms Langhall.*

*Our ancestors chose sites for their towns beside rivers. They built similar bridges, similar hotels and general stores. From one end of Australia to the other, small towns look much the same.*

*Have you read* Angel at My Door, *Ms Conti?*

*Since the plagiarism accusation I have. I borrowed it from the library. It's a good read.*

*You write very convincingly of rape—*

*I thought this was a morning show.*

*—and of the loss of a child. Have you known the loss of a child?*

*To tell you the truth, I've never been fond of gut-spillers – and less fond of those who lap up what's been spilt.*

*You've been something of a mystery woman. I'm sure our viewers would be interested to hear a little about your life.*

*I thought that I was here to talk about* The Winter Boomerang.

'It's Jenny!' Lila screamed.

'You're going senile as well as bald,' Sissy said.

'It's Jenny, and I know where she got that book's title – from bloody old Joe Flanagan.'

*You are pro-abortion, Ms Conti?*

*One of my characters is. I write fiction. It's in the front of the book. 'The characters and events in this book are fictitious and any resemblance to real persons, living or dead, is purely coincidental'*, the one in pink said.

The channel cut to a commercial and the flatmates rose and went to the kitchen to make a sandwich before *Days of Our Lives* came on.

# The Handshake

Away from the cameras and lights and finally convinced that C.J. Langhall was Cara and that Cara had recognised her, Jenny wanted to run. But at least it was over. She'd got through it. Wasn't sure how. Couldn't remember a word she'd said. Had forgotten most of what she'd rehearsed with Jim and Georgie, gone blank as soon as the lights were on her. And their heat had made her head itch. Mortein fly spray or not, that wig was crawling with lice, which during the show had migrated down her neck to her shoulders and were now hopping around in her stomach. But it was over, and thank God.

Georgie was waiting where she'd left her. Waiting with a bloke, and smiling, which pretty much told her that they hadn't watched that fiasco. She walked to her side, still playing Juliana Conti of the fixed smile.

'You did good,' Georgie greeted her.

'You saw it?' Jenny asked and turned with a smile to the male. 'I'll get the truth out of her in the car.'

'You were a breath of fresh air, Miss Conti,' he said.

'Morris Langhall,' Georgie introduced Ms Langhall's husband, and he offered her his hand. She took it.

And she knew. As soon as she gripped it, she knew, and her heart, pounding hard for hours, stopped dead. The whole world stopped dead while she gripped his hand. Always, always, she'd known she'd recognise him by his hands, that it wouldn't matter if he was six or sixty, she'd know him.

And time ticked and she didn't know how much time had ticked. Dropped his hand as if it burned and stepped back, her sight, already blurred by Georgie's glasses, blurring more. Turned, looking for the exit, wanting to run. Didn't know where to run so turned back to look one more time at his face.

He was still there, her own beautiful six year old Jimmy, hiding beneath the years. Knew his eyes, the shape of his mouth, knew his ears. The ugliest little scrap of humanity God had ever seen fit to put on this earth at birth, his head misshapen, face scratched, eye bruised, and lucky to get out of her alive. She'd loved him at first sight. She loved him now and wanted to tell him that he was her own beautiful boy, wanted to hold him to her heart, but she looked again for the way out, her fingers covering trembling lips, pressing their trembling in and unsure for how much longer she could hold her howl inside. Strong fingers. They'd always been strong enough.

Saw Cara twelve feet away, surrounded by a group, and thank God he'd seen her too. 'Nice meeting you,' he said, offering his hand to Georgie, then with a smile that had never altered, he walked to Cara's side. Jenny followed him with eyes that could barely see, followed the blurred image of his back until it merged with the group.

Turned to Georgie then. 'Get me out of here, love.'

Georgie knew the way. 'You did good,' she said. 'If you'd bombed out, I mightn't tell you so, but I wouldn't tell you that you did good.'

Out to the sun then, and thank God for Georgie's darkening glasses. One or two tears got away but she caught them, wiped them determinedly with strong fingers.

'You recognised Cara?' Georgie asked.

'As soon as I saw her.'

'Did she recognise you?'

'I don't know. Probably. How far are we away from the bus depot, Georgie?'

'Nothing is far away in Melbourne, which is why everyone and their dog wants to live here, which makes getting to where you want to go damn near impossible,' Georgie said.

They were in the car before she spoke again. 'I recognised her when they rushed her in. There were two of them waiting for her. I spoke to her. She looked stunned, then smiled and introduced me to her bloke and asked what I was doing there.'

'What did you tell her?'

'That I was Juliana Conti's literary agent. Her husband is a lovely bloke. When they hurried her away, he stuck to my side like glue. "Georgie of the copper hair," he said. She must have mentioned me to him before.'

And Jenny sobbed, a dry triple intake of air sob, as she returned Georgie's glasses and replaced them with her own sunglasses. Began searching then for the pins holding her wig in place.

She'd planned to stay tonight. She'd told Katie she'd see her after school. Couldn't. Not now. She had to get away from Georgie, or she'd end up spilling what she knew. Couldn't. Could never tell her she'd been talking to her own brother. Couldn't.

'I need to go home, love.'

'Close your eyes and relax. I'll take you back to Greensborough, make you a strong coffee and you can watch it on video. You looked nervous when you came on, but you settled down and mostly looked in control. Stop worrying. It's over, Jen.'

Too many pins to remove and, jammed in traffic, Jenny gave up the search, ripped the wig from her head and pitched it over to the back seat. She scratched then, scratched and lifted her flattened hair high.

'Are we heading towards the bus depot?'

'No.'

'I need to go home, love.'

'Why?'

'Don't question me today, Georgie.'

'No one had a hope of recognising you. I had to keep telling myself you were you.'

'Drop me off anywhere. I'll catch a tram.'

'I'll drive you,' Georgie said, and she stopped talking and drove. There was nowhere to park when they got near the depot.

'The walk will do me good.' Jenny's hand was on the door release.

'The bus doesn't leave until three, and I'm not leaving you until you tell me what happened.'

'I'm going to bawl in a minute, that's what's going to happen. I know myself too well and, right now, I know I'm better off by myself. Tell Katie I'm sorry and I'll send her an email.'

Georgie slid the car into a no standing zone. Jenny had the door open and was out before the handbrake was on.

'I hate leaving you like this.'

'I thank God for you. You remember that always, darlin'. Every day of my life, I bless the day that you were born,' she said, then, taking Georgie's outstretched hand, she kissed it, closed the door and walked away fast.

Walked fast around the corner where she got her back to a wall and fought cigarettes from her handbag. Got one out of the packet. Got one between shaking lips, got it lit, then walked on, blowing smoke.

She'd be all right. She was a survivor. She'd get over this. She had to get a seat on the bus. Had to concentrate on that. There should be plenty of empty seats today. She'd be all right once she got home to Jim and closed the doors against the world. Just had to get there, that's all.

The bus was late leaving, and not until she boarded did she consider what she was wearing. There was no one from Woody Creek on it, or no one who looked familiar. She took a seat at the rear, a window seat, then closed her eyes against Melbourne, safe now to think of Jimmy, to embed his adult face into her every brain cell, to entrench the feel of his hand into her every nerve ending. Could still feel his touch. Could still feel his blood pulsing into her.

Tears dripping, she removed her sunglasses, aware that mascara and eyeliner must have been leaking with her tears. Wiped her eyes with her fingers, then with a used tissue. Left black smears on it and told herself to stop crying, that she'd seen him, that she'd touched him, that he was still beautiful.

And married to his sister.

*Dear God, what have I done?*

That's what she'd have to live with for the rest of her life. And how could she live with it? Couldn't. And they couldn't know what they'd done. They had children. Georgie couldn't know. That was the worst part, not being able to tell her.

The trip was always long but today Jenny didn't notice it, didn't know the bus was approaching Kilmore until it was there. Buses had always stopped, opposite the Kilmore public toilets. She didn't want to get out but the driver did, and he wanted to lock the door. Last down those steps, she tailed the few passengers to the toilets where she queued for a cubicle, wanting its paper, not its bowl, and when the crowd cleared, she washed her face and used their toilet paper. Scratchy, hard on the face paper – city councils didn't encourage travellers to help themselves to wads of it.

The bus was still locked when she returned. She lit a cigarette and stood sheltering from the wind behind it until the driver came back. They wasted twenty minutes there, took on one passenger. They dropped off two at the next stop and picked up no replacement. Wasted twenty minutes in Willama where three passengers were offloaded and one boarded, a young chap carrying a backpack, and he looked like a Dobson. Jenny kept her head low.

He wasn't a Dobson. She was the only passenger to disembark in Woody Creek, a pink-clad passenger, and she wished the night darker, wished the fabric of the opportunity shop suit warmer.

The cool change had followed her home, and last night's forecast for showers had been right. Light rain was falling.

Georgie would have phoned Jim. Jenny looked for the white Toyota, a Jap car but made in Australia and a good model, Teddy Hall said. No Toyota, nor any other car in the street, and too much light left in the day, enough to see the pink of that suit. Not a soul about to see it, though, thank God. Tonight Woody Creek looked like a ghost town where the lights had been left burning. The bank had closed its doors ten years ago. The doctor who set up shop there on Wednesdays did a roaring trade. A retirees' town, Woody Creek, and old age demanded pills and potions. Thank God he didn't work nights.

She looked at her watch then walked to the old post office's recessed doorway, unchanged in the seventy years she'd known it. The building was now the community centre. No quilt making, bingo or internet lessons scheduled on Wednesday nights. She backed deep into a corner, remembering a younger back cowering there because she'd failed to make a mad woman love her.

She'd failed as a mother, failed to become a singer, failed to give up smoking too, and in the dark of the recessed doorway, she lit a cigarette and stood blowing smoke to the east, the west, uncertain from which direction the Toyota would come – if it came. Rain angled down in the glow of the streetlight, light reflected on wet bitumen. Not much light at the house which would ever be Maisy's house.

Ten year old Jenny had stood in this doorway staring at Maisy's lights, willing Norman to lose his allocated small change fast to George Macdonald and his poker-playing friends so he'd finish early and she could go home. Should have run across the road and told him she was afraid to stay alone with mad Amber. He might have listened then. Hadn't the night of the ball when she'd tried to tell him his wife was a liar. All gone now.

For ten minutes Jenny hid, waiting for Jim, waiting for the rain to stop falling, and it was heavier now than it had been when she'd got off the bus. Jim would know it was raining. What if he'd fallen in the yard, tripped over by the dogs? It had happened three weeks ago. Georgie would have let him know she'd be on the bus, and there was nothing wrong with his hearing. He'd hear that rain on the roof.

Was he lying out in it? What if he'd fallen last night? She'd spoken to him at seven last night. He'd have no reason to go outside after seven. He would have this morning, though.

She argued with herself for a moment while looking out at the light rain, then she started walking. She'd walked in worse. She'd walked this town long enough to have seen it all – wind, rain, hail and dust storm.

Didn't look at the railway house she'd once called home – had once loved – until Amber came home. Walked by it fast and around the corner into the railway yard. It was darker there, and its darkness made the hotel's lights seem brighter, but she'd have to walk beneath them if she wanted the shelter of that long veranda. She slowed her footsteps, accepting instead the shelter of the paling fence and the overgrown trees behind it. No meals were served at the hotel on Wednesday nights and the drinkers would be drinking, not standing outside watching the rain. A wetting rain, and her padded bra more showerproof than the suit.

Laughing Katie last night, laughing with her mother's mouth, her mother's teeth. Georgie laughing last night. Concerned today. Jenny had no secrets from her, but it would do her no good to find out she'd been speaking to her brother for an hour and hadn't recognised him. He'd recognised her. There was no doubt in Jenny's mind about that. *Georgie of the copper hair.* She was fifty-nine, but never allowed a telltale grey root to mar that copper mane. Still beautiful, regal, and raising Katie the way a girl should be raised, in a beautiful home with a mummy and a daddy and a cat to chase the birds away from her fruit trees.

Jenny looked towards Norman's sad old abandoned station. The occasional goods train still passed through Woody Creek on its way to somewhere else. Never stopped. A busy place once, passengers buying tickets out of this town, stacks of bleeding timber waiting to be loaded. No more mills in town. The bush mill now cut firewood. No more concerts. No more Saturday night picture shows. No balls, no dances. Woody Creek's social life revolved around the community centre, the hotel and the bowling club's pokies.

The changes I've seen, Jenny thought as she walked up to the twin metal lines, stepping carefully over the first of them. The sleepers were old and the dirt and stones filling the spaces between them were never meant to be walked on in high-heeled shoes. Look on the bright side, Jen. You could have been wearing those pink platform sandals.

No bright side to look on tonight. She turned to the west, towards Charlie's crossing, then to the east towards Blunt's. Flat as a tack, this town, and those railway lines looked as they ever had, like grey pencilled lines ruled through the middle of Woody Creek by a monster's hand.

She'd travelled with Jimmy down those lines when he was ten months old. Travelled back with him when he'd been three. Walked him down that long road home to Granny, his sweaty little hand clinging to her own, his tinkling little voice chanting, *Woody Creek stinks*. Had she held his hand too long today? Had she dropped it too fast? She didn't know what she'd done. Could still feel its touch.

He'd been four years old when she'd taken him and the girls down to Armadale, almost six when she'd brought him back. Then the Hoopers had stolen him away.

There was a bright side. She'd seen his face. She'd held his hand . . .

Always she'd looked for him. When she'd caught city trams, she searched the faces of passengers. When she'd been in crowds, in city theatres, she'd looked for him. When he'd been sixteen, she'd looked at schoolboys. When he'd been eighteen she'd looked at young businessmen. Always, she'd looked at their hands, knowing she might not recognise his face but she would know his hands. And she had. She had.

And couldn't even tell Jim. He didn't know about Cara. She'd removed her and the Sydney rape from *The Stray* because Jim didn't know about her.

*What have I done?*

Couldn't go back and undo any of it. Had to forget Jimmy now. She'd shaken the hand of Morris Langhall, of James Morrison Langdon . . .

He'd looked well. He was married to a big name writer. They lived on a twenty-acre property in an English manor house. My flesh, my blood, lives in a five hundred year old manor house. Jenny shook rain from her hair then walked on.

Had Cara recognised Juliana Conti's hand?

She'd spoken about their three children. Elise, still at school, Tracy, a ballet dancer, and Robin. Jenny's own flesh and blood grandson was a surgeon. Itchy-foot had come from a family of doctors and surgeons. *Was a seed of healing passed on to him through my blood?* Itchy-foot had wanted to sing – maybe he'd wanted to write; he'd filled thirteen small leather-covered diaries with his life, and if not for his diaries, Jenny wouldn't have written *Before Her Time.* Had he passed on his seed of writing to Jenny, and she in turn to Cara?

She sought the shelter of a large peppercorn tree, growing forever in the western corner of the railway yard, and looked again at the hotel veranda. It would give her shelter most of the way home and there was no sign of life on that corner. But the western side of Three Pines Road was darker and that pink suit lost its colour in the dark, so she crossed over to the west side and walked on, soaked to the skin now, rain trickling down the back of her neck before she reached a melaleuca that she'd seen planted as a spindly seedling and watched grow into a giant. It kept the rain off.

The dogs were barking. Did they sense she was near? She'd kept two pups from Lorna's last litter. Cara had spoken about her dogs, a pair of border collies, and Jenny had damn near forgotten who she was supposed to be and mentioned her pair of red . . . bitten that sentence short but, the camera on her, she'd had to continue, and the only dog breed that had come to mind had been Pekinese. Loathed those ugly little mutts. Juliana Conti now owned a pair – reddish. Were Pekinese ever reddish?

She'd watched her tongue. Had said nothing that might give away her identity. Her hands could have given her away to Cara, though maybe not. Maybe she'd thought relative, thought the writing seed and hands had come down Juliana's line.

A car went by, spraying water, its stereo shattering the silence of the ghost town. Those pounded rhythms were considered music to the youth of the nineties. There were car stereos in town larger than the cars they were in. She watched it pass, watched its lights painting the wet peppercorn tree into a glistening green fairy land as the car turned right, then the thump-thump rhythm faded and the night was again dark.

At fourteen, she'd been too afraid to walk at night, afraid of the bogymen who hid behind the trees and came out to murder girls. She'd sat on the sports oval fence, swinging her feet to the band music. It's never the bogyman you fear who gets you. It's the ones you don't fear.

She'd feared that morning show, its host, its cameras, then she'd walked on the set and recognised Cara. It had almost undone her. For the first ten minutes the lights had been on her, she'd sat, scared stiff Cara would expose her on national TV.

She crossed the road and Olejoe and Lila were waiting for her at the small gate, yipping and wriggling their pleasure at the sight of her. She patted wet coats, scratched behind wet ears and received a doggy kiss or two.

'Where's Jim?' she said. They ran ahead of her to the back door, and as she opened it, she asked herself how many mothers who had lost their sons ever got to see them again. She had to think how lucky she'd been, then let him go.

Warmth greeted her. The kitchen was always warm. She took

her wet shoes off and walked on wet stockinged feet through to the entrance hall to peer into the sitting room.

And there he was, sound asleep on the couch, his head propped on a pillow, one leg propped over the padded arm rest. He wasn't as good looking as his son. Jim Hooper had never been the best looking boy in Woody Creek, but she'd loved him when he'd been a gangling, big-eared goblin of a boy, and she loved him still, on his back, his long jaw dropped in sleep. Just did, didn't know why.

Should have told him years ago about Cara. But she'd done what she'd done, what she'd deemed right and necessary at the time, and there's not one day, not one second of the past you can alter with should-have-beens and shouldn't-have-dones. You play the cards life deals out to you, play them the best way you can, and win, lose or draw, that game has to be played out to the end.

*A Hand of Cards.* A damn good title. What a story it would have made. *Mother and daughter united on national television.* Shaking her head, she crept down to the bathroom, wanting Jim to sleep until she'd showered, washed her hair and her soul clean.

Half an hour more Jim slept. She was dressing-gown-clad, in the kitchen, making a mug of strong coffee when the lid of the jar fell and rattled on the floor.

'Who's there?' Jim called.

'A burglar, and I've just stolen your every worldly possession.'

'What's the time?'

'After nine,' she said.

'I took two pills so I could drive over and meet the bus,' he said. 'They knocked me for six.'

'Get your hip fixed and you won't need to swallow drugs before you drive,' she said, then added coffee to a second mug.

He was seated on the couch when she entered to place the coffee on the small table between their chairs. He didn't reach for his mug, but for the remote control.

'There's nothing on, on Wednesday nights,' she said.

'I taped a show,' he said, and he hit play.

'You didn't, Jim. You wouldn't do that to me.' Then she heard the music and knew he had. 'Turn it off!'

'Sit still and watch,' he said.

She wanted the remote to kill that tape, but his arms were long and he held it high and at a distance.

'Please turn it off. Today was hell on earth.'

'I plan to blackmail you with it for the rest of my life.'

'Which won't be long if you don't turn that thing off.'

*

And thus we leave them, arguing over the remote control, Jim killing himself laughing as the pink-clad woman fills the screen, her head high, her smile fixed. He hasn't laughed often these past months.

We leave Jenny refusing to look at the screen, sitting head down, drinking hot coffee and crunching a biscuit while an audience applauds. But television screens will draw most eyes. Her eyes are drawn up to peek. She sees pink, sees a stranger with too much dark hair hiding her face. Sees a small woman perched uncomfortably on the edge of a too large chair showing her bare knees and she watches her attempt to cover her knees with her hands – then sees her remember her hands and snatch them away to her sides.

The host asks if she's comfortable. The lady in pink tells him she'd be more comfortable seated with the audience, thank you, and the audience laughs.

Jenny lifts her chin. She's watching the screen now, listening to her voice, and to Cara's. He's by her side. She's safe to watch it.

The lady in pink has found a dangling thread at her knee. She attempts to tuck it out of view and Jenny moans, knowing what comes later, but the station cuts to a commercial.

'Everyone will recognise me,' she says as Jim hits the fast-forward button.

'I didn't. Until you spoke I thought you were the Ms Langhall they'd been advertising every two minutes before the show began. She flew in last night and only agreed to do the show this morning.'

Fast-forwarded commercials flip by in silence, then Cara is back on the screen, and Jim hits play. Well practised at interviews, Cara makes it obvious that she is there to sell her latest book.

And the camera swoops to Juliana. She's attempting to snap off that dangling thread but it unravels, as the hems of shop-bought garments are apt to do – Juliana's expression is all Jenny's. Jim laughs, and again Jenny fights him for the remote control.

There's a close-up of Cara on the screen. As a girl she resembled Jenny. Her hair is shoulder length, its curl gone, its colour now that popular champagne blonde. She sounds English – or sounds like Myrtle. Jenny watches intently as Cara speaks of her years in Sydney, in Melbourne, of her children, her greatest achievements, she says.

'That's enough, Jim!'

'Trust me.'

She's always trusted him, almost always, and he's right. Midway through the torment, survivor Jenny steps into the lady in pink. She plays the game out to the end.

*

*Dare I bid them such an abrupt goodbye? Dangling threads encourage fingers to pick, to poke. Seams can unravel – and surely there is more to tell of Morrie and Cara.*

*Only their return flight details. They leave from Sydney's Kingsford Smith Airport at 18.09 on 28 November. They won't return to Australian shores.*

*Trudy will, and soon. At this moment she and Nick are in a plane over the Indian Ocean. She's five months pregnant with twins and wants them to be born in Australia. By midday tomorrow Vern Hooper's big old house won't feel so empty. There'll be talk and too much laughter when Jim plays his Pink Lady video again.*

*He'll play it on Saturday when Georgie, Paul and Katie arrive . . .*

*Ah, Katie. There must be more to tell of Katie Morgan Dunn.*

*Not one word more, my faithful reader. She is Jenny's tomorrow, and you and I are not going there.*

## MORE BESTSELLING TITLES FROM JOY DETTMAN'S WOODY CREEK SERIES

### Pearl in a Cage (Woody Creek 1)

The first novel in Joy Dettman's sensational Woody Creek series.

On a balmy midsummer's evening in 1923, a young woman – foreign, dishevelled and heavily pregnant – is found unconscious just off the railway tracks in the tiny logging community of Woody Creek.

The town midwife, Gertrude Foote, is roused from her bed when the woman is brought to her door. Try as she might, Gertrude is unable to save her – but the baby lives.

When no relatives come forth to claim the infant, Gertrude's daughter Amber – who has recently lost a son in childbirth – and her husband Norman take the child in. In the ensuing weeks, Norman becomes convinced that God has sent the baby to their door, and in an act of reckless compassion he names the baby Jennifer and registers her in place of his son.

Loved by some but scorned by more – including her stepmother and stepsister who resent the interloper – Jenny survives her childhood and grows into an exquisite and talented young woman. But who were her parents? Why does she so strongly resemble an old photograph of Gertrude's philandering husband? And will she one day fulfil her potential?

Spanning two momentous decades and capturing rural Australia's complex and mysterious heart, *Pearl in a Cage* is an unputdownable novel by one of our most talented storytellers.

**Thorn on the Rose (Woody Creek 2)**

It is 1939 and Jenny Morrison, distraught and just fifteen years of age, has fled the tiny logging community of Woody Creek for a new life in the big smoke.

But four months later she is back – wiser, with an expensive new wardrobe, and bearing another dark secret . . .

She takes refuge with Gertrude, her dependable granny and Woody Creek's indomitable midwife, and settles into a routine in the ever-expanding and chaotic household.

But can she ever put the trauma of her past behind her and realise her dream of becoming a famous singer? Or is she doomed to follow in the footsteps of her tragic and mysterious mother?

Spanning a momentous wartime decade and filled with the joys and heartaches of life in rural Australia, *Thorn on the Rose* is the spellbinding sequel to *Pearl in a Cage*.

**Moth to the Flame (Woody Creek 3)**

In *Moth to the Flame*, Joy Dettman returns with another dazzling tale of the unforgettable characters of Woody Creek.

The year is 1946. The war ended five months ago. Jim Hooper, Jenny Morrison's only love, was lost to that war. And if not for Jenny, he would never have gone.

'An eye for an eye,' Vern Hooper says. An unforgiving man, Vern wants custody of Jenny's son, his only grandson, and is quietly planning his day in court.

Then Jenny's father, Archie Foote, swoops back into town. Archie offers Jenny a tantalising chance at fame and fortune; one way or another he is determined to play a part in her life.

Is Jenny's luck about to change, or is she drawn to trouble like a moth is drawn to the flame?

**Wind in the Wires (Woody Creek 4)**

The wind is whispering in Woody Creek . . . Change is in the air

It's 1958 and Woody Creek is being dragged – kicking and screaming – into the swinging sixties.

Cara and Georgie are now young women but, raised separately, they have never met. They've both inherited their mother's hands, but that's where their similarity ends.

Despite a teenage mistake looming over Cara's future, she still believes in the white wedding and happily ever after myth. Georgie, however, has seen enough of marriage and motherhood, and plans to live her life independent of a man.

But once the sisters are drawn into each other's lives, long-buried secrets are bound to be unearthed, the dramatic consequences of which no-one could have predicted . . .

## Ripples on a Pond (Woody Creek 5)

The old timber town of Woody Creek has a way of getting under people's skin . . .

Woody Creek is preparing for its centenary celebrations – but for many of its townspeople it's just another reminder of the old days, before so-called progress roared through the town, altering everything in its wake.

Not for Georgie though. As the clock ticks over to 1970, she's determined that the new decade will be the one that sees her finally break free.

For Cara, Woody Creek will forever be tied to a devastating mistake that cannot be undone. She's vowed never to set foot in the place again.

Meanwhile, Jenny's estranged son, Jim, has inherited an estate in the United Kingdom and is trying to make a new life for himself. If only he could shake off his one terrible attachment to Australia.

As Woody Creek draws Joy Dettman's much-loved cast of characters back into its grip, confessions, discoveries and truths seem certain to explode in the most shocking of show-downs . . .